THE DRUG RUNNERS

H.C. Hannah

ISBN: 9798662877320

John, this is for you, with love
Thank you for sharing my dreams

ONE

00:05 am, Thursday, September 19
Coast Guard Station Headquarters, Deepwater Harbour, Antigua

The distress call came in at just after midnight. It was taken by Melford, one of two crew members on duty in the comm room that night. He swallowed a bite of an oatmeal and raisin cookie and took a large gulp of lukewarm coffee as he picked up the radio handset. The frantic message was barely audible. Spoken by a male voice with a British accent, it was panic-stricken and urgent. A man on the edge of losing his cool. Melford hurriedly took down important details. The name of the sailing yacht, Atratus, reported to be approximately fifteen nautical miles southwest of Sugar Reef Bay.

Melford paged a launch request to the English Harbour crew who were based out of a small station on the south coast of Antigua. It was one of three locations manned by the Coast Guard, the maritime branch of the Antigua and Barbuda Defence Force.

Returning to the radio handset, Melford asked the captain of the Atratus if he had a DSC radio linked to his navigation equipment.

'No.' The crackled reply was just audible.

Melford frowned. A DSC, or digital selective calling radio, was used to transmit a distress signal to the Coast Guard and other ships within range. When connected to the onboard GPS, it could also send the location of the vessel in distress. If the search and rescue team had this information, they knew exactly where they were headed. Without it, guesswork, search patterns and luck were required.

'Problems… electrics on board,' came a muffled voice through a roar of white noise and static.

'I'm alerting the lifeboat crew now,' Melford said into the handset. 'What sea survival equipment do you have onboard, over?'

He waited for a reply. None came. He tried again.

'Mayday Atratus, do you have a life raft on board, over?'

Radio silence from the yacht.

'Mayday Atratus, this is the Antigua Coast Guard. Do you read, over?'

Melford took a deep breath as he realised he'd lost radio contact with the distraught captain. He glanced at the pair of monitors on the desk in front of him. The one on the left contained radar images; smatterings of coloured dots and blurred shapes against a dark blue background. On the other screen was an electronic chart display of the coastline. A boat-shaped symbol represented every significant vessel within range of the Coast Guard station. The short range coastal tracking system known as the AIS, or automatic identification system, was used extensively in the maritime world for the exchange of navigational information between AIS-equipped receivers, both on and offshore. By clicking on a symbol, information such as the name of the ship it represented, its course and speed, and call sign, could be obtained. But in order to transmit this information, a dedicated VHF transponder was required. As far as Melford could see, the Atratus was either out of range of the Coast Guard station or did not have a functioning transponder. He spoke into the handset once more.

'Mayday Atratus, this is the Antigua Coast Guard. Do you read me?'

There was no response. Not the faintest hiss or a crackle. It was clear the Atratus had suffered some kind of electrical failure and had lost all means of communication. Or the vessel had capsized and was sinking. Or the captain had become incapacitated in some way. Or had been thrown overboard by a giant wave.

As sheets of rain lashed angrily against the shuttered windows of the Coast Guard station, Melford glanced uneasily at a third monitor on the desk which displayed current weather information. Another complication. Outside, a violent storm raged. According to the latest charts, radar images and data alerts, a force ten gale with winds of up to sixty miles an hour was battering the south of the Caribbean island and surrounding area. Somewhere out there in the darkness of the night, the sailing boat Atratus was being tossed and buffeted mercilessly by giant, rolling waves in a blinding mist of driving rain, sea spray and dense white streaks of foam.

The AIS screen showed that there were no other boats in the vicinity of the last reported position of the Atratus. It was hardly surprising. The weather forecast and subsequent warnings had been clear and accurate. A storm was approaching. It was the middle of the hurricane season. Only a foolhardy sailor would leave the safety of harbour in a storm of this intensity. The closest ship to the Atratus was a research and survey vessel sailing under a German flag at least thirty nautical miles away. With a cruising speed of just over three knots, it would take the ship until lunchtime to reach the Atratus. Even so, Melford put out the call, just in case.

'All stations, all stations, all stations, this is the Antigua Coast Guard, Antigua Coast Guard, Antigua Coast Guard. Report received of a fifty-seven foot white vessel Atratus, taking on water. Last reported position fifteen nautical miles southwest of Sugar Reef Bay. All mariners requested to keep a sharp lookout. Assist if possible.'

The telephone rang. Melford reached across the desk and picked it up. He knew who was calling.

'Max,' he said.

'English Harbour,' the coxswain of the rescue boat replied briskly.

Brushing cookie crumbs off the desk, Melford relayed the details.

'Yeah, I just took a Mayday from the captain of a fifty-seven foot sailing vessel, the Atratus, last reported fifteen miles southwest of Sugar Reef Bay.'

'What's he doing out in that storm?' There was a note of disbelief in Max's voice.

'Good question. He's reportedly taking on water and requesting immediate assistance.'

'How many on board?'

'Just him apparently.'

'Is he wearing a lifejacket?'

'I don't know. I lost comms with him minutes after he put out the call. Maybe his electrics are out, or maybe he capsized, I've no idea, but I've told you everything I know.'

'Did you get any information on injuries? Medical needs?'

'No, like I said, the comms went down before I had chance.'

'Any other vessels nearby?'

'None close enough to offer immediate assistance.'

'Okay, thanks Mel. I'll see if I can make contact once we're on our way.'

'Take care out there bro,' Melford said as they hung up. He felt helpless. Although he was the mission coordinator and would stay in touch from the comm room, the rest of the search, rescue and recovery operation was down to the five-strong English Harbour crew who, within less than fifteen minutes, were launching their response boat, an imposing looking thirty-eight foot vessel with an aluminium hull, an enclosed cabin and three powerful outboard engines.

'Did the yacht send a distress alert?' Linroy, one of the crew, shouted to Max at the helm. Cupping his hand behind his ear, Max motioned to Linroy to repeat the question. The powerful roar of the engines, combined with the driving rain and noise of the wind, was almost deafening as the boat rocked and lurched in the dark water of the harbour.

'Was there a distress alert?' Linroy yelled. He stepped into the small cabin and closed the door at the rear, shutting out the storm. Joining Max and the other three crew members, he checked his lifejacket was secure before he took a seat and fastened his safety belt. Colin, the navigator, was already punching buttons on the electronic chart plotter and scribbling various pencil marks on a paper chart of the coastline. He frowned in concentration as he studied the search pattern they would adopt to locate the Atratus.

Alvin, seated at the radar display, was keying in data for the search and rescue mission and tuning out interference from the rain and storm clutter. Shawn, the mechanic, was in charge of the engines and other mechanical components on board. It was down to him to ensure everything functioned properly while they were at sea.

'No distress alert according to Melford,' Max replied as he engaged the throttles and skilfully began manoeuvring the lifeboat through the harbour. He held the wheel firmly as the boat was buffeted by the waves. Rubber wipers flapped back and forth across the windshield in a vain attempt to keep up with the relentless rain. A red light illuminated the area inside the cabin to protect the night vision of the crew. The glare from the radar display and the other electronic screens, the chart plotter and the GPS, were tilted away from Max to enable him to pick out objects on the darkened horizon as clearly as possible. In addition, Colin had a pair of night vision binoculars beside him.

As they advanced through the channel, leaving the lights and safety of the harbour behind, they entered the wide open sea, where the waves became taller and rougher. Passing the final set of channel markers, with their red and green lights blinking rhythmically, the crew of the rescue boat were engulfed in darkness. The moon and stars were obscured by thick, angry storm clouds, churning and boiling in the night sky overhead. The stark glare of their own navigation lights reflected on the white crests of the waves, as the hull of the boat pitched violently over the swells and plunged hard into the troughs.

'Steer two-one-zero magnetic and maintain course,' Colin said, simultaneously studying the chart plotter and the paper chart in front of him. 'What's the name of the vessel again?'

'Atratus,' Max replied.

'When we reach the last known position of the Atratus, we'll start an expanding square search.'

Max nodded. He picked up a radio handset to his left and relayed a brief message to Melford detailing their current position. He confirmed they were en route to the last known position of the Atratus where they would begin the search. He gave Melford the names of the crew on board before asking if there had been any further radio contact from the Atratus. From the Coast Guard station at Deepwater Harbour, Melford acknowledged the message and informed them that he had received nothing more from the yacht.

'I'll see if I can get any response,' Max said.

Remaining on VHF channel 16, the marine international distress frequency, Max attempted to contact the Atratus, prefixing the name of the yacht with the word Mayday. Ten seconds turned to thirty, then sixty, but there was no reply. Max tried again. He knew that during a search and rescue mission like this one, the coxswain, or another member of the lifeboat crew, would endeavour to communicate with the vessel in distress, initially on channel 16. If contact was made, the lifeboat coxswain would inform the captain that help was on the way, with an estimated time of arrival. He, or she, could also ask for additional information from the captain, such as where the vessel was sailing from and where it was going, along with regular updates on the nature of the emergency. If the vessel in distress was still manoeuvrable, the coxswain could give the captain a course to steer in order to guide the two boats towards each other. Working with the position and speed of the vessel in distress, and the wind and the tide, the rescue boat could then determine a point at which the course of the vessel could be intercepted.

Without radio contact with the Atratus, however, this wasn't possible. Max and the rest of the crew had only the last known position of the yacht and the search pattern calculated by Colin in order to try to locate it. The atmosphere in the red glow of the small cabin was tense, although the crew remained calm and composed. As they peered anxiously into the inky black of the night, through the sheets of horizontal rain which glistened in the beam of the searchlights, Shawn voiced what they were all thinking.

'What crazy idiot sets out on a sailboat in a storm like this? The weather warnings have been all over the news for days.'

'There's always someone,' Linroy said, gripping the armrest of his seat as the boat lurched violently to the port side. 'You know my rule, never leave a harbour to look for a harbour. This is one of the worst storms we've been out in for months.'

'Turn to starboard, heading two-two-zero magnetic,' Colin said to Max. The coxswain repeated the new heading back to the navigator as he turned the wheel, changing course as directed.

'This ain't gon' be an easy one.' Linroy spoke again.

'Maybe he'll send up some flares,' Max said, wrestling with the wheel in an effort to stay on course as the boat flopped and bounced over the waves.

'Let's hope,' Linroy replied. Apart from the noise of the engines and the storm, silence resumed in the cabin as the five crew members prepared themselves for the mission ahead. According to Colin, at their current speed it would take them around twenty-five minutes to reach the last known position of the Atratus. He regularly checked the compass heading and a stopwatch, cross-referencing their position on the paper chart with the one displayed on the chart plotter. In addition, he had programmed the approximate coordinates of the last known position of the Atratus into the GPS. After almost thirty minutes from leaving English Harbour, they reached the last known location of the yacht.

'This is it,' Colin said, glancing ahead before returning to the chart. 'Fifteen nautical miles southwest of Sugar Reef Bay. We'll start the search pattern. Max, take up a westerly heading turning five-zero degrees to starboard. New heading two-seven-zero magnetic.'

'Turning five-zero degrees to starboard heading two-seven-zero magnetic,' Max repeated as he began turning the wheel. The rescue boat slowly responded. It was buffeted by the waves as they took up their new heading with every crew member scanning the horizon intently through the darkness. Colin radioed to Melford informing him that they had arrived at the search area, that there was nothing seen and they were commencing the search. He also gave Melford an update on the wind and the tide, the sea state and their forward visibility, which was poor. There was a short acknowledgement from Melford before the radio fell silent again. After a few minutes, Colin checked his stopwatch and gave Max a new heading, turning the rescue boat ninety degrees to starboard.

Soon they were tracking in a northerly direction with the wind behind them.

The expanding square search, as it was known, was conducted by carrying out a series of timed legs from a defined search point, in this case, the last reported position of the yacht Atratus. Each leg increased in length after every other turn. At the end of each leg the rescue boat turned ninety degrees to starboard, keeping speed and course headings constant. The track spacing of each leg equalled the length of the first leg of the search. With Colin announcing new headings every few minutes, the search area expanded, mile by mile. For the westerly and northerly headings, the strong, gusting wind was behind them. The easterly and southerly headings were into wind and took considerably longer. The waves tossed the rescue boat like a child's toy in a bathtub and the rain lashed angrily against the hull.

'I'm seeing nothing so far,' Shawn said to nobody in particular.

'Me neither,' Linroy added grimly. 'Alvin, you getting anything on radar?'

'No.' Alvin shook his head without taking his eyes off the screen. 'But I got a lot of clutter with this storm.' Although the onboard radar was used primarily as an aid to navigation, during search and rescue missions it could be used to locate vessels in distress such as the Atratus.

Colin gave Max a new heading to steer before picking up the radio handset and checking in with Melford. He confirmed their current position and heading, which coincided with what Melford was looking at on the monitor in front of him.

'There's still no sign of the casualty.' Colin concluded his radio communication and replaced the handset in its cradle.

'Wait a sec, what's that ahead?' Shawn said suddenly, leaning into the aisle from his second row seat. 'It looks like a light.'

'Where?' Linroy asked, following Shawn's gaze. He picked up the night vision binoculars and scanned the horizon.

'Straight ahead,' Shawn replied. 'It's maybe a mile or so away.'

'I see it too,' Max said. 'It's an SOS signal: three short flashes followed by three long ones.'

'There's a blip on my screen but it's hard to know exactly what it could be,' Alvin said.

Colin punched more buttons on the GPS, enlarging the area of the Caribbean Sea immediately ahead of them.

'If it's the Atratus, it's further west than we thought,' he said, studying the chart.

As the sturdy response boat laboured valiantly across the rough sea and giant swells towards it, at times the light signal disappeared.

'Maintain course,' Colin said tensely. 'Where's the light gone?'

'I think I have a visual,' Max said.

Sure enough, as the beam of the powerful search lights from the lifeboat penetrated the haze of rain, the white hull of what looked like a sailing yacht bobbed into view before being engulfed by a giant wave and streaks of flying foam. As the wave swelled, the stricken yacht, listing precariously, reappeared. The enormous mast, half of which had broken off in the storm, was being dragged forlornly behind the yacht, along with the remains of shredded sails, attached and unfurled, hopelessly battered by the wind and waves. It had to be the Atratus.

Colin radioed a brief sit-rep to Melford, informing him they had a visual with a vessel fitting the description of the Atratus. With some relief, Melford acknowledged the message. It would be a few more minutes until they reached the yacht, however, and the crew released their safety belts and began making preparations for the rescue. There was an air of tension on board heightened by the lack of comms with the casualty, fuelling the anticipation of not knowing what they were about to encounter. Colin made a final attempt at calling the Atratus on the radio but there was no reply. As they came closer to the yacht, Max pulled back the throttle levers.

'I'll get as near as I can,' he said, 'but with the mast broken and collapsed over the port side of the yacht it's only gonna be possible to approach from the starboard side.'

'We can work with that,' Shawn replied. 'Apart from the damaged mast and sails, the boat looks to be holding up pretty well.'

'Those fancy sailing yachts have sturdy hulls,' Linroy remarked. 'They're built to be ocean-going.' He picked up a handheld radio and slid it into one of the pockets on his cargo pants. If he boarded the Atratus, he'd need to maintain comms with both the Coast Guard station and the rescue boat.

'Signs of life,' Colin said suddenly. 'There's a man at the stern.'

'I see him,' Linroy said.

As Max manoeuvred the lifeboat closer to the Atratus a bead of sweat trickled down the side of his forehead. He looked at the pattern and pitch of the waves in relation to the yacht, which would determine how he would bring the rescue boat alongside. It would make it easier if he could communicate with the captain to explain the plan and invite him to cooperate with them, but without comms, it wasn't possible.

'I'm going out on deck,' Linroy said. As he opened the door to the rear of the cabin, he stepped into a swirling mist of sea spray and rain. Alvin, pulling his safety helmet firmly down on his head, was close behind.

With one hand on the throttle levers and the other on the wheel, Max battled with the waves as he piloted the response boat closer still to the Atratus. The swells tossed the two vessels close together and then apart as Max attempted to move alongside the yacht without colliding with it. They could see the captain on board clearly now. He was soaked through and hanging onto the wheel in the cockpit at the stern. The canvas of the rigid bimini above him was ripped to shreds and he was exposed to the full force of the howling wind and sweeping bands of rain. The plan was to manoeuvre the rescue boat alongside the Atratus, close enough to put Linroy and Alvin on board. Providing the yacht hadn't suffered too much damage and the hull was still intact, they would attach a tow rope and bring the vessel safely back to harbour. It would be a dangerous mission.

Holding firmly to the side of the rescue boat, Linroy and Alvin, already soaked through, waited on deck as Max skilfully piloted the boat as close to the Atratus as he dared. They were joined by Shawn who would remain on the lifeboat ready to throw the towline to his crew mates. The engines roared and subsided over the noise of the wind and rain as Max manipulated the throttle control levers. The two boats rocked violently alongside each other. With every rise and fall and crash of the waves, the crew were showered with a salty, dank mist of sea spray.

Finally, a small amount of luck and a lull in the storm brought the two vessels close enough for Linroy to leap across to the deck of the Atratus. He was followed soon after by Alvin. While Linroy made for the captain of the yacht at the stern, Alvin headed to the bow to look at possibilities for connecting a towline. Even for the experienced crew members, the sea conditions made it a difficult and precarious task. Max radioed to Alvin informing him that he would attempt a couple of mock runs before Shawn threw the towline across, in order for them to get a feel of the strength of the wind and the swell height and direction of the waves as he manoeuvred alongside the yacht. Shawn, at the stern of the rescue boat, kept one eye on Max and the other on Alvin, who was inspecting the cleats on the Atratus.

Linroy had reached the captain of the yacht. Radioing on his handheld, he confirmed that the man was exhausted, dehydrated and suffering from mild hypothermia, but otherwise uninjured and not requiring immediate medical attention. The message was acknowledged by Melford, back at the Coast Guard station, who added an informal comment of encouragement to the crew to hang in there and stay safe.

'Linroy, have you requested a tow, over?' Colin asked from the lifeboat.

'Yeah, he's agreed. We're all set,' Linroy replied. The yacht Atratus was now the responsibility of the rescue crew.

Max wrestled with the rising swells as he commenced the first mock run for transferring the towline. Wrapped in a foil blanket, the pale-faced captain of the Atratus, who insisted on remaining at the helm with Linroy, was slumped on the floor of the cockpit. Exhausted, he leaned against the wood-slatted bench on the starboard side, swigging water from a plastic flask given to him by Linroy. As Max began the second dry run, Shawn and Alvin confirmed they were ready to set up the tow, Shawn from the stern of the rescue boat and Alvin at the bow of the yacht.

Completing the mock run, Max manoeuvred the rescue boat into position for what he hoped was the final time. The waves thrashed against the hulls of both boats and he focused on keeping them apart, but close enough for the towline to be successfully transferred to the Atratus. The thick rope was attached to a buoyant heaving line, which would be used to messenger the heavier towline across the water. Shawn, who had secured himself to the rescue boat to keep his balance, had carefully coiled the heaving line in preparation. He received a nod from Alvin and, as the two boats pitched towards each other, he hurled the line hard to the Atratus. It landed in the middle of the deck as a wave crashed over the side of the yacht. The crews on both vessels watched nervously as Alvin dived for the line. He caught it and held it tightly as the wave swept across the deck and the yacht lurched violently into a trough.

Steadying himself on his hands and knees and barely able to see through the mist of sea spray, Alvin fastened the tow rope as securely as he could to the cleats on the foredeck. When he was satisfied that the line was firmly attached, he signalled to the rest of the crew. Max, who had been maintaining the position of the rescue boat slightly ahead of the Atratus, gave a nod of acknowledgement and slowly opened the throttles. He powered tentatively ahead, taking up the slack in the towline, although the rolling waves prevented any degree of precision handling. In calmer seas, Max knew that to ensure the line didn't come under immediate tension, the manoeuvre needed to be performed as slowly and smoothly as possible. But the towering waves smashing into the hulls of both vessels, and the strong, gusting winds, prevented them from having any hope of a fluid towing operation.

When the rescue boat was a little further ahead of the Atratus, Max pulled back the throttles in order to give Alvin and Shawn a chance to check the line before they began their perilous journey back to English Harbour. The length of the towline was determined by the distance between each wave, with the aim of ensuring that both boats were on the peaks and in the troughs at the same time.

Shawn had lengthened the tow rope to keep the vessels further apart in the rough sea.

The storm had subsided a little but the wind remained strong and the driving rain reduced their forward visibility to no more than a few feet, the mist producing a glare in the powerful navigation lights. Although Alvin had attached the tow rope as securely as possible, there was a risk of the force of the line ripping the cleats out from the deck of the yacht. Max knew he had to limit the towing speed to no more than three or four knots. In addition, there was extra drag from the broken mast and sails trailing along the port side, causing the yacht to slew in one direction. It would be a long, slow and turbulent ride back to English Harbour.

Almost five hours later, the exhausted, windswept and sodden crews of the Atratus and the Coast Guard boat glimpsed the twinkling lights of Antigua in the distance. Max breathed a sigh of relief and felt the pull of the Atratus on the towline behind as it lurched over a wave. He was grateful to be nearing the safety of the harbour at last. It was still raining hard, although the swell from the giant waves and the strength of the wind was finally diminishing.

Dawn was breaking as they approached the welcoming glow of English Harbour, beyond which rose the darkened silhouette of the island's rocky, undulating landscape. Max radioed to Melford to confirm they were entering the channel. The red and green lights of the floating markers blinked intermittently as they made their way into the harbour, red buoys on the starboard side of the channel, green buoys on the port side, although Max knew he could pilot the course in his sleep. The water was much calmer here and the harbour entrance was deep, wide and easy to navigate. The only real danger was the reef extending from Charlotte Point, on the south side. Favouring the opposite side of the channel, closer to Berkeley Point, Max kept an eye on the glimmering lights of a stone-coloured hotel high on the hill ahead of him, aligning them with a course in degrees magnetic on his compass.

As the boats crept into the harbour, Max slowed the speed of the rescue boat to two knots. The speed limit for all marine craft in the harbour was four knots, but he was conscious of the trailing remnants of the broken mast and torn sails and would need to manoeuvre with caution, giving a wide berth to any boats moored nearby. He radioed to Linroy and agreed they would pick up a mooring to which they would secure the yacht, before returning to shore. Linroy replaced his handheld radio into the pocket of his cargo pants and glanced down at the captain of the yacht. The man was still wrapped in the foil blanket and slumped on the deck, leaning awkwardly against the cockpit bench. His eyes were open now and he gazed straight ahead. Linroy checked his breathing; it was regular and his respiratory rate was normal. The man was still alive.

Looking back up, something caught Linroy's eye. He frowned in puzzlement. In the steely grey light of dawn, he could just see inside the shadowy interior of the yacht through the open door leading to the companionway. On the port side a u-shaped bench in expensive cream leather surrounded a wooden-topped table. Secured to the bench with thick nautical rope was a row of large, blue plastic drums, perhaps seven or eight in total. On the table was a line of another four or five, Linroy couldn't quite see the exact number. They were the same blue plastic, probably with a capacity of around fifteen US gallons, tied tightly together with the same thick rope. Whoever had secured the drums looked to have made a decent job of it. The knots had weathered a force ten gale at sea without a single one slipping. The ropes which secured the drums to the bench and table had also held fast.

Still frowning, Linroy stole another glance at the captain. He had given his first name as Oliver but had revealed nothing further, although perhaps that was not uncommon in the circumstances. Linroy considered the picture before him. Something felt wrong. For starters, severe warnings of the approaching storm had been in place for days. Experienced sailors and yachtsmen would have been aware of the ominous forecasts and changes in the weather. They would've hunkered down in the safety of a harbour until the storm had passed. Never leave a harbour to look for a harbour.

Oliver would have needed some kind of sailing experience to pilot a fifty-seven foot yacht singlehandedly out at sea. Why had he not heeded the stark weather cautions and taken note of the warning signs? Instead, he had chosen to brave the storm, risking his life and his expensive yacht, and now also the lives of his rescuers.

And that was the other thing. He was sailing alone. Fine, it wasn't completely out of the ordinary, but the whole point of sailing around the Caribbean on yachts like this one was that it was a social pursuit, usually enjoyed by a group of people. The Atratus was a very nice, expensive yacht, probably worth well over half a million dollars. The sloop should've been drifting lazily around the islands, dropping into exclusive harbours for lobster dinners and boozy night stops. It certainly wasn't made for ferrying around crude plastic drums tied together with industrial-grade rope in force ten conditions. It wasn't a container ship. As Linroy contemplated what might be in the blue plastic drums, the faint sound of alarm bells began to go off in his head.

'Where did you say you were sailing from again?' Linroy asked, his eyes fixed on the rescue boat ahead.

'Saint Lucia,' Oliver replied, referring to one of the islands further south of Antigua.

'That your point of departure?'

Oliver paused before responding.

'No,' he said shortly.

Linroy waited but Oliver remained silent.

'What was your original point of departure?' Linroy asked.

'Port of Brighton.' The reply was abrupt. Linroy knew the port was a small harbour in southwestern Trinidad. He gave it some thought.

'Where were you headed?' he asked.

'Sugar Reef Bay,' Oliver replied.

Sugar Reef Bay was a mile-long stretch of sugar crystal pink sand on the southeastern coast of Antigua, facing the Atlantic. Rising from the beach were tall palms and lush green hills. The bay was home to an exclusive enclave of multimillion dollar beach houses and luxury villas.

'You got your own mooring there?' Linroy asked curiously.

'Yeah.'

'You were almost home then.'

'Yeah. Almost. Before I got caught in this blasted storm.'

'You didn't check the forecast before you set out?'

'Sure. I thought I could make it before the storm hit.' Oliver shivered and tugged the crumpled foil blanket tighter around him.

Linroy considered the route again: the point of departure Trinidad, just off the coast of Venezuela, to a private mooring in an exclusive bay in Antigua, via Saint Lucia. The fact that Oliver was sailing alone, risking life and limb and a rather nice boat in a violent storm. And the fact that the yacht was new, luxurious and — most of all — expensive. And the blue plastic drums. Something was very wrong with this picture.

Keeping half an eye on his dishevelled passenger, Linroy retrieved the handheld from his cargo pants and called the Coast Guard. Melford responded from Deepwater Harbour and Linroy relayed another message. He knew his fellow crew mates would hear and understand.

'Yeah, Coast Guard, we're in the harbour now. About to hit the mooring. We got anyone meeting us back on shore, over?'

There was a pause at the end of the line.

'You need some assistance?'

'Yeah. Might be a good idea.'

'No problem. I'll have Delano meet you there. Anything else, over?'

'Nope. That's all.'

'Got you.'

Melford hung up and Linroy pocketed the handheld. He shot a suspicious glance at Oliver who was staring straight ahead, apparently disinterested and unmoved. But Linroy knew he'd overheard the radio communication.

TWO

6:35 am, Thursday, September 19
Hibiscus Cottage, Mamora Bay, Antigua

It was still early but the storm had kept Delano Reid awake for most of the night. He stood in his kitchen in a pair of navy boxer shorts, scrolling through the headlines on his cell phone as he deposited a generous amount of roasted coffee beans into the bean container of a one-cup coffee machine. It was still raining hard outside. The rays of dawn light splashed a pale grey through the half-open jalousie windows of the small one-bedroom cottage. Delano lived the simple life as far as material possessions went. The coffee machine was probably his most extravagant purchase.

He had one teenage daughter, Tamesha, who was his pride and joy. He doted on her. She was doing great at school, was top in her maths class and had just made the school netball team. She lived with her mother. Delano lived alone. He saw Tamesha every other weekend and occasionally he'd meet her from school too. They'd hang at the beach together before going back to his cottage for grilled shrimp, corn salsa and fried Johnny cakes — Delano loved to cook — followed by chocolate ice cream sundaes with whipped cream, nuts and hot fudge, Tamesha's favourite.

If Delano had his way Tamesha would live with him all the time. His current job wasn't conducive to this longing, although many times he'd considered quitting anyway. He dreamed of investing in a handful of plastic beach chairs and cheap parasols. He'd set up his own enterprise on a beach nearby, renting the chairs and parasols to tourists by the hour. It would at least be a step closer to realising a dream of owning his own beach bar. But for now, the dream was on hold. He wanted to ensure he could provide for Tamesha in every way possible and he was saving for a decent college education for her.

At least he had the cottage. It was a crude little wooden structure painted white with a tin roof on which heavy drops of rain now landed with a loud, metallic echo. The whole place took up no more than four hundred square feet. His bedroom, with an adjoining bathroom, led into a small open-plan kitchen and living area. Dark wooden kitchen cabinets lined one of the walls, shabby and scratched with some of the handles missing from the cupboard doors. A large gas cooker with rust streaks down one side stood by itself against another wall.

The lounge area boasted a small couch, which Delano slept on when Tamesha stayed over, and a bookcase half-filled with scruffy paperbacks and a handful of dog-eared technical manuals he had acquired over the years. The only other item of furniture in the room was a brown formica sideboard unit on which sat a lamp with a sun-bleached shade and an ancient-looking TV. There was no electricity connected to the property and Delano relied on a small generator for power. Although the cottage was linked to the public water supply, like many private residences in Antigua, Delano's principal source of water came from three large tanks. The rainwater collected and stored in the tanks provided him with a sufficient amount for most domestic uses like washing, showering and flushing the toilet. The heavy rainfall overnight would have raised the water level in the tanks considerably, which was always a good thing.

But Delano didn't care how primitive his cottage was, because a step through the mesh screen door from the living area led to a hidden secret. Outside, a wooden deck area overlooked one acre of land which sloped gently down to a generous stretch of beach frontage. The deck area afforded magnificent views of the entire bay, taking in the glittering turquoise sea fringed by soft white sand and luscious palms and foliage. On the opposite side of the bay stood an exclusive, five-star beach resort, while a handful of imposing super yachts were moored in the crystal clear waters below, now bathed in raindrops and glinting in the dawn light. Delano never grew tired of the sweeping panorama and spent many evenings on his deck, beer in hand, contemplating life and imagining his beach bar dream.

As he filled the water container of the coffee machine, he surveyed the bay through his kitchen window. The horseshoe shape of the shoreline had provided a calmer haven for the super yachts from the raging storm overnight, although the usually glassy water of the bay was peppered with large drops of rain and the palm trees along the shoreline swayed wildly in the breeze. Heavy grey storm clouds hung low in the sky over the horizon as the rain continued to beat hard on the metal roof of the cottage.

Suddenly, a shrill sound interrupted the drumming of the rain. It was a call from the Deepwater Coast Guard Station.

'Delano.' As he answered, he set his phone to speaker and placed it back on the kitchen worktop.

'Morning Delano. It's Mel here. Sorry to call so early but I got a case for you.' Delano recognised Melford's voice.

'Oh?' He slid the phone closer to him. 'Where?'

'English Harbour. The lifeboat crew picked up a yacht in distress just after one-thirty this morning. Fifteen miles southwest of Sugar Reef. One on board. Exhausted and dehydrated with a touch of hypothermia but he's otherwise okay. His point of departure was the Port of Brighton.'

'Trinidad?'

'That's right.'

'Anything else?'

'Only that the yacht's chock-full of plastic drums.'

'What's in them?'

'My imagination's running wild but if I was a betting man…'

'All right Mel. I'm on my way. I'll alert the rest of the team and be there in fifteen.'

'Great. The yacht's moored to a buoy in the harbour but one of the day crew will take you guys out to it in a tender. They'll meet you on the shoreline.'

'Thanks. Oh, what's the name of the yacht?'

'Atratus.'

'Atratus?'

'Yep.'

'What kinda name is that? What's wrong with Wind Dancer or Carpe Diem or Serenity?'

'It's Latin.'

'Since when did you become a classical scholar?'

'Since four o-clock this morning when I was waiting for Max and the crew to make it back to the safety of harbour. It means to be clothed in black, like in mourning, or to be darkened, blackened, murky, dingy...'

'I think I get the picture, thanks Mel. That's an uplifting start to the morning.'

'You're welcome. You know I like to furnish you with as much information as possible.'

'I'm sure it'll come in really handy.'

'The other place the word atratus is used, of course, is in the scientific names — again, usually derived from Latin — of various birds, animals, insects and mammals. You know, like Cygnus atratus for the black swan, or...'

'You going anywhere with this, Mel?' Delano asked, smiling to himself.

'Just an extra bit of background which might help with the case.' Delano knew Mel was smiling too.

They said goodbye and hung up. Delano dressed hurriedly in navy cargo pants and a navy t-shirt, and reached for his waterproof jacket. He always took it with him to a job but rarely needed to actually wear it. Today was the exception. It would also help him stay warm. The temperature was considerably cooler than usual. He paged the other members of his seven-strong team and poured a generous supply of freshly brewed coffee into a thermo travel mug. Pulling on his boots, he grabbed his backpack and lifejacket and headed out into the rain.

Officer Delano Reid headed up the small but formidable Tactical and Surveillance Team of the Crime and Drug Squad of the Leeward Islands, otherwise known as the CDSLI. With a distinguished history of military service in the Antigua and Barbuda Defence Force, Officer Reid's previous roles included providing security detail at key government properties, assisting the police with fighting crime, and the tactical training of military and law enforcement personnel. He had been head-hunted for his current role in the CDSLI, an elite task force set up to combat drug trafficking, money laundering and the financing of terrorism.

Lately though, the drug trafficking part of the job had seemed to take precedent over the other two. Conveniently situated on a vital crossroads between the narcotics producers of South America and the hungry consumers of the United States and Europe, Antigua was considered to be a prime transhipment location for narco traffickers. A drug transit zone. A gangster's paradise. Although drug trafficking carried a maximum penalty of life in prison, the rewards mostly far outweighed the risks for anyone willing to take them.

The headquarters of the CDSLI was in Antigua, although there were teams based at various locations throughout the Leeward Islands of the Caribbean, including Anguilla, Saint Martin, Saint Kitts and Nevis, Saint Lucia and Guadeloupe. The myriad secluded harbours and quiet or abandoned airstrips throughout the islands provided traffickers with countless staging areas and cache sites for large quantities of drugs. Delano knew that even the principal airports on the islands afforded a base for extensive networks and connections with drug smugglers. They, in turn, used private and chartered flights to convey clandestine shipments to and from assorted locations throughout the Caribbean and beyond.

The CDSLI worked alongside other partners within the region, such as the Coast Guard, on multi-agency counter-smuggling operations. Between them, they shared intelligence and collaborated with training. In the five years Delano had headed up his team, they had supported the Coast Guard in successfully intercepting a number of marine vessels and aircraft with large shipments of drugs. The team also conducted joint counter-narcotics operations with overseas law enforcement agencies, including the United States Coast Guard and the Drug Enforcement Administration. The amaranthine demand for illegal drugs from North America and Europe ensured that Delano and his comrades would have jobs for life.

It was a ten minute drive to English Harbour. Delano's silver Toyota Hilux pickup rattled and shook as he navigated the uneven tarmac and avoided invisible potholes filled with water. With the exception of a few early risers and commercial vehicles, the roads were deserted. It would be mid-morning before the usual rush hour of tourists in rental cars and SUVs descended on the highways. The wipers of the pickup screeched miserably across the windshield in a vain attempt at providing some form of forward visibility.

With the near-bald tyres of the Toyota splashing through deep puddles, Delano pulled into a small gravel parking lot and cut the engine. He pulled his backpack off the seat next to him and, clutching his travel mug, opened the door and jumped out. Glancing around the lot through the rain, he didn't recognise any of the other vehicles. He was the first to arrive. He jogged down to the slipway of the marina where he spotted the waiting Coast Guard tender and two members of the English Harbour day crew, Lawrence and Connor, wearing matching navy waterproof jackets and tan cargo pants. The wind whistled eerily through the rigging of the sailboats moored in the harbour and halyards slapped noisily against the masts as the three men exchanged early morning pleasantries and comments about the storm. One by one, the remaining members of Delano's team began to arrive.

'So what's the story with the Atratus?' Delano asked when they were assembled in a small semi-circle around Lawrence and Connor. Kitted out in wet weather gear, boots and lifejackets, they stood with their backs to the wind and rain.

'We know about as much as you,' Lawrence said, raising his voice to ensure he could be heard. 'The captain of the yacht isn't saying anything although Linroy thinks he'll talk when you guys show up.'

'Maybe,' Delano said, taking a gulp of coffee. He glanced at the rain-streaked but eager faces of his team and selected three of them to join him in the tender which would take them to the Atratus, secured to a mooring in the harbour.

'Anson, Mitch and Hyacinth, you're with me. Nerissa, Brandon and Edella, take shelter back at headquarters and I'll call you with an update as soon as I know what we're dealing with. Nerissa, check in with Mel at Deepwater Harbour — he should still be at the station — and get the details of the initial distress call from the yacht. Times, locations, all that. Brandon, get started on the paperwork. You know, the usual. Edella, get digging, see what you can find out about the Atratus yacht, who owns it and so on. All we know so far is that the man on board is a British guy going by the name of Oliver.'

The team split up. Three of them retreated to one of the marina buildings where the CDSLI headquarters was situated. The other four climbed into the Coast Guard tender, a small rigid inflatable boat. Lawrence had the outboard motor running, ready to ferry them over to the Atratus. Connor remained on the dockside as they cast off, weaving their way through boats and mooring buoys, into the harbour. After a few minutes, Lawrence reduced the power of the small outboard. Through the rain, they could see the skulking, grey silhouettes of two boats ahead: the battered remains of a large sailing yacht and the Coast Guard rescue boat. As they neared the vessels, Lawrence manoeuvred the RIB alongside the rescue boat where two figures appeared on deck. They were soaked through and looked windswept and exhausted. Lawrence cut the engine and Delano, Anson, Mitch and Hyacinth quickly boarded the larger rescue boat, one after the other. As soon as he had secured the RIB, Lawrence joined them a few minutes later. The faint scent of gasoline hung in the air as Delano and his team were greeted by Max and Shawn. They listened intently as Max summarised the search and rescue mission.

'The captain isn't giving us anything other than his name, and the port of departure and destination,' he said, 'but Linroy's pretty certain this is a case for you guys and I agree with him. Somethin' just ain't right about this.'

'Lead the way,' Delano said, gesturing to the lifeboat crew.

Max stepped aside as Shawn led the CDSLI officers to the port side of the boat which was moored alongside the wreck of the Atratus. With its mainsail and jib ripped to shreds and the remaining part of its broken, twisted mast hanging limply over to one side, the luxurious Beneteau sailing yacht, severely damaged from the storm, was a forlorn sight. On the foredeck, Alvin was coiling ropes and inspecting a cleat. He saluted Delano who returned the courtesy as the team made their way to the stern of the rescue boat.

In the rain-washed cockpit of the Atratus, Linroy sat beside a man in his early forties. He had short, dark hair and a deep suntan. Beneath a silver foil blanket, wrapped loosely around him, he was wearing a black polo shirt, faded by the sun, and grey shorts with what looked like shrimps printed on them. No lifejacket. He was barefoot and shivered slightly in the breeze.

'Morning Linroy,' Delano said cheerily.

'Thanks for coming,' Linroy replied. 'I guess Max brought you up to speed?'

'Yeah, he did. You got anything else for us?'

'Not much,' Linroy shook his head. He turned to the man next to him. 'This is Oliver Jacobs. He was on his way from Brighton Port in Trinidad to Sugar Reef Bay when last night's storm hit.'

'It was a bad one,' Delano remarked. 'You check the weather before you set out Mr. Jacobs?'

'I know better than that,' Oliver said with a faint sneer, avoiding eye contact. His voice was husky with exhaustion and dehydration. 'I've sailed in force tens before. Storms and rough seas don't faze me. If it wasn't for the mast breaking up, a double engine failure, an electrical failure and then a complete loss of comms…'

'You had one or two things go wrong then,' Delano said, draining the last of his coffee.

'You could say that.'

'Important journey was it?' Delano asked. Behind the sneer, Delano could see that Oliver knew the game was up. With his team close behind, Delano stepped to the edge of the rescue boat.

'You know who we are, Mr. Jacobs?'

'I'll take a wild stab in the dark and guess you're the welcoming committee the Coast Guard requested on the way here.'

28

'Very astute,' Delano said, matching the sarcasm. 'Then if you'd be so kind, we'd like your permission to come aboard.' It was a point of courtesy rather than a legal requirement.

Oliver brought his eyes up to meet Delano's. He appeared to be wrestling with the remnants of his conscience, which was apparently as much in tatters as the shredded sails of his yacht. He stood up slowly, pushing himself to his feet with both hands.

'Don't have much choice, do I?' he said with a shrug.

'You're not exactly in a strong position right now, no, Mr. Jacobs,' Delano replied. 'I suggest you make it easy for yourself. It'll work out better in the long run.'

'Fine, come and join the party. Knock yourselves out boys,' Oliver said coolly, but the reckless tone of his voice was laced with a note of fear.

'Boys and *girls*.' A female voice spoke. Oliver narrowed his eyes and peered around Delano in the direction of the voice. Hyacinth's petite frame was swamped in her waterproof jacket, lifejacket and backpack but there was a stubborn glint in her large brown eyes.

'Whatever.' Oliver shrugged again rudely.

The four officers climbed nimbly from the rescue boat onto the yacht, one after the other. Standing in a small group in the cockpit of the Atratus, they were joined by Alvin.

'I sure am glad to see you guys,' he said with a weary smile. 'I've made fast the lines to the mooring and she's secure. The mast's a wreck, what's left of it. It'll need a bit of care when you bring her ashore, but it'll hold for now.'

'Good job Alvin,' Delano replied. 'You too Linroy. We'll take it from here. Go home. Get some well-earned rest.'

As Linroy and Alvin began to climb across to the rescue boat, Delano spoke again. 'Mr. Jacobs, you got anything to say to two of the crew who saved your life this morning, before they disembark?'

'If I'm not mistaken, it's their job. It's what they're paid to do,' Oliver said with disdain.

'Noted,' Delano replied coldly. 'And now you're about to find out what *I'm* paid to do.' He shot a grin at Linroy and Alvin as they stepped off the Atratus onto the lifeboat. They saluted him before joining Max, Colin and Shawn who were preparing to untie from the mooring and return to shore, leaving Lawrence and the RIB with the CDSLI officers, Oliver Jacobs and the Atratus.

Dense, towering clouds scudded across the sky from the east and the steady rainfall continued. A faraway rumble of thunder could be heard over the engines of the rescue boat as it set off towards the marina, its wake gently rocking nearby yachts and fishing boats moored in the harbour. The noise gradually faded into the distance as the boat neared the shore. Surrounded by the other three members of his team, Delano turned to Oliver.

'So Mr. Jacobs, what was the reason for your visit to Trinidad? A little vacation, was it?'

Oliver, still wrapped in the foil blanket which rustled every time he moved, looked away with a bored expression. Delano peered past Oliver through the open door into the saloon of the yacht. He could see the blue plastic drums stacked around the seating area on the port side.

'Brought back a few souvenirs, did you?' Delano asked. The silence continued as Oliver appeared to be contemplating his options.

'What's in the drums, Jacobs?' Delano said. There was a note of impatience in his voice. But still the captain of the Atratus did not reply. Windswept and chilled from the dampness of the morning, Delano wasn't in the mood for dancing. A distant crackle of thunder echoed around the harbour, louder than before. Suddenly he took a step past Oliver in the direction of the saloon.

'Okay stop,' Oliver said in a defeated tone. He knew the game was over. And he had lost. 'The drums are full of cocaine.'

Unmoved by Oliver's admission, Delano paused before responding.

'Quite a stash you've got in there,' he said finally.

'That's nothing.' The reply was suddenly cocky, confident. 'The boat's loaded. Every cupboard, every drawer, the cooker, even the head. Every damn compartment. Four and a half thousand pounds of the stuff. Seventy-five million dollars' worth of cocaine. I'll bet this is the biggest stash you guys have ever seen.'

Delano swallowed hard but remained composed. If Oliver Jacobs was speaking the truth, then this was indeed the biggest payload of cocaine he had encountered on one vessel in the five years he had overseen his team in the CDSLI.

Anson, stocky and well-built, immediately stepped forward. He pushed Oliver roughly, turning him so he was facing away from them, before holding his arms in a vicelike grip. Hyacinth produced a thick tie-wrap and secured it tightly around his wrists. Oliver glanced down over his shoulder at her with a look of contempt.

'Sorry darling, but you're really not my type.'

'Pity,' Hyacinth replied coldly, 'cos I got a whole lot of other implements specially reserved for jackasses like you. Your loss I guess.'

Delano smiled to himself. Hyacinth could hold her own with anyone. He looked at his three team members.

'Let's take a look around.' He turned to Oliver. 'The boat belongs to you?'

'Yeah. So don't touch anything and wipe your feet before you go below deck.'

Ignoring the retort, Delano led the way down the companionway into the open-plan saloon and galley. Little could be seen of the Alpi walnut veneer, the Rovere Aleve flooring and the plush leather seating of the luxurious interior due to the number of blue plastic drums, tied together in rows of four and two. Every window and deck hatch was obscured by the drums, with the only natural daylight from the cockpit behind them. Delano pulled a small flashlight from his pocket and beamed it around the saloon, taking in the sight before him. A small space had been cleared around the control console for access to the instrument panels and the radio. The display screens were dead and the radio was silent. A crumpled paper navigation chart with various markings on it was still attached to the cluttered surface in front of the console. An iPad in a protective case was positioned on a mount next to the chart. Delano guessed it became useless to Oliver when the battery died and he had no means of charging it. Same with the handheld GPS which had been thrown onto the floor in the storm.

As he made his way between the circular walls of blue plastic towards the bow, Delano stepped over a mask and snorkel and one diving glove. The laminate flooring was littered with various items which had fallen from cupboards or had come loose from their housings during the storm. Further along a pair of waterproof Barska binoculars lay next to an underwater camera in waterproof casing. Oliver certainly had all the gear. Delano turned to the little group behind him. They were grateful to be sheltering from the wind and rain outside, including Oliver, who stood sullenly and silently next to Hyacinth.

'Mitch, get some pictures,' Delano said. 'Anson, take a look inside one of these drums. Let's see what we've got. Hyacinth, you okay with your new friend?'

'Never better,' Hyacinth replied with a wry smile.

'Good. I'll take a look through here.' Delano stopped suddenly and turned to Oliver with a puzzled expression.

'You learn Latin at school?'

'Yeah. Why?'

'The Atratus,' Delano replied thoughtfully. 'Why d'you give your boat that name?'

Oliver shrugged.

'It means to be clothed in black, like in mourning, or to be…' Delano went on.

'I know what it means,' Oliver snapped.

'Just liked it did you?'

Oliver ignored the question and Delano let it go. He stepped into the small area leading to the forward cabin straight ahead, with the port and starboard cabins on either side. Oliver had been telling the truth. In the port and starboard cabins, the same blue plastic drums were stacked in twos on the beds of each cabin, held together with the same thick, nautical rope. Delano eased his way into the port cabin, through to the head. It consisted of a toilet and washbasin area, and a separate shower compartment, none of which were visible or usable due to the ominous blue plastic drums stacked on top of each other. Above him was a deck hatch, firmly shut and covered with a mosquito blind. Delano pushed against one of the drums. It felt heavy and not easily moveable. He returned to the small area between the cabins. Back in the galley, Mitch was taking photographs while Anson was prising open the top of one of the blue drums with a large screwdriver. Oliver stood watching them with Hyacinth beside him.

The forward cabin, and the associated head and shower room, had apparently served as Oliver's living quarters for the journey and were the only areas which did not contain any plastic drums. Oliver's personal effects were strewn haphazardly across the unmade bed and over the floor, where they had been thrown during the storm. Delano crossed to the starboard cabin where one of the ropes around the drums had come untied. The drums it had held together were no longer neatly stacked but toppled and laying haphazardly against each other, jolted loose by the storm. The top of one of the drums laying on the mattress of the bed had become detached from the drum. Inside, Delano could just make out rectangular bricks containing white powder. The bricks were wrapped in clear plastic and tightly sealed with duct tape. They were packed in fives and held together with more duct tape.

'Boss.' A voice called from the saloon. It was Anson. 'We got cocaine all right.'

Delano returned to the saloon where Anson had retrieved a bale of five bricks from one of the other drums. With a scalpel blade, he had removed one of the bricks from the bale and carefully slit a piece of the clear plastic wrapping from which he had extracted a sample of the white substance, placing it in an ampoule from a small drug testing kit. The liquid inside the ampoule had turned a deep shade of blue, indicating the presence of cocaine. He held the ampoule up for Delano to inspect. Oliver watched in silence.

'Short of a lab analysis, I'd say that's fairly conclusive,' Delano said.

'What did you find down there?' Anson asked, nodding towards the bow.

'Much of the same in the port and starboard cabins,' Delano replied, glancing at Oliver. He paused as he considered their next move. 'We need to bring this vessel ashore,' he said decisively, 'and get these drums unloaded. Thanks to the storm and Linroy's sharp eyes we just picked up a major-league drug shipment.'

'Connor's on his way over with the tender,' Lawrence stuck his head through the door from the top of the companionway behind Hyacinth and Oliver. 'Thought you'd like to know.'

'That's good timing,' Delano said. 'He can stay here with Mitch and Anson while they finish up. Lawrence, we'll head back to shore with Hyacinth and Jacobs.'

'No problem,' Lawrence replied. 'I'm ready when you are.'

Over the sound of the rain they could hear the roar of an outboard motor as it approached the yacht. Within minutes Connor had tied up alongside and was on the deck of the Atratus.

'The hell's happened to that mast?' he said, joining Lawrence at the top of the companionway. 'Oh my…' His eyes widened at the rows of plastic drums. He gazed around the galley and saloon area before noticing the loose brick of white powder on the chart table. With a look of disdain at Oliver, he said, 'You have any idea how many lives are ruined every day because of lowlife traffickers like you?'

'Sorry pal but I don't think I gave you permission to board,' Oliver said curtly, 'so if you don't get the hell off my boat I'll be reporting you to the Coast Guard for unauthorised boarding and violating my rights.'

'I am the Coast Guard,' Connor replied in a weary tone. 'I can board your pathetic excuse of a shipwreck any time I want and I can look anywhere I want without warning, a warrant or probable cause.'

'You…' Oliver began, but was interrupted by Delano.

'That's enough. Connor, stay here with Anson and Mitch. I'll send Brandon over to give them a hand. When they're done, you and Mitch can take care of the logistics of towing this wreck to the quay so we can offload the cocaine. Jacobs, you're coming back to shore with Lawrence, Hyacinth and me.'

'I hope your officers know what they're doing here,' Oliver said. 'This outfit seems a bit amateurish to me…' He glanced at Connor.

'We're done here,' Delano cut him off again with a warning glare. 'Let's go.'

'See you back at base, boss,' Anson said, without looking up from a pile of documents he had retrieved from one of the stowage compartments.

Lawrence had brought the tender around to the swim platform at the stern. He held it steady for the others to board. Flanked between Delano and Hyacinth, and still with his wrists secured behind his back with the tie-wrap, Oliver sat on a bench at the stern while Lawrence started the motor. He untied the painter and pushed off from the yacht before returning to the helm, where he took the wheel.

'All set?' He turned to Delano.

'We're good,' Delano replied with a nod.

Lawrence gently pushed the throttle forward and guided the RIB around the port side of the Atratus, steering well clear of the remains of the damaged mast. He gradually increased the speed and they felt the cool wind and rain on their faces as the little boat skimmed across the water towards the dock. Overhead, the charcoal grey clouds boiled and churned, casting an oppressive gloom along the horizon. There was a faint echo of another growl of thunder. Oliver Jacobs sat on the bench between the two CDSLI officers, motionless and silent. Staring into the distance, he considered his next move.

THREE

The room was windowless, the only light a purple-tinged glow emitted by low-level LEDs at each corner. It was unofficially known as "the vault" to those who were aware of its existence. The walls were constructed of cinder blocks painted dark grey and the only way in or out was through a heavy steel door, also painted dark grey. The room was furnished with a single item: a metal folding chair anchored to the uneven, brick-paved floor. There was no air-conditioning in the room, the only source of airflow rendered by two wide ventilation grilles near the tops of the walls. The air was clammy with a faint smell of seaweed.

Dressed in dry clothes: a charcoal grey t-shirt and black shorts on loan from the CDSLI, Oliver Jacobs sat on the metal folding chair and studied a cinder block on the wall in front of him. He guessed he was in some kind of underground bunker. He was familiar with the history of English Harbour: during the eighteenth century it was the base for the Royal Navy's operations in the surrounding area. Within the harbour was Nelson's Dockyard where a collection of restored eighteenth and nineteenth century buildings and other historical artefacts from the colonial period of the dockyard were displayed. At the entrance to the harbour was Fort Berkeley, a now ruined fort built in the early eighteenth century to defend the harbour. There were still remnants of its stone walls and ramparts, and a cannon, evoking historical impressions of the colonial era for tourists visiting the area. There was sure to be an abundance of hidden tunnels, bunkers and secret rooms below ground. It was no surprise to Oliver that the CDSLI had commandeered one of these as an interrogation room. Perhaps there were others used as storage areas for seized contraband.

The tie-wrap had been removed and his wrists were now in handcuffs which were attached to the chair. He glanced up as the door opened and Delano and Hyacinth entered. The heavy door slammed shut behind them on its sprung hinges. From somewhere above, but which he had been unable to locate even after his eyes had become accustomed to the dim light, Oliver knew a secret camera was rolling and a hidden microphone recording. He spoke first.

'I'd like to make a telephone call.'

'Maybe. When we're done here,' Hyacinth replied.

'I think you'll find it's my legal entitlement,' Oliver said calmly.

'Oh really?' Hyacinth raised an eyebrow. 'Your legal entitlement? We're not the police. We got different rules.'

'I'm still entitled to my phone call,' Oliver said, narrowing his eyes.

'You're not particularly entitled to anything,' Hyacinth returned frostily. 'Who you wanna talk to? Your mommy?'

'My wife.'

'You're not married,' Hyacinth shot back. 'You wanna make an international call? Someone back home in the UK?'

'No. It's a local call.'

'Local? You gave us a London address when we took your details,' Delano interrupted.

'I need to contact someone here in Antigua.'

'Your lawyer?'

'A friend. But since you mention it, I'm also entitled to legal counsel so I'd like to make that phone call too.'

'Answer our questions first. We'll see how that goes before we decide on whether to grant your request or not,' Delano said.

'I'm not answering anything till I've made my phone call.' Oliver's voice remained calm but in the dim light of the room the colour of his cheeks intensified and beads of sweat began to form on his forehead.

'That's not how it works Jacobs,' Hyacinth said. 'Like I said, we ain't the police. We got different rules.'

'The law's still the law,' Oliver retorted.

'Ah, something we agree on,' Hyacinth said. 'I knew we'd find common ground eventually. Which brings us right on point. What exactly *were* you doing with seventy-five million dollars' worth of cocaine on board your yacht?'

Oliver didn't reply and returned his gaze to the cinder block in the wall.

'Help us out here, Jacobs,' Delano said. 'Things aren't looking good for you. You realise you're facing life in prison if you're found guilty of possession and being concerned with the supply of cocaine, right?'

Oliver remained silent.

'Names, Jacobs,' Hyacinth said. 'Give us the names of your contacts.'

'I'm not giving you anything till I get my phone call.'

'What's the urgency?' Delano asked, slightly curiously.

'It's my right,' Oliver replied.

Delano glanced at Hyacinth and shrugged.

'Better give him his phone call, I guess,' he said. He looked at Oliver. 'We'll make arrangements for you to be taken to a room with a phone. Someone'll be down to escort you.'

Oliver didn't reply. The steel door slammed shut behind Delano and Hyacinth as they left the room. He was alone once more.

'Oliver Robert Randal Jacobs. Born May thirty-first, nineteen seventy-six in London, England. An only child. Studied accountancy at the Queen Mary University of London. Graduated in nineteen ninety-seven with a First class degree, the highest class honours you can get in the UK.'

Edella Martin glanced at her hastily scrawled notes before continuing.

'After graduating Jacobs was headhunted by a number of prestigious financial institutions, but eventually went to work for Miller Kochmann. You've probably heard of them; they're one of the top twenty accounting firms in the world, headquartered in

London but with more than six hundred offices worldwide. They specialise in audit and assurance, tax, advisory and risk.'

She looked at the four blank faces of her co-workers who were stood in a group around a large, free-standing whiteboard. Obviously nobody had heard of Miller Kochmann. No matter. She cleared her throat and continued, pointing to bullet point number six on the whiteboard.

'He appears to have started with considerable promise at the firm but was a bit of a playboy by all accounts. He liked parties, wining, dining and women. Worked hard, played harder. Somewhere along the way, he seems to have gotten caught up in a handful of shady business ventures. I found links to a Dutch businessman by the name of Tobias Anneijes who masqueraded as a dealer of high-end artwork for millionaire clients across Europe. Tobias and his partner, Sonny Duclair, were caught in an undercover operation in December two-thousand for which they served a two year prison sentence. There's also another interesting character in Jacobs's past: a man called Graymond Sharkey.'

'Who?' Anson looked bemused.

'Yeah, you heard me right,' Edella went on, slightly annoyed at the interruption. 'Graymond Sharkey. I got a source who works for some obscure crime unit in London who did a bit of digging for me. According to her, Graymond, a multi-millionaire businessman with his own aviation company in the UK, also dabbled in the art smuggling world way back. But this guy ended up with a lot more on his rap sheet than a bit of stolen art trafficking. In two-thousand he was convicted of a double homicide. He served two life sentences in a max security prison and was released in...' She glanced down at her notes, '...October twenty-sixteen.'

'Jacobs sure has some interesting friends,' Anson remarked. 'How'd he hook up with this Sharkey guy?'

'Jacobs was his accountant,' Edella replied, 'but it seems they hung out quite a lot as friends leading up to and around the time Graymond was convicted of murder.'

'Was Jacobs involved in any way?' Delano asked.

'Doesn't appear to have been. According to my source, other than being Graymond's accountant, he wasn't connected to the murders. What's interesting about this case though is that shortly after Graymond's release in twenty-sixteen, new evidence came to light which led to his exoneration of the crimes. He was pardoned and another man,' another glance at the notes, '…a James Keyes, was found guilty of first-degree murder. There was an accomplice too, a man called Landon Davidson.'

'Bad luck for the Sharkey guy though,' Brandon said, 'serving a life sentence and knowing the whole time that he was innocent. What was the new evidence which came to light?'

'My source told me that James Keyes, or Jimmy as he was known, faked his own death — he was one of the two men Graymond was supposed to have killed — but was severely burned in the process. Some months later he had extensive plastic surgery for full-thickness burns to his face before he relocated to Negril.'

'Negril, Jamaica?' Anson queried.

'Yeah, he had a beach house there and a couple of restaurants. Anyway, a freelance journalist who reported on the original trial back in two-thousand, but wasn't convinced of Graymond's guilt, uncovered confidential patient records from a London clinic. They contained details of the reconstructive surgery Jimmy Keyes had done, but were under a false name. The journalist also discovered one of the pieces of stolen art which went missing at the time Keyes faked his death. It was hanging in the bedroom of his beach house. But I digress…'

'No, carry on, this is gripping stuff,' Brandon said.

'Well, other than the fact that Oliver Jacobs was connected to this guy Graymond Sharkey back then, both professionally and personally, he apparently had nothing to do with the murder case itself.'

'Are they still in touch?' Hyacinth asked.

'I don't know,' Edella replied. 'I'm still following up leads and I didn't want to get distracted from looking into the rest of Jacobs's background.'

'Go on,' Delano said.

'In the summer of two-thousand and one it appears Jacobs left Miller Kochmann to set up his own accountancy firm, OJ Accountancy Limited. The circumstances in which he left Miller Kochmann are obscure and somewhat questionable, but I'm still digging. Anyway, he set up his own accountancy business, with headquarters in London according to the records of the UK's Companies House, but with an interesting smattering of subsidiary offices all over the US and the Caribbean: New York, L.A., Vegas, Chicago, the Cayman Islands and Jamaica.'

'Far be it from me to jump to conclusions, but this has money laundering and tax evasion written all over it,' Anson said.

'You'd think,' Edella nodded, 'but if he's guilty, he's covered his tracks remarkably well. My source back in London has nothing on him and so far I haven't found anything untoward from this end. The business activities of OJ Accountancy Limited all appear to be legitimate. According to public records it's a bona fide company operating well within the law.'

'You've got to be kidding,' Brandon said in disbelief. 'OJ Accountancy sounds like it should practically be heading up the list of corporate scandals.'

'I know,' Edella agreed. 'Either Jacobs is incredibly smart or his company is entirely genuine in order to provide a smokescreen behind which he can conduct his less scrupulous enterprises.'

'That sounds more like it,' Hyacinth interjected.

'Good work Edella,' Delano said. 'Did you get anything on the Atratus?'

'Oh yeah, the boat. As you know, the Atratus is a Beneteau Sense fifty-seven ocean-cruising yacht. It was built in twenty-seventeen, purchased new and registered in Bermuda by OJ Accountancy as an entertainment facility for high net worth clients.'

'Yeah, I'll bet it was.' Brandon's comment was laced with sarcasm.

'I'm guessing Jacobs forgot to mention that he was also planning on using it for the transportation of illegal drugs,' Anson said.

'It doesn't mention anything about that in the business activities listed for OJ Accountancy, no,' Edella said wryly. 'But as with everything else to do with the company, all expense claims relating to the yacht are legit. It checks out on paper, at least.'

'Smart guy,' Delano said.

'Until now,' Hyacinth added.

'He would've gotten away with it if it wasn't for the storm,' Nerissa interrupted, joining the group. She waved a small bundle of papers. 'Full Coast Guard report and transcript of the initial distress call from the Atratus. The guys at Deepwater Harbour faxed it over just now.' Glancing at Delano, she added, 'Mitch also called to let you know that the Atratus is being brought ashore as we speak. He's on board now with Lawrence and Connor. It's in a pretty bad way apparently, but he'll give us a call when it's berthed and the damaged mast has been made safe. Oh, and Lloyd said to tell you Jacobs is back in the vault.'

Lloyd Kelly, who preferred to call himself a Special Consultant of the CDSLI, rather than his official job title of Technical Assistant, took care of the day to day running of the small headquarters of the Tactical and Surveillance Team. A bouncer by night, employed at The Jungle, a somewhat notorious reggae bar in one of the less desirable precincts of St. John's, Lloyd looked as though he belonged in a heavyweight boxing ring rather than the offices of the CDSLI. While much of his job consisted of answering phones and filing reports, he had certain special clearances for access to classified information and was, in some ways, regarded by the team as an honorary eighth member.

Due to his size and stature he was a useful pair of hands when it came to matters of security. He had been more than willing to take a break from the mundane jobs of the morning to escort Oliver to a room with a phone. Lloyd also possessed advanced information technology skills, mostly self-taught, which, if challenged, he preferred to describe as ethical hacking skills.

'Anything interesting or unusual about Jacobs's phone call?' Delano asked.

'Lloyd didn't say,' Nerissa replied. 'Wait a second…' She retraced her steps to the open door and stuck her head into the small reception area outside where Lloyd sat shuffling papers at an L-shaped office desk. He wore a bright blue Hawaiian shirt with hibiscus flowers and palm leaves, and tan shorts. Looming behind him an intimidating-looking rubber plant emerged from a terracotta pot. It was well over six feet tall and took up most of one side of the room.

'Lloyd,' Nerissa signalled for him to join the group. 'Jacobs's phone call, what was it about?'

Lloyd had mastered a look which said he was incredibly busy, but if they simply couldn't manage without him, he'd break off from his pressing workload to facilitate their investigations. Nerissa recognised the look now as, frowning in concentration, he shuffled more important papers before selecting a single sheet. He joined Nerissa and the others in the crew room, clutching the sheet of paper.

'Oliver Jacobs, or OJ as I like to call him,' Lloyd began with a lofty smile as if he was the first to have made the connection between Oliver's initials and the associated acronyms, 'made a call to a local cell phone number registered to a Quincy Moran.'

'Quincy Moran?' Delano said in surprise. 'I know that name.'

'That's Antigua for you,' Lloyd replied. 'Small island.'

'Quincy Moran. Is he related to Max Moran, the coxswain of the English Harbour lifeboat?' Edella asked.

'They're cousins,' Lloyd replied.

'I went to school with Max,' Brandon said. 'We're the same age. Quincy's quite a few years younger than us though, maybe nine or ten.'

'Which would make him, what, twenty-two, twenty-three years old?' Delano asked.

'Twenty-two,' Lloyd confirmed.

'Quincy was always a decent guy,' Brandon added. 'Worked hard at school, polite, well behaved, helped his mom with household chores…'

'Then how is he involved with a drug trafficker like Jacobs?' Nerissa asked.

'People change,' Hyacinth said. 'Sometimes they get sucked into things they shouldn't without even realising it.'

'Well, Quincy's the least likely person I could imagine being involved with drug smuggling, or anything illegal for that matter,' Brandon went on.

'We've all heard that said before about the guiltiest of criminals,' Hyacinth said.

'What else do we know about Quincy?' Delano asked.

'According to his Facebook profile he's a gardener, and an odd job and pool maintenance man at a number of the beach houses and luxury villas up at Sugar Reef Bay, as well as other properties on the island.' Lloyd took up the narrative again. 'I recognise him from his profile picture; I've seen him at The Jungle a few times.'

'Jacobs was headed for a private mooring at Sugar Reef Bay when he was caught in the storm,' Delano said. 'If Quincy is Jacobs's man here in Antigua, his employment at Sugar Reef would certainly provide him with access and a useful little cover story to explain his comings and goings at the bay. What did they discuss? If there's anything which might point to Quincy we'll get him in for questioning.'

'Er, the conversation was actually pretty mundane,' Lloyd said. He sounded mildly disappointed. His few moments of importance were about to descend into an anticlimax.

'It was a code then,' Hyacinth said suspiciously.

'Maybe,' Lloyd went on. 'So Quincy picks up after about the third or fourth ring. He obviously doesn't recognise the number. OJ says: hey Quince, it's Jacobs. I'm just back. Quincy doesn't sound particularly surprised to hear from him cos he says: oh hey Mr. Jacobs, welcome back. How was your trip?

'OJ replies and says: I've had better. I got caught in the storm last night. The yacht's pretty busted up. It's a complete wreck actually. In fact, I ended up being towed by the Coast Guard to English Harbour. He then goes on to say that he'd been held up and wouldn't make it back to the villa today, as planned. He said the CDSLI wanted to ask him a few questions, but that it was nothing. So Quincy boy sounds all concerned, asks OJ if he's okay and so on and if there's anything he needs done up at the villa.'

'Up at the villa?' Edella asked with a puzzled expression.

'So OJ says yeah,' Lloyd continued, ignoring Edella, 'in light of the storm, you know, high winds and heavy rain, he asks if Quincy can go check on the property, give it the once over, make sure everything's okay. In particular, he says, make sure the parasols around the pool area are secure, and if the cushions from the outdoor furniture on the lanai were wet, for Quincy to put them out to dry.'

'You're kidding, right?' Brandon said after a few seconds' silence.

'*This* was the urgent phone call Jacobs had to make?' Anson asked in disbelief. 'He was worried about the cushions on his rattan daybed getting wet? It's a joke.'

'No, it's not a joke, it's a code,' Hyacinth insisted.

'Good luck deciphering that one,' Anson said with a look of amusement.

'Lloyd, other than asking Quincy to carry out a few routine checks around his villa after the storm, did Jacobs give any other instructions or say anything else which might be important?' Delano asked.

'No, that was pretty much it,' Lloyd replied shaking his head. He waved the single sheet of paper at them. 'This is all I got.'

'Did Jacobs give any indication as to the location of the villa mentioned in their conversation?' Delano asked.

'No, but it was obvious Quincy already knew where he was talking about,' Lloyd replied. 'Like I said, Quincy seems to be based mainly up at the million dollar properties in Sugar Reef Bay. My guess is the villa's one of those.'

'Jacobs certainly doesn't own any of the houses up at Sugar Reef,' Edella said. 'I checked. None of the properties are in his name.'

'Maybe he rents one of them,' Hyacinth suggested. 'Want me to go talk to him again, boss?'

'Yeah,' Delano nodded. 'I'm sure Jacobs would be thrilled to receive another visit from you Hyacinth.'

'No problem.' Hyacinth was already heading for the door.

'And Hyacinth,' Delano added.

'Yeah boss?'

'Call Quincy. Get him in for questioning.'

'Got it.'

The cell phone in Delano's pocket buzzed. He answered it as the rest of the team began to disperse. He held up his hand in a signal for them to wait. After a few short acknowledgements, he hung up.

'That was Mitch,' he said. 'The Coast Guard has brought the Atratus ashore. She's docked at the marina. You guys head down there, I'll be right behind you, there's a phone call I need to make.'

FOUR

Max Moran was sprawled on his couch in a pair of checkered boxer shorts watching a football match on TV when his cell phone trilled loudly. He noted the name of the caller before answering.

'Delano, how's it going?' He muted the TV and shifted into a sitting position.

'Sorry to call you Max,' the voice at the end of the line said. 'Hope I didn't wake you?'

'No, I'm just watching a bit of TV before I hit the sack. Everything okay? Have they brought the Atratus ashore yet?'

'Yeah, they've just berthed at the marina. Something's come up that I wanted to run by you.'

'Sure man, what is it?'

'We got Oliver Jacobs in custody, but he wouldn't answer any of our questions until we granted him a phone call. He was adamant it was urgent and wouldn't cooperate with us until we ceded to his request.'

'Bet he wanted to lawyer up before he let you guys anywhere near him,' Max said with a laugh.

'No actually, it wasn't a call to his lawyer.'

'Oh?'

'He dialled the cell phone number belonging to a Quincy Moran.'

'Quincy?' There was a note of disbelief in Max's voice. 'As in my *cousin* Quincy?'

'Yeah.'

There was a pause before Max spoke again.

'That's crazy. There must be some mistake. The hell's he calling Quincy for?'

'I hoped you'd be able to tell me. Jacobs owns — or rents — a villa nearby, possibly up at Sugar Reef Bay. It's likely that he employs Quincy for general maintenance and gardening duties, perhaps along with some of the other residents at Sugar Reef. He asked Quincy to go over to the villa and check it over, but I'm not convinced there wasn't a hidden message somewhere in that seemingly innocent phone call.'

'Quincy does do a bit of handyman work up there,' Max said. 'You know, odd jobs like gardening, pool maintenance, painting and decorating, stuff like that, but as to him being involved in drug trafficking, there's just no way. That ain't Quincy. What exactly did Jacobs say to him?'

'He told Quincy he'd been caught in the storm last night, that his yacht had been badly damaged and he had to be towed back to English Harbour by the Coast Guard. He mentioned that he was being questioned by the CDSLI but didn't elaborate. Quincy asked Jacobs if there was anything he needed doing at the villa. Jacobs told him to check on the parasols around the pool and put any wet cushions from the furniture on the lanai out to dry.'

'That was it?' Max asked in puzzlement. 'Waste of a precious phone call if you ask me. Who gives a damn about parasols and lanai furniture when you're facing life in prison for drug smuggling?'

'Those were my thoughts,' Delano replied. 'Which is why I wondered if you had any idea as to what the call actually meant?'

'None whatsoever. And I know my family,' Max said defensively. 'Quincy's a good guy. He wouldn't know a brick of cocaine if it was right there in front of him. He'd probably think it was a bag of sugar and spoon it into his tea.'

'You sure about that Max?'

'I'm positive Delano. I'll stake my reputation on it. Quincy's got nothing to do with Jacobs or drug trafficking or anything else illegal. He's innocent. Trust me.'

'So you think the call was legit? No hidden meanings? No secret messages embedded in the conversation?'

'Absolutely,' Max replied firmly. 'I'd say you're clutching at straws with this one. Have you spoken to Quincy yet? What does he say about it?'

'Hyacinth's getting him in for questioning, but I thought you might be grateful for the heads up as you handled the rescue last night and, you know, he's family. This call is just a professional courtesy really.'

'I see. Well, thanks man. I appreciate it. If you like I can reach out to him and ask him about his call from Jacobs. If he knows anything he might open up to me more readily than with your officers. I'm certain he's innocent but he may have spotted something up at Jacobs's villa which could be useful.'

Delano considered Max's offer. It would help them out considerably. With the Atratus having just docked at the marina, the team were about to become very busy. Resources were stretched as it was. In addition, they still had to question Oliver Jacobs further and pay a visit to his villa at Sugar Reef Bay, or wherever it was. It was also true that Quincy was far more likely to speak freely with his cousin than with a member of the CDSLI.

'That would help us out a lot,' he said to Max. 'But are you sure you don't mind after being up for most of last night?'

'Not at all,' Max replied. 'I probably won't sleep now anyway until I've talked to Quincy myself. Leave this with me. I'll reach out to him and see if he knows anything. I'll get back to you as soon as I can.'

'Thanks Max, that's a real help. I'll tell Hyacinth to hold off calling him until you've made contact.'

'No problem. I'll be in touch.'

They hung up. Max scrolled through the contacts in his cell phone until he found the number for his cousin. He tapped on the screen and waited.

With the exception of Hyacinth, the other five CDSLI officers stood on a private jetty at English Harbour as Mitch, Lawrence and Connor completed final checks of the Atratus and signed paperwork along with Gary, the dock master. The area immediately surrounding the yacht was cordoned off with black and yellow hazard tape which flapped in the breeze. The rain and heavy grey clouds ensured that the marina was all but deserted. The operation had, for the most part, been undisturbed by prying eyes and unwelcome interest.

'Has to be one of the largest stashes of cocaine I've ever seen on a single yacht,' Gary remarked as he approached the other members of the CDSLI. 'All credit to the Coast Guard. But you've got your work cut out for you now.' He nodded back to the drug-laden Atratus. 'Shame about the boat though, it's a nice one. Offshore rated, fine cruising speeds. Those things are surprisingly comfortable in most sea conditions, although even the larger ships get thrashed about in force tens like last night's storm. I'm guessing that yacht felt more like a coastal boat designed for a party at anchor in a quiet harbour than an ocean-going vessel. Oh and you'll need a semi-truck to transport all those plastic drums back to your HQ.'

'We came prepared,' Delano replied, pointing to a tractor with a large trailer attached. The CDSLI used it to transport larger stashes of contraband and illegal substances seized in drugs busts.

'That's more like it. You should be able to clear the yacht in a couple of trips with that trailer,' Gary said with a nod of approval. 'Take care unloading. And let me know if there's anything else you need. I'll be happy to help.'

'Thanks Gary,' Delano said.

'No problem,' Gary replied. Keeping his head down against the wind and the rain, he strode away in the direction of the marina office.

Fighting against the elements, the team began removing the plastic drums from the wreckage of the Atratus. Brandon reversed the tractor and trailer towards the jetty, close to the yacht. Along with Lawrence and Connor, the CDSLI officers formed a human conveyor belt, rolling the drums across the deck of the yacht and onto two small trailer carts before being wheeled and transferred to the larger trailer. In two trips, they had unloaded the Atratus and transported the cocaine-filled drums to a small forensics laboratory in St. John's. Rochelle Myers, the lab technician, was about to become extremely busy.

Now empty of the drums, the team ripped what was left of the yacht apart. They discovered more loose bricks of cocaine, tightly packaged and concealed in every compartment imaginable. Oliver hadn't been lying; the boat was indeed stuffed full. Wherever they looked, in every cupboard, drawer and locker, even the cooker, they found bricks of white powder. As they stripped the yacht to a shell, they found specially adapted hiding places in the fresh water tanks and the seat floors.

By the time they had finished, the once plush interior of the luxury craft was littered with remnants of shredded leather, cushion stuffing and miscellaneous cupboard doors which had been removed from their hinges. Oliver's personal property had been seized and bagged. Everything from a mask and snorkel to a small first aid kit had been removed from the yacht to be taken into evidence for what was one of the biggest drug busts the CDSLI officers had ever seen.

As the last few items from the Atratus were placed in a crate and loaded into the back of the trailer, Delano gazed around the saloon of the ransacked yacht for one final check. His team had completely gutted it, stripped it bare. They had been ruthless in their search for every last grain of cocaine. He was confident they had confiscated the entire stash, along with any evidence which might point to Oliver's chain of supply and demand. With the sound of the rain still pattering on the deck above, Delano walked slowly through the saloon and the galley. The laminated floor was wet and covered with muddy footprints. There were scratches and dents on the expensive walnut doors leading to the port and starboard cabins. Delano stuck his head into both before glancing around the forward cabin. His team had been thorough. He was satisfied they had everything they needed. Returning to the cockpit, he stepped onto the jetty and gave the order for the yacht to be secured. More black and yellow hazard tape appeared and he left Edella and Brandon tying it to wooden posts along the jetty, sealing off access to the yacht, while he took a call from Hyacinth.

'Hey boss, so I talked to Jacobs about Sugar Reef Bay.'

'I'm listening.'

'We were right, he does have a villa up there — I checked it out on Google Maps, it's one of the grander ones — I've sent the details to your phones. According to Jacobs, he doesn't actually own it. He just rents it. I ran some more background checks on him and it is indeed his contact address in Antigua. It appears he rents properties in every city where OJ Accountancy has offices. In the US he rents apartments in Manhattan and Chicago and one overlooking the Las Vegas Strip. In the Caribbean he's got a luxury beach condo on Cayman Brac and one in Jamaica, and the villa at Sugar Reef Bay.'

'He rents all six simultaneously?' Delano asked in disbelief.

'Yep, the only home he actually appears to own is an apartment in a place called Belgravia in London.'

'So if he just rents the villa in Sugar Reef, who owns it? Is there a rental agency involved?'

'Jacobs says he doesn't rent through an agency but deals direct with the owner, whom he says he's never met.'

'You get a name?'

'Yeah. A guy called Terry Dove.'

'Great. Call Mr. Dove and tell him we need to search his property. We're done here so get him to meet us there in an hour.'

'I'd love to boss, but there's a slight problem with that. I can't find Mr. Dove.'

'What?'

'I've only got his name to go on. According to Jacobs, Terry Dove is a Canadian businessman who doesn't reside in Antigua.'

'Jacobs must have a number for him or some means of contacting him. Did you check through the contacts on Jacobs's cell phone?'

'The battery was dead so we tried charging it but it was damaged by water during the storm. I've stuck it in a bag of rice to try and suck the moisture out, but that could take a day or so. If the rice doesn't work I'll send it to the lab.'

'What about his iPad?'

'We were able to charge that and it's working fine, but all we found was a bunch of marine charts and weather apps on it. There's nothing personal. No contact details, no names, addresses or phone numbers. No messages or emails. Just generic boating and navigating stuff.'

'Any indication as to the route he took from the Port of Brighton?'

'Yeah, the iPad had a GPS receiver. His route checks out, just like he told us. He left Trinidad and sailed north, past Grenada, and Saint

Vincent and the Grenadines, the eastern Caribbean corridor. He berthed for a short time at a little marina in Saint Lucia, presumably to refuel and stock up on supplies, before setting sail for Antigua. He continued in a northerly direction, through the Leeward Islands, passing to the west of Martinique, Dominica and Guadeloupe and then east of Montserrat before he set course for the home strait due north, to a private mooring at Sugar Reef Bay, which is when he got caught in the storm. He sailed under the radar, like a ghost ship, and barely made any radio calls until his Mayday earlier this morning.'

'He's clearly an accomplished sailor,' Delano observed. 'Hyacinth, talk to him again about the owner of his rental property, Terry Dove. Go through as many listings as you can think of — the Yellow pages, business directories — as well as social media sites, Twitter, Facebook, the usual ones. See if you can find anything on a Canadian businessman who rents out high-end properties in the Caribbean. If you don't get lucky and Jacobs doesn't come up with something useful, we'll have to take him with us to the villa.'

'Sure thing boss.'

As he hung up, Delano checked his watch. It had been more than three hours since his conversation with Max. He hoped the lifeboat coxswain hadn't run into trouble in his attempt to contact Quincy. Silently reassuring himself that Max was a highly trained member of the Coast Guard who could take care of himself, Delano dialled the number of Rochelle Myers, the technician at the forensics lab in St. John's.

'Mitch and Nerissa are here with the last few bricks of cocaine from the yacht. I'm signing them into evidence now,' Rochelle confirmed. 'It's probably the biggest drugs bust I've ever seen, by the way. Kudos to the Coast Guard and your officers, Delano.'

'Thanks Rochelle. There may be more work coming your way; we're about to pay a visit to the villa of the guy whose yacht the cocaine was found on.'

'No problem,' Rochelle replied cheerfully. 'I'll make this case a priority. I've arranged for some extra help which should speed things up a little, but I'll get right on with whatever you send us and keep you updated. Mitch and Nerissa are standing right next to me. You wanna talk to them?'

'Yeah, either one of them will do.'

There was a call-waiting tone at Delano's end as Nerissa came on the line.

'Hey boss.'

'Nerissa, when you and Mitch are done at the lab, join the rest of us at Jacobs's villa at Sugar Reef Bay. Hyacinth has sent the location to your phones. I've got a feeling we're gonna need all hands on deck with this one.'

'We'll be there as soon as we can,' Nerissa replied.

They said goodbye and Delano took the call waiting. It was Max. There was a note of anxiety in his voice.

'Quincy's gone AWOL.'

'What?' Delano asked in surprise.

'I talked to him this morning, asked him about his connection to Oliver Jacobs. Quincy confirmed he'd received the call, but all Jacobs said was that he'd been caught in last night's storm and had to be towed back to English Harbour in his boat. Jacobs wasn't sure when he'd make it back to the villa, but in light of the weather he asked Quincy to take a ride up to the property and make a cursory check of the place, especially the outdoor furniture around the pool and the lanai, the parasols and so on. Oh and you were right about it being up at Sugar Reef Bay. Quincy said he knew the CDSLI were asking Jacobs a few questions, but had no idea he was being held in custody for drug trafficking or was involved in anything like that. Said he didn't have a clue what line of business Jacobs was in. But why would he? He's just the gardener.'

'Did Quincy say exactly what work he does at the villa?' Delano asked.

'He told me he tends the garden one afternoon a week and takes care of the pool, like he does at some of the other Sugar Reef properties. Gets paid in cash, obviously. Said Jacobs has been there for the last eighteen months or so, but Quincy did the same work for the previous residents so when Jacobs moved in he just kept him on. Very occasionally Jacobs gets him to do a few maintenance jobs around the place, but Quincy said he hasn't seen him about much lately. I guess that's because Jacobs has been on his little sailing jaunt to Trinidad and back.'

'Which Quincy knew about,' Delano said. It was a statement, not a question.

'Yeah, Quincy said Jacobs did mention he'd be away for a few days, but again, there was nothing unusual about that.'

'You really believe that phone call was innocent?' Delano asked.

'Yeah man, absolutely. Of course I do,' Max replied.

'So Jacobs is potentially facing life in prison and he calls his *pool maintenance man*?' Delano said. 'I'm not buying it, Max. Quincy's not telling you the whole story. He knows something. I'll get Mitch and Nerissa to pick him up on their way back from the lab.'

'That's the problem,' Max said. 'Like I said, he's gone AWOL.'

'What d'you mean *AWOL*?' Delano asked.

'I suggested we meet so he could tell me everything he knew about Jacobs. He said he had a job to finish and then he'd come straight over to my place, but he never showed. I've made a hundred calls to his cell phone but they're going straight to voicemail. I called my Aunt Junella — his mom — but she said he left for work around seven-thirty this morning and she hasn't heard from him since. Not that there's anything unusual about that. She wasn't expecting him back until later tonight. Some nights he doesn't even come home, but there's nothin' unusual about that either.'

'Did your aunt know where he was supposed to be working this morning?'

'No. She said she thought he'd be over at Sugar Reef, but he doesn't always work at the properties there. He does all sorts of stuff, mostly in the south of the island, but he'll go anywhere. When I spoke to him he said he was over near Hamilton Bay.'

'Does he keep employment records?'

'You gotta be kidding me. Quincy's a cash-in-hand kinda guy. The rainforests of the world are safe where his paper trail's concerned. But he's as honest as the next guy. And he's reliable. You can trust him with anything. This ain't like him to just disappear. I don't know what to do, Delano. I'm worried about him.'

'Keep trying his cell,' Delano said. 'I'll ask Hyacinth to question Jacobs again and get Mitch and Nerissa to visit Quincy's mom's place when they're done at the lab.'

'You think something bad's happened to him?' Max asked. There was a note of panic in his voice. 'It's not like him not to show up if he says he'll be somewhere.'

'Don't worry Max, we'll find him. Send me your aunt's home address; I'll have Mitch and Nerissa go straight there from St. John's. And I'll get Hyacinth to put out an alert on Quincy's truck.'

'Thanks man.' Max sounded far from relieved. 'I appreciate it. I guess I'm worrying for nothing. I'm certain he's innocent though. Quincy's one of the most trustworthy guys I know. He'd never be mixed up in anything like this.'

Delano promised he'd keep Max informed and hung up. He called Hyacinth.

'Yeah boss.'

'Quincy Moran's disappeared.'

'Damn. You think he got spooked by Jacobs's phone call and he's holed up somewhere?'

'I'm not sure. He may have gone to ground, but Max swears he's innocent. See if Lloyd can put a trace on his cell and call Mitch and Nerissa — they're still at the forensics lab — ask them to take a ride over to Quincy's mom's place and talk to her. I'll forward the address to their phones. And put out an alert on Quincy's truck. We need to find him.'

'Got it.'

Delano ended the call and turned to where the other three officers were sheltering from the rain under a palm tree. Behind them the forlorn wreckage of the Atratus bobbed in the water beside the jetty. The black and yellow tape fluttered in the breeze, marking the area around the boat as forbidden territory. Once a sleek, proud sailing yacht, she resembled a derelict shell stripped of her former grandeur and luxury. For now, at least, the seafaring days of the Atratus were over.

'Let's get out of here,' Delano said, pulling the hood of his jacket over his head. 'Edella, Anson, meet us at Sugar Reef Bay, Oliver Jacobs's rented villa. The details are on your phones. Brandon and I will pick up Jacobs and Hyacinth on our way over. We'll get Duane too. He can keep an eye on Jacobs.'

FIVE

2:00 pm, Thursday, September 19
V. C. Bird International Airport, Antigua

As the Virgin Atlantic airliner touched down at V. C. Bird International Airport and taxied to the gate, the Captain informed his passengers that in spite of the grey storm clouds and heavy rainfall, the outside temperature was a balmy eighty-five degrees. The worst of the weather had cleared to the west, making way for a return to the cloudless blue skies and dazzling sunshine British tourists looked forward to while on vacation in the Caribbean.

From somewhere near the front of the aircraft a man and a woman joined the line of passengers, eager to disembark after the eight hour flight from London. The man was in his early forties and of average height and build with a toned physique. His brown hair was cropped short and his skin was lightly tanned. He wore a white linen shirt, navy shorts and flip-flops. As they stepped off the aircraft onto the airbridge, he placed a protective hand in the middle of the woman's back. Her olive complexion was accentuated by a white, cotton blouse and smart, tan-coloured pants. The platform wedge sandals on her feet ensured she was almost as tall as her companion. She had deep brown eyes and her long, dark hair was tied neatly in a high ponytail. In the throng of British tourists, the couple entered the crowded terminal building. It was heavily air conditioned and decorated with large, tropical-themed signs welcoming the latest arrivals to Antigua and Barbuda.

Uniformed airport officials guided tourists and residents into lines cordoned off by retractable belt barriers. Each line snaked its way back and forth to a row of passport control booths at the far side of the building. Public address announcements echoed over the buzz of excited chatter reminding passengers to have their passports ready for inspection. The man and woman waited patiently in line with two small black roller cases beside them. They exchanged a few amicable remarks but otherwise stood in silence. They appeared relaxed and carefree.

As they neared the front of the line they were directed to one of the booths by an airport official. The woman presented her passport to the immigration officer. A badge pinned to the front of his shirt had the name Gregory imprinted on it.

'Welcome to Antigua,' he said, checking the passport against the screen in front of him.

'Thanks,' the woman replied. 'Glad to be here.'

'How long will you be staying in Antigua?' Gregory asked without looking up.

'Three weeks.'

'Are you here on vacation?'

'We are.'

'Where are you staying?'

'A friend's villa. Sugar Reef Bay.'

'It's very nice down there.'

'It certainly is.'

Gregory stamped a clean page somewhere in the middle of the passport and returned it to the woman. Everything was in order. She was good to go. Stepping aside, she waited as her companion presented his passport. Gregory proceeded to check the details. He frowned slightly at the screen before inspecting the passport again. He glanced up at the man.

'Is everything okay?' the man asked.

'One moment please sir,' Gregory replied. 'I just need to make a call.' He picked up a cell phone beside him and tapped the screen. The man turned to the woman with a puzzled look. She shrugged her shoulders. Gregory was talking to someone on the phone. As he hung up, two airport officials appeared from nowhere and approached the booth. The younger man, probably in his late thirties, was wearing a hi-vis vest over a white shirt and navy pants. He was carrying a folder and a clipboard with an air of importance. The badge pinned to his vest told everyone his name was Rusty McChannen. He held the lofty title of Deputy Chief

Security Officer. Gregory handed the passport to the other official, the one without the vest. He was older with greying temples and a kind face. He briefly inspected it before speaking to the man beside Gregory's booth.

'Mr. Graymond Sharkey?'

'Yes.'

'Good afternoon sir, my name's Earl. I'm the chief security officer here. My associate Rusty and I are going to have to briefly interrupt your travel plans and ask you to come with us to answer a few questions.'

'Is there a problem?' Graymond asked.

'I hope not,' Earl replied. He glanced at the woman standing close by. 'Are you traveling together?'

'Yes, we are,' Graymond said.

'Husband and wife?'

'Alicia's my girlfriend.'

'If I can take a look at your passport too, ma'am,' Earl said.

The woman retrieved her passport from her handbag and gave it to Earl who studied it for a few seconds.

'Miss Alicia Clayton?'

'That's correct.'

'Thank you.' Earl held on to the passports. 'If you'd both like to come with Rusty and me, there are a few questions we need to ask you.'

'What's this about exactly?' Graymond asked.

'If you'd come with us please sir,' Earl repeated kindly but firmly. He gestured to Graymond and Alicia to follow him as Rusty led the way across the terminal building and through a security door to one side. Graymond shot a glance at Alicia but she shook her head in bewilderment. A few minutes and a few long corridors later, Graymond and Alicia were ushered into a small office with two wooden desks and a wall of metal filing cabinets. At one end of the room a window looked out across the airfield where a turbo-prop aircraft could be seen touching down on the runway through a gap in the blinds. On one wall hung a large cork board onto which a variety of documents had been haphazardly pinned. On the other wall was a world map.

'Take a seat,' Earl said, pointing to two chairs opposite one of the desks. He sat facing them, on the other side of the desk. Rusty took the passports over to the second desk where he immersed himself in a pile of paperwork with a stern expression on his face.

'Just a few questions to begin with, a few formalities,' Earl began as Graymond and Alicia took their seats. 'What's the reason for your visit to Antigua?'

'It's a holiday. A vacation,' Graymond replied.

'How long will you be staying in Antigua?'

'Three weeks.'

'And where will you be staying? A hotel? An apartment?'

'At a friend's villa.'

'Where's the villa?' Earl scribbled notes on a notepad.

'Sugar Reef Bay.'

'D'you have the address?'

'Yeah, the villa's called Villa Bella Casa. It shouldn't be too hard to locate; I understand there are only a handful of properties up at Sugar Reef.'

'Have you been there before?'

'No.'

'Thank you. And you're staying there for the duration of your trip?'

'That was the plan.'

'And what's the name of your friend?'

'Oliver Jacobs,' Graymond replied slowly.

'Thank you.' Earl wrote on the page in front of him. If he recognised the name, he didn't show it.

'Do you mind telling us why we're here?' Graymond asked again.

Earl placed his pen on the desk and leaned back in his chair before replying.

'The name on your passport has triggered an alert put out earlier today by the Crime and Drug Squad of the Leeward Islands. They're known locally as the CDSLI. They're a task force whose primary aim is to combat drug trafficking and money laundering, amongst other things. You may have heard of them?'

'Sorry, I haven't,' Graymond replied. 'What do they want with us?'

'One of the team is on his way over here as we speak,' Earl went on. 'I'm afraid I don't have any more information than that right now.'

'What about our luggage?' Alicia asked.

'We'll take care of your cases, don't worry ma'am,' Earl replied.

Rusty finished shuffling papers and stood up.

'I'll get coffee,' he said. As the door to the office swung shut behind him, Earl's cell phone vibrated on the desk. He checked the message on the screen and tapped a one-word reply before returning his attention to Graymond and Alicia.

'Just a few more things I need to ask you,' he said, picking up his pen again and pulling a form towards him.

He rattled off routine questions which Graymond and Alicia took turns to answer: full names, addresses, dates of birth, occupations. Earl wrote slowly and the form took some time to complete. Rusty returned with the coffees and they took a short break to talk about the recent storm before Earl resumed the question and answer session. He was just finishing up when there was a sharp knock on the door. It opened before access was granted and a man entered. He was a few years younger than the two airport officials, stockily built with a short haircut and red-framed sunglasses perched on his head. He unzipped a rain-soaked waterproof jacket to reveal a navy polo shirt and cargo pants.

'Sorry I'm late Earl, Rusty,' he said removing the jacket and hanging it over a chair. 'Traffic was heavy.'

'I was actually about to thank you for getting here so fast,' Earl replied, rising from his chair. The men shook hands.

'Thanks for your call.' The new guy glanced down at the couple seated on the other side of Earl's desk. 'You must be Graymond and Alicia,' he said, offering his hand to them in turn. 'I'm Brandon Allen, I work with the CDSLI, the Crime and Drug Squad of the

Leeward Islands. Sorry to interrupt your travel plans, but I need to ask you a few questions.'

'We're kind of in practice with that right now,' Graymond replied. 'Go right ahead.'

Brandon pulled up a chair and leaned towards them with his elbows resting on his knees.

'We have a man in custody whom we understand is a friend of yours.'

Graymond shot a glance at Alicia. They briefly made eye contact as Brandon observed them closely.

'You know who I'm talking about?' Brandon asked.

'There can only be one person,' Graymond said quietly. Outside the open window they heard the roar of a jet engine as an aircraft took off.

'Then you know who I'm talking about.' It was a statement this time.

'What's he done?' Graymond asked.

'Oliver Jacobs was arrested early this morning after putting out a Mayday call to the Coast Guard. He was caught on his yacht in a force ten storm out at sea. When the Coast Guard boarded the vessel, they found a large quantity of cocaine on board.'

Graymond and Alicia exchanged further glances but said nothing.

'So Mr. Sharkey, when you and Miss Clayton fly into Antigua on the very day that Mr. Jacobs is arrested for drug trafficking…'

'Yes, I can see where you're going with this,' Graymond said.

'It is a bit of a coincidence, don't you think?'

'Depends on how you look at it, but I assume you've already been through my résumé?' Graymond's former life haunted him in the most unlikely of places.

'We're aware of your past, yes,' Brandon replied. 'But we're only really interested in your connection with Oliver Jacobs.'

'Fine.' Graymond repositioned himself in his chair. 'What exactly do you want to know?'

SIX

2:30 pm, Thursday, September 19
Villa Bella Casa, Sugar Reef Bay, Antigua

Surrounded by lush tropical gardens and gently sloping green lawns, Villa Bella Casa, Oliver Jacobs's Antiguan residence, commanded sweeping views of a perfect crescent beach and the brilliant turquoise of the Caribbean Sea beyond. Situated at the end of a palm tree-lined private road, and sandwiched between the edge of a cliff and wrought iron gates set into eight-foot high white-washed cinder block walls, the villa was the epitome of privacy.

Every beach house and luxury villa at Sugar Reef Bay boasted similar levels of seclusion for discerning owners and residents. Included in the price tag were stunning views of the bay with private moorings for sleek super yachts, some worth more than the palatial dwellings themselves. One of the moorings, currently vacant, had been the anchorage of the Atratus, a very modest sailing craft in comparison to many of the other yachts.

The four CDSLI officers from English Harbour arrived in three separate vehicles, each with their windshield wipers working furiously to keep up with the rain. Oliver had travelled, handcuffed, in a dark blue Ford Explorer with tinted windows and government licence plates. He was accompanied by Hyacinth and Duane, a plain clothes police officer by day and fellow bouncer with Lloyd at The Jungle by night. Other than showing Hyacinth which button to press on the remote control key fob for the electric gates to the villa, Oliver had remained silent for the duration of the journey.

As the wrought iron portcullis opened slowly away from them, the three vehicles inched forward. A sweeping circular driveway, immaculately brick-paved with a three car garage to one side, led to a sprawling, single story villa nestled among palm trees and immaculately tended gardens boasting a colourful display of tropical foliage and exotic plants. Against the gloom of the foaming clouds and overcast sky, the profile of the villa looked imposing. Its gently sloping roofline, designed to withstand the strongest category of hurricane, was constructed of wooden beams and dark wood tiles. The villa itself was a fusion of wood, stone, cinder block and glass. No expense had been spared in its design and construction.

Delano's Toyota truck, the blue Ford Explorer and Edella's silver Hyundai Elantra parked behind each other in front of the villa. Hyacinth jumped out of the front passenger seat of the Explorer and pulled open the rear passenger door.

'Get out,' she barked. Oliver had not been forthcoming as to Quincy's whereabouts and had denied all knowledge of his recent disappearance. Consequently, Hyacinth was still smarting from her lack of progress with this latest interview. Oliver emerged from the back of the SUV, ducking his head in the rain, and was escorted by Duane to the front door of the villa. Hyacinth stood poised to open the door with the key he had provided.

'Any alarm systems we should know about?' she asked, turning to him.

'You can switch it off once you're inside,' he replied in a surly tone. 'The keypad's to the left of the door.'

Hyacinth nodded and turned back to the ornate, oak door. The other four officers watched as she slid the key into the lock and turned the handle. The door opened easily and swung inwards, revealing a grand circular foyer which led to a large, open-plan living room with a wooden vaulted ceiling. Hyacinth immediately turned to her left. The keypad for the alarm was where Oliver had said it would be. The warning bleeps, alerting any intruder that the house was alarmed, had already begun. Hyacinth punched the six digit code dictated to her by Oliver into the keypad. There was a long tone and the bleeps fell silent.

'Are we good?' Hyacinth asked, turning to Oliver.

'Yeah.'

'We need an event history for that,' Delano said, nodding at the keypad.

'I'll call the alarm company,' Hyacinth replied.

'Any other points of security we should know about Jacobs?' Delano asked. Oliver shook his head.

'What kinda surveillance system you got here?'

'One with cameras.'

'Helpful,' Delano replied with a note of frustration.

'Like I said, this is an illegal search.' Oliver spoke with a sneer. 'You need permission from the owner of this property, Terry Dove. He won't be too happy when he finds out you're here without proper authorisation. But what the hell? Makes no difference to me. Snoop around all you want. I guarantee you won't find what you're looking for.'

Delano chose to ignore him. As they entered the large foyer, Oliver glanced down at the polished marble flooring and then at their boots.

'There's a perfectly good doormat. Use it,' he said with a glare at Anson who was immediately behind him. 'I don't want muddy boot prints all over the floor.'

'Don't worry man,' Anson replied, 'I'll let you mop round before we leave.'

Oliver scowled as they made their way into the open-plan living area beyond the foyer. The interior of Villa Bella Casa was luxurious and majestic. The CDSLI officers stood still for a few moments, gazing around them. To their right, through a set of solid oak French doors, was a larger, open-plan family room incorporating a kitchen and dinette. Duane led Oliver through into the room and instructed him to sit down. The patter of the rain on the roof tiles above them was interrupted by Delano's cell phone.

'You at Jacobs's place yet?' They heard Lloyd's voice as Delano put him on speaker.

'We just got here,' Delano replied. 'Why?'

'Somethin' you should know. I put a trace on Quincy's phone, like you asked, but got nothin' on his current location. Either he's removed the battery or it died completely, or he's in some place where there's no signal.'

'Okay.' There was disappointment in Delano's voice.

'But I did try something else,' Lloyd went on. 'I checked his call log with the carrier. There were two outgoing calls made from his cell this morning, and three incoming. The first was an incoming from the cell number of a guy called Jay Palmer. I'll send you his address, he lives in St. John's. Quincy then made an outgoing call to a number belonging to a Latoya Joseph. After that, the call from Jacobs came in, which we know about. And then Max called him, just after ten-thirty.'

'And the final number he dialled?' Delano asked.

'What's weird is not the number, but the place he was calling from. At twelve-twenty this afternoon, he made a second call to Latoya. She answered, they were connected for the grand total of four seconds and then the call ended. But what's interesting is he made the call from your current location: Villa Bella Casa at Sugar Reef Bay.'

'Quincy was here? At Jacobs's villa?'

'Yep. Well, his cell phone was at least. Since then, he hasn't made or received any calls and the last signal emitted by the phone was from the same location a few minutes later. Since then, the phone stopped transmitting so, like I said, either the battery died or it was removed, or he's disappeared to some remote corner of the island.'

'Thanks Lloyd. Send me Latoya's number. We need to know what the calls between her and Quincy were about. Any updates on the alert Hyacinth put out on Quincy's truck?'

'No, nothing. But I'll keep checking.'

They said goodbye and hung up.

'So Quincy was here after all,' Edella said.

'Looks that way.' Delano checked his watch. 'The last call he made, to Latoya Joseph, whoever she is, was from this location just over two hours ago. And then the phone stopped transmitting.'

'He could still be here,' Hyacinth voiced what was in everyone's minds, 'except the surveillance officers posted at the entrance to the access road swear they haven't seen him today.'

'Same as the surveillance team outside the gates to this place,' Edella added. 'No one's been here but us.'

'So how did Quincy make a call on his cell from *inside* these gates?' Anson asked.

'I'll reach out to the alarm company,' Hyacinth said, 'see if the alarm system was deactivated any time before twelve-twenty.'

'The rest of you, we need to ransack this place, tear it apart, brick by brick,' Delano said. 'Hyacinth's right, there's a chance Quincy could still be here. Anson, take the north side,' he pointed to the wooden louvred doors on his left. 'Edella, you take the east side with the pool and lanai; the parasols, the furniture, the cushions, whatever's out there. If Quincy's here, we need to find him. If he's gone, then we need to work out why he came here and where he is now.'

'Quincy's long gone,' Oliver called from the room next door. They heard Duane's harsh response: 'Shut up Jacobs. And sit down.'

As the team split up, Delano stepped through the French doors into the family room where Oliver sat on one of the couches next to Duane. He glared at Oliver before he spoke in a low voice.

'We'll try this again Jacobs: what was Quincy doing here?'

Oliver met Delano's gaze but said nothing.

'Because let's face it,' Delano went on, 'right now you're facing a very long time in prison for a charming little assortment of drugs-related charges. The prison here in Antigua ain't exactly the most savoury place in the world for rich white boys like you, and believe me, I will personally quash any applications you make to transfer to a UK prison before you've even put in a request. Cooperate with us now and things will be a whole lot easier for you later on. What did Quincy come here to do?'

'Nothing,' Oliver said. 'You eavesdropped into my phone conversation. You know how it went. Quincy's a handyman, a gardener, a general dogsbody. I asked him to check on my property after the storm. That was it.'

'I don't believe you,' Delano said quietly. 'You're lying. And when I find out what about, it won't go well for you.'

'Oh man, I'm trembling with fear already,' Oliver said mockingly.

'Boss, you want me to take the front of the villa and the garage when I'm done with the alarm company?' Hyacinth called from the foyer with her phone to one ear.

Delano nodded before turning back to Oliver.

'Where's the video recorder for the surveillance system here Jacobs?'

'Find it yourself,' Oliver replied rudely.

'We can either do this the nice way, or I can tell the magistrate how uncooperative you've been. Any hopes you might have of bail will be instantly denied. Now, where's the recorder with the footage from your cameras?'

'Try the study.' It was a grudging reply.

'And where is that?'

'Oh for goodness sake, you're supposed to be a detective, aren't you?'

Delano continued to look at Oliver in anticipation of an answer to his question.

'Through there,' Oliver said crossly, pointing to a set of double louvred doors leading off the dinette.

As Delano made his way to the study, he dialled one of the numbers Lloyd had forwarded to his phone and waited for a reply.

Villa Bella Casa was immaculately and expensively furnished and took on the feel of a show home, rather than a place which was actually lived in. It was clinical and impersonal. There were no photographs or mementoes. Other than a couple of porn magazines and a sailing journal, there was nothing to reveal Oliver's life, his friends, family, hobbies or interests. But perhaps it wasn't surprising if he only rented the place. It was temporary accommodation, not a permanent home. His accountancy business apparently took him all over the US and the Caribbean. He divided his time between his other rental properties, his London apartment, and the Atratus.

The family room, which incorporated the kitchen and dinette where Duane and Oliver had been instructed to wait, was spacious and elegant with a nod to the colonial era. Neutral shades of white and cream complemented the darker wood of the low slung sofas and large coffee table in the centre of the room. The natural tones were accented with pops of colour from vibrant magenta and aquamarine cushions to colourful paintings of tropical flowers and birds. A set of three glass hurricane lanterns stood neatly arranged on the coffee table. In one corner of the room, positioned to take in the views out to sea, stood an antique brass telescope mounted on a wooden tripod.

Through a set of sliding glass doors which led outside to the covered lanai and pool area, Edella had commenced a methodical search for both Quincy and evidence of whatever he had supposedly been instructed to take care of or retrieve. As she began slitting the cushions of the outdoor seating with a penknife, sending clusters of downy stuffing skimming across the patio and the pool in the breeze, Oliver watched her carefully through the glass.

'What's she doing?' he said with a frown. 'Is that really necessary?'

Duane didn't reply.

'What exactly is she looking for?' Oliver asked, turning to the plain clothes officer.

'You tell me. You're the drug runner; you do the math,' Duane replied curtly.

'But this is ridiculous,' Oliver said. 'As if I'd use my own home as a stash house. Give me some credit here.' He strained forward towards the glass doors.

'Sit down,' Duane ordered.

'Why? I'm not doing anything wrong,' Oliver protested, 'and it looks like I need to get out there and protect my property. Rest assured I'll be sending an itemised bill to the CDSLI for any damage caused to my personal possessions following this completely unwarranted search. I'm sure the owner of this property will be doing the same if any structural damage should occur.'

'Go right ahead,' Duane replied. 'We're always needing scrap paper.'

Oliver looked back at Edella. She had abandoned the cushions and was inspecting one of the parasols, which was down but unsecured and flapping in the breeze. She began wrestling with it in an attempt to put it up.

'What's she doing now?' Oliver said tensely. 'Oh no, not like that…' Shaking his head in apparent despair, he turned to Duane. 'Can I please go out there and demonstrate how to put up a parasol? It's obvious she doesn't have a clue. She'll break it. It's part of a set. D'you have any idea how much those darn things cost? Trust a woman to break it.'

'Sit down,' Duane said again, more harshly this time. Oliver, who was beginning to annoy him, gave him a beseeching look but obediently sat back down on the sofa. He appeared to be genuinely concerned about the parasols. Duane hoped Edella would find whatever secret they held as Oliver continued to watch the officer in uneasy silence. There were occasional noises from other parts of the villa as the other officers searched each room. Oliver winced at the sound of every crash and bang.

'What's the matter?' Duane asked. 'Worried they'll find your little cache?'

'I've already told you, they won't find a damn thing cos there's nothing here to find,' Oliver snapped. 'And like I said, this is a rental property. It's not my shit here, all right? It's someone else's. And every time one of your clumsy jackass co-workers breaks something, I'm sitting here adding up how many thousands of dollars you're going to be paying the owner of this place.'

'You mean Terry Dove, a.k.a. Oliver Jacobs?' Anson said entering the room from across the foyer where he had been searching the master suite. He was carrying a plastic wallet containing what looked like a passport and a sheaf of documents.

'What?' Oliver swivelled on the couch in surprise to face him.

Anson tipped the contents of the wallet onto the coffee table in front of them.

'Boss,' he called in the direction of the rooms leading off the dinette, 'I've got something.'

Delano appeared and joined the three men as Anson arranged the documents on the table. The passport had a navy blue cover with the Royal Arms of Canada emblazoned on the front. The words "Passport Passeport" were inscribed below the coat of arms, with the word "Canada" above. Anson picked it up and turned to the personal data page inside. It had been issued to a Terrence Everard Dove of Ottawa, Canada the previous year. Terrence's passport photograph bore an astonishing likeness to Oliver.

'That your evil twin, Jacobs?' Anson asked. 'Or would you prefer Terry?'

Oliver scowled.

'What else you got Anson?' Delano said, picking up some of the papers.

'Documents from a safe concealed behind a picture in the master suite,' Anson replied.

'You broke into the safe?' Oliver asked indignantly. 'Then you'll find the details of my lawyer in those documents. You can call him right now, get him to come here and see what you vandals have done to my property, never mind this illegal search.'

'Sorry man, I'd be happy to call him but cell reception's non-existent out here,' Delano said, holding up his phone.

'Damn you,' Oliver muttered under his breath. 'There's nothing wrong with the reception.'

'So according to these papers the legal owner of this place is a Mr. Terrence Dove,' Anson began.

'In effect, you're renting the villa from yourself, Jacobs,' Delano said. 'How imaginative. Why would you do that I wonder? Money laundering perhaps? Tax evasion? Anonymity?'

'My lawyer,' Oliver said defiantly. 'Now.'

'Any other fake IDs in the safe, Anson?' Delano asked.

'Just Terry's so far,' Anson replied, 'but I'm not done back there. I just thought you'd like to see these for starters. I'll let you know if I find anything else.' He nodded at Duane and made his way back to the foyer in the direction of the master suite.

Delano took snapshots on his phone of the passport and documents Anson had retrieved from the safe and forwarded them to Lloyd for a background search on Terrence Dove. Delano knew it would be exhaustive. Lloyd prided himself on being thorough, leaving no stone unturned. There were bills, bank statements, invoices and other official-looking documents, most of them in the name of Terrence Dove, although a few were in Oliver's own name.

As Delano was placing the passport and documents back into the plastic wallet, his phone rang. Ignoring a raised eyebrow from Oliver which he assumed was in light of his comment about cellular reception, he answered it. The call was from Nerissa. She and Mitch were just leaving the home of Quincy's mother, Junella Moran.

'Mama Moran told us pretty much everything Max told you,' Nerissa said. 'Quincy left for work around seven-thirty this morning and she hasn't seen or heard from him since, but there's nothing unusual about that. Sometimes he'd be home for lunch if he was working close by, but most of the time he wouldn't get back until late, if at all. Some nights he'd stay over with friends, or he'd go to his girlfriend's place. His mom wasn't in the least bit worried that something might be wrong until Max called her and then we showed up. Now she's pretty frantic but has no idea where he is and there's nothing at her place to suggest where he might be. We've been through all his belongings and made a thorough search of his room but we got nothing.'

'Did Quincy's mom know where he was working today?' Delano asked.

'No. She thought maybe he could've been at Sugar Reef, but she wasn't certain. When I suggested he might've been working over at Hamilton Bay, she said it was entirely possible, but again, didn't know for sure.'

'What about employment records?'

'Max was right, they don't exist. We found nothing so much as a bank statement or transaction receipt. Quincy only ever gets paid in cash it seems. According to his mom, he has a little black book with names and phone numbers of the people he does work for but it wasn't at the house so he's probably got it with him. We also got a number and an address for his girlfriend, Latoya Joseph.'

'I talked to Latoya earlier myself. Quincy called her twice this morning, which she confirmed. The second call was the last call he made before his phone went dead, moments later.'

'That's interesting.'

'How far out are you from Sugar Reef?'

'About five minutes.'

'Good. When you get here take a little tour of Sugar Reef Bay and start talking to the other residents. See if anyone saw or heard anything or has any information on Quincy.'

'Will do boss. We'll see you later.'

Delano hung up. He was about to leave the room when he remembered something.

'I found your video recorder by the way,' he said, turning to Oliver.

Oliver ignored the comment.

'There was nothing on its hard drive. All the surveillance footage had been conveniently erased. Interesting that, isn't it?'

'I said you wouldn't find anything,' Oliver replied with a faint smile.

'So that's what you wanted Quincy to do, erase the surveillance footage from your video recorder's hard drive,' Delano said. 'Why? What camera footage could possibly need to be deleted so urgently?'

'I didn't ask Quincy to erase any camera footage. He's a lowlife handyman not a security expert,' Oliver said nastily.

'It wasn't about the parasols, was it?' Delano went on. 'It was a coded message to tell Quincy you'd been caught and to ask him to get rid of any evidence at your property which might incriminate you further.'

'You're barking up the wrong tree bro,' Oliver replied. 'You're wasting your time, all of you. You know exactly what I said to Quincy, you were eavesdropping into my phone call and my lawyer will be questioning the legal ramifications of that, by the way. All I asked Quincy to do was check on my property after the storm. Why is that such a problem to you?'

'Because people in custody for narco trafficking generally call their lawyers first, not their gardeners,' Delano said curtly. 'And one other thing, where's your computer?'

'You were snooping around in my study, you tell me.'

'There's no computer in there,' Delano replied. 'Where is it?'

'If it's not in the study, I have no idea.'

'Come on Jacobs. Where's your computer?'

'I've already told you. It's in the study. If you can't find it then either you're completely blind, or stupid, or most likely both, or it's mysteriously vanished into thin air.'

'Another of Quincy's little tasks while he was here, was it?' Delano said with a touch of frustration. 'Erase the surveillance footage and get rid of the computer. A very neat little backup plan. Where is Quincy now, Jacobs?'

'Like I said, you're the detective. Why don't you do your job instead of standing here asking me dumb questions?'

Ignoring the remark, Delano made his way through to the foyer where he closed the French doors and called the surveillance officers stationed at the entrance of the access road to Sugar Reef Bay. It was the only road in and out and provided the sole means of access to the five luxury properties. Villa Bella Casa was the very last one at the end of the peninsula. The officers had documented the small number of people who had passed them since they took up their posts soon after ten-thirty that morning: a resident of one of the properties, a delivery driver and a couple of lost tourists. Quincy Moran had not been among them. The officers had a recent photograph of Quincy and were adamant, as they had been when they spoke to the CDSLI team on their arrival, that Quincy hadn't passed them in either direction.

Delano thanked them and took a walk in the rain to the officers who were sitting in an unmarked car outside the wrought iron gates to the villa. They repeated what they had confirmed to the team earlier that afternoon: nobody had gone in or out all day.

'Is there any way Quincy got to the villa *before* the surveillance officers arrived?' Hyacinth queried when Delano returned to the villa. She had completed a thorough search of the garage which contained a few tools, a ride-on lawnmower and a black Toyota Land Cruiser, but nothing connected to the earlier drug bust.

'It depends on where he was coming from,' Delano replied. 'The surveillance officers arrived at their posts at Sugar Reef around ten-thirty, around the time I called Max. If Quincy was over at Hamilton Bay when Jacobs called him at nine-forty, he could probably have made it here before the officers arrived, but according to Max he didn't do that. When they spoke at just after ten-thirty, Quincy told Max he was still at Hamilton Bay and would head over to Max's place as soon as he was done. Except we know he never showed up.'

'Quincy could have been lying,' Hyacinth suggested. 'Maybe he came straight here after Jacobs's call and lied to Max about where he was.'

'It's possible,' Delano replied. 'We need to find out if anyone saw Quincy at Hamilton Bay this morning. And we still have to answer the question of where he is now.' There was a pause before Delano asked: 'Did you have any luck with the alarm company?'

'No.' Hyacinth spoke in an exasperated tone. 'They were less than helpful, obstructive even. I couldn't get anywhere with them. They wanted passcodes, mothers' maiden names, shoe sizes and a whole bunch of other stuff. Told me I needed all sorts of warrants and so on before they'd release any information related to the security system. Client confidentiality. I asked Lloyd to see what he could do. He'll probably end up hacking into their database, which I'm guessing will be almost as impenetrable as their phone operators.'

'What about Jacobs? He any help?'

'You're kidding, right?' Hyacinth pulled a face.

'We'll give Lloyd until the end of the day before we turn nasty with the security firm,' Delano said. 'Is there any way we can tell if the system's been deactivated today from the keypad by the door?'

'No, I checked. I'm guessing Jacobs chose it purposely for its simplicity. It has no data stored on it; it's simply a device to activate and deactivate the alarm. And it's not connected to the surveillance system either.'

'It almost seems as if Jacobs anticipated this scenario and prepared himself accordingly,' Delano said. They were interrupted by his cell phone. An anxious voice spoke at the end of the line. It was Max.

'Delano, any news?'

'Max, you're on speaker. Hyacinth is here too. No, I've got nothing, other than the last known location of Quincy's cell phone. We traced it to Oliver Jacobs's villa here at Sugar Reef.'

'Quincy was at Jacobs's villa?'

'Looks that way. The last signal emitted from his cell was just after twelve-twenty today. Minutes before that he made a call to Latoya Joseph. I understand she's his girlfriend.'

'Quincy called Latoya? From Jacobs's villa? I can't believe it. Are you there now, at the villa I mean?'

'Ransacking the place as we speak.'

'Found anything?'

'Not so far, apart from fake ID: fake passports, documents, that kind of thing, but we're still looking.'

'I don't understand,' Max sounded perplexed. 'Why would Quincy go to the villa without coming to me first? And why call Latoya from there?'

'Latoya doesn't know for certain what Quincy wanted to talk to her about,' Delano replied.

'Communication was never great between those two.'

'It's not that. When Latoya answered, Quincy didn't say a word. And after four seconds he hung up.'

'Say what?'

'Quincy made two calls to Latoya's number this morning. The first was at eight-twenty and lasted two minutes. According to Latoya, he called to apologise after an argument last night.'

'Sounds about right,' Max said. 'They're always fighting about something. The rest of the family can hardly keep up. What was it this time?'

'According to Latoya, Quincy thought she was cheating on him, seeing someone behind his back.'

'Cheating? With who?'

'Latoya didn't know and apparently Quincy wouldn't say. But she said she wasn't seeing anybody else and his accusations were completely unfounded.'

'I'd be inclined to agree with Latoya. She's a good girl. Definitely not the cheating type. And anyway, that's the first I've heard of it. But you're sayin' the second time Quincy called her, he said nothing and then hung up?'

'Yeah. Latoya says she answered, but there was silence at the other end of the line. She said Quincy's name a couple of times, but there was no reply and then the line went dead. She thinks he was probably calling with another grovelling apology and changed his mind. But since that call, Quincy's gone offline. He hasn't made or received any calls and we can't trace his cell.'

'That's weird. But if he *was* up at Sugar Reef, surely someone spotted him around that time, or maybe they saw his truck?'

'That's another missing piece of the puzzle. The officers posted at the bottom of the access road and outside the gates of Jacobs's property are adamant Quincy hasn't been near this place all day. They've been stationed here since ten-thirty this morning.'

'Then they were at their posts even before I called Quincy to ask him about Jacobs,' Max said.

'But not before Jacobs called Quincy.'

'I hear what you're saying, but I just can't believe Quincy's involved,' Max replied. 'He told me he was on another job at the time anyway. Like I said, it was somewhere over near Hamilton Bay. He said he'd been there since first thing this morning, so there's no way he could've made it to Jacobs's villa before your surveillance people showed up. It's at least a thirty minute drive from Hamilton Bay to Sugar Reef Bay; he couldn't have got there until eleven at the earliest.'

There was a pause before Delano spoke.

'Is there a chance he lied to you about his whereabouts this morning?'

'No. No way.'

'Maybe he somehow evaded the officers guarding the access road and the gates to the villa?' Hyacinth joined the conversation.

'It's hard to see how anyone could have slipped past them without being seen.' Delano said.

'Unless there's another way in,' Hyacinth suggested.

'But I'm telling you, *Quincy wasn't there*,' Max's voice said insistently.

'We want to believe you Max, but his cell phone *was* here and that's the problem,' Delano replied gently.

'Which property at Sugar Reef belongs to Jacobs?' Max asked after a pause.

'Villa Bella Casa. It's one of the larger, grander ones, the last one at the end of the access road.'

'The one on the peninsula?' Max queried. 'The single storey one, all wood and glass and white-washed concrete? Only visible from the sea?'

'Yeah, that's the one.'

'Then there isn't another way in,' Max went on. 'Haven't you seen the sheer drop around the edge of the garden of that place, and the rocky terrain below? That cliff is impossible to climb. Even Quincy wouldn't risk it. He's athletic but he ain't crazy. Scaling that cliff would be a suicide mission.'

'I guess you're right about that,' Delano replied. 'It's the whole point of the location of the villa, after all. It's not just about the stunning views; Sugar Reef Bay properties afford complete security and privacy. It's simply not possible to approach from any direction other than the access road.'

'If your surveillance officers have no record of Quincy arriving at or leaving Sugar Reef Bay, then he wasn't at Jacobs's villa,' Max said.

'So how do we explain the location of the signal from his cell phone when he called Latoya?' Delano asked.

'I don't know,' Max replied. 'Maybe it was stolen.'

'Or maybe Quincy was brought here against his will,' Hyacinth volunteered.

'If that's the case, then someone would surely have had to have got to him before Max,' Delano said. 'And perhaps even before Jacobs.'

'Well, we know Jacobs's Mayday call from the Atratus was put out on VHF channel sixteen, which is a public channel monitored twenty-four hours a day, primarily by Coast Guards around the world, but anyone can listen in if they have a radio receiver and an antenna to pick up the signal,' Max began.

'So if anyone was tracking Jacobs's yacht and heard him put out the call, they would also know that he was picked up by the Coast Guard early this morning,' Hyacinth continued.

'Exactly. If they were watching from a vantage point as we towed the Atratus to the mooring at English Harbour they would've seen everything,' Max went on, 'including you guys unloading the drums of cocaine from the yacht.'

'Perhaps Quincy was needed for access to this place,' Hyacinth said suddenly. 'Jacobs might have given Quincy one of those remote controlled key fobs for the electric gates. Who would know that? Anyone who was watching him could have seen him come and go through the gates.'

'If I owned a place like that I wouldn't just let the gardener come and go as he pleased,' Max said.

'It's only access to the grounds of the property,' Delano pointed out, 'not the villa itself. I think it'd be quite acceptable for the gardener to have access to the garden, especially if the owner was away for a few days and wanted someone to keep an eye on the place. But I'm still not convinced Quincy's just the gardener. Or the handyman or pool boy.'

'He had nothing to do with the drugs bust,' Max said firmly.

'Let's say the key fob was given to Quincy by Jacobs,' Hyacinth said, 'just so Quincy could keep an eye on things while Jacobs was away. When Jacobs called Quincy this morning, it was clear he knew Quincy would have access to the grounds, even if not to the villa itself.'

'All right, I'll go along with that,' Max said.

'If someone was watching the Atratus being towed into English Harbour this morning, having listened into Jacobs's Mayday call to the Coast Guard,' Hyacinth continued, 'and that same someone knew Quincy was in possession of the access fob for the gates to the villa, they could have accosted Quincy soon after he left his mom's house this morning, around seven-thirty. They may not even have known that Jacobs would try to call Quincy, but that's okay because by that time they could have been up to Sugar Reef Bay and in and out of the villa hours before the surveillance officers arrived. It would've been fairly easy to evade most of the residents at that hour too. And even if they were seen, if Quincy and his captor — or captors — were suitably disguised, no one would suspect a thing.'

'Except that theory still doesn't explain how a call came to be made from Quincy's cell phone at the villa much later in the day,' Delano said.

'True.' Hyacinth nodded with disappointment.

'But then again, I can't think of any other explanation for Quincy to lie to me about where he was — or where he'd been — other than that he was under duress,' Max said.

'How did he sound when you spoke to him?' Delano asked. 'You think he could have been under pressure to act normally to avoid any suspicion on your part?'

Max thought for a moment before answering the question.

'Now I think of it, perhaps he did sound a little — I don't know — tense? Uneasy? I guess at the time I just assumed he was busy or caught up with something at work. But if he was being threatened, or…' Max struggled to finish the sentence. 'Oh man, poor Quincy. This could be bad. There's no chance he's still somewhere at the villa, is there?'

'It's looking less and less likely,' Delano replied. 'But we're turning the place upside down. If he's here, we'll find him. We can't jump to conclusions yet, we're just speculating and that's not always a good thing to do. The only evidence we have so far is a phone call made from an impossible location at an impossible time. But I'm certain there'll be a perfectly reasonable explanation as to how Quincy did it. We just need a few more puzzle pieces.'

'Jacobs must have some sort of security system at the villa?' Max asked.

'Yeah, there's an alarm system here. And there are security cameras around the exterior of the property,' Delano replied, 'but all the footage on the hard drive of Jacobs's video recorder has been mysteriously erased. I'll have to get it back to HQ and see if Lloyd can recover anything from it.'

'You know Delano, I feel partly to blame for Quincy's disappearance,' Max said suddenly. 'If he's come to any harm, I'll never forgive myself. And neither will my aunt. I shoulda known something was wrong when I spoke to him this morning. If only he'd said something, or given some kind of indication that he was in trouble. Maybe he did. Maybe I missed it…'

'Don't blame yourself Max,' Delano said. 'It's not your fault. There's no way you, or anyone, could've known that he may have been in danger. And I say *may have* because right now we have absolutely no evidence of that.'

'Yeah, I realise I'm probably overreacting. There must be something I can do to help though.'

'Maybe there is. You know Quincy's friends and family better than any of us, they're *your* family too. Talk to them, see if they know anything. Perhaps something he said one time, even just a passing comment. We'll follow up with our own lines of inquiry, but you may come across something we don't due to your family connections. Have you gotten any sleep at all today, by the way?'

'Not much, no,' Max replied. 'But I'd rather be helping you guys if I can. Keep me informed. He's my cousin, man. Like you said, he's family.' Max's commanding voice, usually brimming with confidence and authority, quivered slightly.

'You'll be the first to hear if we have any news,' Delano reassured him.

'Poor Max,' Hyacinth said as Delano ended the call. 'He must be out of his mind with worry, not to mention exhausted after being up all night rescuing Jacobs.'

Delano didn't appear to be listening.

'What's up, boss?'

'That camera,' Delano said, approaching a small surveillance camera mounted just under the overhang of the roof at the front of the villa. 'It looks like… Someone's sprayed over the lens, blinded the camera.'

Hyacinth was close behind. She looked up at the camera.

'The whole lens is obscured with black paint,' she said in surprise.

'Let's check the others,' Delano said. They made their way around the property in a clockwise direction, searching for and inspecting the lenses of each surveillance camera. They counted ten in total, strategically placed; Oliver was clearly a paranoid individual. The lens of every camera had been masked by black spray paint.

'I hope Lloyd can recover the footage that was erased from the hard drive,' Delano said, 'because someone went to great lengths to disable the camera system and prevent anyone from seeing what was recorded.'

SEVEN

5:30 pm, Thursday, September 19
V. C. Bird International Airport

Almost three hours after introducing himself to Graymond Sharkey and Alicia Clayton, Brandon was firmly of the opinion that the couple were telling the truth and had nothing to hide. Their story checked out on all counts and he received the report from airport security that their luggage was clean. In addition, Lloyd had run exhaustive background checks on them both and had found nothing so much as a parking ticket for either of them. Financial records, travel history, employment history, friends, family and other personal information had been thoroughly researched and triple-checked. Graymond and Alicia were upstanding citizens with unblemished records. The details of Graymond's exoneration for the double homicide of which he was convicted in 2000 were clear-cut and unequivocal. The case was closed and there was nothing further for debate.

Along with the rest of the information Lloyd had sent over and the interviews he had conducted face to face with Graymond and Alicia, Brandon was convinced that they were innocent of any involvement with Oliver Jacobs's current situation. Although Oliver and Graymond had resumed contact after Graymond's release from prison in 2016, and had remained friends since then, Brandon noted that Graymond no longer employed Oliver's accountancy services. Graymond was a businessman and the CEO of his own aviation company, GS Executive Aviation Ltd. The day to day operations of the business were extensive and ranged from a private jet charter service to ab initio lessons for private pilots. The company was profitable with all revenue accounted for. Graymond filed his tax returns on time and donated considerable contributions of cash to environmentally friendly projects and green initiatives as a gesture towards offsetting the carbon footprint made by his company.

In a brief conversation with Delano, who was still at Villa Bella Casa with Oliver Jacobs and the rest of the team, Brandon relayed his findings, supported by the background information provided by Lloyd.

'I'm certain they're innocent,' Brandon said. 'I don't believe either of them are involved in Jacobs's drug trafficking racket in any way.'

'You mean it's a complete coincidence that they fly into Antigua on the very day he's caught with seventy-five million dollars' worth of cocaine on his yacht?' Delano asked cynically.

'Sure, I know how it sounds, but I really believe it's a genuine coincidence,' Brandon said with conviction, adding, 'and you know how I feel about coincidences.'

'Yeah, I do,' Delano replied. 'And I agree with you. There's no such thing.'

'Except today,' Brandon said firmly. 'And if you need even more to convince you, I've got it.'

'Try me,' Delano said. 'I'm listening.'

'Okay then. Alicia Clayton, the girlfriend, is a freelance journalist back in the UK. Lloyd has sent links to a number of her articles. She's investigated scores of different stories and it seems she's even been instrumental in solving a few crimes; everything from grand larceny to homicide. Graymond's own acquittal is testament to her relentless search for the truth. According to Lloyd's report, she used to be the crime editor of a major national newspaper in the UK before she struck out on her own.'

'Good for her but that doesn't put her above suspicion. I'll need more than that.'

'Then listen to this,' Brandon continued. 'Remember last year the police closed the cold case for the murder at the old Rock Palm Resort hotel? The one where a woman's body was found on the beach, back in ninety-five, just before we got slammed by Hurricane Luis?'

'Sure I do. That was big news, it was in the headlines for days, I remember reading the official police reports. It was huge for the police department; that case had been unsolved for twenty-three years with no fresh leads. And obviously it was a huge relief for the Rapley family.'

'Well then, you may recall two people who were particularly instrumental in solving the murder…'

'Wait, yes I do, I recognise the names now, Graymond Sharkey and Alicia Clayton. But how did those two get involved?'

'This is the thing which will convince you of these guys' innocence,' Brandon said. 'Alicia used to vacation in Antigua every year with her parents when she was a girl. They stayed at the same place every year: Rock Palm Resort. Apparently her father had business connections with the owner, Carlos Jaxen.'

'I remember Carlos. Nice guy. American, wasn't he? Always treated his staff well. They were some of the best paid on the island. Real shame what happened to the resort after the hurricane devastated the place.'

'Yeah, it was. I think some international luxury resort company has big plans for the site now but I haven't been there in a while. Anyway, back in ninety-five, Leon Fayer was the general manager of the old hotel, Rock Palm Resort…'

'Leon Fayer? As in Leon, now GM of the West Beach Club?' Delano interrupted. 'Recently won some big travel and tourism award for services to the Caribbean tourist industry?'

'The very same,' Brandon replied.

'I know Leon. He has a beautiful family. His granddaughters and Tamesha are at the same school. Kindest man you ever met. Always got time for everyone. Does he still teach cricket in his free time to the local school kids?'

'Yeah, Leon's one of the good guys,' Brandon went on. 'I called him earlier as his name also came up in the cold case report. It seems he knows Alicia very well and was more than happy to vouch for her. Even offered to stake his name and reputation on the fact that she and Graymond were innocent.'

'Seriously?' Delano asked.

'Yeah. According to him they go back a long way — more than thirty years — from when Alicia and her parents used to vacation at Rock Palm Resort every year.'

'Of course,' Delano said. 'They must've gotten to know each other pretty well.'

'They did. What's more, Alicia and her parents were staying at the old hotel on the night of the murder, in ninety-five. It was the last night before all the tourists were evacuated off the island before Hurricane Luis made landfall.'

'I remember it like it was yesterday.'

'Alicia was only fifteen or sixteen at the time, but she was there in the immediate aftermath of the murder, before the tourists were whisked away from the hotel to the airport. I'm not sure how it happened, but something relating to the murder washed up on her shore again, twenty-three years later, which compelled her — and Graymond — to return to the beach at Rock Palm, where it all happened. The rest is history; you know the outcome.'

'That was *her*?' Delano asked in surprise.

'Yeah. Think you need to offer her a job, boss. She sounds like someone we could use on this team.'

'I'll look forward to meeting her.'

'But anyway, Leon — and a number of other former Rock Palm employees — are prepared to vouch for both Alicia and Graymond with favourable character references all round.'

'Can't argue with that.'

'I agree. Oh and I almost forgot, Leon has insisted that they stay at the West Beach Club. Obviously they can't stay at Jacobs's villa as originally planned. Leon's given strict instructions to let him know as soon as we're done here and he'll send a taxi to give them a ride back to the resort.'

'Friends in high places,' Delano murmured. 'Well then, I guess those two are cleared of any involvement with Jacobs.'

'I'd say they are,' Brandon said, 'but it'd probably be worth keeping in touch with them while they're here. They may be of some help to us. Has Jacobs mentioned them to you at all?'

'No. He hasn't. Not yet, at least. I'll talk to him about them. And I agree with you Brandon. They might be useful to us. Did they seem surprised when they learned why they were stopped at the airport?'

'No, not really,' Brandon said. 'They said they had no idea he was involved in narco trafficking, but Graymond admitted that

Jacobs was no saint. He didn't elaborate but implied that Jacobs's professional conduct was less than scrupulous, hence why he no longer employs Jacobs as his accountant.'

'So they know what he's about,' Delano said.

'Yeah, for sure.'

'Then wish them a pleasant evening, send them on their way to the West Beach Club and tell them we'll be in touch. I'll have another chat with Jacobs, let him know his guests have arrived.'

EIGHT

6:30 pm, Thursday, September 19
Villa Bella Casa, Sugar Reef Bay

By the time the six CDSLI officers had completed a thorough search of Villa Bella Casa, the sun was setting and the pale light of dusk was swiftly turning to darkness. The team reconvened in the large family room and Duane moved Oliver to one of the bedrooms on the south side of the villa.

'Find anything?' Oliver asked with a sneer as he was guided out of the room by the plain clothes officer. His question was ignored but Oliver was not deterred. 'Like I said, you're wasting your time. There's nothing here.'

The rain had finally stopped, and the clouds were clearing to the west. A few stars were visible in the night sky, twinkling serenely after the maelstrom of the storm which had engulfed the island for the last twenty-four hours.

'What do we have so far?' Delano asked.

There was a brief silence. Hyacinth suppressed a yawn. Anson spoke first.

'From the safe in the master bedroom: fake ID including a passport and a whole bunch of documents in the name of Terrence Everard Dove, a Canadian citizen.' He held up the plastic wallet. 'Lloyd's run a series of background searches. Terry Dove is a cleverly created alter ego to whom the title deeds of this villa, and a number of other properties and assets, belong. On paper, Oliver Jacobs rents this place from Terry Dove. Except Oliver Jacobs *is* Terry Dove.'

'Why would Jacobs go to the trouble of renting a property from himself under a false name?' Hyacinth asked frowning.

'I can think of a few reasons,' Anson replied, 'but I'm guessing it's either for some financial gain or to maintain anonymity, keeping his real name off the record.'

'Oliver Jacobs *is* his real name, right?' Nerissa asked suddenly.

'According to Lloyd it is,' Anson said. 'Oliver Jacobs is a bona fide British citizen with a watertight background.'

'If his background is as watertight as his yacht right now then that's not exactly convincing,' Mitch said wryly.

'Very funny Mitch,' Delano said with a smile, 'but Lloyd's correct. And I have sources who can confirm that. A British couple flew into Antigua on a Virgin Atlantic flight from London this afternoon: Graymond Sharkey and Alicia Clayton. They're friends of Jacobs.'

'The same Graymond Sharkey Edella told us about this morning?' Hyacinth asked. 'Wasn't Jacobs his accountant?'

'He was. Many years ago. Jacobs worked as Graymond's accountant back in the nineties, but that all ended when Graymond was sent to prison. These days they're just friends.'

'What about the woman?' Nerissa asked.

'Alicia? She's Graymond's girlfriend,' Delano replied. 'An investigative journalist.'

'Are they connected to this morning's drugs bust in any way?' Mitch asked.

'No, although according to Brandon they're aware of Jacobs's corrupt business dealings and weren't surprised to hear of his involvement with drug smuggling.'

'Why are they in Antigua?' Edella asked.

'They're here on vacation for three weeks,' Delano replied. 'Jacobs invited them to stay at his villa. Apparently he's been insisting they come out here ever since he moved to Sugar Reef eighteen months ago.'

'And we're absolutely certain they're not involved?' Anson said.

Delano summarised his earlier conversation with Brandon, backed up further by additional research from Lloyd.

'Impressive,' Mitch said after Delano finished with an outline of the Rock Palm Resort cold case. Most of the team had read the police reports and agreed that an endorsement from Leon Fayer was worth its weight in gold.

'I've informed Jacobs his visitors have arrived,' Delano went on. 'He's asked to speak with Graymond.'

'What for?' Anson asked. 'To get him to sign his bail bond?'

'Quite possibly,' Delano replied. 'Due to the considerable quantity of cocaine he was attempting to smuggle onto the island, it's likely the court will only grant bail if there are two sureties to sign the recognisance, along with Jacobs himself. I've arranged for Graymond and Alicia to meet with Jacobs at our headquarters first thing tomorrow, along with his lawyer. It's up to them how they decide to proceed. What else do we have? Edella, you get anything from around the pool and lanai?'

'Nothing,' Edella said with a firm shake of her head, 'and you can see what I did to the place.' She gestured to the lanai and swimming pool area, illuminated by the lights of the villa. It looked like an abandoned building site. Stone plant pots had been overturned, ornamental palms and shrubs lay uprooted, surrounded by piles of earth, while stuffing from the shredded cushions of the lanai furniture drifted across the surface of the pool in white, wispy clumps. Four parasols lay on their sides, the canopies torn into shreds.

'Nothing?' Delano asked.

'Nothing at all,' Edella replied. 'If Jacobs asked Quincy to secure the parasols and hang a bunch of cushions out to dry, neither of those things were done, so either Quincy has a short memory and forgot what he'd been asked to do, or he completely disregarded Jacobs's instructions, or they were a coded message for something else, as we suspected. But if that's the case, I've no idea what they meant. If Quincy was supposed to retrieve something, I guess he was successful because I'm tellin' you, it's clean as a whistle out there. There's no evidence of drugs and nothing to connect Jacobs to any narco-related activity whatsoever.'

'Speaking of Quincy, what's the latest on his whereabouts?' Mitch asked suddenly.

'There was a call made from his cell phone at twelve-twenty this afternoon, from this location, to his girlfriend, Latoya,' Delano replied. 'It lasted all of four seconds, during which time he said nothing. Then he hung up.'

'What?' Anson frowned.

Delano brought the others up to speed with the latest theories on how Quincy's cell phone had managed to emit a signal from the villa without Quincy himself apparently being physically present at the time.

'The only thing we know for certain is that Quincy's cell was inside the gates of this place at twelve-twenty today,' Delano said. 'The problem is that the surveillance officers posted at the entrance of the access road to Sugar Reef Bay and outside the gates swear they haven't seen Quincy, either entering *or* leaving the place.'

'So if he *was* here, then he somehow managed to evade four surveillance officers,' Hyacinth added.

'We know he didn't drive here in his truck,' Delano continued, 'and the officers at the end of the road are positive there hasn't been a vehicle in which Quincy might have been concealed as a passenger — or hostage — either. But even if such a vehicle made it past the officers down there, no one's been through the gates to the villa except us.'

'And the event history of the alarm system?' Mitch asked.

'Lloyd's working on that,' Delano replied. 'The security company is being less than cooperative. Their legal people are using every loophole in the book — in the name of client confidentiality — to prevent us from gaining access to their records. Something tells me the company isn't operating on the right side of the law either but we'll save that excitement for another day.'

'Surely they can just tell us whether the alarm system for Villa Bella Casa was activated earlier today or not?' Edella said.

'You'd think,' Delano replied with a note of frustration.

'Are any of Jacobs's devices linked to the alarm system?' Mitch asked.

'According to Lloyd, there's nothing interesting on Jacobs's iPad and his cell phone is still in a bag of rice drying out. I've looked everywhere for a computer or laptop belonging to Jacobs, but there wasn't one on his yacht and there isn't one here either.'

'If Quincy bypassed all four surveillance officers, hypothetically speaking,' Edella said, 'and somehow made it through the gates to this place undetected, what exactly did he do here and where did he go?'

'I can think of a few things,' Hyacinth said. 'If Jacobs and Quincy were in league, they could have planned for a scenario just like this one. Jacobs's innocent phone call asking Quincy to check on the parasols might have been a pre-arranged code telling him to destroy or get rid of any evidence connected to the drugs. If Quincy somehow managed to breach all the security and make it in here without being seen, one of his first jobs appears to have been to blind all the surveillance cameras. At some point he also erased the data on the video recorder's hard drive, and removed Jacobs's computer or laptop and any other external hard drives or electronic devices — and evidence of drugs, incriminating evidence etcetera — before disappearing.'

'Well if that's the case then he appears to have succeeded,' Edella said.

'How do we know all that was done today though?' Mitch asked. 'What evidence do we have that the cameras weren't sprayed weeks ago?'

'The paint over the lenses is fresh,' Delano said. 'And I mean fresh since the storm. The cameras were coated with a layer of dust, sand and other garden debris flying around in the wind. If you look closely at each lens, the paint was sprayed *on top* of all that. It has to have been done within the last few hours. Ergo, although we have no proof, it makes sense that the hard drive was erased at the same time.'

'For a humble odd job man Quincy sure made an expert job of cleaning up,' Mitch said. 'And he sure as hell ain't here now, so he successfully managed to evade our surveillance people too. Edella's right. Perhaps Jacobs's one phone call wasn't so stupid after all.'

'If all four surveillance officers are adamant Quincy didn't pass them in either direction, how d'he do it?' Edella asked. 'How did he get in here, in broad daylight, without anyone seeing him? And how did he leave? Who is he, some kind of Houdini?'

'Unless he never came to Sugar Reef and was never at the villa at all,' Mitch said. 'Just because his cell phone was here, it doesn't mean he was too.'

'That's what we thought,' Hyacinth said. 'Maybe Quincy gave his phone to someone else, or it was stolen.'

'For what reason? Access to this place?' Mitch asked.

'You don't need a cell phone to get in,' Hyacinth replied. 'Just the key fob for the electric gates and the six digit code to deactivate the alarm system once you're inside.'

'Access to the safe then?' Mitch suggested.

'It's a combination lock,' Anson said. He held up a stethoscope. 'I used this to break in. Again, no cell phone required.'

'If Quincy's phone wasn't needed for access to anything, then perhaps the call was set up as a red herring,' Nerissa said, 'to mislead us into thinking he was here when he wasn't at all.'

'You mean he gave his phone to someone else to make the call to Latoya, knowing we'd pick up on it?' Anson asked.

'Something like that,' Nerissa shrugged. 'Or as Hyacinth said, it was stolen.'

'Whoever it was — Quincy or someone else — I'd love to know how they got in and out of here without being seen,' Mitch said. 'There *has* to be another way into the grounds of this place besides through those gates.'

'Hyacinth and I took a walk around the perimeter,' Delano said. 'The whole of the front of the villa is protected by eight-foot high walls and the wrought iron entrance gates, which require a key fob to open them and have been in full view of the surveillance crew for the entire day. As you know, there's one road in and one road out. And that's it. The other three sides are even more impregnable. The precipice which falls away from the gardens surrounding the property would present a serious challenge to the most daring climber. Max says that from a boat on the water looking towards land, the cliff face looks insurmountable. It's a sheer drop. Not only that, it's covered in thick foliage and vegetation. There's simply no way anyone could approach the villa from the cliff sides. And as if that wasn't enough to put someone off, at the foot of the cliff leading to that narrow stretch of sand just visible from up here, are manchineel trees.'

'Then count me out from seeing if it can be done,' Anson said.

The manchineel tree, also known as the beach apple, was well known throughout the Caribbean and Central America. The shiny green leaves and fruit of the trees, which grew to almost fifty feet tall, bore a superficial resemblance to those of an apple tree. The fruit, pale green in colour, was poisonous, along with every other part of the tree. The milky white sap of the manchineel contained a potent skin irritant. Any native of Antigua knew that standing underneath one of the trees during a rainstorm caused blistering if the milky substance came into contact with the skin. The sap had even been known to damage the paint on cars.

'So it's safe to rule out access to this place from anywhere other than the access road and the gates,' Nerissa said.

'What about the security cameras?' Edella asked.

'There are ten in total,' Delano said, 'strategically mounted around the villa and grounds. But all data from the network video recorder's hard drive has been erased. There doesn't appear to be any kind of back-up system either. If there was, it's gone. Then again, even if the recorder hadn't been tampered with, as every single camera has been masked with black spray paint I'm not even sure the footage would be of any use to us, assuming Lloyd's able to retrieve it.'

'Why would anyone spray the cameras if they're going to delete the footage anyway?' Edella asked, frowning.

'Why spray the cameras at all?' Anson asked. 'Why not just cut the wires instead?'

'It's not that simple,' Delano said. 'The surveillance system's wired due to the number of cameras and the size of the property. It's state of the art and would've cost a small fortune to install and set up. The cameras have been expertly wired, probably with standard ethernet cable; it would be fiddly and time-consuming to try to cut the network cable connected to each camera. Some of the cameras are also hard to reach, in spite of the fact that the villa's a single storey building. If Quincy was up against time, it would be much quicker and easier to just spray the cameras with the paint.'

'It still doesn't make sense,' Anson said, 'but if that's why Jacobs sent Quincy — or someone else — here, to delete incriminating footage, then I'd love to know what it was. I hope Lloyd can employ his dark arts to recover the data.'

'We'll get it back to headquarters tonight and he can start on it first thing in the morning,' Delano said.

'I don't think we should write off the fact that Jacobs may have sent Quincy — or whoever — here to retrieve something as well as to erase the footage and spray the cameras,' Hyacinth said suddenly.

'Until we know for sure what happened here this morning we can't rule anything out,' Delano nodded.

'You have any idea what time that camera footage was erased?' Nerissa asked.

'No, but I'm hoping Lloyd will figure that out too.'

'Any fingerprints?' Hyacinth asked.

'I've dusted for prints around the study, but there's only one set and that belongs to Jacobs. If anyone else was here, they wore gloves or wiped the place clean and covered their tracks.'

'What if there was someone else already here at the villa the whole time?' Nerissa said suddenly. 'Someone who didn't need to evade the surveillance officers because he, or she, was already here? Perhaps Quincy wasn't supposed to come by at all, but just to relay a message to the person who was already here. If Jacobs had called that person direct, we'd have instantly been alerted to the fact that he, or she, was here. By calling Quincy first, and getting him to relay the message, Jacobs bought himself, and whoever else was involved, valuable time to dispose of anything incriminating and get out of here.'

'So you're saying that Quincy was just a go-between?' Anson said. 'A messenger between Jacobs and someone else?'

'Exactly,' Nerissa nodded. 'All Quincy would need to do would be to call the person up here at the villa — on another phone, obviously, not his own — to let him, or her, know that it was time to clean house and get out of there. That could've been done well before the surveillance officers arrived at ten-thirty.'

'And the call made from Quincy's phone to Latoya at twelve-twenty?' Mitch asked.

Nerissa paused.

'However we look at this, that phone call is a headache,' Hyacinth said.

'Was the call a code in itself, d'you think?' Anson asked.

'A code for whom? Latoya?' Hyacinth said.

'I doubt that,' Delano replied. 'She's mad at Quincy but otherwise doesn't seem to have any idea what this is about. And she denies knowing where he might be now. Mitch, Nerissa, you get anything from the other Sugar Reef Bay residents?'

'We visited each of the properties as soon as we got here from Quincy's mom's place,' Nerissa began. 'Including Villa Bella Casa, there are five properties along the Sugar Reef headland in total, all worth well over a million US dollars. We started with the large house closest to the entrance of the access road. It's owned by a retired couple, British expats. They've been home all day but hadn't noticed anything unusual. They've never met Jacobs, although they'd passed him in his SUV a few times; he drives a black Toyota Land Cruiser. They said he always seemed pleasant enough, you know, waved, smiled, that kinda thing, but kept himself to himself. He doesn't have many visitors and never caused any trouble. To all intents and purposes he's the perfect neighbour. Quincy takes care of their garden and pool maintenance too. Gets paid in cash. It's convenient all round. They said he's polite, courteous and a hard worker. According to them, he was here at Sugar Reef a couple of days ago, but they haven't seen him or his truck since. The next house along is a luxury holiday rental. A family from Connecticut are staying there — renting the place for two weeks — but they left early this morning to visit Nelson's Dockyard and only just got back so they weren't much help.'

Mitch took up the narrative for the remaining two properties.

'The third house is a pretty nice villa on the opposite side of the road but it was shut up and unoccupied. According to the British couple, it's owned by a wealthy Texan businessman who rarely visits the place. The last property before you get to Villa

Bella Casa is owned by Paul Griffiths, the CEO of a multinational pharmaceutical company. The house is a Caribbean bolthole for him, his wife and their three kids. The wife and kids were getting ready to leave for the airport for a return flight to New York when we knocked, but we spoke to Paul.

'He wasn't overly keen to talk to us, but confirmed that Quincy took care of their pool and garden and kept an eye on the place when they were back in the States. Said Quincy was mostly reliable, did his job well and was always paid in cash with generous tips. Oh, and he was great with the kids; they adored him apparently. Quincy was last at their property two days ago, on Tuesday, and was his usual upbeat self, wishing them a safe trip back to New York and so on. The family had never met Jacobs and knew little about him, even though their property's next door to his. Paul said that although now and again the odd vehicle drove by, Jacobs rarely had visitors. They'd never witnessed any disturbances and sometimes they weren't even sure whether he was home or not. The family have been there for the last month but neither Paul nor his wife had noticed anything out of the ordinary.

'Paul did mention he'd been out for most of the morning. He left Sugar Reef around nine and returned around one forty-five that afternoon. Says he met a friend for a drink, an old sailing buddy who has a yacht berthed at English Harbour. Paul's clearly visible on various surveillance cameras leaving Sugar Reef Bay in his Jeep and the officers at the entrance to the access road confirmed he arrived back at the time he says he did.'

'None of the residents we spoke to admitted to being involved with Jacobs in any way,' Nerissa concluded. 'In fact, most of them said they barely knew him. It was a different story with Quincy though. He's well-known, well-liked and hard working. He's obviously created a niche market for himself, maintaining gardens and pools at high end properties. Just like this place, the grounds of the other houses up here are immaculately maintained. Quincy obviously takes pride in his job. But no one's seen him or his truck at all today. We asked to take a look at any surveillance footage from security cameras, particularly those with a view of the access road, which, according to all the residents, is the only way in or out of Sugar Reef Bay. Most of the properties have cameras overlooking the entrances to their driveways. Quincy didn't show up on anyone's footage. It confirms the witness testimonies that he really hasn't been here in the last forty-eight hours.'

'And yet his cell phone emitted a signal from this very location,' Hyacinth said.

'Well he's definitely not here now and neither is his phone,' Anson said. 'We've turned this place upside down and haven't found a thing. We've found nothing to connect Jacobs to any cartel or drug trafficking organisation. In fact, other than the fake ID, there's nothing illegal here at all, not even so much as a few grams of cocaine.'

Hyacinth was dialling Quincy's number. She shook her head.

'Straight to voicemail.'

'I think we're done here for now.' Delano spoke for the rest of the team. 'It's time to pack up and go home.'

As the last vehicle of the small convoy made its way down the narrow access road of Sugar Reef Bay, the wrought iron gates of Villa Bella Casa closed silently behind them. A dark-coloured SUV with government licence plates was parked to one side of the entrance. The night surveillance crew had taken over, watching and waiting. Tree frogs and crickets chirruped noisily in the warm night air over the rhythmic sound of the waves lapping on the wide, crescent-shaped beach below. As the convoy turned left onto the main road, Hyacinth, seated in the rear of the dark blue Ford Explorer, cast a sideways glance at her fellow passenger. Still wearing handcuffs, Oliver Jacobs sat motionless, staring straight ahead. He had a strange expression on his face. It was difficult to interpret. Perhaps it was one of puzzlement. Or bemusement. Hyacinth couldn't work out which. He turned his head slowly towards her. His dark eyes glinted and his lips curled into a chilling smile. And Hyacinth knew their search at the villa wasn't over.

NINE

7:00 pm, Thursday, September 19
The West Beach Club, Antigua

Frank had received strict instructions from Leon Fayer, general
manager of the exclusive West Beach Club resort, to take extra
special care of the esteemed guests he was dispatched to meet at
the airport. Frank was just happy to get some work. Thanks to the
storm, business had been slow over the last few days. Other than
the routine airport pickups, his more lucrative driving work —
sightseeing tours, excursions, taxi rides to and from bars, clubs and
restaurants, and so on — had been curtailed due to tourists opting
to hunker down and stay put. Although the West Beach Club paid
him a basic wage, Frank relied on the tips from generous tourists
to sustain a better quality of life. This week he was woefully down
on his luck.

He recognised the couple who now approached his ancient but
immaculately maintained Toyota minivan. They had stayed at the
West Beach Club the previous year, around the same time. As far
as Frank could recall, they had also been instrumental in solving
the notorious Rock Palm Resort cold case which had baffled the
Antigua Police Force and numerous detectives for over twenty
years.

He checked their names on the paper Leon had given him —
Graymond Sharkey and Alicia Clayton — and introduced himself
with a warm welcome to Antigua before taking their cases and
placing them in the trunk of the minivan. The sliding door to the
passenger seats was open and Frank gestured to the couple to make
themselves comfortable. The usual excitement typical of British
and American tourists which Frank had become accustomed to
seemed to be lacking. As the couple climbed into the back of the
minivan they were solemn and distracted. Frank jumped into the
driver's seat, placed his phone in the central console and decided to

refrain from the usual spiel on seafood restaurants, sunset cruises and his expertly tailored tour of the island. Instead, he left them to their thoughts while he navigated a mob of holiday representatives, airport officials and animated tourists as he drove to the airport exit road.

The traffic on the highway heading south was heavy due to roadworks. Frank wasn't sure what was going on with the road as they inched forward, but he knew of a few potholes which could do with some attention for starters. Further inland, the traffic thinned out. Dimmed porch lights from one-storey houses and low-rise buildings spilled onto the streets, casting long shadows. Locals, young and old, lingered by the side of the road, or on verandahs with partially completed concrete balustrades, taking in the warm night air. The lilting rhythm of reggae music rose in a crescendo before fading into nothing, along with the aroma of cooking from a roadside snack bar selling ackee and saltfish and chicken curry. The minivan was heading west now. The wooden houses and shacks became further apart and were soon replaced by a darkened landscape of rainforest-covered hills, thick with tropical foliage and lush vegetation.

At last the meandering strip of tarmac began a gentle descent towards the coast. Beneath twinkling stars and a pale opaline moon in the clear night sky, the glittering lights of a cruise ship, far out at sea, moved slowly across the horizon. Frank took a right onto a palm tree-lined road where a large sign, illuminated by two powerful floodlights, welcomed the latest arrivals to the exclusive West Beach Club. Frank waved at the guard stationed in the gatehouse who saluted in return. The minivan wound its way slowly through well-lit gardens, immaculately landscaped and replete with fruit trees and tropical plants.

For the first time during the journey, Frank overheard the couple exchange remarks from the seat behind.

'I'm not sure why, but I'm kind of relieved we're staying here instead of Jacobs's place.' The woman, Alicia, spoke first.

'Yeah, I guess I am too,' her companion, Graymond, replied, 'although I was hoping to see the villa. It sounds impressive. Jacobs has been talking about it for months. And now we're finally here he's gone and got himself busted.'

'You think he's guilty?' Alicia asked.

Disappointingly for Frank, they had reached the hotel and Graymond hadn't responded. Frank's curious side wondered who Jacobs was and why he might be guilty. Clearly the couple in the backseat of his minivan had a reputation for solving crimes. Perhaps this was the reason for their visit to Antigua. Rumours travelled like wildfire around the island and Frank was always happy to be the bearer of gossip, good or bad, fact or fiction. As his grandmother used to say, the important thing was not to let the truth stand in the way of a good story. Frank reluctantly slowed the minivan to a halt outside the brightly lit entrance of the West Beach Club and the conversation between his two passengers was over too soon. He opened the driver's door and the minivan was instantly infused with the warm night air, along with a cacophony of crickets and tree frogs, and the melodic sounds of a steel drum band. Frank jogged around to the other side where he slid open the passenger door. Alicia and Graymond climbed out as Frank retrieved their cases.

A porter in a tan shirt and matching chinos wheeled a brass luggage trolley towards them. He welcomed the couple to the West Beach Club and helped Frank with the suitcases. Frank wished Graymond and Alicia a pleasant vacation — if that's what it really was, he thought to himself privately — and immediately regretted not furnishing them with his wealth of knowledge and insight about the island as Graymond tipped him generously.

'Thank you, sir, much appreciated,' he said, resisting the urge to open his hand to see if the note was a ten or a twenty before he'd returned to the driver's seat and shut the door.

'This way Miss Clayton, Mr. Sharkey.' The porter gestured for Graymond and Alicia to follow him into the spacious, open-plan reception area. The West Beach Club had a modern, stylish vibe, with an abundance of driftwood, stucco and marble. Large ceiling fans rotated with a faint swish under a vaulted ceiling. Comfortable sofas with cushions of turquoise and coral surrounded glass-topped tables. Tall ceramic vases filled with colourful displays of tropical plants added a further splash of colour to the neutral shades of the walls and floor. A stunning arrangement of vibrant red laceleafs, birds of paradise, and magenta bougainvillea, encompassed in palm leaves, sat on a table in the middle of the reception area.

Suddenly, a voice from somewhere over the far side called their names loudly.

'Alicia! Graymond! Welcome! Welcome back!'

They turned in the direction of the voice to see a smartly dressed man in a white, short-sleeved shirt and pale green pants hurrying towards them.

'Leon!' Alicia said excitedly. They embraced before Leon Fayer, the general manager, turned to Graymond and shook his hand warmly with a beaming smile.

'Good to see you again Leon,' Graymond said, 'and thanks for vouching for us earlier. Your word carries considerable weight with airport officials apparently.'

'Not at all,' Leon said warmly. 'It's the least I could do. And I'm so sorry you encountered that... little problem... right after a long haul flight from London. I hope it wasn't too unpleasant for you. I only wish I could've stepped in to help sooner but I trust everything's okay now? I'm sorry, I haven't had a chance to catch up with Earl yet. He's generally a reasonable guy. Same goes for the CDSLI; they have a very good reputation. Of course I vouched wholeheartedly for you both and always will.'

'Leon, you've gone beyond anything we'd ask of you,' Alicia reassured him, 'and as for accommodating us here at the West Beach Club, I don't know what to say. It's...'

'I'm just so pleased you're here,' Leon replied, steering them towards one of the sofas. 'Take a seat and I'll get us some rum punches. Ah, here they are, perfect timing Kaleisha. And can you check Miss Clayton and Mr. Sharkey in please? They're staying in one of the executive villas on the beach.'

A member of the reception team appeared with a tray containing two hot face towels and two large glasses of rum punch. She placed them on the glass table top in front of Graymond and Alicia before acknowledging Leon's instructions with a nod and a smile.

'Thanks Kaleisha,' Leon said as he joined Alicia on one of the sofas. He was in his early sixties, although his energy and enthusiasm suggested he was much younger. He was still in good shape with a toned, athletic physique and his short, cropped hair was only slightly greying at the temples.

'Tomorrow you must tell me what this is all about,' Leon said with a serious note in his voice, 'but tonight I have a table reserved for you in the restaurant whenever you're ready for dinner. Roslyn's the maître d' on duty tonight; she's looking forward to seeing you again. She was so excited when I told her you were coming.'

'We're looking forward to seeing her too,' Alicia replied taking a sip of the rum punch. 'How is she? Is she well? And how's Violet? And Angella?'

'All still here,' Leon replied with a grin, 'just the same as ever. And we still talk about the Rock Palm magic show, even now.'

Alicia smiled at Leon's reference to the Rock Palm Resort cold case which she and Graymond had become involved in the previous September. The allusion prompted the memory of another key player in the twenty-three year old mystery.

'How's Owen Rapley doing?' she asked suddenly.

'Owen's doing great,' Leon replied. 'He's been a groundsman at the West Beach Club for nearly a year now and is one of my most hard-working employees here. I hope you don't mind but I saw him in passing this afternoon and mentioned to him that you were on your way here.'

'Oh of course not,' Alicia said.

'And you do know, I suppose, that…' Leon was suddenly interrupted by a man's voice. It sounded familiar. The accent was distinctly British.

'*Alicia*! You're *here*! *Finally*!'

'Er, as I was about to say, you do know that Owen has a friend visiting from England right now?' Leon continued, unable to hide a faint look of amusement.

Alicia and Graymond turned to see a man of roughly the same age hurrying towards them. He was dressed in a khaki safari shirt tucked into a pair of matching shorts. On his feet were a pair of white canvas espadrilles and he wore a thick, gold-plated curb chain around his neck. Following close behind was a clean-shaven man wearing a tan shirt and tan chino shorts, the uniform worn by the estates team of the West Beach Club.

'*Spencer*?' Alicia said in confusion, turning to the man in the safari attire. 'What are *you* doing here?'

'*Surprise!*' Spencer beamed, revealing an impressive set of perfect white teeth.

'I thought you were coming in late November, to avoid the hurricane season,' Alicia said.

'I was,' Spencer replied, 'but I thought I'd change my flights at the last minute so I could be here at the same time as you and Gray.' He embraced Alicia in a tight bear hug planting a kiss on each side of her face.

'Oh, that's… wonderful,' Alicia said, somewhat taken aback. She tried to recall the time she had made the grave mistake of furnishing Spencer with the dates she and Graymond would be in Antigua.

'I knew you'd be pleased,' Spencer replied excitedly, pulling away slightly but unwilling to completely let go. 'I kinda picked up the vibes that you wanted me to join you guys out here.'

'Really?' Alicia looked astonished. She attempted to extricate herself from Spencer's arms.

'That obvious, was it Spencer?' Graymond cast an amused look in Alicia's direction. 'You know Alicia far too well!'

'Oh hey Gray,' Spencer said casually. 'How was your er, flight?'

'Fine thanks,' Graymond replied. 'Are you staying here Spencer?'

'Yeah, with Owen,' Spencer replied, turning to his companion dressed in the estates uniform. The man gave Alicia and Graymond a shy smile and raised a hand in an acknowledging wave. 'What about you?' Spencer asked. 'I thought you were staying in some fancy million dollar pad on the other side of the island?'

'Last minute change of plans,' Alicia said quickly. She turned to Spencer's companion. 'Owen, it's so nice to see you again. How are you?'

'I'm good,' he replied. 'It's great to see you guys again too. I'll never be able to thank you enough for what you did for me last year.'

'You don't need to thank us for anything,' Alicia replied kindly. 'All Gray and I did was uncover the truth.'

It was another reference to the Rock Palm Resort cold case in which Owen Rapley had been the prime suspect, although he was never convicted due to a lack of evidence. Owen, once the tennis coach and manager of the sports facilities at the hotel, had found himself out of a job when the resort was destroyed by a hurricane. Worse, he found himself unemployable after witnesses reported seeing him on the beach late at night with the young woman who was murdered at the hotel. Twenty-three years on the streets of St. John's, migrating from one homeless shelter to another had brought Owen, an innocent man, to the point of despair. Spencer, who possessed credentials most suited to tracking Owen down, was instructed by Alicia to find him in order to tell him that the hunt for the real killer was all but over. It was during this time that Owen and Spencer became firm friends, and Leon, Owen's former boss, offered him employment once more, this time as part of the estates team at the West Beach Club.

'How's the job, Owen?' Alicia asked.

'Goin' well thanks,' Owen replied, glancing towards Leon for a look of approval.

'It's going very well,' Leon said. 'Owen's one of our star team players at the West Beach Club. There's also quite a demand for tennis lessons among the guests these days. I've even had to reduce the hours he works for the estates crew.'

'That's great news,' Alicia said. 'Congratulations Owen.'

'Thanks,' Owen replied shyly.

'So what are your plans over the next few days Alicia?' Spencer rejoined the conversation.

'Oh we've got a varied itinerary,' Alicia replied vaguely.

Although Spencer's inquisitive nature could be annoying at times, it was the reason they had met and had subsequently become friends. Spencer had been a homeless man, wasted on drugs and alcohol at the time. He was the sole witness to a jewellery store heist in Hatton Garden, although he was instantly dismissed by the police as a reliable one. Alicia, a reporter, had more faith in the emaciated street vagrant's testimony, however. In exchange for coffee and bagels, she extracted details of the theft from her newest informant. After further validation, she was proved correct. Thanks to Spencer's account of the events, alongside Alicia's background checks with trusted sources, and copious amounts of coffee and bagels, all four perpetrators of the heist were caught and almost all of the stolen gems recovered.

Since that time, Spencer's worth had been proved a number of other times as a reliable informant for the reporter, however Alicia had grown fond of Spencer and had encouraged him to get off the streets and spend his fifty-thousand pound reward money on the best detox programme money could buy. Sixty days and copious counselling sessions and gym workouts later, Spencer Warne emerged from the five-star rehab centre a changed man. He was drug-free and with a renewed zest for life. The final touch to his transformation had been extensive dental treatment with the remaining money. Years of neglect due to heroin and alcohol addiction had led to appalling dentition which Spencer had been keen to rectify.

But the biggest challenge was yet to come. Spencer had needed a job. Alicia pulled yet more strings and Spencer found himself hired at the very store in Hatton Garden opposite which he had lay slumped in a vile sleeping bag on the night of the heist. His employment at the store, along with his trademark inquisitive nature, had led to the discovery of an unusual piece of jewellery which, in turn, had led to Antigua, and the denouement of the unsolved murder case at Rock Palm Resort.

Spencer may have overcome his addiction to drugs and alcohol, but his greatest weakness remained: his affection for Alicia. In spite of previous girlfriends, Spencer made no secret of his unrequited love for the investigative journalist, much to the amusement of Graymond and occasional exasperation of Alicia.

'What are you two doing this evening?' Alicia asked Spencer and Owen.

'We thought we'd hang out in St. John's for a while before heading over to The Jungle,' Spencer replied. 'Why don't you join us? Owen knows one of the bouncers, Lloyd. He's got us VIP passes.'

'VIP passes for The Jungle?' Alicia was familiar with the reggae bar and its unsavoury reputation. 'Isn't that a contradiction in terms?'

Spencer frowned in confusion. Before Alicia had chance to clarify the meaning behind her comment, Owen interrupted. He was holding his cell phone.

'I just got a message from Lloyd; something's come up in his day job and he's stuck at the office. Doesn't know what time he'll get away.'

'Oh no,' Spencer said. 'I thought that only happened in London. What's so urgent about his day job? What does he do?'

'He works for the CDSLI,' Owen replied.

'Who?' Spencer asked.

'The Crime and Drug Squad of the Leeward Islands.' Alicia answered the question. 'And yes, they happen to be very busy right now so I'm not surprised Lloyd's pulling an all-nighter.'

'How do you know about the drug squad here?' Spencer asked suspiciously.

'I'm a journalist, Spencer,' Alicia replied, 'and since you asked, if you're heading to The Jungle tonight you may as well make yourself useful and keep your ear to the ground.'

'About what exactly? You know I'm on vacation, right?'

'You'll know what about when you hear something. And as far as interfering where everyone else's business is concerned, I don't think you're ever on vacation, Spencer.'

'I ought to be offended,' Spencer said in protest, 'but I'll let it go this time.' He turned to Owen. 'Know anyone else who can get us on the VIP list at The Jungle?'

'Yeah man, no worries,' Owen replied. He was already scrolling through an extensive contacts list on his phone.

'Spencer, what VIP list are you on about exactly?' Alicia asked with amusement. 'We are talking about the same place here, aren't we? Because the last time I checked, The Jungle reggae bar was about as exclusive as the public toilets in the Oxford Street McDonalds.'

'Then you should give it another look some time Alicia,' Spencer replied. 'The Jungle is pretty up and coming these days with locals *and* tourists. Very popular place. I doubt they'd let you in anyway. You've gotta know the right people and all that.'

'Oh what a shame,' Alicia said drolly.

'But if you change your mind I'll be happy to pull some strings.'

'Thanks. I'll get back to you on that.'

'We'll see you later,' Spencer said, adding, 'and I'll keep my ear to the ground for... what again?'

'You'll know,' Alicia replied.

As Spencer and Owen made their exit, Graymond and Alicia turned to an amused Leon.

'As I was saying,' he began, 'you did know that Owen has a friend staying with him right now?'

'When Spencer told me he was coming to Antigua, he said he'd be avoiding the hurricane season and heading out here in late November,' Alicia said. 'He certainly kept his change of plans quiet.'

'The change of plans is partly my fault, I'm afraid,' Leon went on apologetically. 'As you know, we have three or four cabins for staff which are tucked away towards the rear of the property. They're temporary accommodation really, for emergencies and things. A couple of them are used for storage. Errol, the groundsman who's been staying in the cabin next to Owen is on vacation for a couple of weeks, visiting family in Montserrat. I knew Spencer was planning a trip so I suggested to Owen that he might like to take the other cabin while Errol's away. Spencer snapped up the offer right away and booked his flights. I was aware his time here would coincide with your dates, but of course, the original plan was that you'd be staying with Gray's friend, so I didn't think it would be of any consequence to you. I also assumed Spencer would let you know ahead of time, rather than surprise you like this!'

'Don't worry Leon,' Alicia said. 'He won't be any trouble. Spencer's perfectly capable of taking care of his own itinerary. I'm glad he and Owen are still in touch.'

'It's good for Owen too,' Leon added. 'He's doing well now, but it wasn't easy for him when he first started here. When you've been homeless, living rough on the streets for over twenty years, it's a bit of a culture shock to suddenly find yourself in full-time employment again.'

'I appreciate what you did for him, Leon,' Alicia said. 'You gave him a second chance.'

'After the nightmare he went through, he deserved every bit of it,' Leon said. 'The rest of the estates team here have been wonderful with him too. He's a success story. Thanks to you.'

'Thanks to everyone,' Alicia said.

'Now, it's time for the two of you to relax and get ready for dinner,' Leon said, guiding them to the wide, tree-lined pathway which led to the beach. 'You're in the Caribbean now, on vacation.'

'One last thing Leon.' Graymond spoke.

'Of course. Name it.'

'We'll need a taxi to the CDSLI headquarters at English Harbour tomorrow morning.'

'For what time?'

'The meeting's at eight.'

'Frank will be outside the reception at seven-thirty.'

They thanked Leon and said goodnight before making their way to their villa. The path to the beach meandered through tropical foliage and tall palm trees, swaying gently in the breeze. Low level path lights cast a glow at their feet. Crickets and tree frogs chirruped enthusiastically while the steel drum band in the distance played an upbeat rendition of Cat Stevens's Wild World. Graymond reached for Alicia's hand and squeezed it tightly.

'I'm sorry about Jacobs disrupting everything like this,' he said.

'It's not your fault Gray,' Alicia replied. 'You know why he wants to meet tomorrow?'

'Not exactly, no.'

'You think he's guilty of those drug trafficking charges?'

'Probably.'

'Then perhaps he wants to discuss bail bonds with you.'

'Maybe. Maybe not.'

'Then what?'

'I'm not sure. Jacobs has got himself in plenty of scrapes before and he's never asked me to post bail for him, ever. He's a firm believer in taking responsibility for his actions. I know he'd never drag anyone else into a predicament he'd created of his own volition. I've always admired him for that. My guess is there's another reason he wants to meet with us. As to what that is, I've no idea, but I do know Jacobs. And if there's something he needs to tell us, then we need to hear it.'

TEN

10:15 pm, Thursday, September 19
Hibiscus Cottage, Mamora Bay

Delano stood on the wooden deck of his cottage gazing across the bay. He had changed into a clean white shirt and faded blue jeans. The lights from the sprawling beach resort on the opposite shore cast long reflections over the dark water. One of the super yachts moored close to the beach beneath the cottage appeared to have some kind of party on board. The other yachts in the bay were dark and silent, bobbing gently on the water.

Delano took a long sip from a bottle of his favourite local beer, Wadadli, and savoured the cool, refreshing malt. His thoughts ran through the events of the day, from Melford's telephone call early that morning, to Oliver Jacobs and the wreckage of the Atratus, brought to safety through the storm by Max and his crew. Delano considered the bales of cocaine on board — worth tens of millions of dollars — packed tightly into the blue plastic drums; he thought about Villa Bella Casa at Sugar Reef Bay, the deleted surveillance footage and the camera lenses, deliberately masked with black spray paint. He thought about the neighbours, who had seen and heard nothing, and he contemplated Oliver's one phone call to Quincy, asking him to secure the parasols around the pool and put the soft furnishings out to dry. What did it all mean? Was the phone call really a coded message or was it intended to divert attention from elsewhere?

And where was Quincy now? Did he make the call to Latoya from Villa Bella Casa, or was it someone else? Delano had spoken to both Latoya and Junella Moran, Quincy's mother, neither of whom appeared to have any idea as to what had happened to him. Max had reached out to a wide circle of friends and family members, but no one had heard from Quincy and no one knew of his current whereabouts. Although the last signal emitted from

Quincy's cell phone was from Sugar Reef Bay, and the last call made was from within the grounds of Villa Bella Casa, it didn't unequivocally confirm that Quincy had been there himself.

But if he *was* at the villa, what exactly was he was doing there? The parasols, although down, had not been secured and were flapping wildly in the breeze when the CDSLI arrived. The cushions from the lanai furniture were soaked through; no attempt had been made to put them out to dry. Quincy certainly hadn't carried out any of Oliver's instructions. But if Oliver's message was really about asking Quincy to take care of the surveillance footage, whatever it contained, then why take the trouble to spray the camera lenses first if he was going to erase all the data anyway? It didn't make sense. Delano knew Lloyd was working into the night in an effort to recover the deleted footage from the video recorder's hard drive. He had promised to call Delano with updates.

Even more puzzling was how Quincy made it in and out of the gates to the villa undetected, assuming he was there at all. No one had seen him come or go, even though the gates and entrance road had been closely guarded. In addition, neither Quincy, nor a vehicle in which he might have been travelling, had been picked up on the surveillance footage from any of the other residences at Sugar Reef Bay. Quincy was a ghost. As far as the signal from his cell phone went, Delano acknowledged that the chances of the battery simply being dead and Quincy simply being unable to charge it were diminishing by the minute. And then there was the disappearance of his truck. So far, they had been unable to locate it.

Delano's thoughts were interrupted by the buzz of his cell phone in his pocket. He glanced at the screen before answering. It was Wendell Rivera, an officer with the Antigua Police Force. His raspy voice barked out of Delano's handset with a hollow apology.

'Delano, sorry to call at this time of night but I'm on a narrow stretch of beach at the bottom of the cliffs near Tamarind Point.' The police officer sounded slightly breathless. In the background Delano could hear the ocean and some kind of commotion.

'What's going on Wendell?' Delano asked.

'A couple of nosy tourists out exploring reported the wreckage of a vehicle down on the rocks near Tamarind Point, you know, west of Sugar Reef Bay,' Wendell began. 'They'd been walking along the same path the previous day and swear the truck wasn't there then so they thought they'd better call it in, in case it had washed up on the rocks or somethin'. The vehicle's a dark blue Ford Ranger pickup, quite an old one, with a double cab. The reason I'm callin' you is I saw the CDSLI put out an alert on the same truck earlier today. It's registered to a Quincy Moran. Mean anything to you?'

Delano fell silent at the mention of Quincy's name.

'Quincy Moran? Yeah. It does mean something,' he replied slowly. 'Any idea how the truck got down there?'

'There's evidence of fresh tyre tracks and broken trees and bushes at the top of the cliff. Looks like it went straight off the edge.'

'I didn't think the road up there went anywhere near the cliff edge at Tamarind Point.'

'The main road doesn't, but there's a small dirt track you can take a couple of miles or so before you get to the Sugar Reef Bay turning. The track doesn't lead anywhere, just winds its way along the cliff top for a bit until you reach a dead end. It once led to a small cabin. Apart from the dirt track there's just a vague footpath which the occasional tourist stumbles upon every now and then. I've no idea why anyone would be driving along there — pretty pointless if you ask me — but it looks as though he lost control of his truck and careered off the track to the edge of the cliff before taking a nose-dive. It's difficult to work out exactly what happened but we'll be able to see more when it gets light.'

'Any sign of a body?'

'Nah, we're still lookin'. It's pretty treacherous down here and it ain't easy in the dark. We may have to call off the search until morning. I've contacted the next of kin, a Junella Moran, Quincy's mom, and sent a couple of officers over there. She said Quincy's been missing since this morning. Last person to hear from him was his girlfriend, Latoya. Said he called her around lunchtime but hung up after a few seconds. He didn't say nothin' and nobody's had contact with him since. His mom said you guys had been in touch and were lookin' for him too.'

'Your men get a look at the truck yet?'

'We're goin' through the wreckage now. Like I said, it's precarious out here in the dark. So far we've found no blood or evidence of anyone being in the vehicle when it hit the rocks, so either the driver was thrown clear, or there was never anyone in the cab in the first place.'

'Never anyone in the cab?' Delano queried. 'What d'you mean? The truck just drove itself off the edge of the cliff?'

'You gotta cover all the scenarios my brother,' Wendell replied in a condescending tone. 'Anyway, the vehicle's a bit scruffy inside, windows are all smashed and the doors are busted in, like you'd expect. There was a tarpaulin over the rear of the truck which was ripped to shreds by the rocks on the way down. Most of the contents were thrown clear, but we found a few old garden tools still stuck in there. I understand Quincy was a local handyman and gardener.'

'He was. Any evidence of drugs?'

'Not so far. I'm guessing that's why the CDSLI's involved?'

'Yeah. Hey, you mind if I swing by and take a look at the place where the truck came off the road?'

Wendell hesitated. It was clear he disliked the idea of an officer more senior than himself paying a visit to his crime scene. He hastily recovered his manners with a reluctant reply.

'You can if you want I suppose. I'll tell you now, there's not a lot to see, but you can take a look around if you're so inclined. I'm down on the rocks with the truck, but I'll head back up. You'll see the blue lights from a way off.'

'Appreciate it. I just want to get a feel for what happened.'

Delano hung up and called Anson and then Edella, asking them to meet him at the top of the cliff near Tamarind Point. Back inside the cottage, he grabbed his backpack and waterproof jacket and was on his way out when his cell phone rang again. It was Hyacinth.

'Hey boss, you at home?'

'I'm just heading back out to Tamarind Point. They found Quincy's truck at the bottom of the cliff.'

'No kidding? How'd it end up there?'

'We don't know yet. A couple of tourists spotted the wreckage and called it in. Wendell and his team are at the scene now.'

'Any sign of Quincy?'

'Not so far.'

'You need any help boss?'

'I've asked Anson and Edella to join me. There's no need for us all to show up. Get some rest Hyacinth.'

'That's the problem boss. I can't. Something's bothering me.'

'What's up?'

'It's just something about Jacobs's villa. It's been bothering me all night. It just doesn't… It wasn't… Something's wrong. I think we should go back to the villa.'

'What, now?'

'Yeah. Now. We're not done there. Something didn't add up this afternoon but I couldn't work out what. I kept going over and over in my mind what it could be. It finally came to me just now.'

'I'm listening.'

'You have a cistern, right boss?'

'What?'

'You got a cistern for collecting and storing rainwater, right? On your roof, or next to your house, or below ground or somewhere… But you got a cistern, like most other homes in the Caribbean.'

'Yeah, I got three large water tanks next to my cottage. Why?'

'Villa Bella Casa has a cistern too, right? All the big, posh houses do. I saw the conveyance system for the rainwater, all the guttering and downpipes coming off the roof. I didn't see any water storage tanks above ground so I'm guessing Jacobs has a below ground cistern somewhere under the villa. The conveyance system should direct the rainwater collected from the roof into the cistern.'

'Go on.'

'Well, see boss, there's a problem. When we were searching Jacobs's villa it was raining. Hard. One of those typical Caribbean rainstorms.'

'Yeah…'

'But the thing I don't get is that the rainwater from the guttering *wasn't flowing into the cistern.*'

'So you're saying that…'

'I know it was raining hard, and maybe the conveyance system couldn't keep up, but the cistern wasn't taking in any water at all. Who has a rainwater harvesting system that doesn't collect any water? The cistern can't be full. So why, if the villa has a perfectly good network of gutters and downpipes to collect rainwater and channel it into the cistern, is the water just overflowing into the garden?'

Hyacinth had a point. Roof-catchment cistern systems were used to collect and store rainwater for household and other domestic uses. For more than three centuries rainwater harvesting had been one of most important means of domestic water supply throughout the Caribbean and was by no means a new idea; it was employed by both Greek and Roman civilisations as well as inhabitants of the Pacific Islands before western influences caught on, but the same basic principles from these bygone days continued to be used in modern day roof-catchment systems.

The cistern system utilised in Antigua and other Caribbean islands was one of the most innovative and cost effective ways of capturing and storing large quantities of rainwater. A basic cistern system had four major components: a catchment area, generally a rooftop or pavement; a conveyance system, made up of a network of gutters and pipes designed to move the water from the catchment area into a storage device and finally, a distribution system. To reduce the risk of overwhelming the system during a rainstorm, an overflow pipe was always installed from inside the cistern.

Household storage cisterns were capable of providing a sufficient water supply for most domestic uses and the use of rainwater was an effective way of lessening demand on the public water supply system. A cistern also provided a convenient buffer in times of emergency or shortfall in the public water supply. For most Caribbean home owners, the cistern was merely an addition to the house and could even be incorporated into building structures, such as in basements or under porches. The amount of water in a cistern was a constant topic of conversation; islanders were always happy when it rained.

Delano agreed with Hyacinth that a villa as majestic as Villa Bella Casa should undoubtedly have an elaborate rainwater harvesting system with an adequately sized cistern to store the water collected. In the larger, more expensive properties being constructed in Antigua, Delano knew that common household planning provided for around fifty to seventy-five gallons of water a day per person. The size of a cistern was often based on a storage capacity equal to one quarter of the annual domestic water needs of a household, or a three month supply of stored water. Therefore, if a household's annual water needs was 100,000 gallons a year, the recommended cistern size to accompany the property would be designed and constructed with a twenty-five thousand gallon storage capacity.

In spite of the well-known adage "you pay for a large cistern once and a small one forever," with the implication that a smaller cistern would require the homeowner to purchase public water should the stored supply run dry, many households could not afford the initial outlay for a large cistern. In the case of Villa Bella Casa, which would undoubtedly have a cistern with sufficient storage capacity to carry the household through extended periods of low rainfall, money would have been of no object to the original owner.

A quick calculation in his head confirmed to Delano that in the original designs and planning for Villa Bella Casa, the annual water needs would most likely have been estimated to be between 140,000 and 150,000 gallons a year. The cistern would therefore have been constructed with a storage capacity of between thirty-five thousand and thirty-seven thousand gallons. Based on those figures, he estimated the volume of the cistern to be around five thousand cubic feet. Delano knew that most cisterns in the newer, grander properties on the island were either a square or a rectangle, were typically located below ground and were constructed of various materials including cinder blocks, reinforced concrete, fibreglass or steel. The cistern would then supply water to the household through a standard pressurised plumbing system.

'Jacobs's cistern, it has to be a fair size,' Hyacinth was saying. 'It's gotta be what, twenty-five, thirty foot long? Twelve foot high? Somethin' like that, at least.'

Delano was impressed. She'd done her homework before calling him. And she had a point.

'But did anyone locate the access point to the cistern? A manhole cover or a concrete lid, or some kind of hatch leading underground?' Hyacinth asked. 'I didn't see anything like that when I searched outside. There was nothing in the garage either. Any of the others mention anything?'

'No one reported seeing an opening to the cistern,' Delano replied. 'In fact, there was no mention of the cistern at all, but you're right Hyacinth, there's got to be one there somewhere. If the access point isn't in the garden…'

'Then it must be somewhere inside the villa.' Hyacinth finished the sentence. 'But where? We searched the whole place, top to bottom.'

'We need to go back and locate the cistern, and find out what's wrong with the conveyance system,' Delano said. 'Call the rest of the team: Mitch, Nerissa and Brandon. Tell them to meet you at the villa and start from the beginning. Anson, Edella and I will join you as soon as we're done at Tamarind Point.'

'Do we need to inform Jacobs?' Hyacinth asked tentatively.

'Absolutely not,' Delano replied. They said goodnight with Hyacinth promising to call with any updates from the villa on the location of the cistern.

Delano shut and locked the door to his cottage and made his way across the yard to his pickup. A light rainfall had begun again as he jumped into the cab and started the engine. He flicked the windshield wipers on but the rubber blades had almost completely disintegrated. It was going to be a long night.

ELEVEN

11:05 pm, Thursday, September 19
The Jungle reggae bar and club, St. John's

A concrete floor, a crudely built wooden structure, warehouse-style, with large, rusted ceiling fans and enormous speakers hanging from timber joists formed the familiar surroundings of The Jungle reggae bar and club. Poster-sized prints of Bob Marley and other reggae royalty hung on every wall and were bathed in red and purple spotlights which moved in wide, circular arcs. The joint was packed with locals and tourists. Towards the rear of the club the crowd was more densely populated around a stage where a soloist with long dreadlocks, a faded t-shirt and denim jeans, was accompanied by a band wearing similar garb as they belted out a rendition of Sun Is Shining. Behind the bar, another crude wooden construction which stretched along the entire length of one wall, were shelves containing every imaginable size, shape and colour of bottles, lined up side by side. In the centre of the wall was a large, tarnished mirror. Next to it hung an extensive rum-based cocktail menu scrawled on a blackboard, with prices in Eastern Caribbean dollars, and a sign advising the club's distinguished patrons of the "Rules of the Jungle." These, clearly more guidelines than rules actually designed to be implemented in any way, informed interested parties that the management would not tolerate drugs, pimps or prostitutes, hoodlums or hooligans, bandanas, skullcaps or weapons of any kind.

At one end of the bar, closest to the stage, stood two men — a local and a tourist — drinking Coca-Cola from glass tumblers. They were immersed in animated conversation and appeared to be well acquainted. Suddenly, a group of locals wearing bandanas and dark glasses sauntered past the two men, just as the white man turned towards the stage. He jostled one of the locals and Coca-Cola sloshed out of the tumbler he was holding, drenching the man's sleeveless vest, a faded garment emblazoned with the slogan "Make Love Not War." The tumbler smashed across the floor in front of the man. Bathed in a haze of marijuana, he turned angrily towards the white man and delivered an impassioned sermon of profanities. The white man's drinking companion stepped quickly between them.

'Hey Vinnie, chill man. Spencer's cool.'

'Owen?' Vinnie tilted his dark glasses and his annoyed expression immediately transformed into a friendly smile. 'Heyyyyy, what up man?'

The two men engaged in some kind of elaborate handshake gesture before Owen turned to Spencer and introduced him to Vinnie and his crew. Owen's endorsement had clearly brought out the big-hearted side of Vinnie who immediately apologised to Spencer for the outburst and offered to buy him another drink.

'Thanks mate, but I'm fine,' Spencer replied. Vinnie insisted on the fresh drink and signalled to the barman.

'So how d'you know my homeboy Owen?' Vinnie asked. Before Spencer could answer the question, Owen was already launching into a reply over the cacophony of the reggae band and noisy chatter.

'He's the guy I told you about Vinnie, the one who came lookin' for me when I was down on the streets, told me they'd found who'd murdered Anastasia. If it wasn't for Spencer, I wouldn't be here right now. He saved my life man, him and Alicia, the one who worked it all out and found Anastasia's killer.'

Spencer blushed but appreciated the favourable character reference which had clearly earned a seal of approval from Vinnie and his homeboys. The replacement drink arrived and suddenly they were engaged in animated chatter, although Spencer struggled to understand the local patois. After a few minutes, he realised they were talking about a man called Quincy who had been involved in some kind of altercation with Vinnie and his crew the previous week. The conversation rapidly moved on to a drug bust which had taken place that morning. According to local gossip, which travelled fast on the island, the Coast Guard had been called to a yacht in distress in the early hours of the morning.

The yacht was found to have been carrying a significant stash of cocaine. No one knew who was on board the yacht or how many people were rescued, nor the exact quantity of cocaine seized, but conjecture and numerous theories were being bandied about as to which cartel was involved and what had happened to the drugs.

'The yacht's still moored down at English Harbour,' Jett, one of Vinnie's boys was saying. He appeared to be the person with the most inside information. 'It's got this weird name.'

'Weird?' Vinnie asked. 'Weird how?'

'Weird like it ain't a proper yacht name like Sundowner or Wave Runner.'

'What is it then?' Owen asked.

'It's…' Jett paused to remember. 'It's somethin' like Stratus. Or maybe Atlas or… Artus… It's one of them.'

'Stratus?' Vinnie frowned. 'Ain't that a type of cloud?'

'Could be,' Jett shrugged.

'You sure you heard right?' Another of Vinnie's boys spoke.

'Yeah Richie, I heard right,' Jett said defensively.

'How much blow?' Vinnie asked.

'I heard somethin' in the region of seventy-five million dollars,' Jett replied.

'EC or US?'

'US.'

'No shit,' Vinnie said in awe. 'That's crazy, man.'

'Must be a shipment from one of the big cartels,' Richie ventured. 'They'll be wantin' their drugs back. The narcs had better watch out.'

Spencer assumed Richie must be talking about the Antiguan drug enforcement agency which one of the other locals had referred to as the CDSLI. He suddenly recalled his earlier conversation at the West Beach Club with Alicia. She had used the same acronym although he couldn't remember exactly what it stood for and didn't like to ask. What had she told him? *Keep your ear to the ground. You'll know when you hear something.* Was this what he was supposed to be hearing? He tried to listen in to what was being said although the reggae music booming through the overhead speakers and the local patois put him at a distinct disadvantage. Suddenly Vinnie had to take an urgent call and the conversation ended abruptly. With his phone clamped to one ear, he gave Spencer a comradely slap on the back as he squeezed past a group of tourists next to the bar, his entourage close behind.

Spencer took a sip of his replacement drink and leaned closer to Owen.

'What were they talking about?' He spoke loudly in Owen's ear. 'Did some kind of drugs bust go down this morning?'

'Yeah, it was big according to Jett,' Owen yelled back. 'The Coast Guard picked up a yacht in distress a few miles offshore. They're always picking up small time drug runners but this has to be one of their biggest busts to date. Richie thinks the drugs are probably linked to one of the major South American cartels or DTOs.'

'DTOs?'

'Drug trafficking organisations.'

'Which one?'

'Who knows? I don't get involved with that shit these days. I'm clean and I'm stayin' that way. Never goin' back there again.'

'Same here.' Spencer couldn't agree more. 'What does CDSLI stand for again?'

'They're the drug squad,' Owen replied. 'Can't remember what the letters are for though… The drug squad of the Leeward Islands, somethin' like that. I forget what the C's for…'

'Community? Crime?'

'Yeah crime, that's it. They basically work with the Coast Guard and the police, the DEA, other agencies and so on, to tackle the drugs problem here. The island's sort of a halfway house between South America, you know, where they produce all the drugs, and the United States. I think a lot of the drugs that end up across the Atlantic also come through here and some of the other islands nearby.'

'Isn't that who your friend works for? The CDSLI?' Spencer asked.

'You mean Lloyd? Yeah, he does. He's a tech geek. A hacker, basically. What Lloyd don't know about computers ain't worth knowing. Next time we're here I'll introduce you. He has a side hustle here as a bouncer most nights. He must be working somethin' big tonight. He never misses a weekend, they're the busiest times.'

Spencer was about to ask Owen if he thought Lloyd was working on the same case that Vinnie and his crew had been discussing when two men, apparently more friends of Owen, approached. Owen introduced Spencer as his "brother from England" before engaging in another unintelligible conversation, a mixture of broken English and patois. Spencer tried to listen for key words, but they appeared to be talking about a cricket match and he quickly lost interest. His mind drifted to the gossip surrounding the early morning drug bust which had taken place while he, and most of the rest of the island, was sleeping. He wondered if it might be linked to the case Alicia was interested in.

As the conversation between Owen and his friends seemed to digress to the altercation at the club the previous week between Vinnie and his homeboys and the man called Quincy, Spencer excused himself. The dispute was apparently still to be resolved and therefore remained a hot topic at The Jungle. Bored with the local small talk, Spencer pushed through the crowds to the rear of the club, to where he found a crude wooden door with a gent's bathroom sign on it. The band had just resumed their set after a short break. From the confines of a squalid cubicle Spencer hummed along to a reggae song he didn't know and decided to invest in a pocket guide to the language of Antigua.

00:10 am, Friday, September 20
CDSLI Headquarters, English Harbour

Lloyd massaged his temples and took a thirsty gulp from a can of Rockstar Zero Carb, his sixth in the same number of hours. Sure, his heart rate was probably teetering on the brink of ventricular fibrillation thanks to the caffeine, but he needed to focus. For the sixth time that night he scrutinised the ingredients list on the side of the can and reassured himself that the beverage did in fact also provide him with additional health benefits. The constituents of the energy drink consisted of an herbal blend of guarana, ginseng, ginkgo and milk thistle, whatever they were. He'd look them up one day.

On a desk in front of him was the network video recorder which Delano had retrieved from Oliver Jacobs's villa the previous afternoon, along with Jacobs's iPad and cell phone, still encased in a bag of rice. The NVR was plugged into an iMac, one of two on the desk. The other iMac sat across to Lloyd's right. It had a larger, twenty-seven inch screen which displayed a convoluted array of open text terminals, chat windows and text editors. In one corner was a rapidly moving time plot and an elaborate-looking graph. In the other, an early episode of Friends was playing, without sound, like a silent movie.

Returning to the video recorder and the smaller iMac, Lloyd pecked at the keyboard. He had taken the liberty of decamping from his desk under the giant rubber plant in reception to the crew room, for extra space. The home of the CDSLI headquarters had once been a warehouse of some kind, which had formed part of a group of abandoned dockyard buildings. From the outside it was constructed of brick and sandstone with floor-to-ceiling, metal-framed jalousie windows which overlooked the harbour. Inside were a series of smaller rooms and a large open-plan space, the CDSLI's main crew room. The hardwood floors and wooden vertical beams gave an historical nod to the building's past, while old factory pendant lights with copper dome shades hung from supporting joists which ran along the length of the ceiling.

At one end of the room an assortment of wooden desks faced each other. At the other stood the whiteboard covered in scrawled notes, papers and photographs. Next to the whiteboard, the two iMacs, an oversized hard drive and Oliver's electronic devices sat on a larger desk. Beside it, various manuals and reference books were stacked haphazardly on a freestanding bookshelf. Hanging on the wall behind the desk was a large map of the Caribbean islands and miscellaneous lists of Coast Guard protocols and procedures, airport security information and sundry bulletins from an alphabet soup of crime and drug enforcement agencies. On the opposite side of the room a faded brown leather couch and a threadbare Persian rug provided the only semblance of soft furnishing comfort.

Hunched over the desk under the light of one of the copper shades, Lloyd continued to attack the keyboard of the smaller iMac while occasionally glancing across towards its big brother. He chuckled at a scene from the Friends episode currently playing before returning to his data recovery assignment.

'Come on baby,' he said under his breath as he typed furiously, aware that time was of the essence. He, Lloyd Kelly, Special Consultant to the Tactical and Surveillance Team of the CDSLI, would not be letting the side down any time tonight. He knew he was getting closer to accessing the files. Suddenly, he pressed the return key with a flourish and an image flickered into life on the screen.

'Got you,' he muttered with satisfaction as more pop-up images began to appear, one by one, on the display. It was the deleted surveillance footage from the hard drive of Oliver Jacobs's video recorder. Wiping beads of sweat from his forehead with the back of his hand, Lloyd exhaled loudly. There were ten images in total, one from each of the ten security cameras located at various points around Villa Bella Casa. Lloyd could see that the cameras had been set to record continuously, 24/7. Each image contained a date and time and the camera number in the bottom right hand corner.

He double-clicked on the image in the top left corner of the desktop, enlarging it to full screen view. It displayed footage from camera one, located at the front of the villa to the right of the front door. He clicked the playback button shown on the screen and selected the start time to the early hours of Thursday, September 19, the previous day. Setting the playback speed to fast forward, Lloyd took a long sip of the Rockstar Zero Carb and leaned back in his chair to watch. The first part of the playback took place in the dark, but the camera's infra-red LEDs provided a night vision recording with a range of up to approximately ten metres away.

The front garden of Villa Bella Casa was deserted, although the high winds from the storm were battering a palm tree and a group of tall tropical plants in one corner of the shot. As daylight broke, the wind became calmer and the infra-red images turned to high quality colour ones. The area within range of camera one was still and silent. Lloyd yawned and glanced at the Friends episode on the screen beside him. It was one of his favourites. Lloyd had seen all 236 episodes countless times. Suddenly there was a movement on the display in front of him. He returned his gaze to the camera image and slowed the playback speed, noting the time at the bottom of the screen. It was 11:43 am. From the right side of the screen a figure approached the camera cautiously. It was a man wearing a black t-shirt and black pants. Lloyd leaned in closer. The camera's wide angle lens caught the man's face clearly. It was Quincy Moran.

'So you were there after all my brother,' Lloyd said in a loud whisper. Delano's hunch had been correct. Lloyd watched as Quincy moved closer to the camera. He had an emotionless expression on his face. The look in his eyes seemed cold and indifferent, but perhaps it could also be interpreted as one of fear. As Lloyd gazed at the screen, Quincy's arm came up towards the camera lens. In his hand was a circular aerosol can of black spray paint. He tilted it towards the camera, applied pressure to the nozzle and the screen went dark. Lloyd was left staring at a black square as camera one continued rolling blind. The time at the bottom of the image clicked over to 11:44 am. And Quincy was gone.

Minimising the full-screen display, Lloyd returned to the ten camera images. He clicked on the second image which showed footage from camera two. As before, he selected playback in fast forward mode and settled in his chair to watch. The footage was from a slightly different aspect but still from the front of the villa. The infra-red images from the night vision camera changed to colour as the sun came up. It was a similar story to camera one and, as the time at the bottom corner of the screen approached 11:30 am, Lloyd slowed the playback speed and leaned forwards in his chair. At precisely 11:42 am, the figure of a man wearing the same black t-shirt and black pants approached the camera. Lloyd tensed slightly, watching the man's face intently. There was the same hollow expression in his eyes. Fear or indifference? Suddenly, Quincy glanced behind him but Lloyd couldn't see what had caught his attention. It was outside the range of the camera angle. Perhaps one of the other cameras had picked it up. He would work methodically through them all. There was no one else in the shot; Quincy appeared to be working alone. He turned back to the camera where, once again, he raised the aerosol canister, shook it quickly and sprayed the lens. The image went black and Quincy vanished from the screen. The time was still 11:42 am, exactly one minute before the first camera had been sprayed.

Lloyd surveyed the footage from camera three, located on the north side of the villa, with particular heed to what might have caught Quincy's attention in camera two, but the images revealed nothing. Perhaps it was just the noise of the wind in the trees or an animal in the bushes. Quincy went through the now familiar motions, spraying the lens of camera three with the aerosol exactly two minutes before the time he sprayed camera two. He was apparently making his way around the property in an anticlockwise direction. By the time Lloyd reached camera six, which covered a section of the pool and the garden from the lanai on the east side of the villa, it was clear that Quincy knew the location of all ten cameras. There were four to go.

Suddenly there was a change in proceedings. Camera seven threw Lloyd a curveball. He had been fast forwarding the video footage towards noon when, at 11:34 am, precisely eight minutes before Quincy had walked up to camera one, he could be seen approaching camera seven. The camera was pointing in an easterly direction and overlooked the rear garden, from somewhere on the southeast side of the villa. At 11:35 am the lens was masked by the black paint. A minute later, at 11:36 am, Quincy was visible on camera eight, located on the south side. He had apparently started the job at camera seven, moving clockwise to camera nine before changing course, returning to camera six, from where he continued in an anticlockwise direction to camera one. At 11:43 am, camera ten, attached to the garage overlooking the circular driveway at the front of the property, was the final camera to be sprayed with black paint. Lloyd was left staring at a screen with ten blank squares. The dates and times at the bottom of each square showed that the cameras continued rolling, but recorded nothing. Whatever happened next in the grounds of Villa Bella Casa remained a mystery, known only to Quincy.

It was a clever thing to do, Lloyd thought to himself. Quincy had clearly planned his moves ahead of time and had arrived at OJ's villa pre-armed with the can of black spray paint. Quincy, or OJ, or both, had apparently anticipated that the deleted surveillance footage may be recovered at some point if the NVR got into the wrong hands, such as those belonging to law enforcement personnel. Care had been taken to ensure that if this should happen, they were still one step ahead. But why not simply remove the NVR component itself instead of going to the trouble of deleting the footage and leaving it at the villa for the CDSLI to find?

Lloyd continued watching until finally, at 12:56 pm, the date, time and camera number disappeared from each of the ten squares simultaneously. The surveillance footage had been erased and the NVR disconnected from the power. The evidence from the footage showed that only Quincy had been present at Villa Bella Casa that morning. As he made his way from camera to camera, carefully spraying each lens as he went, he seemed to be working alone. But other than vandalism to a private property, which OJ surely wouldn't be pressing charges for, the elusive handyman remained innocent of any crime.

There was nothing more to be gained from the surveillance footage and Lloyd turned his attention to the larger iMac. He squinted at the lines of colourful text and syntax highlighting in one of the open text terminals before he began typing, fixated on the screen. It was his second challenge of the night. The event history for the alarm system of Villa Bella Casa was only accessible on Oliver's computer, which they hadn't found at the villa. Potentially,

Oliver also had the means of accessing it on his cell phone, but that was temporarily out of action and encased within a bag of rice. The alarm company had refused to cooperate on grounds of client confidentiality and was therefore facing a court order to comply unless Lloyd was able to hack into the database and retrieve the event history of the villa's alarm system.

There was no recorded history for the movements of the electric gates at the front of the villa, although in Lloyd's mind this was not now important. Recorded times of any activation or deactivation of the alarm system would be useful to them though. Lloyd had video footage of Quincy at Villa Bella Casa after Oliver's phone call to him from custody. He now needed evidence of Quincy entering the property.

After a flurry of furious typing and two cans of Rockstar Zero Carb later, Lloyd surveyed the screen of the iMac for a few seconds before leaning back in his chair with a smug look of satisfaction. He was in. The entire database of the alarm company was in front of him. He minimised the Friends episode in the corner of the screen and rapidly navigated through names, addresses, client records, employee records and miscellaneous system settings until he found what he needed: the account for Villa Bella Casa at Sugar Reef Bay. It was registered in the client's name, a Mr. Terrence Dove, and contained detailed information about the alarm system.

Lloyd scrolled through a comprehensive list of headings: security, cameras, detectors, utility outputs, home automation, video clips and notifications until he found what he was looking for. He clicked on event history. At the top of the screen was the previous day's date: September 19. Beneath the date were details of when the alarm system had been activated and deactivated and whether by means of the keypad by the front door or a key fob.

The top and most recent entry showed that the alarm had been deactivated with Keypad #1 at 23:04 that night. He was aware the team had returned to the villa for some reason. They must still be there, he thought to himself. The entries below detailed the times the alarm system had been activated and deactivated by the CDSLI earlier that day, which correlated with the times the team had been at the villa. But as Lloyd's gaze moved to the fourth line down, he realised the alarm had been deactivated and reactivated prior to the time the CDSLI had arrived.

The entry log in the database clearly stated that someone had punched the six digit code into the keypad by the front door at precisely 12:59, exactly three minutes after the surveillance footage was erased from the hard drive of Oliver Jacobs's NVR. The alarm had been deactivated earlier that day at 11:45, minutes after camera ten was sprayed with black paint, when someone had entered the villa through the front door.

'Damn Lloyd, you're good,' he muttered to himself. He scanned the times again. The record of the alarm system being set and unset couldn't lie. It was right there in front of him in the highly classified database of the security company. There was no mistaking, someone had been inside Jacobs's villa earlier that day. And now Lloyd knew the name of that person and exactly how long he had spent inside the property, to the nearest minute. Once Quincy had sprayed camera ten on the front of the garage, he had let himself through the front door with what was presumably his own key, and deactivated the alarm system. He could then move freely about inside the villa without arousing suspicion. The only thing Lloyd still wasn't clear on was how Quincy had actually made it into the grounds of Villa Bella Casa in the first place. Clearly he didn't enter through the electric gates as the officers posted immediately outside had been there for at least one hour before Quincy showed up.

'Has to be another way in,' Lloyd thought to himself. He looked at the time of day Quincy had approached each camera. It was a sure giveaway as to the rough location of the alternative entrance. Quincy had initially approached the villa from somewhere on the south side. Lloyd reached for his cell phone and dialled Delano's number.

'Lloyd, what've you got?' Delano took a while to pick up and sounded distracted.

'Delano?' Lloyd said. 'You at OJ's villa?'

'No, I'm not. I'm heading over there in a minute.'

'Sorry man, did I wake you?'

'No, I wasn't asleep. You find anything?'

'Yeah, I did. You were right boss. Quincy arrived at OJ's villa around eleven-thirty yesterday morning. And it was Quincy who sprayed the lenses of the security cameras with black paint.'

'So he *was* there.'

'He's on the footage, clear as day. Didn't do much to disguise himself. I guess he hoped no one would be able to retrieve the video footage, although the fact that he went round spraying the cameras first sort of says he was aware of the possibility that it might happen and wanted to be doubly sure no one found out what he was up to at the villa.'

'Anyone with him?'

'No. No one else shows up on the camera footage anyway. Looks like he was alone.'

'Any sound?'

'Nope, just the silent movie.'

'Thanks Lloyd.'

'Oh that's just the intro. I haven't got to the good part yet. After vandalising the cameras, Quincy let himself into the villa and deactivated the alarm system. This was at precisely eleven forty-five according to the alarm company's database.'

'You breached their firewalls then?'

'Of course.'

'How long did Quincy spend inside the villa?'

'The alarm was unset for little more than an hour. It seems Quincy's final job was to erase the surveillance footage. The time recorded on the footage, before the NVR was disconnected from the power supply, was twelve fifty-six, three minutes before the alarm system for the villa was reactivated, again using the keypad at the front door — Quincy obviously knows the code — at which point I'm guessing he'd done everything he needed to before disappearing.'

'If he's not still at the villa then where'd he go?' Delano asked.

'Good question. But I have an idea. It all comes down to the order in which he blinded the cameras.'

'What?'

'If he came in through the front gates — which we know didn't happen because your officers were right outside the whole time — he'd have started his little graffiti rampage with camera ten and then moved on to camera one, working his way around the villa in a clockwise direction until he reached camera nine, on the south side. But he didn't do that. According to the times shown on the camera footage, the first camera lens he sprayed was number seven, on the southeast side of the garden. He then worked his way round clockwise to camera nine before doubling back, this time going anticlockwise from camera six all the way round the north side, to the front. Like I said, the last camera he sprayed was number ten, which is mounted on the garage.'

'So Quincy initially approached the villa from the back?'

'That's what it looks like.'

'But that's… impossible. The perimeter of the garden is thick with bushes and foliage. It's impenetrable. And beyond the foliage is a sheer drop right off the cliff, which is covered with even thicker foliage and vegetation, all the way down to a thin strip of sand which is essentially just a small cove. I'm not even sure you could reach it by boat.'

'I know, it's a puzzle, I had a look at a satellite image of the place. But the camera doesn't lie. Quincy was there, for sure. And he approached from the cliff side.'

'Thanks Lloyd. Appreciate you staying late.'

'Any time.' From his end of the line, Lloyd heard loud voices and the faint sound of an engine.

'Where the hell are you Delano? What's all the commotion about in the background?'

'I'm at Tamarind Point with Anson and Edella. A couple of tourists spotted the wreckage of a Ford Ranger pickup on the rocks at the foot of the cliff.'

'Isn't that…'

'Quincy's pickup? Yeah. It is. Or was.'

'Any sign of Quincy?'

'No. Not yet. It looks like the pickup went over the edge of the cliff at speed. It's pretty busted up. If Quincy was inside when it happened it's unlikely he survived the force of the impact on the rocks below.'

'Could he have been thrown clear?'

'Maybe. But there's no sign of a body so far.'

'Into the sea?'

'Unlikely. The rocks stretch far out into the water at this point.'

'Anything I can do to help?'

'Go home, get some rest.'

They said goodnight. Draining his eighth can of the Rockstar energy drink, Lloyd shut down the computer programs and tossed the empty can into the trash. He thought about Delano at the scene of the wreckage of Quincy Moran's pickup truck. If Quincy's body was found on the rocks below, they may never know the real reason he'd been to Villa Bella Casa the previous day. Or how he made it inside the gates undetected.

TWELVE

00:50 am, Friday, September 20
Tamarind Point, Antigua

Under the stark glare of portable flood lights, Delano, Anson and Edella stood on the top of the cliff at Tamarind Point looking down at the rocks below. They were surrounded by uniformed police officers, police patrol vehicles with flashing blue and red lights and an abundance of crime scene tape. There were sounds of voices crackling over radios and the waves crashing on the rocks at the bottom of the cliff. It had started to rain hard again. Large droplets of water caught in the beam of the floodlights formed puddles which merged into channels on either side of the road.

Fully clothed in bright yellow waterproofs and looking more like a commercial fisherman than a police officer, Wendell Rivera approached the group of CDSLI officers. He had returned to the top of the cliff from the small stretch of beach and rocks below.

'Traces of cocaine. In the cab of the pickup,' he said. 'Still no sign of Quincy though. And this rain's not helping things either. If Quincy's body *was* thrown clear it may wash up further along the coastline. Depends on the current. My guys are just finishing off down there, but there's not much more we can do until it gets light.'

'Any other thoughts on how the truck ended up down there?' Delano asked.

'It's pretty busted up from the rocks, but there's still nothing to suggest why it came off the dirt track and went over the cliff edge,' Wendell replied, wiping drops of rain from the side of his face. 'Mechanically it appears to have been in good working order. We haven't found any faulty or malfunctioning parts so far. The brakes, steering, engine, and nuts and bolts of the vehicle all seem fine.'

'This is an odd place for a pickup to suddenly plunge over the edge of the cliff,' Delano said, indicating the tyre marks a few feet away surrounded by metal posts and crime scene tape. 'I mean, why here? There are no skid marks to suggest sudden sharp braking, there's no evidence that he lost control of the vehicle and no explanation as to why he would suddenly deviate from the dirt track. If it was slippery, there'd be signs of skidding, but the tyre marks just come straight off the track and over the edge.'

'If Quincy *was* in the pickup maybe he was unconscious,' Edella volunteered.

'I don't think so,' Wendell replied brusquely. 'There's no evidence of fresh blood or any kind of trauma inside the cab. It's clean. I'd say there was nobody in that truck when it went over the cliff.'

'Maybe he ran it off the edge to make us *think* he was in it,' Anson said.

'Or to hide evidence of the traces of cocaine in the cab,' Edella added. 'Or both.'

'He sure picked a remote spot if he wanted us to find his truck and think he was gone,' Delano said. He turned to Wendell. 'Any witnesses?'

'Nope.' Wendell shook his head. 'Not so far anyway. Like I said, it's fairly remote up here. If it wasn't for those nosy tourists we may not have found the truck for days or even weeks. It's almost impossible to spot from the water, as if Quincy *didn't* want his truck to be found.'

'Any sign there was another vehicle involved?' Delano asked. 'Could Quincy have been meeting someone up here? Any other tyre tracks nearby?'

'Nothing,' Wendell replied. 'We covered as wide a search area as we could before it started raining. Now any hope of finding fresh tracks will be completely washed away. Literally and metaphorically. But I'm confident there wasn't another vehicle up here.'

'Any idea what time this all happened?'

'Sometime yesterday's all I got. So far, the last known location of Quincy's truck was when he left his mom's at seven-thirty yesterday morning.'

'We're following the same leads,' Delano said. 'He was reportedly doing some work over at a property at Hamilton Bay yesterday morning, but I've just received new evidence as to his whereabouts between eleven-thirty and one p.m. yesterday. He was caught on the surveillance footage from one of the houses at Sugar Reef Bay: Villa Bella Casa. It's the last villa at the end of the peninsula.'

'Sugar Reef? Yeah, I know it,' Wendell said with a measure of contempt. 'It's where the filthy rich expats build their vulgar mansions. What's a lowlife like Quincy doing up there? He a rent boy or somethin'?'

'He's a handyman and a gardener,' Delano replied. 'He does work for a lot of the homeowners up at Sugar Reef as well as other locations on the island. He's reportedly very good at his job.'

'I'll bet he is,' Wendell scoffed.

'As a handyman.'

'Of course.'

'We took a look at that cabin at the end of the track down there.' Delano changed the subject.

'Oh yeah?' There was slight annoyance in Wendell's voice. Delano's attendance at *his* crime scene was beginning to irritate him.

'It's pretty derelict and looks as though no one's been there in years,' Delano continued regardless. 'There were a couple of wooden benches and an old table inside, and some coils of frayed rope, but the place is thick with dust and cobwebs and there's dense undergrowth outside leading up to the door. It's unlikely Quincy was headed there. I'm inclined to agree with you, it looks as though he was trying to dispose of his pickup.'

Wendell was interrupted by a call on his radio. Excusing himself, he turned his back to the rain and spoke into the handheld.

'There's nothing else to be done here for now,' Delano said to Anson and Edella. 'Let's head over to Villa Bella Casa and join the others.'

'Happy with that,' Edella said, throwing a look of disgust in Wendell's direction.

Delano waved at Wendell as they walked to their vehicles, parked further along the dirt track. Wendell, still talking into his radio, gave an officious nod and quickly returned to his conversation.

'Boss, remind me why we're going back to the villa in the middle of the night when we spent all afternoon there and found nothing,' Anson said wearily. 'I think I'd rather stay here with Wendell and his lobsterman outfit. What are we looking for exactly?'

'The cistern,' Delano replied.

'The *cistern*?' Anson asked in a puzzled tone.

'A villa like that, it's gotta have a fairly large cistern. We didn't find any water storage tanks in the grounds and the rainwater from the gutters was overflowing straight into the garden. So where's the cistern and why isn't it collecting any water? Did either of you see a manhole or trapdoor which might lead to a cistern or water storage tank?'

Anson and Edella confessed that they hadn't but agreed that a place the size and magnitude of Villa Bella Casa would probably have been constructed with its own rainwater collection and storage system in addition to being connected to the public supply. They reached their vehicles and set off slowly along the dirt track towards the main road. Delano led the way with Anson and Edella following close behind. At the intersection they turned right towards Sugar Reef Bay. It was a short journey to the villa, affording little time to contemplate two baffling questions: where was Quincy Moran and where was the cistern of Villa Bella Casa?

01:30 am, Friday, September 20
Villa Bella Casa, Sugar Reef Bay

The two police officers working the night shift outside the gates of Villa Bella Casa waved the three vehicles through. There was ample space on the large driveway where the dark blue Ford Explorer, the pool vehicle for the CDSLI, was already parked. There were lights on in most of the windows of the single storey property, casting a warm golden glow across the rain-soaked brick paving. Delano, Anson and Edella hurried through the rain to the front door and let themselves in. They were once more in the grand circular foyer of the villa.

'Good to see you guys.' Hyacinth appeared from the family room to the right of the foyer.

'You too,' Delano said, shaking the rain off his jacket. 'Where are the others? Have you found anything?'

'Not yet.' Hyacinth appeared slightly crestfallen. 'I'll let the rest of them know you're here.'

She picked up her handheld radio from the table and informed the other three that Delano, Anson and Edella had arrived. Within five minutes, all seven members of the team had assembled in the family room. With Oliver remaining in custody at the CDSLI headquarters in English Harbour, Duane's presence was not required. The mood was despondent as they sat on the sofas surrounding the large coffee table in the centre of the room.

'If I thought we were wasting precious time here this afternoon, we're definitely wasting it now,' Mitch said, frowning in Hyacinth's direction.

'Couldn't agree more,' Brandon added. 'We've searched everywhere. Twice. Three times. There's nothing here.'

Nerissa remained silent, although it was clear she shared the same sentiment as the other two.

'Then where's the darn cistern?' Hyacinth asked defiantly.

'How many times Hyacinth? There isn't one,' Mitch said with a frustrated sigh. 'If there was we would've found it by now. It's not like we're looking for buried treasure. Cisterns are generally built to be accessed easily. If there was one here, it'd be pretty obvious where it was.'

'So what's the conveyance system from the roof for then?' Hyacinth went on.

'They're called downpipes and gutters,' Brandon replied. 'Every building has them. They're used to channel rainwater from the roof, but they don't have to lead to a cistern. They can just run to drains in the ground.'

'There aren't any drains, I checked,' Hyacinth said indignantly. 'The guttering's overflowing into puddles of water around the villa. I'm telling you, that's not right. There's got to be a cistern here somewhere.'

Brandon shrugged and raised his hands in vexation. He changed the subject. 'What's the word from Tamarind Point?'

Delano relayed what they knew so far about Quincy's battered pickup, noting the absence of skid marks off the dirt track, the presence of cocaine in the cab, and the absence of a body or any signs of blood, injury or trauma.

'There's no evidence at all to suggest Quincy was inside the truck when it went over the cliff edge,' Delano said. 'The opposite in fact.'

'So where is he?' Brandon asked.

'I've no idea. We keep looking until we've found him though.'

'I talked to Jacobs again before we came here,' Hyacinth said. 'If he knows of Quincy's whereabouts then he's not talking.'

'There's a surprise.'

Delano also apprised the team of Lloyd's findings: the successful recovery of the surveillance footage revealing Quincy's movements at the villa the previous day and the event history of the alarm system, which confirmed that Quincy had entered the property at a quarter to twelve and had left a minute before one o'clock.

'What on earth was he doing in here for more than an hour?' Nerissa asked, glancing around as if the walls would reply. 'The place is immaculate and we've found no trace of drugs.'

'Maybe he was cleaning up,' Anson suggested.

'We know he was deleting the surveillance footage for one thing,' Mitch said.

'That's hardly going to take an hour,' Nerissa replied.

'Well we know what he *wasn't* doing,' Edella said, recalling her search around the pool and lanai the previous day. 'We know he wasn't tying up the parasols and putting the cushions out to dry.'

'Maybe he went for a quick swim and mixed himself a cocktail from the drinks bar over there,' Brandon volunteered.

'Or maybe he was in the cistern.' The voice was firm, insistent.

'You're boring me now Hyacinth,' Mitch said with a yawn.

'Fine, you guys go home,' Hyacinth said, standing up. 'I'm staying until I've found the cistern.'

Mitch rolled his eyes at Brandon before turning to Delano.

'Seriously boss. Let's call this off. We're wasting our time. It's late and we've a lot of work to do tomorrow.'

Delano looked around the room at his team. They'd been working since six o'clock the previous morning. They were exhausted and had found nothing at the villa. It was tempting to call it a night and send them home to rest, but Hyacinth's determined expression and a niggling doubt in the back of his own mind stopped him.

'We stay here,' he said resolutely. 'We keep looking.'

'But for *what*?' Mitch asked with a note of desperation in his voice.

'For anything,' Delano replied. He stood up. 'And everything. The remnants of Quincy's cocktail, a pair of wet swimming shorts, the imaginary cistern. We make one more thorough search of this place. Now. Tonight.'

As the team reluctantly spread out to commence one final search of the villa, Mitch murmured something about Quincy swimming buck naked before he disappeared through to the master suite.

'Thanks boss,' Hyacinth said softly as she passed Delano on her way to the rooms on the east side of the property.

'You better pray we find something,' Delano replied. With the rest of the team dispersed elsewhere around the villa, he decided to remain in a central location, in the family room with the kitchen and dinette. He stood still and looked around him. The sailing journals lay haphazardly on top of the porn magazines on the coffee table, beside the hurricane lanterns. He glanced over to the bare walls where the colourful paintings had hung; they were now stacked in a pile against the kitchen island. Walking over to each wall, he tapped in various places. There was no change in resonance. The walls were solid.

He turned back to the large coffee table in the middle of the room, surrounded by the sofas. The previous day, the furniture had been moved to one side of the room and the large rug in the centre had been rolled up to reveal the wooden floor underneath. If the property had been constructed with a cistern, the only realistic place for it to be was below ground, due to the fact that there was no other water storage tank anywhere else on the site. But yesterday's search had revealed nothing. No hidden trapdoor, no secret wormhole or access hatch.

Delano gazed around the kitchen and dinette. The kitchen cupboards and range cooker were integrated into the wall. There was a large island with a marble worktop in the centre, but it was attached to the tiled floor. The furniture and rug in the dinette had also been removed, and the floor and walls examined, but to no avail.

With a sigh, Delano turned back towards the family room. Over on the far side was a circular dining room on an elevated platform with a set of circular steps leading up to it. Through a set of wooden louvred blinds, a large window overlooked the driveway and gardens out front. In the centre of the room stood a large circular dining table surrounded by six high-backed dining chairs. The dining table itself was an eye-catching piece of furniture. A circular glass top, almost seven feet in diameter, with thick, bevelled edges, rested on top of what appeared to be one solid piece of the root of a tree. The wood, most likely reclaimed teak, was in an upside-down position with the roots pointing upwards and outwards, supporting the glass top. The wide trunk of the tree, at least two feet across, formed the base of the table and was planted firmly on the floor of the dining room. Not only was it a solid piece of furniture and extremely heavy, it appeared to have been attached to the floor in some way and was the only item that the team had been unable to move the previous afternoon.

Delano's gaze rested on the table but he knew it would be too heavy for him to move by himself. The bank of light switches on the wall to the right of the dining room suddenly caught his attention. There were four switches almost flush to the wall plate in the "on" position. Without thinking, he strode across to them and flipped them all off. The lights in the family room and dining room went out, but the lights from the kitchen and dinette remained on. They were controlled by another bank of light switches in the kitchen, which Delano could see from across the room.

Mitch, who had been in the master suite, appeared in the foyer as Delano flipped the first switch to the "on" position. Nothing happened. The family room and dining room remained in darkness.

'All good in there boss?' Mitch called out. Delano flipped the light off and then on again. Still nothing happened.

'What's this light switch for?' Delano asked. Mitch joined him and inspected the bank of switches on the wall.

'It doesn't turn on any lights in this room?' Mitch asked looking around.

'No.' Delano flipped the switch next to it and the main light in the dining room came on. Delano flipped it off and moved to the next switch which controlled the chandelier in the centre of the family room. The final switch was for the wall lights in the family room. He flipped all the lights off and returned to the first switch.

'Maybe it's for an outside light,' Mitch suggested.

'But the switches for the lanai and pool area are in the room leading off the foyer,' Delano replied, 'and the lights for outside the front of the villa are next to the alarm keypad.'

'Then perhaps it's a spare,' Mitch shrugged. 'A redundant switch.'

'That's a bit strange though, don't you think?' Delano said. He flipped the switch on and off as he looked around the room with a puzzled expression. Suddenly Brandon and Hyacinth entered the dinette from the rooms on the south side of the villa.

'I'm sorry Hyacinth,' Brandon was saying, 'I totally respect you as an agent but this time I really think you're mistaken…'

'What're you doing boss?' Hyacinth interrupted her fellow officer.

'Trying to work out what this switch is for,' Delano replied. 'What's the point of it? Every other light switch in this place has a purpose: to turn on a light. Except this one. When you switch it on and off, nothing happens.'

The four of them stood gazing around the room as Delano continued flipping the switch. Suddenly, Brandon walked towards the darkened dining room, ascending the steps to the elevated floor level.

'Wait a minute,' he said in a low voice. He was looking down at the wooden floor. 'Every time that switch goes on, I can see a chink of light shining through a piece of the floor over here.'

As Delano flipped the switch on and off, the other two joined Brandon on the elevated platform. The three agents stood staring down at the wooden boards.

'There's definitely a light coming on down there, beneath the floor,' Brandon said. 'And it's in time with you flipping that switch on and off, boss. There's another room down there. We never saw it yesterday because it was daylight, even though it was overcast and dismal outside. But now it's completely dark and there are no other lights on in the room, it's clearly visible.'

Leaving the light switch on, Delano stepped up into the dining room. He looked around before finally turning his gaze to the floor.

'You're right, there's definitely a light on in the space beneath this room,' he said, 'but the question is, how do we get down there? Is there a secret entrance somewhere?'

'If there is I doubt it's in here,' Brandon said. 'It must be outside.'

'Who searched this room yesterday?' Hyacinth asked suddenly.

'I did,' Anson said, appearing from behind them. 'What's the problem?'

'There's another room under this floor,' Hyacinth replied. 'You see anything yesterday that might have been the entrance?'

'Say what?' Anson asked with a confused expression. 'A *room*? Under *here*?'

He followed the gaze of his co-workers to the chinks of light through the wooden boards.

'Hyacinth, you're right. There *is* a room down there.' Anson's eyes widened in amazement. 'I never saw it yesterday. How could I have missed it?'

'It wasn't your fault,' Hyacinth said. 'It was daylight when we searched before. You can only really see the light through the floor when the rest of the room is in darkness. But how do we get down there?'

'I didn't see anything in here which looked like a secret door when I searched,' Anson said, 'and I was pretty thorough, although obviously not thorough enough.' His voice tailed off, almost apologetically.

'It doesn't matter Anson,' Delano said. 'Perhaps it's better we didn't find this yesterday. Jacobs was here then. It may be to our advantage that he doesn't know we've found his secret room for now.'

'Yeah, perhaps,' Anson replied. He appeared to recall something. 'The only thing I couldn't move yesterday was that table. It seems to be attached to the floor somehow. It just wouldn't budge. I guess I dismissed it at the time, but who has a table welded to the floor?'

'It is a bit strange,' Mitch agreed. He stepped forward and applied some sideways force to the table. Brandon joined him and pushed on the glass top while Mitch attempted to move the teak base below. Nothing happened. The table stayed put. As they stood up, sweating and panting from the strain, Hyacinth inspected the table.

'Maybe there's another way,' she said, almost to herself. She held the bevelled edge of the glass top firmly in both hands and twisted it in a clockwise position. It held fast. She shifted her body weight and tried twisting it in the opposite direction. To her surprise, it suddenly began to move. There was a faint whirring sound, as if a small electric motor had just been activated. And then the table top began moving by itself. It turned slowly in an anticlockwise direction, and then the floor underneath the thick base of the tree root began to twist upwards in a corkscrew motion, raising the whole table. Hyacinth stepped back in alarm as the table continued turning and moving upwards. Supporting the elevated piece of floor beneath the table was a thick metal rod, which appeared to be powered by the electric motor.

The five of them stood silently watching until the table stopped turning completely, high above the floor, the tree roots supporting the glass top spread out as if they were branches. The base of the floor had risen enough to reveal a gap of roughly three feet. The metal rod was in the centre of the hole and a crude wooden stepladder on one side stretched downwards to the floor of the secret room.

Mitch dropped to his hands and knees and peered into the hole.

'Oh man,' he said suddenly. He sat up and turned to the other three. There was a look of alarm on his face.

'What is it?' Brandon asked.

'Hyacinth, I owe you an apology,' Mitch said quietly. 'It's the below ground cistern. But you were right, it's not used to store water.'

'Apology accepted. What's down there?' Hyacinth asked. She dropped to her knees beside him. As she peered through the gap a look of horror came into her eyes. Her question hung in the sultry air, an eternal ellipsis, unanswered. They had finally discovered the secret of Villa Bella Casa.

THIRTEEN

03:05 am, Friday, September 20
Abandoned airstrip, undisclosed location, south of Miami, Florida

In spite of the early hour of the morning, the mercury was still hitting the mid-eighties. Circular patches of sweat were forming rapidly around the armpits of Johann Ryan's pressed white shirt as he hurried across the apron to where the silhouette of an ancient-looking aircraft stood in darkness. He was carrying two large brown suitcases which appeared as timeworn and battered as the aircraft itself. It was a clear, still night and the silvery glow of a crescent moon hung suspended in the midst of a myriad brilliant stars. The only sounds were the crickets chirruping enthusiastically in the tall grass at the side of the apron and Johann's footsteps crunching on loose stones as he walked quickly across the concrete.

Johann reached the aircraft, placed the suitcases on the ground and paused for breath. After a few moments, he lifted the cases again with some effort, lugging them up the steps and through the cargo door on the port side, into the aircraft. The cases were heavy and he half-lifted, half-threw them onto two faded leather seats at the rear. Wiping his brow, he turned and made his way back down the steps. Breathing heavily, he strode across the apron towards one of two dilapidated hangars. His path was illuminated by the dim glow of a flashlight. The dark shadow of the derelict building loomed imposingly over the broken concrete of the apron and two crudely paved, weed-strewn runways beyond.

Johann disappeared into the hangar before returning a few minutes later. He was carrying two more brown suitcases of the same size. Propelled by the momentum of the cases swinging at his side and eager to reach the aircraft as quickly as possible to deposit the weighty load, he walked briskly. After a final trip back to the hangar to collect the last two suitcases, he stashed them in the cabin before retreating back down the steps. He walked around the aircraft, closing the wing lockers in the wings and the cargo hatches in the nose cone, which were also loaded with bags and cases of varying shapes and sizes. Reaching the steps to the cargo door once more, Johann disappeared back inside the cabin. He squeezed between a haphazard collection of grey duffle bags and suitcases on the seats and the floor of the cabin. The bags were zipped tightly shut and bursting at the seams. The zipper on one of the bags had come slightly open revealing a stack of hundred dollar bills. Johann stopped to push it back into the bag. He forced the zipper closed and squeezed past the front passenger seats to the cockpit where he retrieved a large canvas backpack. He placed it on one of the sheepskin-clad seats up front and rummaged around in the bottom until he found what he was looking for.

Turning, he squeezed his way back through the cabin between the cases and bags to the cargo door, clutching a stainless steel thermos flask. He sat down heavily on the floor of the cabin at the top of the steps and unscrewed the lid of the flask before pouring a dark-coloured liquid into the inverted cap. He placed the flask on the floor beside him and took a long drink of the warm liquid, savouring the rich flavour of Colombian coffee beans laced with a generous measure of Captain Morgan dark rum.

Johann Ryan was in his mid-sixties — although could probably pass for being in his late-fifties — and lamented the fact that these days he was the official baggage handler as well as the captain of every flight he piloted. He'd been a keen sportsman and swimmer in his youth and throughout most of his life. He'd been fit, toned and muscular. But the stress and hectic lifestyle of recent years — and the love of food — had steadily curtailed these interests, leading to a decline in fitness levels and a slight, but noticeable, gain in weight. Even so, Johann had managed to hold onto a thick head of hair and the handsome, boyish looks of his youth.

Taking another long sip of the spiked coffee, he stared out into the night, listening to the cheerful noise of the crickets and, a little further away, the hiss and chitter and whistle of insects from a nearby swamp. He tried not to think about the flight ahead of him. At least he had a decent aircraft. It looked a little old and tired, but it flew well. The 1977 Cessna 404 Titan had been purchased from a dealer in Miami for one hundred and fifty thousand dollars and was, in Johann's opinion, a bargain. Mechanically, the twin-engined, propeller-driven aircraft was in good shape due to the fact that Johann was a competent engineer and mechanic, as well as a pilot. The fuselage and wings were showing a few signs of rust and decay, but somehow the Cessna managed to stay airborne during flight. The one thing in Johann's favour was that he was an outstanding pilot with considerable flying experience; he knew he could bring the aircraft down and land it safely in any emergency scenario. The interior of the aircraft was tatty and shabby with its tan leather seats configured for nine passengers and two pilots, although for the most part there were never any passengers and there was never a co-pilot in the righthand seat. Johann nearly always flew alone.

Almost two years earlier, Johann had been an airline captain with an impressive résumé spanning more than forty years within commercial aviation. That is until one day when, out of the blue, he was made redundant by the airline. Technically, the circumstances of his redundancy package were determined by the fact that the airline had gone bust as opposed to an abundance of younger, up and coming pilots. But of the dozen or so airlines Johann had been employed by during his extensive flying career, it was the third airline to become insolvent and the third time he had suddenly found himself out of a job.

This time around it was a dreary afternoon in midwinter. It had been an uneventful flight back to the UK from Hurghada, Egypt, where they had left warmer, sunnier climes behind them five hours earlier. From the flight deck, Captain Ryan and his first officer watched the autopilot of the Boeing airliner execute a perfect landing at Stansted Airport, before they were directed to a gate at the far side of the airport by the air traffic controller. Upon their arrival at the unusually remote location, the airliner, loaded with sunburned holidaymakers in shorts and flip flops, was suddenly surrounded by airport security vehicles escorted by two police cars with flashing blue lights. The convoy approached the aircraft at speed and screeched to a halt, akin to a Hollywood action movie.

Johann peered out of the cockpit window to watch the events on the tarmac below. As the passengers disembarked, airport officials leaped out of their cars with court order documents in their hands, grounding the aircraft with immediate effect. They entered the cockpit as Johann completed his paperwork, but he knew the deal. With a heavy heart he wished his young first officer well as he picked up his backpack and walked down the steps of the airliner onto the tarmac for the last time. He had just turned sixty-three and any hope of finding another flying job, except perhaps fishery patrols in Scotland or night cargo to the Continent, was now a rapidly fading dream.

It was early afternoon and, as dusk fell, Johann trudged to his car, an ageing black BMW 3 Series. He didn't see the point in stopping by the crew room to say goodbye to any fellow pilots who might still be hanging around and he decided to avoid the management staff at all costs. The ops department could mail him his tax documents by post.

As Johann reached his car, a light drizzle had begun. The air was cold and damp. He pulled his lanyard over his head, throwing it on the seat beside him with his backpack, as he got in. He started the engine and reversed out of the parking space, ignoring the twenty mile hour speed limit as he headed for the exit. He joined a slow-moving ribbon of taillights heading northbound on the motorway, but he was in no hurry to get home. His latest wife — the third in twenty years — a flight attendant, had left him the previous week for a first officer with a rival airline. Not that Johann was particularly broken up about it. He wasn't happy with her anyway. She didn't appreciate him and there had never been a whole lot of love to go round. He was better off without her. He pulled onto the forecourt of a gas station a few miles from home to pick up some fuel and a microwaveable chicken balti for two, with extra rice. The intention was to eat half tonight and half the next night, but Johann knew that wouldn't happen.

Flying had been Johann's life, his everything. He'd been an airline captain, he'd had status, respect and admiration as he strode through the airport terminals in his pilot's uniform with four-bar epaulettes. And now suddenly, it was gone. It had all been taken from him. But, unlike the previous two redundancies, this time he had a plan. Or, more specifically, he had a friend who had a plan. And so it was, five months later, that Johann found himself in the seat of another Boeing airliner. It wasn't the captain's seat on the flight deck up front; it was a passenger seat in coach between two large Antiguan women.

Johann had taken early retirement and cashed in his pension and the rest of his savings. He'd sold his house and his car, a few items of furniture and most of his possessions, save for a few clothes. He'd purchased a one-way ticket to Antigua, his favourite Caribbean island, and now he was leaving the miserable British weather and his soon-to-be ex-wife — who would be getting as little as possible of his small, hard-earned fortune — for year-round sunshine and busty beach babes half his age wearing little more than string bikinis.

Johann cleared customs at V. C. Bird International without a hitch. He made his way to the baggage carousel from which he retrieved one oversized suitcase before heading to the information desk, as instructed by his friend. It was surprising how chance meetings could change the course of a life. A few years earlier, perhaps four or five, Johann couldn't remember exactly, he'd been doing some flying work out of Miami International Airport. Late one hot, humid night, unable to sleep due to a faulty air conditioning unit in his rented apartment, he'd found himself in a strip club in Downtown Miami where he was invited to join a small group of men who were clearly having a good time. They comprised a mix of nationalities: Americans, Colombians, Jamaicans and a couple of Antiguans. Whoever they were and whatever they did, there appeared to be no shortage of cash. Johann's tab was taken care of and, along with his new friends, he enjoyed the finest top shelf champagne and women.

When his work contract based out of Miami came to an end, Johann returned to an airline job back in the UK, but remained in touch with a couple of the men from the strip club. And so, five months earlier, when he had lamented the loss of his job and his somewhat liberating renewed single status, one of the men had suggested that he might consider a clean break and start a new life someplace else.

'No chance of that happening,' Johann had replied forlornly. 'I'm sixty-three. Unless I fly night cargo or take some crappy fisheries patrol job, my flying career's over.'

His friend had insisted otherwise, however, with a suggestion, no, an offer, of some flying work which had left Johann temporarily speechless. The details were scant, but it was a generous offer and far too good to turn down. And Johann wasn't exactly in a position to be choosy anyway; he needed a job. According to the friend, the work involved flying various cargo items and the occasional passenger throughout the Caribbean with the odd trip to Miami now and then. The job also entailed scenic flights around the island for tourists, as required. Johann would be based in Antigua where temporary accommodation would be provided on his arrival, along with a car and, of course, his own aircraft.

In addition, the friend had offered to take care of all the paperwork, including some sort of residency permit and a United States Federal Aviation Administration, or FAA, licence conversion, which was required for any flying work undertaken in Antigua and the Caribbean. Apparently, the friend had contacts in the Antiguan government and could pull strings. The necessary paperwork was of no consequence to the friend and easily sorted. It was a miraculous turn of events! Within hours, Johann's hopeless, desperate situation had been transformed to one of promise, prospects and excitement. Not even in his wildest dreams could he have envisaged such good fortune. A new life in the sunshine beckoned, a far cry from the misery and emptiness of his soon-to-be old life back in England. All he had to do was buy a one-way ticket to Antigua and pack his bags. The friend would take care of the rest.

Half-wheeling, half-dragging his suitcase behind him, Johann hurried through the crowds — mostly tourists — towards the information desk with a buzz of fear and excitement. He spotted his friend immediately: he was in his late thirties and dressed in a white, short-sleeved shirt and navy pants. He was carrying a folder and a clipboard and looked as though he had an important role. He had once mentioned that he worked at the airport, although Johann wasn't exactly sure of his official title. He appeared to be engaged in an animated conversation with one of the girls behind the information desk. Over the shirt he was wearing a hi-vis vest with a badge pinned to it which read: Rusty McChannen, Deputy Chief Security Officer.

Rusty had been true to his word. All the paperwork was in order, including a newly issued FAA licence in Johann's name. Johann queried the fact that he should perhaps have been present in some way to obtain the document, or that he should have completed some kind of flight test or taken an exam, but Rusty had assured him this wasn't necessary and that everything was aboveboard. Rusty had presented Johann with a set of keys attached to a metal keyring: the first key was for a room for which Rusty had paid two months' rent upfront; the second was for a car, an old, beat-up Subaru Station Wagon which had cost less than a thousand dollars and had more than one hundred thousand miles on the clock. Johann's new office did not require a key. It was a 1977 Cessna 404 Titan aircraft, white with retro brown and orange stripes along the fuselage and across the horizontal stabiliser. It was parked halfway along runway ten, the original but now disused runway of V. C. Bird International, alongside an impressive lineup of biz jets which ferried the rich, famous and anonymous around the globe.

The only area in which Johann felt Rusty could have improved upon with the relocation package was the accommodation. His new lodgings was a small room in a wooden bungalow situated just off the airport perimeter road. It belonged to a woman in her fifties called Twila who worked as a cleaner by day. It was anyone's guess as to what forms of employment she engaged in by night and Johann was careful not to find out.

The place was a dive with a strong odour of rancid fish and a bathroom so unsanitary that Johann felt the only suitable method of disinfection would be to burn it to the ground and start over. The most alarming aspect of his new lodgings however, was the considerable interest shown in him by Twila, clearly in awe of the fact that her latest tenant was a pilot. Unfortunately for her, she was a far cry from the bikini-clad femme fatale of Johann's dreams and the attraction remained steadfastly unrequited. To his horror, her advances became more and more brazen until he decided he'd had enough. Early one morning, he left Twila a month's rent in a brown envelope on the kitchen worktop with a note to inform her he was leaving.

He loaded his cases into the Subaru and drove to St. John's where he checked into a hotel. Forty dollars a night paid for a room and breakfast. He then took a trip to a real estate agent where he put in an offer for a recently refurbished one bedroom condo with an ocean view. He paid the asking price of one hundred and fifty thousand dollars with cash upfront on the proviso that he could move into the furnished condo within a fortnight. After ten days he realised this was an unrealistic expectation for a country which operated on island time, so he bribed the real estate agent to give him the keys to the unoccupied condo and he moved in anyway. His new home was part of a residential complex in the northwest of the island with access to communal gardens and a communal swimming pool.

As the days passed, Johann began to settle into his new life in the sun and the memories of the life he had left behind began to fade. The ever-accommodating Rusty informed Johann that the official documentation for his new air charter company, JHR Airways, for which Rusty was a silent partner, had been completed and that Johann Harcourt Ryan was now the chief executive. Johann even had his own business headquarters, a small wooden hut with a tin roof on the edge of the disused runway ten. A rather plain-looking sign on the door advertised scenic flights around Antigua and Barbuda and other neighbouring islands. If only his ex-wives could see him now.

Other than the minimalistic sign, Johann's only objection was to the bargain-basement prices at which Rusty was advertising the scenic flights compared to the other tour companies, but he decided not to raise the issue and appreciated that a startup business needed to be competitively priced. Once he'd established himself as the best scenic pilot on the island, he'd persuade Rusty to agree to a price increase. Johann was a competent pilot with a natural talent and thousands of flying hours. In the past he'd also been an instructor and an accomplished aerobatics pilot before pursuing his airline career. He may be getting on in years but experience counted for a lot. He knew he could fly well and vowed never to take the job — or the views which went with it — for granted.

Over the first few weeks, business was inevitably slow. Johann made the occasional flight to other islands for various contacts and business associates of Rusty, as well as a few scenic flights around the Antigua coastline for miscellaneous groups of tourists, but he knew his current level of work would not be enough to sustain the business. He was already planning to buy Rusty out altogether one day. Johann knew he owed Rusty big time, but Rusty was managing the bookings and calling the shots, and didn't appear to be concerned about the sparse workload. Occasionally Johann wondered what Rusty could possibly be gaining from such an investment and, indeed, what kind of a job he had at the airport which enabled him to put up the necessary capital required to bankroll an aircraft worth nearly a quarter of a million dollars. Late one afternoon, however, those questions were answered. Rusty's motives and end game became clear. And Johann realised it was too late to change his mind and back out. Rusty had been shrewd, Johann had been naive. And now he was left with no choice but to carry on. But the more he considered things, the more he realised there was a silver lining in every cloud.

Johann had been paid in cash for his most recent cargo flight from Puerto Rico to Antigua which had been arranged, as usual, by Rusty. The cargo consisted of eight large brown suitcases which a middle-aged Hispanic man who spoke little English insisted on taking airside on a trolley, all the way to the Cessna. The cases felt heavy to Johann as he placed them in the wing lockers; four in the port wing and four in the starboard. He checked the load sheet, which detailed the precise weight of the suitcases, and briefly wondered what they contained before he said adiós to the man and climbed into the aircraft.

Following a clearance from air traffic control, Johann took off, commencing a steep climb away from the airfield. He admired the setting sun over to the west, which cast bright rays of orange light across the ocean, before he set a course for a southeasterly heading towards Antigua. At a cruising speed of one-eighty knots, the flight time would be just under two hours. Darkness fell quickly at sea level and, from five and a half thousand feet, Johann surveyed the twinkling lights of the streets and houses of Puerto Rico. He flew almost directly overhead the small island of Culebra, an island-municipality of Puerto Rico and part of the Virgin Islands geographically, the lights of which he could just make out ahead of him on his port side. He cleared the archipelago to the east and flew on in darkness. The route took him overhead Saint Kitts and Nevis and finally to the more populated, brightly lit island of Antigua where he commenced a gentle descent and requested permission to land at V. C. Bird International.

Johann touched down smoothly and continued rolling to the end of the runway where he vacated and taxied to his usual parking spot, halfway along the old runway ten. It was almost nine p.m. and the last flight of the day was lining up for takeoff, a British Airways flight bound for London. By now, Johann was familiar with the flight schedules and the airlines which operated out of the airport. The majority of flights were to or from neighbouring islands; the others were international flights with London, New York and Miami being the most popular destinations. Johann shut down the engines of the Cessna, unfastened his seat belt and pulled a clipboard onto his knees from the seat beside him. In the yellow glow of the cabin lights, he quickly completed the documentation for the flight. As he flipped through the pages attached to the clipboard, his eye caught the load sheet once more and he wondered what was in the eight brown suitcases.

Placing the clipboard back on the seat beside him, Johann stood up and made his way to the rear of the aircraft where he opened the cargo door and let down the steps. The hot, humid night air instantly engulfed him, along with the chirrups of tree frogs and crickets, which were briefly drowned out by the roar of the British Airways jet as it took off into the darkness.

The old runway ten was deserted which wasn't unusual for that time of night. Johann was supposed to call Rusty as soon as he shut down the aircraft, but he was aware that Rusty could easily track his flight anyway and would know the minute the Cessna touched down. Glancing quickly around him, Johann walked to the port wing, opened the wing locker and hauled out one of the suitcases. He placed it on the tarmac and inspected the fasteners, simple spring-loaded toggle latches. The case wasn't locked. He popped the clasps, which sprung open easily, and lifted the lid of the case. He looked down at the contents inside and his worst fears were realised.

Inside the case were rectangular packages of a white-coloured substance, tightly packed and wrapped in clear plastic. Leaving the case open, he stood up and pulled another case out of the wing locker. He glanced towards the airport and saw the silhouette of a black SUV making its way towards runway ten. It was still a fair distance away but Johann knew it was headed in his direction. There wasn't much time. He placed the second case on the tarmac and popped the latches as before. Lifting the lid, he expected to see more packages of white powder, but the contents of this suitcase were different. This time, the case contained vacuum-sealed bundles of one hundred dollar bills, held together with mustard-coloured currency straps. Johann had no idea of the total value of the dollars, but he guessed it could be millions. And that was just in one suitcase.

Johann looked back at the first suitcase before checking the progress of the black SUV. It was close now. Closer than Johann had expected. With his heart pounding in his chest, he flipped the lid of the first suitcase shut and was about to close the second when the SUV screeched to a halt beside the Cessna and a man dressed all in black jumped out of the passenger side.

'What're you doing with those cases?' he called out to Johann before noticing the open wing locker.

'I thought I'd start unloading, help a bit,' Johann replied. He could hear his voice trembling.

'On whose orders?' the man asked, skirting the wing of the aircraft.

'Rusty's.' Johann tried to sound casual.

'Oh really?' The man wasn't convinced. He pulled a cell phone out of his pocket and tapped the screen. He raised the phone to his ear and waited. After a few seconds, someone answered.

'It's Glen. You tell your pilot to start unloading the cases?'

He listened and nodded before replying. It was short and sharp.

'That's what I thought. Yeah. What you want me to do?'

Instructions were given at the end of the line which Glen acknowledged before placing the phone back in his pocket.

'You're lying,' Glen said unpleasantly.

'I'm sure that's what Rusty told me to do,' Johann said. 'I guess I misunderstood. But the cases are all...'

'Shut up and get in.' Glen yanked open one of the rear doors of the SUV and gestured for Johann to climb inside.

'What?'

'Get in the car. Now.'

'But what about...'

'Get in the damn car,' Glen said again. As he spoke, he pulled one side of his jacket away from his body. Attached to his belt, Johann could clearly see a holster containing a handgun.

'Get in,' Glen said, signalling to the door.

'What about my things? My flight bag and stuff?'

'You won't be needing those right now. Shut up and get in the car or you won't be needing your flight bag *ever*.'

Johann wasn't sure how serious Glen was. The best course of action was probably just to cooperate. Perhaps it was all a big misunderstanding. He walked as calmly as he could towards the SUV and got in. Glen slammed the door behind him. Johann looked over to his left and realised there was someone else in the car besides the driver. Someone else with a gun which was pointed right at him. Nobody spoke. The driver shifted the SUV into gear and sped off back towards the main terminal leaving Glen with the Cessna and the suitcases. The SUV had nearly reached the main runway when the driver turned right and then left onto a small service road which ran parallel to runway ten. They crossed the threshold of the main runway and continued towards the northeastern side of the airport where they passed between the main terminal building and a row of hangars.

The driver turned into a small parking lot next to one of the hangars and pulled up beside a similar-sized black SUV. He had barely come to a stop before the front passenger door opened and someone got in, turning to face Johann. It was Rusty.

'Good evening Johann,' Rusty said with a smile. 'How was your flight from Puerto Rico?'

'Fine,' Johann replied. 'What's going on Rusty?'

'Tell me something. Is it usual procedure back in England for pilots to rummage through the cargo they've been entrusted with?'

'Not unless they've a reason to suspect that the cargo contains something dangerous or which might put the flight at risk,' Johann replied steadily.

'Oh. Okay.' Rusty nodded in understanding. He frowned. 'So then, I'm curious, wouldn't it be more logical for the pilot to inspect the cargo *before* taking off?'

'Er yeah, in most circumstances it would.' Johann silently chastised himself for the schoolboy error.

'So what could possibly be gained from examining the cargo *after* you've landed?' Rusty continued.

'I think it was just a misunderstanding,' Johann replied.

'Oh I'm sorry,' Rusty said. 'Was I not clear when I asked you to contact me as soon as you'd landed so I could send a vehicle to unload the cargo? I don't recall telling you to remove the suitcases from the hold and open them right there on the tarmac.'

Johann remained silent. He felt bitterly betrayed. Rusty hadn't hired him to fly tourists around the island. That was a cover, a tawdry facade for Rusty's sleazy little drug-running outfit. Johann had always tried to live his life with honesty and integrity. While some of his fellow airline pilots smuggled various items of contraband through customs, Johann was always at the front of the line to inform officials of any items to declare. While his previous three marriages had ended, without exception, as a result of his ex-wives cheating on him, Johann had remained faithful to the end. But now he found himself unwittingly in the middle of a drug-trafficking operation. A sudden thought struck him.

'Those cargo flights I flew for you last week,' he said to Rusty, 'the ones from Jamaica and the one to Miami. What was in those duffle bags?'

'You're paid to fly, not to ask questions,' Rusty snapped.

'I have a right to know if the cargo's legal though.'

'You don't have any rights at all Johann.'

'I think I do and I don't want to have anything to do with this — this whole…'

'Is that so?' As Rusty spoke he reached inside his jacket and pulled out a large Manila envelope. He passed it to Johann. 'You might like to think about that for a moment.'

Johann took the envelope.

'What's this?' he asked nervously.

'Take a look,' Rusty shrugged.

Johann peered inside. The envelope contained about six sheets of A4-sized paper. He slid them out and examined the top one. It was a grainy colour image of a man carrying two duffle bags through the cargo door of an aircraft. Johann took a deep breath and flipped to the second page on which was printed another colour photograph. Same man, same aircraft, different day, different cargo. But Johann recognised himself and the Cessna Titan. The other pages contained similar images, most of which had been taken by a camera with a long range zoom lens from somewhere near the terminal at V. C. Bird International. A couple of the photographs had been snapped at an airport in Miami.

'This is blackmail,' Johann said quietly, tossing the photographs on the seat beside him.

'Precautionary measures,' Rusty said casually.

'Count me out,' Johann said. 'I don't want a part of this. Find someone else Rusty. I'm going home to London.' He reached for the handle of the door.

'Not so fast Captain Ryan,' Rusty said. 'You're not going anywhere. Don't even think about opening that door.'

'Why not? What are you going to do?' Johann asked defiantly. 'If you want to threaten me, go ahead. Like I said, I don't want any part of this. Let me go or I'm taking this to the police.'

Rusty laughed out loud. He produced another grainy photograph and held it up for Johann to see. It was a picture of two men, one of whom had his back to the camera. Johann didn't recognise the other man.

'Sorry, no idea who they are,' he said, shaking his head. 'Never seen either of them before.'

'You might not know them, but I should probably just mention that the man on the left, the one with his back to the camera, knows all about you,' Rusty replied.

'What?' Johann asked in surprise. 'Who is he?'

'Alejandro Ortega.'

'Sorry, that name doesn't ring any bells.'

'Alejandro Ortega is one of the most powerful Colombian drug lords and head of the Ramirez Cartel, one of the most formidable drug cartels in the world. Any bells ringing now? Alarm bells perhaps?'

Johann shook his head slowly.

'Ah, well, you see the thing is Johann, that while the police won't give a damn about some little snitch who goes to them with zero proof to back up his story, Alejandro might care a bit more about one of his employees who steps out of line.'

'I don't work for Alejandro, whoever he is,' Johann replied obstinately.

'I'm afraid you do. Who d'you think funded your relocation to Antigua and provided the cash for your aircraft?'

'But, this is… It's all wrong. You tricked me,' Johann said quietly.

'You certainly appeared quite willing to accept the job offer and relocation package from my point of view.'

'Yes, but you weren't upfront with the truth.'

'I told you you'd be flying cargo around the Caribbean. I think that was a perfectly truthful, accurate description of the work you're doing. Anyway, before you decide on your next move, you might be interested to know that the last time one of Alejandro's employees stepped out of line, there was a terrible accident…' Rusty produced a final photograph of what looked like a hulk of twisted metal and broken glass on a dirt road somewhere in the middle of a desert landscape. The contorted mass had clearly once been some kind of vehicle but was unrecognisable in the picture. Johann gasped in horror at one side of the photograph where the body of a man had been thrown clear of the car. The body, wearing blue jeans and a pink and white striped shirt, lay at an awkward angle with its left arm twisted underneath. Johann's gaze shifted to the man's head and he suddenly felt an overwhelming wave of nausea. One side of the head had been ripped away from the other side, revealing a broad, V-shaped split between the man's eyes. His skull was completely smashed and chunks of white brain matter lay next to his head in a large pool of blood.

Johann looked away quickly. The image was disturbing, like something out of a macabre horror movie. Except he knew it was real.

'Tragic,' Rusty was saying, shaking his head in mock sympathy.

'You sick bastard,' Johann said coldly.

'Decision's yours, Captain Ryan,' Rusty said in a cheery manner.

'Oh sure it is,' Johann said sarcastically. 'Just give me a moment while I consider my options…'

'Take all the time you need,' Rusty replied, 'oh and I almost forgot, here's your backpay for the last few weeks.' He tossed a thick bundle of one hundred dollar bills at Johann. The bundle consisted of three stacks of bills held together with strips of brown paper. Each stack was almost five inches high. Suddenly Johann knew Rusty had him right where he wanted him. The plan had been set in motion from the moment Johann had set foot in Antigua. If he walked away now, he'd be looking over his shoulder for the rest of his life. He had no choice but to give in. He glanced at the stacks of bills and made a rough calculation in his head. If all the bills in each bundle were one hundred dollar notes, he guessed he was looking at around a hundred thousand dollars per stack. Which meant that he had something in the region of three hundred thousand dollars right there in front of him. Over a quarter of a million dollars for just over a month's work. Johann did a few more calculations. He'd always been pretty good at mathematics. If Rusty was paying him that kind of money, he'd be making something in the region of seventy-five thousand dollars a week. Fifty-two weeks in a year. Four million US dollars a year. Rusty was still talking, but Johann was barely listening.

'Obviously this is just a little sweetener, a golden hello, sort of a welcome aboard. Alejandro always rewards loyalty with generosity. And there's more to come, Johann, much more. D'you really think it was an accident we met in that strip joint in Miami back in twenty-fourteen?'

'What?'

'According to Bob Harrison you were one of the best pilots he'd ever seen.'

An airline captain and skilled aerobatics pilot himself, Bob Harrison had been Johann's line manager during his time in Miami.

'You know Bob?' Johann asked.

'Oh sure, he's a good friend of mine,' Rusty replied. 'He told me all about you. Said your flying abilities were second to none; there wasn't an airstrip you couldn't negotiate or a crosswind you couldn't handle. We kept half an eye on you when you returned to England, and when you were made redundant back in January it was the obvious thing to do to get you out here. Clearly I can't *force* you to work for us Johann, but it would be a terrible shame if you turned down what I consider to be a very generous employment package. It would be tragic, in fact.'

'Cut the crap Rusty,' Johann said dispassionately. 'You know I don't have a choice here.'

'Well I wouldn't like to influence you either way,' Rusty replied. He glanced at his watch and waited. Johann's mind was in turmoil, but at the centre of it all was the money. Johann wasn't sure he'd ever been in proximity to quite so much cash in his life. He'd weathered three redundancies and two divorces where his ex-wives had clamoured for as much of his wealth as they could get their greedy little manicured paws on. From across the pond, his soon-to-be third ex-wife had already started divorce proceedings along with wholly unrealistic demands where his finances were concerned. Obviously he'd need to hide his most recent earnings carefully until the divorce was finalised.

Like a gaudy carousel going round in front of his eyes, Johann considered the last sixty-three years of his life: the good times, the bad, the highs, the lows, the friends, the ex-wives, his family, the airline career… Sure, he was a gifted pilot but what else did he have to show for his part in the world exactly? What was the point of it all? Had he actually gained anything from being honest and principled? What did anyone gain from living a virtuous life? Had he really had fun and lived life to the full?

At that moment, it was as if some faceless voice was speaking to him, some invisible force was coaxing him. The gaudy carousel turned to glittering images of wealth and excess: opulent villas, sleek private jets, chauffeur-driven supercars, champagne, parties, beautiful girls and he, Johann Harcourt Ryan, at the centre of it all. Wasn't that what life was really about? Money, riches, pleasure, passion, possessions, living the dream. And now it was his for the taking.

It took less than a minute for the appalling idea of drug-running to be vanquished by the thrill and excitement of a life of excess. There was a silver lining in every cloud. Suddenly it didn't matter anymore that Rusty had priced the scenic tours offered by JHR Airways so low compared to the other tour companies. Johann didn't need the cash now anyway, the company was just a front for the drug trafficking. Suddenly it didn't matter if he received poor ratings on Tripadvisor for the occasional lewd remark and sexual innuendo to his female passengers. And suddenly it didn't matter if tourists bypassed JHR Airways for more professional tour companies. Hell, it didn't matter if he never received another damn booking. Johann suddenly realised that this was Rusty's aim all along: he had priced the scenic flights so cheaply that hardly anyone would consider flying with JHR Airways with the whole "you get what you pay for" mentality of modern society. Which is precisely what Rusty wanted in order to ensure that Johann was free for his main flying work: trafficking drugs and money. JHR

Airways scenic flights was never meant to make a profit. It was only ever a facade for the drug running. For a second, a faint smile played on Johann's lips. It was troubled, laced with guilt and self-reproach, but it was enough for Rusty to know that Johann had made his choice.

'I'll be in touch,' he said to Johann. He opened the passenger door and got out, closing the door behind him. The driver started the engine, shifted into gear and pulled away, out of the parking lot. They sat in silence and Johann realised they were back on the service road which ran parallel to runway ten, heading towards a small parking lot at the other end where his Subaru Station Wagon was parked. It was one of the only cars left in the lot at the late hour. The SUV pulled up immediately behind it and the driver waited in silence. Clutching the bundle of one hundred dollar bills, Johann got out. He closed the door behind him and the SUV took off into the darkness. Johann stood alone next to his car. He could see his keys in the ignition and his flight bag and backpack on the rear seat. He got in. Throwing the bundle of cash on the passenger seat beside him as if it was a pile of old flying magazines, he turned the key and started the engine.

There was a small supermarket along the road leading to the gated complex where his condo was situated. Johann parked the Subaru outside and made his way into the store. A few late night shoppers meandered along the aisles with half-empty trolleys while supermarket employees stacked shelves. Johann made his way to a small area at the back of the store where a sign hanging over the aisle read: Beer, Wine and Liquor. He chose a bottle of cheap rum from a limited selection and headed for the checkout. He'd never been much of a drinker, but now was surely cause for celebration. Or perhaps to alleviate a guilty conscience. Johann wasn't sure and he didn't really care. He paid for the rum with change from his wallet and headed back to the Subaru which, for the first time ever, he had locked. As he got in and started the engine he cast a brief glance over to where a large aeronautical chart now lay open, spread across the passenger seat. He reversed out of the parking lot and drove home.

FOURTEEN

03:20 am, Friday, September 20
Abandoned airstrip, undisclosed location, south of Miami, Florida

Sitting at the top of the steps of the Cessna, Johann downed the last of the coffee and rum from the thermos. He remembered that night at V. C. Bird International, when Rusty had handed him the three hundred thousand dollars in the back of the black SUV, as if it was yesterday. His conscience had slowly been eroded since that time. Sometimes he wondered if it had gone completely. It didn't matter though, did it? He was living the dream now, wasn't he?

Sure, he was now a very rich man, but with the wealth came new problems, including what to do with all the cash. He rented a number of storage units in Antigua and Miami on a month-to-month payment system, just in case he needed to move the money quickly. Both places had parking right outside each unit and twenty-four hour access. The units were climate-controlled to protect the paper bills from humidity. He knew the locations of every surveillance camera around the storage facilities and how to avoid them. He also knew Leonard, a guy in Miami who took care of the rest of the cash for a considerable slice of the pie. Johann wasn't exactly sure what Leonard did with the money, but tried his best to keep up with the myriad shell corporations and deposits in offshore tax havens which Leonard had set up.

Johann could afford anything he wanted, but aside from drinking a bit more, his lifestyle hadn't changed much. He still drove the Subaru and lived in the same condo. If people noticed that he had suddenly come into money, questions would be asked. He needed to keep a low profile. He dreamed of taking all his cash and just disappearing one day. But Rusty would find him. Alejandro Ortega's cartel had infiltrated just about every organisation throughout the Caribbean that Johann could think of, from police departments to airport security to border control. He may have had millions, but sometimes Johann found himself longing for the freedom of his old life, with all the trials and tribulations and financial challenges which went with it.

Suddenly, he felt his cell phone buzz in his pocket. He pulled it out and glanced at the screen before answering.

'What d'you want Rusty?'

'Where are you?' The familiar voice at the other end spoke quickly.

'Miami.'

'When will you be back in Antigua?'

'Around ten-thirty.'

'Good, I've got another job lined up for you.'

'What? I've been up all night.'

'Don't worry, it's not until later this afternoon. Get a couple of hours' sleep when you get back. It'll be worth it. There're girls.'

'Yeah?'

'Meet me outside the Pavilion Café at three. Usual routine. I'm the pilot, you're the passenger, a buddy of mine just coming along for the ride.'

'Where are we going?'

'Just the usual scenic tour crap we normally do. If the girls are impressed we might head down to Montserrat. Maybe even land, I haven't decided yet.'

'These girls, they're friends of yours?'

'Friends of friends.'

Any friends of Rusty were people in positions of wealth or status from whom Rusty could benefit in some way.

'Okay, I can be there.' Johann liked to give himself the illusion of choice, at least.

'Just be sure to make me look like a damn good pilot,' Rusty added.

'Yeah, don't worry about that.'

'And don't drink too much this time. I need to know you're not going to screw up and have us all killed.'

'Have I ever let you down Rusty?'

'No, but that's not the point.'

'I promise I'll only have one drink. Two at the most.'

'Good. Make sure of that. I'll see you at the Pavilion, three o'clock sharp.'

'See you there,' Johann replied, but Rusty had already hung up.

Johann went to take a sip of the rum-infused coffee before he realised the thermos was empty. The flight that afternoon would be straight-forward enough but he could really do without it after a seven hour flight from Miami to Antigua. Rusty called the shots, however, and if Rusty had set up the flight, then Johann had no choice but to comply. By virtue of the fact that Rusty worked at the airport, albeit as a security official, he liked to expand his role now and again to impress, particularly when there were girls involved. Over drinks or dinner and at parties, Rusty would, from time to time, casually drop into the conversation that he was a pilot. He'd learned some aviation jargon and the fact that if there was one thing which impressed women, it was a man who could fly an aircraft.

The first time he'd casually remarked that he was an ace pilot and had flown all over the United States and the Caribbean, he'd had a few too many cocktails. He'd also just happened to mention that he had his own aircraft and suddenly he was the man of the moment. The women were all over him and he was lapping up the attention until one of them said something which stopped him cold. She suggested he took them all up for a flight. What to do? He'd only ever taken one flying lesson in his life during which he had somehow managed to put the aircraft into an incipient spin. The instructor had had to seize the controls to prevent them from descending into a death spiral.

Across the terrace, Rusty had spotted Johann, sipping his cocktail alone, staring out to sea. And Rusty had had an idea. It was a little outrageous perhaps, but nonetheless, if it worked it would save face with the girls who were now clamouring for a seat on what was becoming something of a sensational flight. It had to work.

Later that night, Rusty informed Johann of his plan. Wearing four-bar epaulettes and a golden wings badge pinned to his shirt, Rusty would take the captain's seat on the left of the Cessna's cockpit and Johann, in a casual shirt and jeans, would sit on the right, on the co-pilot's side. Rusty would inform the girls that his friend had asked to come along for the ride and that he, Rusty would perhaps even allow his friend to fly the aircraft some of the way, with Rusty following through on the controls, naturally. Rusty would give a short flight brief to his passengers, which Johann would write out for him ahead of time. Johann would go along with Rusty and pretend he was enthralled by Rusty's skills as a talented pilot. In reality, Johann would have full control of the aircraft, but as far as the girls were concerned, it would appear as though Rusty was doing all the flying.

Johann wasn't keen on the idea until Rusty reminded him that he wasn't exactly in a strong negotiating position and Johann reluctantly agreed to the plan. In addition, Rusty knew he could persuade Johann to do just about anything if women were involved. To make the whole thing as convincing as possible however, Johann pointed out that Rusty would need to communicate with air traffic control on the radio. It was a comment which Johann immediately regretted; he suddenly found himself tasked with an intensive training course on radiotelephony communications until Rusty sounded vaguely like a competent pilot.

That first flight itself was a success. Johann flew expertly with a perfect takeoff and landing while Rusty put on an Oscar-winning act as a professional pilot. His radio communications with air traffic control were reasonably convincing and, most importantly, the girls were in awe. Together, Rusty and Johann pulled it off and Rusty was keen to get some mileage out of his latest ruse. It was important to keep it off the radar as far as the airport was concerned however, and Johann was sworn to secrecy. Rusty wasn't sure how things would go down if Earl, his boss, learned that he was passing himself off as a pilot to impress women.

These days, Johann and Rusty had the whole sham down to a fine art between them, although their last flight to Saint Barts had involved copious amounts of champagne being served throughout lunch. As far as Rusty could see, this was the only downside to the whole thing. In order to keep up the act of being a professional pilot, he was obliged to abstain from alcohol. Johann, on the other hand, was masquerading as the passenger and could consume as much as he wanted. To Rusty's horror and in spite of his thinly veiled threats, this was a frequent occurrence. The last time they conducted such a flight, Johann's alcohol intake far exceeded any drink-drive limit, let alone drink-fly limit and Rusty was concerned that Johann's inability to pilot the aircraft back to Antigua would expose their little stunt. Unwilling to admit to their female passengers what was really going on, he reluctantly allowed Johann to take off, fearing for their lives. Somehow, Johann managed a faultless departure, a smooth flight and one of the softest touchdowns Rusty could remember. Johann truly was an exceptional pilot.

But now, in the tropical heat of the Miami night, Johann reluctantly replaced the cap of the empty flask and stood up wearily. He descended the steps onto the apron where, after a cursory glance around him, he unzipped his flies and proceeded to empty his bladder. He was never keen on the idea of using the emergency peeing device stowed in the cockpit. It was almost three-thirty and time to get moving.

He climbed back into the cabin and pulled the steps and cargo door shut behind him. Picking up the thermos, he made his way between the duffle bags and suitcases to the cockpit. He threw the flask into his backpack and sat down heavily into the left hand seat, securing his seatbelt loosely around his middle before commencing a somewhat abridged version of the preflight checks. It was routine for Johann by now. He had completed the trip to and from the abandoned airfield countless times. As for the Cessna, he manoeuvred the aircraft as effortlessly as if it was merely an extension of his own body.

Johann started the twin engines one at a time and rapidly scanned the gauges and instruments in front of him. He positioned his headset and adjusted the microphone in front of his mouth, although he always kept radio calls to a minimum. He switched on the electrics and, as the lights of the cockpit came alive, he deftly pushed buttons, turned knobs and manipulated controls until the checks were complete. He was full of fuel and, along with the duffle bags and suitcases, Johann was also aware that the Cessna weighed considerably more than its maximum takeoff weight limit. It wasn't the first time. In fact, it was the norm. He'd loaded the cargo as carefully as he could in an attempt to keep the weight and balance of the aircraft in check but it was a common problem which he frequently had to overcome.

He had learned that Rusty, or indeed anyone tasked with the job of determining the amount of cargo for each flight, apparently had no idea about the risks of an overloaded aircraft. Arguing the point had proven fruitless and Johann regularly found himself uttering a brief prayer on takeoff as the Cessna skimmed the tops of trees and bushes in an attempt to get airborne, the stall warner shrieking hysterically at him. So far each takeoff had been successful and Johann grew bolder with each flight. But he knew the day would come when the aircraft would be so overloaded it simply wouldn't make it off the ground, or would struggle a few feet into the air before stalling into an uncontrollable descent, crash-landing back onto the runway or into a field or swamp beyond.

As Johann eased the throttles away from him, the noise of the engines grew louder and the aircraft began rolling forwards. The wind was light and although he would have a slight headwind on the way back to Antigua, it would have little impact on the overall flight time. Assuming he could get airborne, he anticipated an uneventful trip, as usual. Aside from the weight issue, the flight was legal, almost. In the darkness of the early hours, Johann would cruise at low level, under the radar, across uninhabited terrain and sea and coastline before climbing to around nine thousand feet somewhere near Key West International Airport from which a flight plan to Antigua had been filed. An anonymous employee at the airport, whom Johann had never met, would activate the flight plan and the flight would suddenly be on the radar, legal, aboveboard. *I'll take care of the paper shuffling, you just fly the damn plane,* Rusty had frequently reminded Johann.

Over two years, Rusty had kept his word and these days, Johann actually found himself believing he might never be caught. It seemed the Ramirez Cartel, and the powerful drug lord Alejandro

Ortega, had tentacles in every transport hub, every government agency, every police department and every other jurisdiction which mattered. Strings were pulled, palms were greased, deals were made and anyone who stepped out of line wound up as a tragic accident, the details of which were neatly covered up. Evidence would mysteriously vanish, witnesses would unexplainably disappear, but everyone would look the other way.

The Cessna Titan taxied across the apron towards the threshold of the crudely paved runway. There was little light from the crescent moon, but Johann was more than familiar with the layout of the disused airstrip and could navigate the taxiways from the feel of the uneven concrete beneath the wheels of the aircraft. He lined up for takeoff and glanced across to his right, to the derelict hangars which stood dark and silent. To his left was thick undergrowth masking swamps and marshland. There was no one around for miles. He was alone. Even the sky above would be deserted in the early hours of the morning, save for a handful of cargo flights and the occasional passenger jet heading north from South America.

Johann scanned the gauges and instruments for a final time and checked his watch. His right hand pushed the throttles of both engines forward and the RPM needles began to dial clockwise around the gauges. Johann released the brakes and the Cessna began to roll, gathering speed. As the engine noise increased, the wheels rattled over the paved runway and Johann stared intently ahead, glancing at the airspeed indicator every few seconds. He knew the speed necessary for takeoff at maximum weight but the aircraft was heavier than this. And the heavier the aircraft, the greater the speed required to get airborne. The current weight of the Cessna was beyond anything written in the pilot's operating handbook. This kind of flying relied not on textbook knowledge, but on experience, the feel of the aircraft and the pilot's own willingness to take risks. And the greatest risk of all was an engine failure on takeoff.

Sure, Johann knew the exact length of the runway. He knew the airfield elevation was a few feet above sea level and the air temperature was eighty-four degrees. These were essential components which determined the performance of an aircraft. He had been over the calculations many times in his head, like always. But even so, no pilot in his right mind would ever take off with an aircraft this much over the weight limit.

The throttles were at full power and the engines roared as the Cessna continued gathering speed, moving closer towards the end of the runway beyond which was an alligator-infested swamp. Beads of sweat ran down Johann's forehead. His right hand was steady on the throttles, his left hand on the yoke. As the speed increased, he gently eased the yoke back, feeling for the aircraft's desire to fly. Through the darkness the end of the runway loomed closer and he held his breath. He eased the yoke back still further, blinking the sweat out of his eyes. He had nearly reached the end of the runway.

Suddenly, he felt the lift from the airflow over the wings. The stall warner shrieked loudly as he felt the nose wheel and then the main wheels struggle to leave the runway. He took a shallow breath. The undercarriage skimmed the long grass at the end; the Cessna was barely airborne under the weight of the cargo. He gradually increased the climb rate, little by little, wiping the sweat from his eyes. Finally, he retracted the landing gear and made a shallow turn onto the heading for Key West. Within a minute he had reached his low-level cruising altitude. He settled in for the flight back to Antigua.

FIFTEEN

03:30 am, Friday, September 20
Villa Bella Casa, Sugar Reef Bay

The body lay face up and fully clothed in the middle of the concrete floor of the cistern. There were dark ligature marks around the neck, which was bloated and swollen. The eyes were puffy and partially open with pinpoint marks, reddish purple in colour, on the eyeballs. There was a trickle of dried blood at one corner of the mouth from an abrasion on the lower lip, which was swollen, cracked and bloody. A gash covered in dark, dried blood could be seen on the right side of the forehead, perhaps from some kind of blunt force trauma or a fall to the ground.

Suddenly, the game had changed. The images from the surveillance cameras of Villa Bella Casa had suggested that he had been working alone, but now they knew that there must have been someone else with him, the murderer, his killer, who remained off camera the whole time. Which meant that two people had managed to evade the officers at the access road and the villa gates.

'Strangulation or blunt force trauma?' Mitch's voice broke the silence.

'ME's on her way,' Edella called from above, 'and the police are en route too.'

'Thanks Edella,' Delano replied.

As well as determining the cause of death, the medical examiner would also provide an accurate estimation of the time of death, although Delano and the other members of the CDSLI knew that the corpse of Quincy Moran could not be more than fifteen hours old. The ambient temperature in the below ground cistern was cool compared to the room directly above. Although rigor mortis had set in and the corpse was stiff and immobile, the coolness of the air had slowed the onset of decomposition and thus, the smell which accompanied rotting flesh. In addition, the air was dry thanks to a small dehumidifier humming quietly in one corner which would also help to delay putrefaction. Above the dehumidifier was the inlet by which rainwater from the roof would normally have flowed into the cistern, but it had been carefully sealed off. Someone had intended the cistern to remain completely dry. The reason for this became clear as, in the dimness of the single light bulb which illuminated the secret underground space, Delano, Hyacinth and Mitch gazed around them. The other four members of the CDSLI peered through the gap between the circular base of the floor under the table and the floor of the dining room.

The cistern was constructed of concrete, probably cast-in-place and reinforced with steel rods, although it was impossible to tell for certain. The interior walls and floor of the cistern were smooth and looked as though they'd been coated with some kind of cement plaster and a cement-base sealant to protect against leakage. Lining three of the four walls were neat stacks of United States dollar bills held together with mustard-coloured currency bands.

'Mustard bill straps,' Delano commented. 'The bills are in one hundreds.'

The rectangular-shaped cistern was large in proportion to the size of the villa, as Delano had suspected it would be. The storage capacity of a rainwater cistern depended on several factors: the amount of rainfall, the roof-catchment area available for collecting that rainfall, the daily water requirements of the household and the amount of cash available to build the cistern. All except the first of these factors could be controlled to some extent by the owner of the cistern. When it came to Villa Bella Casa, cash had clearly been of no object. Like the rest of the place, no expense had been spared with the construction of the cistern. Delano estimated its dimensions to be roughly twenty-five feet long, eighteen feet wide and twelve feet high, giving the space a storage capacity of approximately forty thousand US gallons. The stacks of bulk currency stretched the length and breadth of each wall and were of various heights.

'How much d'you think we're looking at here boss?' Mitch asked.

'I'd say close to one hundred million dollars,' Delano replied. Mitch gave a low whistle.

'Where's the rest of it then?' Hyacinth said.

Mitch looked at her in disbelief.

'What d'you mean *the rest of it*?' he asked incredulously. 'Isn't this enough for you Hyacinth?'

'To be honest, no,' Hyacinth replied bluntly. 'Sure, there's a lot here, but think about it. We've just seized Jacobs's yacht with a payload of nearly four and a half thousand pounds of cocaine worth close to seventy-five million US dollars. I don't know how long he's been doing this, or how often he makes the sailing trips down to Trinidad, or what he does with the cash he gets from this little enterprise, but if he's moving that much cocaine in one shipment alone I'm thinking he should have a lot more currency kicking around than what we're looking at here. Where's he hiding it?'

'You mean where else *here*? At the villa?' Mitch asked.

'Probably not.' Delano spoke. 'But I'm inclined to agree with Hyacinth on the amount of currency we'd expect to find; there should be more. As to where, it's doubtful Jacobs would spread it around his property for the very reason we demonstrated yesterday: the risk of a thorough search should he ever be caught redhanded. The more hiding places, the greater the chance of one of them being discovered. I'd say this is it as far as the villa's concerned.'

'Perhaps this is a temporary stash site till Jacobs moves it on to someplace else,' Nerissa suggested from above.

'Which could be anywhere,' Delano said. 'Jacobs is lawyering up but we'll have another crack at him later today.'

'Don't suppose Quincy's got his cell phone on him, does he?' Brandon asked through the gap in the ceiling.

Mitch pulled out a pair of disposable gloves and put them on. He kneeled next to the body and gently patted the pockets of the shirt and jeans. He shook his head.

'Nope. No phone,' he said, glancing up at the rest of them, 'unless it's in one of the back pockets of his jeans, but we can't move the body until the ME gets here.'

'What about the keys to his truck?' Edella asked. Mitch patted the body up and down once more, sliding his hand carefully into each pocket. When he reached the top pocket of Quincy's shirt, he paused before pulling out a crumpled piece of paper. He unfolded it and held it up for Delano and Hyacinth to examine. It contained scribbled notes in list form, written in black ink.

'Looks like yesterday's work schedule,' Mitch said.

'Eight a.m., Hamilton Bay, JP villa.' Hyacinth began reading aloud. 'Ten a.m., Falmouth, LT. One p.m., Willoughby. Three-thirty p.m., Sugar Reef.'

'Quincy's day didn't exactly go according to plan then,' Brandon said from above.

Mitch took a snapshot of the paper with his phone before refolding it and replacing it in Quincy's top pocket.

'What's JP and LT?' Edella asked. 'Some kind of a code for something?'

'They could be the initials of Quincy's employers, or the owners of the properties he worked at,' Delano replied. 'Remember the first call Quincy received yesterday morning? It was from someone called Jay Palmer. In light of the fact that Quincy's first job of the day was allegedly at Hamilton Bay, it's possible it was at a property belonging to Jay Palmer.'

'Maybe Jay Palmer was calling to let him know what work needed doing there,' Hyacinth suggested.

'As for LT, I've no idea what those initials might stand for,' Delano went on.

'We should check for property owners around the Falmouth area, or Falmouth Harbour, with the initials LT,' Nerissa said. 'There aren't any initials next to Willoughby; you think he means Willoughby *Bay*? Perhaps he had work at more than one property there and was employed by multiple owners. Same goes for Sugar Reef Bay. He seems to have structured his day geographically, starting at Hamilton Bay and working his way east to Sugar Reef.'

'Until Jacobs threw a spanner in the works and asked him to go check on this place,' Mitch said.

'Could Jacobs have set him up?' Hyacinth asked, staring at Quincy's lifeless body.

The question was left unanswered as Nerissa announced the arrival of Lianne Henderson, the medical examiner, and three police officers known to Delano and his team.

'Wendell Rivera's on his way over from Tamarind Point,' one of the officers said with a slight grimace. 'Apparently this is connected to the case he's working there.'

The officers and Lianne climbed down the stepladder into the cistern and Nerissa and Brandon passed various kit bags and items of equipment to them from above. Delano brought them up to speed with the circumstances surrounding the discovery of Quincy's body before they set to work processing the crime scene. Mitch and Hyacinth climbed the stepladder up to the dining room but Delano hung back.

'Cause of death?' he queried as Lianne knelt by Quincy's body, placing her medical bag beside her. She was approximately forty years old and petite in stature. She wore her thick hair scraped back from her face in a tight bun and was dressed in a navy boiler suit with her name embroidered on the front pocket. As she knelt, she spent a few moments examining the body before responding.

'You're asking if it was blunt force trauma or strangulation, right?' she said as one of the police officers began taking photographs.

'Yeah,' Delano replied.

'Obviously you'll need to wait for my final report before you quote me, but I'd probably say…' Lianne paused and looked back down at the body. 'This laceration on the side of Quincy's head occurred prior to death; you can tell by the amount of dried blood we've got here. So it's logical to assume that the blow to the head wasn't fatal, and the killer finished the job with a rope round his neck.' Lianne examined the head and neck more closely before producing a pair of tweezers and a plastic evidence bag.

'There are clear ligature marks on his neck here and here which suggest the killer used a fairly thick piece of rope,' she continued. 'Looks like we've got a few fibres from the rope too; we'll get them analysed and see what we've got.'

'Thanks Lianne,' Delano said. 'I'll leave you to it.'

He exchanged a few words with the three police officers who were busy taking photographs, video footage and gathering evidence, before he climbed the stepladder into the dining room, rejoining the rest of the team.

'Poor Quincy,' Edella said. 'I feel so sorry for his family. His mom will be heartbroken. I guess she had no idea he was mixed up in all this.'

She was interrupted by Brandon who held his cell phone out to Delano.

'It's Max. For you boss. Says he's tried to call you a few times but it keeps going to voicemail.'

'Thanks. I doubt there's any cell reception down in the cistern.' Delano took the phone from Brandon. 'Max, hi, how are you?'

'Delano, I heard they found Quincy's truck.'

'Yeah, they did. The police are on their way back to your aunt's house. There's more bad news I'm afraid.'

'What? What's happened?'

'We found Quincy's body.'

There was a brief silence at the end of the line.

'I'm so sorry Max,' Delano said.

'Did they find it at the bottom of the cliff?' Delano could hear Max struggling to maintain composure.

'No, they didn't. It's possible Quincy was never anywhere near Tamarind Point, where his truck was found. We discovered his body in the below ground cistern at Villa Bella Casa.'

'What? Oliver Jacobs's place up at Sugar Reef?'

'Yeah. It looks like Quincy was murdered.'

'Murdered? H — how?' Max could hardly get the words out.

'He was strangled.' Delano decided to keep the details scant. Max was distressed enough and the police were en route to break the news with more detail to the family.

'I — I just can't believe this,' Max said through broken sobs. 'I can't believe it. How could this happen Delano? What am I gonna say to my aunt?'

'The police are on their way to talk to you and your aunt right now,' Delano said gently, 'and the forensics team are in the cistern working up the crime scene as we speak.'

'But *who* Delano?' Max sobbed. 'Who did this?'

'I don't know Max. And, as you know, this is out of my jurisdiction now. It's over to the police. It's my job to follow up on the cocaine, but you know I'll keep abreast of any information relating to Quincy as well.'

'Thanks Delano. I appreciate that. Oh and I meant to say, I reached out to as many of Quincy's friends and family members as I could to see if anyone knew anything which might be helpful.'

'Any luck?'

'Not really. No one knew much at all although there was something…'

'Go on.'

'I'm not sure if it's relevant but apparently Quincy was involved in some kind of altercation last week at The Jungle, that reggae club in St. John's.'

'Yeah, I know it. Sleazy place. Lloyd's a bouncer there. Likes to keep his hand in with the underworld.'

'I'm not sure what the fight was about, but apparently it was with some guy named Vinnie Trickett.'

'I know him,' Delano said. 'He's a lowlife drug pusher. Runs a fairly slick operation selling drugs on street corners and further afield — to the far corners of the island — through social media and text messages and so on.'

'What was Quincy doing getting mixed up with him? This doesn't sound good.'

'I'll check in with Lloyd, see if he's heard anything before we start jumping to conclusions.'

'Yeah, of course. Well, other than that, I got nothing,' Max said sombrely. 'Oh Delano, the police have just arrived. Latoya's here too with Aunt Junella and me, and a few other family members have stopped by. I just don't know how my aunt's going to take this.'

'Go and be with your family. And take care yourself Max,' Delano said. 'We got this.' He promised to stay in touch and they said goodbye. The rest of the team were moving furniture to clear a path from the front door to the entrance of the cistern in preparation for the removal of Quincy's body and the one hundred dollar bill stacks. The discovery of Quincy's body had muddied the waters somewhat. A routine drugs bust had led to a homicide which would mean a joint investigation with the Antigua Police Department.

Delano wondered how much Oliver Jacobs, back in his temporary cell at the CDSLI headquarters, knew of Quincy's demise. Had he personally organised the hit? If so, how had he set it up from the confines of his cell? He'd been in custody since his unexpected rescue and subsequent arrest. His only contact with anyone on the outside had been with Quincy himself. And now Quincy was dead.

But if Oliver Jacobs hadn't been responsible for orchestrating Quincy's murder, someone else must have known about his phone call to Quincy. Or perhaps someone predicted the course of events after the drug bust on the Atratus and Oliver's arrest. While details of the bust hadn't been made public, anyone could have listened into Oliver's Mayday call to the Coast Guard on channel sixteen and headed to English Harbour to wait for the arrival of the Atratus. Someone, somewhere had been watching and planning. Someone, somewhere knew about the one hundred million dollars in Oliver's cistern. And someone, somewhere, had made contact with Quincy, luring him to Villa Bella Casa. Whether Quincy went under duress or of his own free will, Delano wasn't sure. One thing he was certain of though, was that Quincy's killer hadn't planned on the CDSLI's discovery of the cistern, and thus Quincy's body and the hundred million dollars. Delano knew that every move the team made was being watched. And he intended to find out by whom.

SIXTEEN

08:00 am, Friday, September 20
CDSLI Headquarters, English Harbour

The man in handcuffs, sitting at a crudely constructed wooden table, was not the man Graymond and Alicia had been expecting to see when Lloyd ushered them into the small interview room. Although they had remained in touch, the last time Graymond had seen his former accountant in the flesh — at a Mexican joint on the outskirts of London back in 2016 — the physical effects of nearly two decades of alcohol, cocaine and all-night parties were beginning to manifest themselves in Oliver Jacobs. The borderline obese forty year old was popping pills for high blood pressure, high cholesterol and various other self-inflicted ailments. For a brief moment, on that drab November evening in 2016, Graymond had actually lamented the state his friend was in.

Nearly three years later, however, Oliver Jacobs was a different man. Tanned and toned, with biceps and muscular thighs bulging under temporary prison clothes: a dark blue scrubs-like shirt and pants, Oliver was the picture of vitality and health. His short cropped hair lacked any signs of greying around his temples and was obviously dyed. He wouldn't have looked out of place on the cover of a men's fitness magazine.

'Jacobs, what the hell happened to you?' Graymond exclaimed as he took a seat on the other side of the table. The room was basic with whitewashed walls and a wooden floor. Rays of sunlight streamed through a large window crisscrossed with steel bars overlooking the dockyard.

'Gee thanks. Aloha to you too Gray,' Oliver replied. 'I suppose you could say island life suits me. These days I swim a lot, run a lot, sail a lot… There's nothing like spending time out on the ocean to reflect on the true meaning of life.' He shifted his gaze to Alicia who slid gracefully into a chair beside Graymond. 'Ahh, the lovely Alicia. How are you beautiful?'

'Oh, you know, kicking back and relaxing with a cocktail on the first day of my vacation, soaking up the sunshine, starting work on my tan…'

'Just as feisty as ever I see,' Oliver replied with a smile. 'You always were my kind of woman. It's a shame Gray got to you first, but if you ever fancy something a little bit more *exciting,* call me. You know where I am.'

'I sure do know where you are Jacobs,' Alicia replied wryly, 'and what could be more tempting than a first date in a prison cell? It beats a candlelit dinner in a fancy restaurant any day.'

'I have handcuffs.' Oliver winked, raising his manacled wrists off the table.

'Yes, you do,' Alicia replied. 'Which brings us nicely to the question of why we're here.'

'Ah, yes, that. Well, first of all I suppose I need to apologise,' Oliver began. 'I mean, I feel bad, inviting you guys out here to stay with me and then getting arrested on the day you arrive. Bad form on my part I'm afraid. But fear not, it's only a temporary disruption to our plans.' He turned to the man sitting beside him. 'This is my lawyer, Harvey Webster. He's the best damn defence lawyer on the island. I guarantee he'll have me out of this place in a couple of hours.'

Harvey stood up hastily and shook hands with Graymond before turning to Alicia who offered her hand. He was wearing a pale pink shirt, open at the neck, beneath an expensive-looking charcoal linen suit. A neatly trimmed goatee and sideburns were the only hair on his otherwise bald head. His dark brown eyes, which assumed a distinctly serious expression, peered through oversized square-frame glasses which would have been more fitting on the catwalk of a fashion show than in a crude interview room at the CDSLI headquarters.

'Harvey Webster. Pleasure to meet you both,' he said in a deep voice.

'Webster, these are friends of mine: Graymond Sharkey and Alicia Clayton.' Oliver looked at each of them in turn as he made the introductions. 'Actually, before we were friends I was Gray's accountant. But then he went and got himself banged up in a supermax for a double murder.'

Harvey barely flinched.

'Turns out he didn't do it after all though,' Oliver went on cheerfully. 'Served all seventeen miserable years of his life sentence for nothing. We all knew he was innocent, of course.' He winked at Graymond.

'I really appreciated your loyalty back then Jacobs.' The reply was laced with sarcasm. 'You visited me how many times over those seventeen years?'

'A couple? Three maybe?'

'Try once.'

'I was busy back then,' Oliver protested. 'I did write you on a regular basis though.'

'That's strange. I only received one letter from you the whole time I was inside.'

'Really? I could've sworn it was more than that. I guess the letters got lost in the mail.'

'That must be it,' Graymond replied. 'Anyway Jacobs, you asked to see us. Stop wasting our time and tell us why we're here.'

Harvey gave Oliver a warning look before he replied.

'Don't worry, they're trustworthy,' Oliver said. 'It's why they're here.' He turned back to Graymond and Alicia. 'Where was I? Oh yes, my apologies, once again, for…'

'Yeah all right Jacobs, you don't need to keep sugarcoating this with apologies, we were questioned at the airport yesterday when we arrived. We have some idea what this is about.'

'You were questioned *already*?' Oliver asked in surprise. 'By whom? Surely not one of those interfering busybodies from the drug squad?'

'Minutes after we stepped off the plane we were escorted from passport control by security,' Graymond replied. 'And yes, we were interviewed by the CDSLI.'

'I had no idea,' Oliver said, genuinely surprised. 'No one tells me anything around here. I'm truly sorry about that.'

'Sure you are,' Alicia said.

'What's going on Jacobs?' Graymond asked. 'And I mean *really* what's going on?'

Oliver was about to reply when the door opened and a man stuck his head into the room. He glanced beyond Graymond and Alicia towards Harvey.

'Mr. Webster, sorry to interrupt but could I talk to you for a moment please?'

'Sure Delano.' Harvey got to his feet. 'I'll be back in a minute.' He gave Oliver another warning stare as he strode across the room to where the man held the door open for him. Once it had closed behind them, Oliver leaned forwards in his chair. He looked earnestly at Graymond and Alicia.

'Okay, I'll be straight with you. I'm in trouble and I need your help.'

'I think we get that,' Graymond said.

'I'm serious Gray. I've got more enemies than I can keep track of these days and very few friends. In fact, right now you're the only people I can trust.'

'Spare us the emotional crap, Jacobs.'

'All right, but at least hear me out,' Oliver went on. '*You* were once on this side of the table, wrongfully convicted of a crime you didn't commit.'

'Yeah, but Jacobs, that's just it, I was *wrongfully* convicted. Don't try telling me you thought that white powder they found on your boat was laundry detergent.'

'Okay, so maybe the cargo wasn't *entirely* lawful...'

'Not *entirely lawful?* For heaven's sake Jacobs, you had seventy-five million dollars' worth of cocaine on board.'

'All right, all right.' Oliver held up his hands. 'If it helps, I did everything I could not to call out the Coast Guard in that storm.'

'Oh well that makes it all okay then. Come on though Jacobs, drug running? Really? I know your past isn't exactly wholesome, and I guessed your seemingly innocent life out here wasn't completely kosher either, but I didn't actually believe you'd sink to the murky depths of narco trafficking.'

'If you're not interested in my side of the story then you may as well leave now,' Oliver said crossly. 'But you're nothing more than a hypocrite, Sharkey. You might not be guilty of murder but I know your past better than most; fraud, tax evasion, smuggling high end art and antiquities… Do I need to go on? You can sit there and judge me all you like, but at the end of the day you're no better than I am.'

'That's in the *past*,' Graymond retorted angrily. He stood up, sending his chair flying. 'I've done my time, as you've so helpfully reminded everyone, so don't talk to me about…'

'Gray, sit down,' Alicia said quickly. She retrieved his chair from the side of the room and placed it upright next to the table. '*Both* of you need to chill.' She looked straight at Oliver as Graymond reluctantly took his seat.

'Jacobs, we know what you've done so there's no point trying to sell us a bunch of lies. What d'you want from us? You looking for someone to post bail for you?'

'That *was* one of the things I was planning on asking you, but Webster just told me the magistrate will likely be denying all requests for bail,' Oliver replied. 'Apparently the man from the CDSLI in charge of the investigation, Delano Reid, the guy who just stuck his head in the door, informed Webster himself this morning. I'll probably have to remain in custody for now.'

'Are you a flight risk or something?' Graymond asked. 'They think you'll pose a serious threat to others…?'

'Who knows? Maybe it's something to do with the fact that Delano hasn't exactly taken to me.'

'Why on earth would that be I wonder?' Alicia said. Oliver ignored the sarcasm.

'It's probably more to do with the sheer quantity of cocaine you had on board your yacht,' Graymond said. 'What's your lawyer's take on this? If he's the best on the island…'

'Well obviously I have as much of a constitutional right to bail as the next person, so we're still going ahead and applying to the court…'

'Which will have to find substantial grounds for rejecting bail,' Alicia added.

'Correct. But Gray's right, the amount of cocaine they found on my boat does rather put me in the serious offences league so to speak. Webster says if bail *is* denied, he'll appeal, naturally, but it'll take time. Legal stuff always does. Anyway, Webster says there're strings he can pull, so it's a case of wait and see. If anyone can get results, he can. Sure, he's expensive but he comes highly recommended and I'll pay whatever it takes. I can afford it.'

'What about your consular representative from the British High Commission?' Alicia asked. 'Can they do anything?'

'Apparently they only do welfare stuff; make sure I'm being fairly treated and so on. They don't get involved in legal matters.'

'Have you been contacted by anyone from the High Commission yet?' Alicia asked.

'Yeah, some lady called me.'

'And?'

'I told her to shove it.'

'You what?'

'What was she gonna do anyway? Check they've given me a toothbrush?'

'That's not really the point Jacobs,' Alicia replied wearily. 'The idea is that they're on your side. They're sort of like your advocate when it comes to things like health issues, security concerns, the way you're treated in prison — which I can't imagine would be very pretty out here — things like that. It's their duty to provide help to any British National who gets arrested in a foreign country, no matter what for. You may need them.'

'Meh. I'll take my chances,' Oliver said with a shrug. 'I'd rather have you guys on my side.'

'To do what exactly?' Graymond asked. 'If we can't post bail for you…'

'I need you to find someone,' Oliver replied, suddenly lowering his voice.

'*Find someone*?' Alicia asked.

'Yeah.'

'Who?'

'My gardener. Well, he sort of does other jobs too. He's sort of a gardener, handyman and pool maintenance man combined.'

'Sorry, did I just hear you right?' Graymond asked with a frown. 'You're about to go down for possession and trafficking of a class A drug and you're worried about finding your pool maintenance guy?'

'You got it.'

'But — why?' Alicia asked.

'When I was first arrested and taken into custody, and the CDSLI granted me my phone call — well, technically I had to ask for it and Webster will be raising the issue with the court, naturally — I called Quincy, that's my maintenance guy's name. I told him to go check on the villa. You know, in light of the storm, gale force winds and heavy rain, I thought it would be a good idea for him to go check on my property, make sure everything was okay.'

'Since when did a phone call to your gardener become more important than one to your lawyer after being arrested?' Graymond asked. 'I'm speaking from personal experience here.'

'Yeah, I get that. Delano said the same. But that one phone call thing is a total myth anyway. It only happens in the movies and on TV. In reality you can make as many damn phone calls as you want. I knew they were always gonna let me call my lawyer so I thought I'd talk to Quincy first and get him to go to the villa, make sure nothing had been damaged by the storm.'

'I'm still struggling to appreciate your order of priorities here,' Graymond said.

'Hear me out man.'

'Okay then. So you call up Quincy and ask him to go check on your villa. What happened next?'

'He never went.'

'How do you know?' Alicia asked after a moment's pause.

'When I called him first thing yesterday morning, he told me he was on a job, but that he'd drop everything and head straight to the villa.'

'How d'you know he didn't do just that?'

'Because when I went to the villa with the CDSLI yesterday afternoon I could tell he hadn't been.'

'*How?*' Alicia asked.

'Because he hadn't done anything I'd asked him to.'

'Such as?'

'Securing the parasols round the pool, putting the soft furnishings from the wicker chairs on the lanai out to dry, stuff like that…'

'Oh come on Jacobs,' Graymond interrupted. 'You seriously think he's gonna head over to the house of a man who's just been arrested for possession of cocaine to tie up a few parasols and plump a few cushions? Last thing he'd want to be is mixed up in that kinda thing. He probably got spooked and went to ground after he took your call. If I was him, I wouldn't want to be found anywhere near your villa — a crime scene hotbed — with the police crawling all over it.'

'No, he wouldn't do that. He knew the CDSLI were questioning me but he didn't know why and he didn't know anything about the cocaine,' Oliver replied firmly. 'He promised he'd go check on the place for me.'

'Of course he did,' Graymond said wearily.

'You're not getting it Gray,' Oliver said with a note of frustration. 'Quincy promised me he'd go and he meant it. He wouldn't promise and then not show up.'

'You really believe that, don't you?' Graymond said. He almost felt sorry for Oliver.

'Yeah. I do. But whatever you think of me, the fact of the matter is Quincy never made it to the villa. And that's a problem. Something's wrong.'

'Why d'you want us to find him so badly?' Alicia asked.

'I'm worried about him,' Oliver replied. 'He's a good guy. The last thing I want is for something to have happened to him because of me. I just want to know he's okay, that's all.'

'Since when have you ever cared about the consequences of your actions affecting other people?' Graymond asked with a note of disbelief.

'Maybe I *have* changed,' Oliver shrugged. 'Like I told you, I've had a lot of time to reflect on things.'

'I'm sorry but I'm just not buying this,' Graymond said. 'And anyway, if your lawyer's so good, why don't you employ his services to find your handyman and leave us out of this?'

'I'd rather not get Webster involved if you don't mind,' Oliver replied. 'Let him focus on the drugs charges and my bail application, and if it comes to it, I hope you guys will agree to sign my bail bond but right now, I just need you to find Quincy. That's the priority and you're the only ones I trust with this. Track him down and find him, like you've found other people before. Whatever it takes. And before you ask, I will pay you very, very well.'

'Forget the payment thing Jacobs,' Alicia said. 'I'm not sure I want any of your drugs money anyway. Something tells me you're still not being entirely truthful with us. What is it you're not saying?'

Alicia watched the man across the table carefully. For the briefest of moments, a strange look flashed across Oliver's face before he quickly regained his composure and resumed his steely gaze.

'Okay, well there are a couple of things,' he said slowly, 'but I'm not sure if they're relevant or not.'

'Such as?' Graymond asked.

'When I went to my villa with the CDSLI yesterday, Delano asked to see my laptop and the surveillance footage on my security system recorder.'

'As expected.'

'Of course. Well, he found the video recorder, but all the surveillance footage had been erased from the hard drive. And my laptop wasn't there. It was missing.'

'You think Quincy had something to do with it?' Graymond asked.

'No, I don't. Not at all.'

'But Delano thinks otherwise,' Alicia said. It was more of a statement than a question.

'Yes.'

'I might be inclined to agree with him given the circumstances,' Alicia added.

'What reason would Quincy have for deleting the footage and taking your laptop?' Graymond asked.

'That's just it. He wouldn't have any reason. He wouldn't have even known about them anyway.'

'What was on your surveillance footage?' Graymond asked.

'Nothing,' Oliver replied firmly. 'As you know, I've been away the last few days, down in Trinidad. The villa's been all shut up.'

'Could anyone else have been there?' Alicia asked.

'No. No one. And when I'm home it's just me by my lonesome self.'

'Who else has access?' Graymond asked.

'Just Quincy.'

'He has access to the villa itself?' Alicia queried.

'Yes.'

'So now I'm curious,' Alicia said. 'I know many homeowners who employ a handyman, a gardener, a pool maintenance man. But of those homeowners, I don't think I know any who give such people unrestricted access to the properties themselves. How is it that Quincy has access to your villa?'

'It's mainly because I'm often away,' Oliver replied. 'I just like to know there's someone here with a means of entry to the villa, just in case. Like I said, I don't have many friends. Quincy may just be a maintenance man, but he's trustworthy and knows the place inside out; he was the gardener for the previous owner too. Plus some of the control switches for the garden lights and so on are inside the villa. I like him to have access to those too, just in case there's a problem when I'm away.'

'So if not Quincy, who else might have erased the surveillance footage and taken your laptop, and why?' Graymond asked.

'I honestly have no clue.'

'Oh come on Jacobs,' Alicia said impatiently. 'You must have some idea. Friends, business acquaintances, sailing buddies…?'

'I really don't have any of those.'

'Who's your contact in Antigua?' Graymond asked.

'You mean for the cocaine shipments?'

'No, for your barber's. Of course I mean for the cocaine shipments.'

'What does this have to do with Quincy?' Oliver asked cautiously.

'Everything and nothing right now,' Graymond replied. 'But if you want us to help you, you'll have to trust us and tell us everything you know.'

'Okay. I trust you. But this doesn't go any further than this room. Understood?'

'Like I said, you'll have to trust us. Who's your contact?'

'All right then. He goes by the name of Ray, but I think that's probably an alias.'

'Last name?'

'I just know him as Ray.'

'How did you meet Ray?' Alicia asked.

'In a bar.'

'Here in Antigua?'

'No. Jamaica. About a year ago. Ray's British though. An expat.'

'How does he communicate with you?'

'Sometimes he calls but it's mostly through text messages.'

'You have his number?'

'It probably won't help, he uses a different burner every time.'

'So enlighten us Jacobs, tell us how this works,' Graymond said.

'It's pretty simple really. The cocaine originates primarily in Colombia and usually traverses Venezuela before it's taken across to Trinidad. When there's a shipment of cocaine ready to be collected, Ray sends me the details a few days ahead by text; the location and time of the pickup and so on. And then I sail down to Trinidad on the Atratus, my yacht. You two would love it by the way, it's a fifty-seven foot Beneteau with cruising speeds of up to…'

'Get back on point Jacobs,' Alicia said sharply.

'Sorry. Where was I? Oh yeah, Trinidad. I sail down there in my yacht — it usually takes about two to three days, depending on the sea conditions and the weather — and meet my contact, a hispanic guy who goes by the name of Ernesto. The pickup's usually at the Port of Brighton — it's a very small port in southwestern Trinidad — although it changes from time to time. Ernesto and I, and sometimes a couple of other guys, load the cocaine onto the Atratus — it's packed in bales and stashed in plastic containers — and then I set sail back to Antigua. There's a small marina in Saint Lucia where I stop for fuel, water, food and extra supplies if I need them. There's usually just enough time for a quick sundowner with the marina owner who gets a generous payoff of cocaine in exchange for his cooperation and silence. It's a nice little arrangement. And then I set sail for the second leg of the journey.

'I always time my arrival to get back here at night, when it's dark. I've a mooring in the bay at Sugar Reef. If you saw the other yachts moored nearby you'd understand that it's very private and very exclusive, perfect for a clandestine transaction of illicit substances and currency between two parties. Once I'm back at the mooring, I send Ray a text message. This is the slightly creepy part: within minutes an old fishing trawler appears out of nowhere, like a ghost ship. It moors alongside the yacht and two guys jump on board and start offloading the drugs onto the trawler. When everything's been transferred, they dump the bundles of cash onto the Atratus and disappear back into the darkness.'

'And that's it?' Alicia asked.

'Pretty much. After that I secure the yacht and swim to shore.'

'What about the cash?' Graymond asked.

'I leave it stashed in lockers on the yacht and come back the next night with a small RIB to retrieve it. It's pretty safe out there in the bay.'

'You take it back to your villa or someplace else?'

'The villa. The money's stored there temporarily until I move it.'

'The CDSLI searched your villa yesterday,' Alicia said.

'They didn't find the money.'

'Did Quincy know about the money?' Graymond asked.

Before Oliver had a chance to respond the door opened and Delano entered with Harvey and a man in a police uniform. He was stockily built with a serious, almost threatening glare. The CDSLI officer introduced himself to Graymond and Alicia as he pulled two chairs up to the table from the other side of the room.

'Pleasure to meet you both,' Delano said. 'This is Officer Wendell Rivera,' he gestured to the stocky man in the police uniform, 'he has a few questions for Mr. Jacobs. First though, I'd like to extend my apologies, on behalf of the CDSLI, for your experience at the airport yesterday afternoon.'

'It's no problem at all,' Graymond replied. 'Your officer Brandon was very kind.'

'And the security staff at the airport treated you with courtesy?'

'Earl and Rusty were very professional.'

'Oh, you met Earl and Rusty did you?' Wendell tutted and rolled his eyes as he sank heavily into his chair. 'They're a fine pair, aren't they? More of a comedy duo than airport security professionals if you ask me. I doubt Earl could run more than a few yards in a real emergency and as for Rusty and his damn clipboard…'

'I realise it wasn't the greatest start to your vacation,' Delano interrupted quickly, 'but we had to follow up all lines of inquiry after the Coast Guard rescued Mr. Jacobs here.' He cast a brief glance in Oliver's direction.

'We completely understand,' Alicia said.

'I feel particularly contrite about it all though as your reputations precede you here in Antigua,' Delano added.

'Oh?' Alicia asked in puzzlement.

'I'm reliably informed that you're a respected investigative journalist back in the UK and have been partly responsible for solving a number of crimes there. I'm also aware of your involvement in closing the notorious Rock Palm Resort cold case last year which had gone unsolved for what, twenty-two, twenty-three years?'

'Twenty-three.'

'I hear you were both instrumental in that,' Delano went on. 'In addition, you're very highly regarded by an esteemed mutual friend, Leon Fayer.'

'Leon's a very good friend,' Alicia replied with a smile.

'He tells me he's known you and your parents for over thirty years. You guys go back a long way.'

'This is all very lovely,' Oliver interrupted, 'but I'd quite like to continue the meeting with my lawyer, his time for which I am paying *by the hour*. You've already interrupted proceedings once Officer Reid, so if you don't mind…'

'Don't worry Oliver, I won't bill you for this hour,' Harvey said. 'Delano's here to talk to you with Officer Rivera anyway. There have been a couple of developments.'

'What developments?' Oliver looked from Harvey to Delano to Wendell, and back to Harvey. Wendell, clearly keen to take charge and assert his authority as soon as possible, paused before speaking and looked suspiciously at Graymond and Alicia.

'They're my friends and they're staying,' Oliver said firmly. 'What developments?'

'We can leave the room if you wish,' Graymond offered, sensing Wendell's hesitation.

'Yes, I don't think I can allow…' Wendell began but was immediately cut off by Oliver.

'They're staying,' he snarled. 'If you've got a problem with that then I've got a problem with answering your questions.'

'In light of their involvement with the Rock Palm Resort cold case, I think it would be absolutely fine for Miss Clayton and Mr. Sharkey to stay,' Delano said hastily. 'They may even have a few thoughts of their own.'

Wendell scowled.

'I'm the officer in charge of this case Delano, and I'm afraid…'

Once more, Oliver cut his sentence off: 'Good. That's settled. Now, what developments are you talking about? Have you found Quincy yet?'

'It's interesting you should ask that Mr. Jacobs,' Delano began before Wendell could object further to Graymond and Alicia's presence. 'Because as a matter of fact we have.'

'Oh thank heavens,' Oliver said. There was a measure of relief in his voice. 'Where is he? Can I talk to him?'

'I'm afraid not.'

'Delano's right,' Wendell recovered himself and was anxious not to miss out on any more of the conversation. 'That won't be possible.'

'What? Why?' Oliver asked.

'Quincy's dead.' Wendell uttered the words without feeling.

'*What?*' Oliver asked in horror.

'He was found in the early hours of this morning, murdered,' Wendell went on. 'You wouldn't happen to know anything about that, would you Jacobs?'

'Hold up. Quincy's been *murdered?*' Oliver appeared genuinely shocked. Either he was an accomplished actor or this really was the first he knew about it. '*How?*'

'He was hit on the head with a blunt object and strangled,' Wendell replied, almost enjoying himself.

'But — *why?*'

'I was hoping you'd tell us.'

'I — I don't know why. How could I possibly know anything? I've been locked up in this hell hole for the last twenty-four hours.'

'All this place gives you is an alibi for the crime itself,' Wendell replied. 'It doesn't absolve you from orchestrating the hit.'

'You think *I* had something to do with Quincy's murder?' Oliver shook his head defiantly. 'This is absolutely ridiculous. You couldn't be further from the truth. Where did you find him?'

'See that's the other thing,' Wendell went on. 'We found his body in your below ground cistern. Along with over one hundred million dollars. Oh and you might like to get your guttering looked at. I think there's a blockage somewhere. The rainwater's not going into your cistern, it's just overflowing into the garden.'

Oliver stared straight ahead for a moment. So they had discovered the cistern. He looked crushed, defeated. But his expression was perhaps also one of surprise — shock, even — at the news of Quincy's death.

'I knew something was wrong yesterday,' Oliver said. 'I *told* you something was wrong.' He glanced at Delano. 'I knew Quincy hadn't been to the villa.'

'Quincy *did* go to the villa.' Delano's tone was softer than Wendell's. 'We managed to retrieve the deleted surveillance footage from your video recorder. Quincy was there all right. He sprayed your security cameras with black paint before deactivating the alarm system and letting himself in.'

'You're lying,' Oliver said in a low voice.

'Afraid I'm not Jacobs. And neither is the camera footage. It's all there, along with the deactivation and reactivation times of the alarm system, to which Quincy obviously knew the code.'

'So you get him to spray the cameras, delete the surveillance footage and take your computer.' Wendell attempted to regain control of the interrogation. 'But then something happens. Quincy wasn't the only one at the villa, was he? Who else was there Jacobs?'

'How do *I* know?' Oliver replied, suddenly angry. 'If you hacked into my surveillance footage you should be able to see that for yourselves. And as for asking Quincy to spray the security cameras with paint and *then* delete the footage, what would be the point of that? For starters I *asked* Quincy to go to my villa, so it's not like he needed to hide the fact that he was there. He was *supposed* to be there. And there'd be no reason to erase the camera footage. There was nothing on it anyway. I've been away for the last week. The place has been shut up and unoccupied. The most exciting thing you'd see on *that* would be a bird flying past or Quincy scooping a few leaves out of the pool.'

'Oliver, Quincy didn't venture anywhere near the pool on the footage we recovered,' Delano replied. 'He was much more interested in the cameras. If *you* didn't ask him to spray them, then who did?'

'I've no idea,' Oliver said obstinately.

'Who was at your villa with Quincy?' Wendell asked again.

197

'I don't *know*!' Oliver almost screamed. He lifted his handcuffed hands and slammed them back down on the table with a crash. The police officer annoyed him even more than Delano.

'I think you've pushed this far enough,' Harvey interrupted. 'My client has made it very clear that he neither instructed his gardener to carry out the acts recorded on his surveillance system, nor indeed to subsequently delete the related footage. Unless you've got anything useful to add, I think we're done here.'

'We're certainly not done here,' Wendell said, standing up. 'I'd also like an explanation from Mr. Jacobs as to the origin of the money we found in the cistern at his villa, an estimated one hundred million US dollars.'

'Don't know anything about that either,' Oliver shrugged.

'Oh come on Jacobs,' Wendell said. 'You're wasting my time. And everyone else's. Where'd the money come from?'

'Officer Riviera, or whatever your name is, if I knew the answer to that question, I'd tell you, but I have absolutely no idea about any money in my cistern. It's news to me,' Oliver replied. 'I appreciate your solving the mystery of why the rainwater was flooding into the garden though. I'd often wondered about that. I'll get my maintenance man onto it right away. Oh wait, he's dead.'

'I'm fed up with listening to your crap Jacobs,' Wendell replied coldly. 'Just tell me where the money's from.'

'That's enough Wendell,' Harvey said. 'My client has already given you his answer. And anyway, isn't the money the CDSLI's jurisdiction?'

'It's a joint investigation,' Wendell snapped. He glared at Harvey before looking directly at Oliver. He spoke in a low, threatening tone. 'I know you're lying. And the next time I see you I'll have the evidence I need to prove it.'

'I can hardly wait for that moment,' Oliver replied. 'Now then, moving on, what's happening about my bail application?'

Wendell appeared unable to get any more words out. Delano answered the question.

'That's a matter for the court. Magistrate Gerald Darroux will consider your application at ten o'clock. Don't get your hopes up though.'

'Then we'll be appealing,' Oliver said with a shrug. 'Won't we Webster?'

'Let's see what Magistrate Darroux says first,' Harvey replied calmly.

'Miss Clayton, Mr. Sharkey, it was a pleasure to meet you both, in spite of these unpleasant circumstances,' Delano said, as he pushed back his chair and stood up. 'I'm sure we'll have the opportunity to talk again soon.'

'I'm sure we will,' Graymond replied. With a parting glare at Oliver, Wendell muttered goodbye to the four still seated around the table and followed Delano out of the room. Harvey's cell phone buzzed on the table. He picked it up and glanced at the screen with a frown.

'I'd better reply to this,' he said apologetically. 'Excuse me everyone, I'll be back in a couple of minutes.' He hurried outside and when the door had clicked shut behind him Alicia spoke.

'Well, Jacobs?'

'I can't believe Quincy's dead,' Oliver replied.

'You didn't know about that?' Alicia asked.

'*No!*' Oliver said in an offended tone. 'Of course I didn't.'

'What was he doing spraying the security cameras at your villa?' Graymond asked.

'How do *I* know?' Oliver replied. 'I've been stuck here since yesterday morning. Quincy must've been threatened somehow. He wouldn't willingly do that. He was loyal; he'd *never* betray me.'

'I guess you don't need us to find him anymore though,' Alicia said.

'No, I need you more than ever now.' Oliver stared at her intently.

'What for?' Graymond asked.

'I need you to find Quincy's killer.'

'What?' Alicia asked, shocked.

'No way Jacobs,' Graymond cut in. 'There's no way we're getting involved with this.'

'Please,' Oliver said. 'You solved the Rock Palm murder. It was all over the news out here. I need you guys to do the same again and find out who killed Quincy.'

'No way,' Graymond said again firmly. 'First of all, we're on vacation. Second, the Rock Palm murder was a cold case, over twenty years old and Alicia was directly involved with it. This, on the other hand, is an active investigation with a team of police officers assigned to it. You've got to let them handle it.'

'I don't think so,' Oliver replied. 'I don't trust that jerk Wendell one bit. Would *you*?'

'That's not the point Jacobs,' Alicia said. 'Gray and I can't investigate a murder here in Antigua. It's as simple as that.'

'And we're on vacation anyway,' Graymond said again.

'Come on guys,' Oliver pleaded.

'How do we know you're telling the truth about all this anyway?' Alicia said. 'How do we know you didn't send Quincy to your villa under false pretences to check on the property when really you'd arranged for someone to have him murdered?'

'Why would I do that?' Oliver asked.

'Because Quincy knew something that could incriminate you further in this whole thing and you needed to have him silenced,' Graymond replied.

Oliver paused for a moment before speaking calmly and quietly. He looked directly at Graymond and Alicia, making eye contact.

'You have to believe me,' he began. 'I'm being completely honest with you. Fine, I might be a worthless drug trafficker who was caught redhanded with a boatload of cocaine, but I'm innocent of Quincy's murder. I have no idea who's behind this, no idea who'd want him dead. I really did ask him to go to my villa to check on things — not for any other reason — and apart from you and the CDSLI officers, I've spoken to no one. And I have no idea who else knew that Quincy went to the villa yesterday morning. As far as I'm concerned the only people privy to this information were the CDSLI officers themselves.'

'That's great Jacobs, but you need to tell that to your lawyer and Officer Rivera, not us,' Graymond replied, standing up. 'We're on vacation. Come on Alicia.'

'Gray, *please*,' Oliver said.

'Gray's right, Quincy's murder is a matter for the police, not us,' Alicia said. 'I'm sorry but we can't help you out with this. If you need us to post bail, you know where we are.'

Oliver remained silent as Graymond and Alicia left the room. They nodded to the man outside the door who'd introduced himself as Lloyd Kelly, Special Consultant to the CDSLI. He directed them towards the reception area.

'You think Jacobs is telling the truth?' Alicia asked when they were out of earshot.

'Usually I'd say no,' Graymond replied, 'but this time, I'm not so sure.'

SEVENTEEN

08:55 am, Friday, September 20
St. John's Magistrates' Court, Antigua

Magistrate Gerald Darroux was suffering from a bad cold and had already decided that he wasn't feeling gracious to anyone that morning, least of all the nefarious miscreants who should know better than to break the law. Already running a fever, on his arrival at the court building, Magistrate Darroux had been irked to discover that the air conditioning unit had still not been repaired from the previous week.

'We're working until eleven and then everyone's going home,' he had snapped to Anne, the court clerk, as she handed him a printed list of the cases he was due to hear that morning. 'We'll have staff passing out in the heat. This building's unfit for purpose.'

'I'll contact the Ministry of Works again,' Anne had replied. She knew better than to disagree with anything Magistrate Darroux proposed and none of the staff ever complained at the early finishes anyway, especially on Fridays. The magistrate frowned at the list he held in his hands before striding purposefully towards his office. It was the usual rubbish: summary offences, minor assaults, petty theft, public disorder and so on. There were the usual repeat offenders; sometimes he didn't know why he bothered. But one case caught his eye. He scanned the details which had been submitted by the CDSLI. They outlined a drugs bust which had gone down in the early hours of the previous morning on a yacht at English Harbour. The captain of the yacht, a man by the name of Oliver Jacobs, was due to appear in court that morning on charges of possession, intent to transfer, being concerned with the supply of cocaine and the trafficking of over two thousand kilograms of the class A drug. The magistrate's eyes nearly popped out of his head when he read the amount of cocaine the drug squad had seized from the yacht. Gerald reached for a tissue to blow his nose and continued reading. The frown on his face intensified. When he had finished reading the details of the case, he placed the papers on the desk in front of him, ignoring the rest of the list.

Gerald's next birthday heralded his retirement and he was counting down the hours and minutes until that hallowed day arrived. One of the things Gerald was looking forward to most about his retirement was spending time with his five grandchildren who were aged between two and twenty-two. A year ago, Gerald had six grandchildren. But one devastating night, his third grandchild, eighteen year old Dylan, had taken a lethal cocktail of drugs which had resulted in his death. The person who had supplied the drugs which had killed Gerald's grandson had never been caught, although Gerald had a fairly good idea of the man's identity. But now Gerald had a serious problem with anyone who brought drugs to the island. Suppressing a violent sneeze, he opened one of his desk drawers and pulled out a thick pad of duplicate forms. He picked up a pen and began to fill in the blank form on the top. His first hearing wasn't until nine-fifteen. In light of the fact that the court building would be closing early, it made sense to get ahead with the paperwork. At the top of the form, Gerald entered the name: Oliver Robert Randal Jacobs. Underneath, in large block capital letters, he scrawled the words: BAIL DENIED.

10:10 am, Friday, September 20
CDSLI Headquarters, English Harbour

Four of the seven-strong team had reconvened in the crew room at the CDSLI headquarters to discuss the morning's events. The other three officers, Anson, Mitch and Edella, had returned to Oliver's villa to oversee proceedings as the stacks of hundred dollar bills concealed in the cistern were loaded into an armoured truck. Escorted by police vehicles, the truck would transport the money back to the CDSLI headquarters to be counted and checked for authenticity. Nerissa, who had spent the morning tracing Quincy's movements leading up to his death the previous day, began with a summary, accompanied by bulleted notes and a map of the island pinned to the whiteboard. The others sipped strong coffee as she talked.

'We know Quincy left his mom's house on Jonas Road at seven-thirty yesterday morning. I tracked down a couple of witnesses at Hamilton Bay who saw him arrive in his truck around seven forty-five. He was there to do gardening at a holiday rental, a villa owned by someone with the initials JP, which matches the work schedule we found in Quincy's shirt pocket. Delano, you were right, JP stands for Jay Palmer. He's an American who owns a restaurant in St. John's. Jay told me he's employed Quincy to take care of the pool and garden of his villa for the last couple of years. Apparently Quincy's been completely reliable and great at his job up until about six months ago. Since then, he started not showing up for work on time — or at all — leaving off early, or only doing half a job and making stupid mistakes.'

'Such as?' Delano asked.

'According to Jay there was one time he put the wrong chemical in the pool. It affected the water so bad that the guests renting the villa couldn't use it for half their vacation. Jay told me it cost him a bunch of money to put right and the guests gave the villa a scathing review, understandably. Jay gave me a couple of other examples where Quincy's been off his game, said he's given Quincy plenty of ultimatums and even tried talking to him to find out why things were going downhill, but Quincy just clammed up and refused to talk. Jay called Quincy at around ten past eight yesterday morning — which matches Quincy's phone records — to check Quincy was actually at the villa doing what he was supposed to be doing.

'One of the neighbours also spotted Quincy in the garden. She saw him around eight-thirty, said he was on his cell having an intense discussion with someone. We know the phone records have him placing a call to his girlfriend, Latoya, at eight-twenty. The neighbour says she saw him on the phone again about an hour later: Jacobs's call. According to the neighbour and a couple of other witnesses, Quincy left Hamilton Bay just after ten-thirty in his truck.'

'Well, he wasn't heading over to Max's place because Max says he never showed. And now we know he didn't just drop everything after Jacobs's call to rush off to the villa to spruce up the lanai furniture,' Hyacinth remarked.

'No, but there's a reason for that,' Nerissa went on. 'Even though Jacobs says Quincy promised he'd go straight to the villa, something happened which prevented him from leaving: Jay Palmer showed up unexpectedly.'

'A surprise visit to check on Quincy?' Brandon asked.

'You could call it that. Even though they'd spoken on the phone and Quincy had assured Jay the work would be done, past experience meant that Jay no longer trusted Quincy, so he drove down to Hamilton Bay to check for himself. Says he arrived just before ten, soon after Jacobs's call to Quincy. He stayed for about half an hour so even if Quincy was planning on leaving for Sugar Reef, now he was stuck. He couldn't go anywhere until Jay left.'

'I wonder what changed in Quincy's life six months ago to cause such a noticeable deterioration in his work,' Delano said.

'Drugs?' Hyacinth suggested.

'Max is adamant Quincy never touched them. He told me himself Quincy was so naive he'd probably mistake a bag of cocaine for a bag of sugar.'

'Relationship problems with Latoya?'

'Perhaps. He was certainly distracted with her call that morning, although according to Max that was nothing new. Nerissa, what else did you get from Jay Palmer? Did he just have a problem with Quincy's work or d'you think there was something else going on? Surely if you're unhappy with your pool guy you just let him go and find someone else?'

'You'd think,' Nerissa nodded. 'I ran a background on Jay. He's an American businessman from New Jersey. Three years ago he moved to Antigua where he invested a substantial amount of money into a restaurant in St. John's. The venture provided a number of jobs for locals, in exchange for residency and citizenship. Apart from a parking ticket back in the States, his record's clean and he has no prior convictions. He lives with his partner, Ingrid, a former model from Norway, in a nice house in Cedar Valley overlooking the golf course. I'm still looking into the financial records for the restaurant business as well as his personal finances. I have noticed a number of discrepancies with the restaurant accounts but I'll need to dig a little deeper to see exactly what's going on. I did speak to one of the staff who worked there though, Bryce, the restaurant manager. He said business hadn't been going well lately.'

'I know Quincy's murder isn't technically our case, but you think Jay had something to do with it?' Hyacinth asked.

'The fact that he was simply unhappy with Quincy's work doesn't exactly give motive enough,' Delano replied. 'But Wendell might be interested in him.'

'I did ask Jay about his movements yesterday,' Nerissa volunteered. 'Sure, like Hyacinth said, I know the murder's not our case, but I figured that whatever happened to Quincy would be closely connected to our own investigations. Jay told me he was in his office at home until around nine-fifteen when he drove to Hamilton Bay. He stayed for an hour doing various jobs around the place and generally keeping an eye on Quincy, and left just before ten-thirty. He says he drove straight home and went back to work in his office there for a couple of hours.'

'Can his partner vouch for him?' Delano asked.

'No, she was on the golf course all morning with a couple of friends, but there was something… I spoke to the lady who cleans Jay's house in Cedar Valley. She said she was there all yesterday morning, cleaning, and didn't see Jay's car arrive back until after one o'clock.'

'So if *he* says he was back in his office by eleven, but he didn't actually get home until one, where'd he go?' Delano asked. 'And why lie about it?'

'Jay swears he came straight home and insists his cleaning lady's mistaken.'

'Is there any CCTV footage to back up either statement?' Hyacinth asked.

'I checked. Jay doesn't have any cameras around his property and the only other camera nearby has apparently been broken for months,' Nerissa replied.

'I can understand a discrepancy of thirty minutes or so,' Delano said, 'but we're talking almost two hours here. It's Jay's cleaning lady's word against his.'

'Exactly,' Nerissa agreed. 'Two hours is a significant amount of time. And I don't see why his cleaner would have any reason to lie. The opposite in fact, she could lose her job over this.'

'So if she's telling the truth and Jay's lying, any idea as to where he was between ten forty-five and one o'clock?'

'No. Not so far.'

'What about the rest of his day?'

'At around two o'clock he says he drove to the restaurant to check on the lunch shift. The staff on duty yesterday confirmed he was there until around four-thirty, when Jay says he drove to Fort Bay Beach for a run. He was alone, but we can check for any witnesses once we get the time of Quincy's death from the ME. After the beach, Jay said he returned to his office until around six-thirty when he went back to the restaurant to oversee the evening shift.'

'He's clearly a very hands-on kinda guy with his business,' Delano commented.

'The staff said the same,' Nerissa said. 'According to them he's quite controlling and likes to be involved with the minutiae of the running of the place. Anyway, they confirmed he was there until just after midnight. He was one of the last to leave and says he drove straight home. Ingrid was already asleep and can't say for sure what time he got back.'

'Thanks Nerissa,' Delano said. 'And you're right, Quincy's murder is closely connected to our own case, for sure. I spoke to Wendell about running a joint investigation on this but, as you might guess, he wasn't too keen.'

'I'm sure he'll be even less keen to know we've been doing his job for him,' Hyacinth said with a smirk. 'And let's be honest, the feeling's mutual. I'm not too keen on working with him either.'

'He's not the easiest to get along with,' Delano acknowledged. 'But the two cases are inextricably linked. And unfortunately we need him on our side.' He turned to Nerissa. 'Were there any witnesses for Quincy's movements after he left Hamilton Bay?'

'Not that I've found.' Nerissa shook her head. 'The next thing we know is he was spraying camera seven at Jacobs's villa shortly after eleven-thirty.'

'So even though it only takes around thirty minutes to drive from Hamilton Bay to Sugar Reef Bay, it took Quincy nearly an hour,' Delano said.

'There seems to be a trend forming here,' Hyacinth remarked. 'Everyone seems to be taking ages to get anywhere. Did they shut the roads yesterday, or did I miss a major traffic problem? It's puzzling.'

'Maybe Quincy stopped somewhere on the drive over to Jacobs's villa,' Brandon suggested.

'What if he left for Sugar Reef Bay as soon as he could,' Hyacinth said, 'in other words as soon as he thought Jay Palmer was a safe distance away and definitely not coming back. But as he neared the access road to Sugar Reef and saw the plain clothes officers parked there, he realised he couldn't get to Jacobs's villa without being stopped and questioned. But he knows another way in. So he turns his truck round and heads for the alternate route.'

'If he's going there to check on the property at Jacobs's request, why not just go up to the plain clothes guys and tell them what he's doing?' Brandon asked. 'All they'd need to do was give us a quick call to confirm he was legit before letting him through. They'd probably even escort him up there.'

'Which was probably the very last thing he wanted,' Nerissa said.

'I agree,' Hyacinth said. 'If that's what happened, it confirms that Quincy's visit wasn't anything to do with parasols and soft furnishings, as I suspected from the start. In spite of Jacobs's seemingly innocent request, Quincy knew what it was really about, hence his unwillingness to approach the officers at the access road. He couldn't let them know what he was actually up to. Ergo, the reason it took him a whole hour to get to Villa Bella Casa was because he had to take an alternative route, which took more time.'

'Don't forget there was someone else too,' Delano added. 'His killer. If Quincy did indeed know another way up to the villa, perhaps he met his murderer at the clifftop near Tamarind Point — either willingly or he was coerced — in order to show him, or her, the alternate route. It would explain why his pickup was disposed of later, to ensure he had no means of escape.'

'What if Jay Palmer didn't drive away from Hamilton Bay after all?' Brandon said. 'Maybe he parked up a little way out from his place at Hamilton Bay, just to make sure Quincy didn't sneak off early again. We know Jay's done that before. Suppose this time though, when he sees Quincy drive past a few minutes later, it's the final straw, it's one time too many. He's outraged and decides to follow Quincy and see what he's up to, where he's going. From a distance, he watches Quincy turn his truck round to avoid the officers at the Sugar Reef access road and decides to confront him, forcing him off the road and up the dirt track to the top of the cliff to explain himself.

'But by this time Quincy's getting pretty anxious about carrying out Jacobs's instructions at the villa. After realising the access road is under police surveillance, perhaps he panics and tells Jay about the cistern and the money, just to get him off his back. Maybe he even makes some kind of deal with Jay. If the restaurant was in trouble financially, the money Quincy could have offered Jay to leave him alone would've made all the restaurant's cash flow problems go away. So Quincy shows Jay the cistern at Villa Bella Casa and Jay realises just how much money there is. That's more than enough motive for him to want Quincy dead. He takes care of Quincy and closes up the cistern before he returns to the cliff where he drives Quincy's truck over the edge, jumping clear at the last moment, in an attempt to make it look like an accident. Finally, he drives back to his house to change and tidy himself up in time to head over to his restaurant for two o'clock.'

'That's a very plausible theory Brandon,' Hyacinth said.

'Except Wendell said they didn't find evidence of any other vehicles at the top of the cliff,' Nerissa interrupted.

'Maybe Jay parked further down the track,' Brandon said.

'Talk to him again Nerissa,' Delano said. 'Try not to tread on Wendell's toes while you're at it, but we need to find out where he was between ten-forty five and one o'clock.' He glanced round at the others. 'What else do we have?'

'Ten a.m., Falmouth, LT, as written on the screwed up piece of paper in Quincy's pocket,' Brandon said. 'I made some calls; LT stands for Luiza Torres. She's a dentist with her own dental clinic in St. John's. I spoke to her between patients. She said she has a house in Turtle Bay, a smart little residential area on the peninsular at the outer edge of Falmouth Harbour. The house has a pool and a well established tropical garden with palms and shrubs. She paid Quincy to come by once a week for an hour or two, mainly to look after the pool. He'd also do whatever was needed in the garden as she has little time to work on it herself. She had no complaints about his reliability or the work he did for her. She was at work yesterday from eight-thirty until six seeing patients.'

'So far Jay Palmer's the only one who had a problem with Quincy,' Delano observed.

'Actually no,' Hyacinth said. 'I spoke to a couple of residents at Willoughby Bay who own beach houses there: a Larry Roth and a Jennifer Wilcox. Quincy did work for both of them — the usual pool maintenance, gardening, odd jobs and such — and was due at their properties at one and two p.m. respectively yesterday. They told pretty much the same story as Jay. Up until around six months ago Quincy was the perfect handyman, but then they began to notice a change. He was increasingly unreliable, not showing up for work, not doing the work properly and was generally becoming more of a liability. After Quincy was a no-show yesterday, both Larry and Jennifer were at the point of letting him go.'

'Alibis?' Delano asked.

'Yes, for both,' Hyacinth nodded and glanced down at a page of hastily scribbled notes. 'Larry runs a little business doing boat tours and snorkelling expeditions out of Jolly Harbour. The man who usually drives the boat was sick yesterday so Larry had to do the tour himself. A party of eight had booked a boat trip from eight till three. In spite of the weather, they insisted on going, so Larry was out on the ocean waves the whole day, the perfect alibi. As for Jennifer, she runs a preschool and nursery just outside St. John's. She was there from seven-thirty until five-thirty with witnesses; staff, parents and an army of three year olds. Don't think I'd wanna argue with them.'

The remark drew a chuckle from her co-workers.

'Is it worth noting that the only people who hadn't noticed a deterioration in Quincy's work were the owners of the Sugar Reef Bay properties?' Brandon asked.

'And the dentist, Luiza Torres,' Nerissa added.

'She's probably too busy to notice,' Hyacinth said.

'What about alibis for the Sugar Reef Bay residents, just out of interest?' Delano asked.

'To recap: there are five properties at Sugar Reef Bay in total, one being Jacobs's villa.' Brandon flipped through a small notebook as he spoke. He stopped halfway through and turned back a page. 'If we take it from the access road entrance, the first house belongs to the retired British expats…'

Nerissa interrupted again: 'Believe me, it ain't them, they don't need no alibi. They're so frail and elderly I doubt they'd even make it up to Villa Bella Casa, let alone strangle a strong, fit, twenty-two year old man when they got there.'

'Who's next?' Delano asked.

'The second property is a holiday rental. The owner's out of the country and the place is managed by a local agency. The family who are currently staying at the property spent the day at Nelson's Dockyard,' Brandon continued. 'We can rule them out. The third house is the villa owned by the Texan businessman which was all shut up; nothing going on there. The fourth property, the one next to Villa Bella Casa, is owned by a man called Paul Griffiths; he's the pharmaceutical CEO.'

'His wife and kids were just getting ready to leave for the airport when Mitch and I knocked on the door,' Nerissa said.

'Wife and kids?' Delano said suddenly. 'Paul wasn't going with them?'

'He was staying on a few more days,' Nerissa replied. 'He told us he occasionally uses the property to entertain clients and business associates, four of whom are due to arrive today. Incidentally, aside from the family from Connecticut who spent the day at Nelson's Dockyard, he's the only Sugar Reef resident who left the Bay before the plain clothes officers arrived. He's clearly visible on at least two surveillance cameras driving away from his home around nine yesterday morning. He returned at one forty-five, as confirmed by the officers at the entrance to the access road.'

'My notes say he was meeting a friend at English Harbour,' Brandon said.

'An old sailing buddy according to him.'

'Any idea *where* at English Harbour they met?' Hyacinth asked.

'He said it was on his friend's boat, the Blue Moon, berthed in the harbour.'

'I'll check names of boats currently berthed in the harbour,' Hyacinth said. 'And I'll pull yesterday's surveillance footage of all vehicles in the area and parked nearby, see if our pharmacy CEO's Jeep was there between the times he said.'

'While you're at it run some background checks on Mr. Griffiths,' Delano added. 'See if he's got any prior convictions or past connections with Jacobs.'

'Sure thing,' Hyacinth nodded. There was a pause before Nerissa spoke quietly.

'How are Quincy's family holding up, boss? I know you spoke with Max earlier today.'

'The police went to Junella Moran's home in the early hours of this morning to inform her that Quincy's body had been found,' Delano replied. 'Max called me back a little later. He was with the rest of the family at his aunt's home. She's understandably distraught. First she hears her son's pickup's been found at the bottom of a cliff, then within a matter of hours the police deliver the news that he's been found in a cistern, strangled to death. As a parent I don't know how I'd take that kind of information.'

'What about Quincy's girlfriend, Latoya?' Hyacinth asked.

'I talked to her again too. Like Junella and Max and the rest of the family, she's devastated. She and Quincy may not have had the smoothest of relationships according to Max, but even so, they were apparently very fond of each other. She also agreed with Max that Quincy never took drugs and would never have had anything to do with drug trafficking.'

'And how's Max?' Brandon asked.

'He's taking it pretty badly too,' Delano replied. 'Says he and Quincy were close. Quincy looked up to him like an older brother and Max adored Quincy. He told me he's taking a few days off to be there for his aunt and the rest of the family.'

'If they were close, surely he has an idea as to who might have done this?' Hyacinth asked.

Delano shook his head.

'Max is at a loss to know who's responsible for his cousin's death. Although they were close, it seems that Quincy had some secrets after all, which makes this even more painful for Max.'

'And to think he was part of the crew who rescued Jacobs in that storm on Saturday night,' Nerissa said.

'That must really suck for him,' Hyacinth added.

'He did mention that Quincy was involved in an altercation at The Jungle,' Delano said suddenly.

'Isn't that the dive bar in St. John's where Lloyd moonlights as a bouncer?' Hyacinth asked. 'Someone please remind me why he works there again,' she said with disdain. 'Sure, I guess he needs the money, but there are nicer places.'

'He says he likes to keep his hand in with the underworld.'

'Sometimes I feel like we do enough of that already. Who was the altercation with?'

'Vinnie Trickett.'

'There's a surprise.' Hyacinth rolled her eyes.

'I can go talk to him,' Brandon volunteered.

'By all means, but be clear what you're questioning him about,' Delano said, adding wryly, 'for Wendell's benefit.'

'Sure, I get it. We're not investigating Quincy's murder but whether Vinnie the street king has any information relating to the drug bust on the Atratus,' Brandon said. 'But obviously if our line of questioning happens to digress, then it goes where it goes.'

'Exactly,' Delano replied. 'We should also check in with Lloyd about the altercation, see if he knows anything.'

'Where is Lloyd?' Brandon asked. 'He wasn't under his rubber plant this morning.'

'He's setting up next door for the arrival of the money truck. He said he'd come through when he's done.'

'There's something about Quincy that just doesn't add up,' Nerissa said. 'I feel like we're talking about two different people here. It's as if he was leading a double life. To his family he was a hard-working, virtuous young man, yet he clearly knew about the money in Oliver Jacobs's cistern and was involved in some way. And then there's the altercation with Vinnie Trickett. No one gets mixed up with that dirtbag unless they're on the wrong side of the law.'

'Let's give Quincy the benefit of the doubt for a moment,' Brandon said. 'Suppose he's innocent and really was just checking on the parasols and lanai furniture at the villa when he accidentally stumbled into someone else while he was there. Realising he'd now be able to identify them, their only choice was to get him to spray the cameras around the villa with black paint; even if the surveillance footage was recovered, there'd be nothing to see. And then, of course, they had to get rid of Quincy himself, to make sure there were no loose ends.'

'If Quincy was innocent, why didn't he just walk right up to those surveillance officers at the gates?' Hyacinth said. 'Whatever his reasons were, he steered clear. Because he had something to hide.'

They were interrupted by the phone on the desk beside Delano. He answered it and they waited as the caller seemed to do most of the talking with Delano making occasional noises of acknowledgement.

'Thanks Mitch, that's good work. We'll see you soon.' He hung up before turning to the rest of them. 'The money from the cistern's been loaded into the armoured truck and they're on their way here. Mitch thinks the hundred dollar bills are genuine, but the machine will confirm that for sure.'

As he finished speaking, the door opened behind them and Lloyd entered. He looked surprisingly fresh considering he had spent half the night hacking into Oliver's hard drive and the security company's database. The blue Hawaiian shirt had been replaced by a clean one, black with a bamboo orchid print.

'Room next door's ready for the cash from OJ's villa,' he said with a grin. 'Don't suppose we have an ETA do we? I can't wait to see what a hundred million dollars looks like.'

'The armoured truck's just left Sugar Reef Bay,' Delano replied.

'You think OJ's handyman was after the money and got caught in the act?' Lloyd asked.

'Too soon to tell.'

'Sure, you need to follow up on a few leads first.' Lloyd nodded with understanding.

'You may be able to help us with one,' Delano said. 'Quincy had an altercation with Vinnie Trickett at The Jungle last week. Know anything about that?'

'Yeah, I remember it,' Lloyd replied, frowning as he recalled the event. 'I was on the doors. It was busy that night. Had to pull Quincy out of there as Vinnie's crew would've had him in the hospital,' he paused before adding, 'but I guess that's better than the mortuary. Anyway, I've no idea what the fight was about and Quincy didn't stick around after so I never found out. He hasn't been back to The Jungle since.'

'Any witnesses?' Delano asked.

'Plenty.'

'So you keep a list of people who come through the doors or something?' Nerissa asked.

'Yeah right,' Lloyd replied with an amused look. 'We're talking about The Jungle here Nerissa, not a kindergarten with a teacher calling out names from a register.'

'Sorry, I shoulda known that,' Nerissa laughed.

'What about surveillance?' Brandon asked. 'Cameras and such?'

'Cameras?' Lloyd scoffed. 'Like I said, it's The Jungle. What happens at The Jungle stays at The Jungle. What more can I say?'

'In that case Brandon, it's over to you to go talk to Vinnie and his crew,' Delano said.

'Good luck with that,' Lloyd chuckled. He muttered something about having more work to be getting on with and disappeared through the door to the reception area. Hyacinth, who had been talking on the phone, hung up.

'That was Rochelle at the forensics lab in St. John's. She's run a bunch of tests on the white powder we seized from the Atratus yesterday, the usual, gas chromatography, mass spectrometry and so on. The powder tested positive for cocaine, with a purity in excess of seventy percent.'

'That would render a street value somewhere in the region of two hundred million dollars, at a guess,' Brandon said. 'Not bad for one week's work.'

'That's probably pocket money for Jacobs,' Hyacinth retorted. 'Rochelle's also been through the rest of the contents we retrieved from the Atratus as well as Jacobs's personal effects. There was nothing of note other than traces of cocaine on most items.'

Suddenly Lloyd burst through the door with a look of alarm on his face.

'Delano, Mitch just called…'

The four members of the CDSLI turned to face him. His voice shook as he spoke.

'The truck and police cars en route from Jacobs's villa were stopped and held up at gunpoint just now. There were masked men with sawed-off shotguns. The four police officers… they're dead…'

'Oh my gosh' Nerissa said. She brought a hand to her mouth. 'What about the others?'

Lloyd swallowed hard.

'Mitch is injured, but not seriously. Edella took a gunshot wound to the chest but she's alive, just. Mitch is with her now and the EMTs are on their way.'

'And Anson?' Delano asked calmly.

Lloyd went to speak and found he couldn't.

'Is Anson okay?' Nerissa said, her voice trembling.

Lloyd swallowed and shook his head. He spoke quietly.

'No, he's not. Anson didn't make it.'

EIGHTEEN

10:40 am, Friday, September 20
V. C. Bird International Airport

Seven hours and ten minutes after taking off from the disused runway in Miami, Johann Ryan's Cessna Titan touched down on runway zero seven at V. C. Bird International. The landing was executed with Johann's usual finesse; the aircraft kissed the tarmac and Johann taxied rapidly towards the end of the runway. He turned right onto the old runway ten, as directed by air traffic control, to his usual parking spot about halfway down. He manoeuvred the aircraft between a sleek Learjet and a rather tatty looking Britten-Norman Islander, which was probably older than the Cessna, before shutting down the engines.

He removed his headset, unlatched his seatbelt and reached across to his backpack where he fumbled around for a large bottle of Captain Morgan dark rum. It clinked against the steel flask as he retrieved it from the backpack. At the same moment, his cell phone began to ring. He shot a glance at the screen and groaned inwardly. He knew he couldn't ignore it. He put the caller on speaker as he unscrewed the bottle cap.

'Yeah Rusty.'

As he lifted the bottle to his lips, a familiar voice spoke. 'Put the rum away Johann.'

Johann paused, the bottle halfway to his mouth.

'I said put it away.' The voice was firm and insistent.

'Okay, okay,' Johann replied with a note of frustration. He reluctantly screwed the cap back on the bottle and tossed it onto his backpack. 'I've been flying for seven hours man, I need to rehydrate.'

'Lamont's on his way over.' Rusty ignored the protest. 'Sit tight till he reaches you. The airport's busy today. You gotta unload quickly and discreetly.'

'Where's Glen?' Johann reached beside his seat and pulled the clipboard with the aircraft documents onto his knees.

'He's overseeing a job near English Harbour. He'll probably be out of the office for most of today, so to speak. Lamont will take care of your cargo. He'll be with you in two minutes.'

Johann knew better than to ask what felonious enterprise Glen might be overseeing, but guessed he'd find out soon enough, either through word of mouth or, as on occasion, through the local news.

'All set for this afternoon?' Rusty asked, changing the subject.

'Yeah. Three o'clock at the Pavilion. And you said there'd be girls, right?' Johann replied. His mouth was parched and he gazed longingly at the half full bottle of rum beside him as he scribbled the flight time on the papers attached to the clipboard.

'Yes, there are girls,' Rusty said impatiently, 'which is why your job is to make me look like a damn good pilot, remember?'

'I remember,' Johann replied with a frown.

'I gotta go,' Rusty said, signing off. 'I'll see you later.'

The call ended and Johann finished the paperwork. He gazed straight ahead out of the windshield, too tired to move. From his left, in the direction of the terminal, he spotted a silver Ford Transit cargo van headed his way. It was a lefthand drive van with two men up front. As it approached, Johann could make out the words written along the side. They were in black typeface with elaborate swashes which said CulinAir Catering Inc. There was an emblem of an aircraft beneath the words, part of a slick company logo, except Johann was familiar with the airport catering companies which serviced the airlines operating out of the airport. CulinAir Catering Inc. wasn't one of them.

The Ford Transit slowed to a halt in front of the Cessna and backed in beside it. The Learjet, parked further along, concealed the next few minutes of activity from the airport surveillance cameras, mounted high up on the terminal building. Two men in matching navy shirts and pants jumped out of the catering van. Navy baseball caps were pulled low over their eyes and they kept their heads down as they approached the Cessna. Johann hauled himself out of the seat and made his way through the cabin to the rear, squeezing between the suitcases and duffle bags. He opened the cargo door and let down the steps as Lamont and his companion approached.

'Start unloading,' Lamont barked impatiently at Johann. He glanced at the other man. 'Emil, you take the wing lockers and the nose cone. Work fast.'

'Got it,' Emil nodded. He began unlatching the port wing lockers.

'What're *you* waiting for?' Lamont said, turning back to Johann. 'Come on, get a move on with the bags or I'll call Rusty.'

Johann quickly hauled two of the duffle bags from the seats immediately behind him and threw them out onto the tarmac towards Lamont who jumped backwards. He looked up angrily at Johann.

'Watch out, man,' he hissed. He picked up the bags and placed them in the catering van. Johann retrieved two more duffle bags from the cabin, this time carrying them down the steps and laying them on the tarmac. It was clear the two men were on edge. As they unloaded the aircraft they remained silent, focusing on the job, casting uneasy glances back towards the terminal building and to the headquarters of the aviation company opposite, a smart, single storey building with a tin roof.

Johann's muscles, still stiff from the seven hour flight, ached furiously. In the heat of the mid-morning sun he wiped sweat from his forehead as he worked. It was hard to keep up with Lamont who was younger and fitter and quite frankly had the easier job. When Emil had finished unloading the cargo from the wings and nose cone, he joined Johann inside the cabin and passed the last remaining suitcases down to Lamont. In less than ten minutes, the Cessna had been emptied of its payload. Emil disappeared to the rear of the catering van and returned almost immediately with two large black duffle bags. He placed them at the bottom of the aircraft steps.

'Rusty tells me you've got a scenic flight booked later today,' Lamont said as he rolled the side door of the catering van shut.

'Yeah, that's right,' Johann muttered, eyeing the bags at his feet.

'Well, have a good one,' Lamont said, 'come on Emil, let's get going.' He jogged round to the driver's side as Emil climbed into the passenger's seat without so much as a second glance in Johann's direction. Lamont started the engine and Johann heard him shift into gear. He stepped on the gas pedal and the van edged out around the side of the Learjet before speeding off towards the terminal building.

Johann glanced around before making his way back inside the aircraft cabin. A small Gulfstream jet taxied past, heading towards the main runway. On the other side, an airport minivan with a flashing orange beacon on its roof held its position, allowing the jet to pass, before turning in the opposite direction towards the eastern end of runway ten where the Pavilion Café was situated. Johann reached across the front seat for his backpack on which lay the bottle of rum. With sweaty, shaking hands, he unscrewed the cap and put the bottle to his lips. He closed his eyes as he felt the warm, sweet liquid in his throat. With the next few sips he savoured the smoothness of the burnt caramel. Mustering what was left of his willpower, he replaced the cap, threw the bottle into his backpack and slung it over his shoulder. He secured the window latches before walking back through the cabin to the cargo door. He needed to refuel before the afternoon flight with Rusty and his party, but a shower and a few hours' sleep were higher on the list of priorities.

He shut the door before making a cursory walk round the aircraft to ensure Emil had fastened the wing and nose cone hatches properly. He returned to the port wing where the two duffle bags sat on the tarmac. This was the part he dreaded the most. He picked the bags up and, doing his best to appear casual, crossed the old runway towards the service road on the opposite side. Beyond was the parking lot where his Station Wagon baked in the heat of the late morning sun. A hazy shimmer hovered over the ground as Johann walked quickly in an attempt to make the two bags crammed with one hundred dollar bills look as though they contained nothing more than the weight of a couple of changes of clothes. Johann knew serious questions would be asked if anyone found out what was really inside the bags. He nodded at the driver of an airport security van and tried to control his breathing. Once he reached the service road, he slowed his pace a little. His shirt was drenched with sweat and the muscles in his arms burned with the weight of the bags.

He reached his car, which was parked in a corner of the lot, and threw the bags in the trunk. Sometimes he despised the money. Maybe he should make a series of anonymous donations to charity and just give the whole lot away. But he knew such obscene amounts would be traced and questions would be asked. He closed the trunk of the Subaru and glanced quickly around again before getting in and starting the engine. As he reached the exit, the familiar debate raged in his mind: turn left and go straight home, or turn right and deposit the bags in the storage unit. He was hot and exhausted, but he couldn't risk the cash being discovered in the trunk of his car. He shifted into gear and made a right turn.

In an effort to stay awake, he turned on the radio. A local breaking news bulletin was in progress. He increased the volume as the reporter summarised details of an armoured truck which had been held at gunpoint by a group of five men wearing black masks. The truck was a government vehicle with a police escort en route from a private residence at Sugar Reef Bay to the headquarters of the Crime and Drug Squad of the Leeward Islands at English Harbour. Four police officers and one CDSLI officer were reported dead, while two other officers had been critically injured. There were also reports of a civilian casualty who appeared to have been mixed up in the holdup, but information was scant. Details were still coming in as to how the events of the morning had unfolded, why the truck had been targeted and who exactly was behind the whole operation, although Johann thought he had a pretty good idea. Sure, Glen and his fellow mercenaries were the foot soldiers on the ground doing the dirty work, but Rusty McChannen called the shots.

NINETEEN

Hyacinth and Lloyd remained at the CDSLI headquarters while Delano, Brandon and Nerissa set out to where Anson, Mitch and Edella, and the police escort officers, had been held at gunpoint. The location was a deserted stretch of road along a cliff top roughly halfway between Sugar Reef Bay and English Harbour. When the three CDSLI officers arrived, Wendell was already at the scene of the crime, barking orders to a small group of law enforcement officers, forensic specialists and other uniformed personnel. Two police cars, an unmarked government car and two ambulances were parked haphazardly around the police escort cars which had been involved in the shooting and were peppered with bullet holes. The windshield of one of the cars was shattered and both had punctured tyres. A breakdown truck was en route.

As they gazed in shock at the carnage around them, Delano noticed Lianne Henderson, the ME who had been called to examine Quincy's body earlier that morning. She was crouched over one of the bodies which lay in a pool of blood at the side of the road.

'Nerissa, Brandon,' Delano said, pointing in the ME's direction. 'It's Anson.'

'Oh Delano.' Nerissa fought back tears. 'I don't think I'm ready to go over there right now.'

'It's okay,' Delano said gently, 'I'll go speak to Lianne. You find Mitch and Edella. Brandon, catch up with Wendell, see what he's got so far.'

Nerissa nodded and set off in the direction of the ambulances.

'Delano, how many police officers were escorting the truck?' Brandon asked, looking around him. He appeared to be counting something.

'Four in total.'

'None of them made it, right?'

'Not according to Lloyd.'

'And Mitch and Edella?'

'Still alive. Edella's in a critical condition; Mitch has minor injuries.'

'Four police officers and Anson makes five,' Brandon said. He was staring a little further away, to where a light blue sedan was parked. It had a shattered windshield and the hood was spattered with an uneven line of bullet holes. The driver's side door was open and shot up with more bullet holes. Beside the car lay another body.

'There are six bodies, Delano,' Brandon said. He nodded towards the body laying motionlessly by the sedan. 'Who's that over there?'

Delano squinted in the bright sunlight to where Brandon was pointing.

'I don't know,' he replied. 'See if Wendell has an ID yet.'

'Yeah. I will.'

The two men split up. As he crossed the road towards Lianne, Delano glanced at the ambulances. A paramedic was standing by the rear doors of the first ambulance making preparations to leave the scene. Beside the second ambulance Nerissa was talking to Mitch who sat upright on a stretcher, his right arm in a sling. Another paramedic was attempting to take a blood pressure on his left arm. He winced as the cuff tightened. Delano continued walking to Lianne who was crouched over the body of his fellow officer. When he reached the side of the road, he knelt beside her. She finished what she was doing before turning to Delano.

'I'm so sorry,' she said.

'Thanks,' he replied. 'Cause of death?'

'Multiple gunshot wounds to the chest, close range, probably with some kind of crude sawed-off shotgun. Bottom line, Anson didn't stand a chance. I'm so sorry Delano.'

'Anything else noteworthy?' Delano tried to ignore his emotions and stay on point.

'Not really. All four police officers were also shot at close range with what appear to be bullets of the same calibre, but don't quote me on that until the lab have processed the evidence conclusively.'

'And the sixth body?'

'I haven't got to him yet. From what I understand, he's a civilian who came round the corner shortly after the shooting began and inadvertently got caught in the line of fire.'

'Thanks Lianne. And I guess you haven't had chance to conduct a postmortem on Quincy yet?'

'You guess correctly Officer Reid,' Lianne said with a faint smile. 'We'd barely got him back to the mortuary before we took this call. But I'll be in touch, I promise.'

'I appreciate it,' Delano said. As he stood up, the body lying next to the blue sedan caught his eye. The sixth victim. Nearby, a police photographer snapped shots from various angles. Delano crossed the road to where the ambulances were parked. He approached the paramedic with the first ambulance and introduced himself.

'Will she be okay?' he asked, nodding towards Edella who lay motionless on the stretcher inside, attached to monitors and a ventilator with an assortment of wires and tubes.

'She's critically injured with gunshot wounds to the right side of her chest,' the paramedic replied. She spoke with a sense of urgency. 'We need to get her back to the hospital right away. When we got here, she had a tension pneumothorax, a collapsed lung. My co-worker performed a needle decompression through her chest wall to allow the air in her pleural cavity to escape, but she needs to be seen by a doctor in the ER for more treatment.'

'Here's my number,' Delano said, passing her a small card. 'Will you ask the nurses to call me with any updates?'

'Of course.' The paramedic shut the rear doors of the ambulance as she spoke. She took the card and placed it in her pocket. 'We have to go now.'

Delano nodded and stepped back as she walked around to the driver's side door. He turned to the other ambulance where Mitch lay on his stretcher talking to Nerissa. He looked pale and shaken but smiled as Delano approached.

'Hey boss.'

'How are you Mitch?'

'I'm alive. For that I'm thankful.'

'Your arm?' Delano nodded at the sling.

'It's nothing,' Mitch replied stoically. 'I took a bullet to the shoulder. It was a through and through and missed all the major vessels according to the paramedics. I'll be fine. How's Edella?' He glanced at the other ambulance which was just leaving, its red and white lights flashing as it manoeuvred slowly around the blue sedan.

'Not good,' Delano replied. 'She needs urgent hospital treatment. I've asked for the nurses to contact me as soon as they have more information. What happened Mitch?'

'I — I don't know. One minute we were driving along, the next this black, unmarked SUV suddenly came up from behind. We heard what sounded like shots being fired and in the sideview mirror I saw the police car behind us swerve. The SUV overtook us and pulled up right ahead of the front car. Everything happened so fast. These masked men jumped out of the SUV, they were all in black with black balaclavas, carrying sawed-off shotguns. They shot up the front police car, took out the two officers and then ran over to the truck.'

Mitch paused.

'What happened next?' Delano asked.

'Two of them approached the driver's door, where Anson was sitting. They managed to open the door and started shooting. One of them pulled him out of the truck. Edella was in the middle and I was on the passenger's side, furthest away from the shooters. I yanked my door open and grabbed Edella, but she'd been hit pretty bad. I felt something hit my shoulder hard before I dragged Edella out of the truck and into those bushes at the side of the road. I couldn't get to Anson.'

Mitch's voice faltered.

'The shooters jumped into the cab of the truck and drove off behind the SUV. I couldn't see the rear of the SUV to get a plate. I called nine-one-one and then you guys. Edella was still alive but losing consciousness — I knew she'd been hit badly — but when I saw Anson and the police officers...'

Mitch broke off.

'I couldn't save them Delano.' He blinked back tears and looked away.

'Mitch, there was nothing you could've done,' Delano said gently.

'It's not your fault,' Nerissa added.

'I don't know,' Mitch replied shaking his head. 'I should've been more prepared for something like this. We should've been ready. We were too casual. We were...'

'Mitch,' Delano said sternly. 'You can blame yourself and go over this in your mind a thousand times. It won't bring Anson or the police officers back. You need to get some rest.'

Mitch looked at Delano defiantly.

'There's no way I'm going anywhere. I'm staying here, staying with you.' Wincing in pain, he reached across and ripped off his blood pressure cuff and the rest of his monitoring before swinging his legs down off the stretcher. Standing, he steadied himself on the side of the stretcher. The paramedic hurried over to him.

'Officer Kirland, please get back on the stretcher and leave your monitoring attached, we're not done yet,' he said insistently.

'Thanks for your help, but we are done,' Mitch said. 'I'm fine. I don't need any more medical attention.'

'Mitch, you do,' Nerissa said. 'Listen to the paramedic. Please.'

'I'm *fine*,' Mitch said angrily.

'Mitch, please,' Nerissa protested.

'How is he really?' Delano spoke to the paramedic.

The paramedic sighed in resignation before responding.

'He's lost some blood and has considerable soft-tissue damage to his right shoulder. I've patched it up and cleaned the wound the best I can but he needs antibiotics and an x-ray, at the very least.'

'I'm staying here boss,' Mitch said. 'I can't leave now.'

'Mitch, you really do need to listen to the paramedic's advice,' Delano said firmly.

'No,' Mitch replied. 'I'm not going to the hospital.'

The paramedic raised his hands in frustration.

'Fine. Then we'll make a deal,' Delano said. He had trained his team himself and knew he was partly to blame for Mitch's defiance and determination to stay on the case in spite of his injuries. 'When we find the truck, you'll take yourself to the hospital and get checked out. You'll get your x-rays and your shot of antibiotics and comply with whatever the doctors tell you. Do we have a deal?'

'Almost,' Mitch replied. 'I'll go when we find the truck *and* its contents *and* the masked shooters.'

Delano sighed.

'All right then,' he said. He nodded at the paramedic. 'Don't worry, we'll keep a close eye on him. If we're worried we'll send him straight to the hospital. Thanks for all you've done.'

'Call us if you have any concerns,' the paramedic replied as he began packing the stretcher back into the ambulance.

Brandon approached the group of CDSLI officers. He surveyed Mitch's sling and pale countenance.

'You okay man?' he asked.

'I'm fine,' Mitch replied shortly. 'I saw you talking to Wendell. Does he have anything yet?'

Brandon nodded unsmilingly. 'He's convinced it's an inside job, quite rightly in my opinion. But quite wrongly, he thinks the leak's come from the CDSLI. He's refusing to share any information with us until, in his words, we've cleaned our house and found the mole.'

'I'll talk to him,' Delano said.

'I did get something though,' Brandon added. 'I spoke to the forensics guy over there by the blue sedan. They have an ID for the sixth victim.'

The four of them glanced towards the civilian casualty further along the road. With her medical examiner's bag beside her, Lianne Henderson was kneeling next to the body.

'They know who it is?' Nerissa asked.

'His name's Leon Fayer.'

TWENTY

As the remaining five agents and Lloyd reconvened, the mood back in the crew room was sombre but with a quiet determination to continue the investigation with greater fervour than ever. Hyacinth and Lloyd had wasted no time following up on a number of other leads relating to the case. They had information to share, but first they demanded to know how Edella was and how exactly the clifftop road hijacking had gone down. Mitch, who winced as Hyacinth gave him a hug, recounted the events of the morning with Delano and Brandon filling in what they knew so far.

'Any witnesses?' Hyacinth asked.

'None,' Delano replied. 'But there was an innocent civilian who unwittingly drove round the corner straight into the hijackers' line of fire.'

'That's bad timing,' Hyacinth said. 'Did the police get an ID yet?'

There was a pause as Hyacinth waited for the answer. Her eyes met Delano's.

'Someone you know?' she asked quietly.

'I'm afraid so,' Delano replied. 'His name's Leon Fayer. He's — he *was*,' Delano corrected himself, 'the general manager of the West Beach Club, the five star hotel over near Hamilton Bay.'

'He was the one who vouched for Jacobs's British friends, right?' Hyacinth said.

'Yes, he was,' Delano nodded.

'Could this incident be connected in any way?'

'I don't think so. I don't see how…'

There was a short pause before Hyacinth spoke again.

'Didn't you mention that Leon's granddaughters go to the same school as Tamesha, your daughter?'

'Yeah, they do.' For the first time that morning, Delano struggled to keep his emotions in check. He spoke quickly. 'I talked to Leon's wife, Betsy. She said he was on his way to the West Beach Club. He'd spent the morning at home and was supposed to be taking the day off today, but he had a few things to sort at the hotel and was going in for a couple of hours.'

'Oh man, that's awful,' Lloyd said. 'So it looks like he just happened to be in the wrong place at the wrong time? And he wasn't even supposed to be going into work anyway. That's bad luck. How's his wife holding up?'

'Surprisingly well,' Delano replied. 'She's strong. She'll keep it together for everyone else. Leon meant a lot to many people, including me.'

'I'm so sorry boss,' Hyacinth said. 'If there's anything we can do...'

'You're already doing it,' Delano said. 'For Anson's sake *and* for Leon's sake, let's find the men who did this and, more importantly, the bastard who paid them. Bottom line, the guys who hit the truck this morning are just guns for hire, nothing more. There's someone behind this whole thing, behind Quincy's murder and now the murders of Anson and Leon. The motive is clear: it's about the drugs and the money. We don't exactly have the most definitive suspect list right now, but let's look again at who we do have and see which of those people also had means and opportunity. It's clearly someone with considerable weight to throw around and who knows how to mobilise the right people to get things done quickly.'

'I still think Jacobs is involved somehow,' Mitch said. 'Even if he's not directly pulling strings from his cell, I'll bet he knows who is.'

'Jacobs may well be involved, but he didn't know the details of the truck moving the money this morning so it has to be an inside job.' Nerissa spoke for the first time since they had returned to the crew room. 'Someone has to have leaked the route and departure time of the truck from Villa Bella Casa. That info definitely didn't come from us, so Wendell had better go back to his own team and start hunting down the source of the leak.'

'It doesn't necessarily have to be an inside job,' Lloyd said suddenly. 'Think about it: any one of the residents of Sugar Reef Bay would know the time the truck left OJ's villa and it would be easy enough to guess its intended destination. If they knew about OJ and Quincy and the cistern, they wouldn't need a degree in rocket science to work out what was in an armoured truck flanked by police escort vehicles either. All it would take would be a couple of phone calls to mobilise a hit squad — who were probably on standby anyway — to take out the police and CDSLI officers and hijack the truck.'

'I checked the alibi of Paul Griffiths — the CEO of the pharmaceutical company and Jacobs's neighbour at Sugar Reef — for yesterday morning around the time Quincy went missing,' Hyacinth added. 'Remember Paul told us he was meeting an old sea dog of his on a boat berthed at English Harbour called the Blue Moon? Well, get this, there are no boats called Blue Moon moored at English Harbour, or at any of the other marinas around the island for that matter. Lloyd managed to get hold of CCTV footage from the main harbours. Guess what? Neither Paul, nor his Jeep, show up on any of the surveillance cameras around English Harbour or any of the other boatyards. He lied to us.'

'So where *did* he go then?' Mitch asked.

'Good question,' Hyacinth said. 'We tracked him down to a small boutique hotel near Nonsuch Bay where he was seen entering the gift shop there around nine-fifteen.'

'He went to a *gift shop*?' Brandon said in surprise. 'What the...'

'It gets better,' Hyacinth went on. 'A few minutes later, he was seen leaving the gift shop with Elena, the Spanish lady who runs it. She hung a sign on the door before they walked off together.'

'You mean *together*?' Nerissa asked. Hyacinth nodded.

'That's low,' Nerissa said with disdain. 'His wife and kids hadn't even left the island.'

'Lloyd also ran some background checks on him.' Hyacinth glanced at Lloyd who picked up an iPad from the desk beside him and took over the narrative.

'I was primarily looking for connections with drug cartels, any prior criminal convictions or past connections with OJ,' he began, 'but I found nothing of interest to us. He's a well-respected CEO and he and his wife are upstanding members of their community. They attend a whole bunch of charity functions every year and give generously to all of them. They're model citizens and in many ways are the perfect couple with the perfect family. There was just one thing though.'

'Other than his affair you mean?' Nerissa said.

Lloyd nodded. The others waited as Lloyd scrolled up on the screen of the iPad and turned it towards them.

'Is that a bank statement?' Mitch asked, frowning.

'Correct. It's from one of Paul Griffiths's bank accounts, one of which his wife is not a joint account holder and doubtless knows anything about. You'll notice that there's an outgoing payment of fifty-thousand US dollars to a bank account in Antigua, a personal checking account with one of the commercial banks here. The account's in the name of Quincy Moran. Previous statements show that Paul's been making regular payments to this account for the past five months. We cross-referenced the payments with online statements from the checking account and, sure enough, the deposits from Paul's account matched.'

'It's safe to assume that Paul Griffiths was having an affair with Elena, the Spanish gift shop lady, Quincy found out about it and was blackmailing him,' Hyacinth said. 'Which gives us a whole other motive for Quincy's murder. But if Paul subsequently found out about the contents of the cistern and guessed that the truck headed for Villa Bella Casa this morning was en route to collect the cash, it also gives him motive for the hit on Anson and the rest of the crew on their way back here.'

'Before you ask, Duane's picking up Paul as we speak to bring him in for questioning,' Lloyd added.

'Good work you two,' Delano said.

'There's one other thing,' Lloyd continued. He exchanged the iPad for a battered-looking cell phone which he extracted from a bowl of uncooked rice. 'OJ's cell phone. I managed to dry it out enough to retrieve his calls and messages. There was an app for his alarm system which corresponded with the details I obtained from the security company, as well as an app for his surveillance system. It had all the standard stuff: a live stream, instant intruder alert, night vision and links to the cloud for storage and playback of the footage.'

'If that phone hadn't been water-logged you could've saved yourself a whole bunch of time,' Brandon said.

'Comes with the job of Special Consultant,' Lloyd shrugged casually. The others smiled at each other as he continued. 'Anyway, aside from those two apps, the phone had all the usual ones, you know, weather, news, a couple of stocks and shares apps, but otherwise there was nothing of interest. In fact, it was quite boring. As far as emails go, they were pretty mundane too. Most were the usual rubbish you'd expect to find in anyone's email account; services and utilities and so on, mainly relating to his properties here and elsewhere, along with all the typical junk mail. Messages-wise, it seems that while he had a considerable number of business associates, there were few friends and acquaintances with whom he communicated regularly. It's logical to assume he used a separate phone, probably a burner, for the drug trafficking side of things. It wasn't listed in his possessions you guys retrieved from the yacht so he probably tossed it over the side when he knew the Coast Guard was on the way.'

'What about calls?' Delano asked.

'Ah. I was getting to that,' Lloyd said. 'It's the only interesting part. The day before he was caught in the storm, OJ made a couple of calls to a cell number with a seven-five-eight area code.'

'Saint Lucia?' Brandon asked.

'Correct. We traced the number to a Marcus Holland. He owns a marina there. He denied knowing anyone by the name of Oliver Jacobs, or having ever had a sailing yacht called the Atratus berthed in his marina, but it's my guess this was OJ's port of call to refuel and restock with food and water on his way back to Antigua. I'm sure Marcus took a nice little backhander and asked no questions in return. There was probably also an extra little sweetener of white powder for Marcus's silence; he was as tight-lipped as they come.'

'CCTV?' Brandon asked.

'You can always rely on the surveillance cameras,' Lloyd replied cheerfully. He picked up the iPad again and tapped onto the screen. It showed black and white footage of a small marina with a few modest-sized yachts and sailing craft berthed along the jetty. The date at the top was the day before the night of the storm. With his thumb and index finger, Lloyd zoomed into footage of a sailing yacht manoeuvring into a berth at the far side of the marina. He waited a few seconds before freezing the image and zooming in further. He held it up for the rest of the team. There was no mistaking the yacht in question: it was the Atratus. The image was blurry but they could just make out the helmsman: it was Oliver Jacobs.

'We spoke to Bobby, the CDSLI officer down in Saint Lucia, and he's headed over to the marina to take Marcus Holland in for questioning,' Hyacinth said.

'There was nothing else useful on OJ's cell and it isn't linked to any other devices, so we still don't know what was on his laptop,' Lloyd added. He glanced at his watch. 'That's all I've got. If you guys don't have anything else for me right now, there're a few jobs I need to finish up next door.'

'You mean like watering that giant rubber plant?' Brandon asked with a straight face.

'Very funny,' Lloyd replied. Unable to think of a witty riposte, he placed the iPad on the desk and disappeared through to the reception.

'I guess the only person who knows what's on Jacobs's laptop, other than Jacobs himself, is Quincy's murderer,' Mitch said. 'There's a reason it was taken from Jacobs's study.'

Delano excused himself to take a call on his phone. He listened and nodded for a few minutes before thanking the caller and hanging up.

'That was Jessie, Wendell's second-in-command,' he said to the rest of the team. 'She knows Wendell's not the greatest when it comes to sharing. As he's otherwise engaged with the events of this morning, she called to check in and make sure we'd been kept up to speed with what they had on Quincy's pickup.'

'Anything new?' Brandon asked.

'Not really.' Delano shook his head. 'We know the pickup went over the edge of the cliff some time after ten-thirty yesterday morning, when Quincy was seen leaving Hamilton Bay, but before eight-thirty yesterday evening, when the tourists spotted the wreckage down on the rocks. Forensics found evidence of cocaine in the cab but no signs of blood or trauma, concluding that there was no one inside when it plunged over the cliff. The only DNA found in the cab belonged to Quincy and his girlfriend, Latoya. She gave a statement to the police and said that she was a frequent passenger in the truck.

'Jessie said they found no evidence of any other vehicles along the dirt track at the top of the cliff. There are numerous tyre tracks further down though, where the track joins the main road, and it's an impossible task to identify them all. The most likely theory the police are working on is that someone — possibly Quincy's killer — knew he was en route from Hamilton Bay to Sugar Reef Bay and maybe even followed him there. Somewhere near Tamarind Point Quincy was forced to abandon his pickup and take his captor to Villa Bella Casa by the alternative route, assuming there really is one, either in another vehicle or on foot. Later that day, Quincy's captor returned to the pickup and, knowing that Quincy was dead, drove the pickup to the top of the cliff and put it in drive before jumping out at the last minute. There are two possible reasons for dumping Quincy's truck: the first is that it contained some kind of incriminating evidence which needed to be disposed of. The second and most likely reason is that Quincy's killer wasn't expecting Quincy's body to be discovered so quickly. The pickup on the rocks was intended to be a red herring which again, Jessie suspects wasn't supposed to be found quite so fast.

'She thinks the killer intended for it to be spotted eventually, possibly with the aim of leading the police to conclude that Quincy was in his truck when it went over the edge, that his body was thrown clear, dashed on the rocks and washed out to sea. Their attention would be diverted elsewhere, on a wild goose chase, with the Coast Guard and search and rescue teams out at sea searching for his body for days. Which would buy the killer yet more time to remove the cash from Jacobs's cistern and stow it safely elsewhere.'

'Suspects?' Hyacinth asked.

'That's the other reason for Jessie's call. So far they've drawn a complete blank, but Wendell mentioned we'd spoken to a few people they might be interested in.'

'Oh okay, so Wendell only gets one of his gofers to call us with information when he needs some himself,' Brandon said hotly. 'Why doesn't he do his own legwork for a change?'

'Forget Wendell,' Delano said. 'We're in this together. We need to pool our information. There's a lot at stake.'

'So who do we have?' Brandon asked. He picked up a black marker pen ready to scrawl on the whiteboard.

'Paul Griffiths, the pharmaceutical CEO, has motive and opportunity,' Hyacinth volunteered. 'Quincy was blackmailing him and we know he was unaccounted for around the time Quincy was murdered with only Elena, his Spanish gift shop lover, to vouch for him. We have him on camera leaving the hotel gift shop in Nonsuch Bay at around nine-fifteen yesterday morning. He returned to Sugar Reef at one-forty five. Unfortunately there are no cameras overlooking the parking lot at the boutique hotel at Nonsuch Bay so we haven't been able to obtain any footage of Paul's Jeep arriving or leaving. We know Paul is familiar with Sugar Reef Bay and owns the property next to Jacobs's villa. He may have got wind of what Jacobs was up to and wanted a slice of the pie for himself. He's also wealthy in his own right and would have been able to pay for the hit on the truck this morning.'

'Then there's Jay Palmer, the American businessman and restaurateur.' Nerissa took over the narrative. 'He had a beef with Quincy over his unreliability and substandard work which has cost Jay money and ratings in the past. We know he called Quincy that morning and drove over to his property at Hamilton Bay where Quincy was working. In addition, Jay has no alibi between ten forty-five and one o'clock that afternoon. We know he left his house again just before two, when he drove to his restaurant in St. John's. I checked Jay's financial records both here and in the States. His restaurant in St.

John's may appear to be successful, but the books say otherwise. The establishment is massively in debt and just last month Jay took out a loan to pay the staff wages. It's a similar story for his investments and business interests elsewhere. He's made some bad decisions and has lived beyond his means for some time now. He's on the verge of losing the restaurant, his home in Cedar Valley, his lifestyle and his reputation. It's fair to say the money in Jacobs's cistern would've been a tempting prospect to Jay Palmer and would've put an end to his cashflow problems. The only obstacle in his way was Quincy.'

'So Jay has motive, opportunity, and no alibi,' Hyacinth said, as Brandon wrote furiously on the whiteboard.

'He's probably also capable of organising the hit squad to take out the truck,' Nerissa added.

'And then there's our favourite neighbourhood pusher, Vinnie Trickett,' Brandon said, pausing from the writing. 'I'll pay him a visit this afternoon, see if I can jog his memory about the altercation with Quincy at The Jungle.'

'Isn't that a usual Friday night occurrence where Vinnie's concerned?' Mitch asked.

'It is for Vinnie, but not for Quincy,' Brandon replied. 'According to Max, Quincy was always pretty even-tempered and was rarely involved in anything so much as a minor scuffle, least of all a serious fight with the notorious crime lord of St. John's.'

'Vinnie Trickett's just a lowlife candyman, the scum of the streets,' Mitch said. 'Sure, he might have threatened Quincy and even had him murdered, but you really think he's big enough and clever enough to arrange a hit on a truck carrying a hundred million dollars?'

'Definitely not,' Brandon said, 'but he might know someone who is.'

'Brandon's right,' Delano added. 'Finding Quincy's killer is the key to finding who's responsible for the hit on the truck and the murder of Anson, Leon and the four police officers. Sure, the three suspects we have so far all have motives for Quincy's murder — Jay and Paul are without alibis and Vinnie doubtless has a whole crew of hatchet men at his disposal — but there's more to this than just a dispute with a local handyman. Which brings me to our fourth suspect…'

'Oliver Jacobs,' Brandon said as he wrote the name in block capitals and underlined it.

'This whole thing started when he put out his Mayday call to the Coast Guard during the storm in the early hours of yesterday morning,' Delano said. 'It was the catalyst to everything else which started to unravel around him. The shipment of cocaine was found on *his* yacht; Quincy's body and the hundred million dollars were found in *his* cistern. Jacobs knows far more than he's saying.'

'I think we should talk to him again,' Hyacinth said.

'What about his lawyer?' Nerissa queried, raising an eyebrow.

'Forget the lawyer,' Mitch said harshly. 'Anson's dead because of Jacobs, along with Leon and four good men. I'm with you Hyacinth. Let's put the pressure on him again.'

'Wait a minute,' Delano said raising a hand. 'Mitch, you're lucky I'm even allowing you to be here after what you went through this morning. There's no way you're interviewing Jacobs right now.' He paused. 'Nerissa, go with Hyacinth. Tell Jacobs his lawyer's been held up in court.'

'Sure thing boss,' Nerissa replied. As she and Hyacinth left the room, Delano's cell phone rang again.

'It's the hospital,' he said, glancing at the screen.

There was a tense silence as Delano listened to the person at the end of the line. The call was brief and to the point. Delano thanked the caller and hung up. He glanced around at the remaining members of his team before he finally spoke.

'That was one of the nurses from the ER. Edella's taken a turn for the worst. It's not looking good.'

TWENTY-ONE

1:55 pm, Friday, September 20
CDSLI Headquarters, English Harbour

'Aside from the fact that this is completely illegal and my lawyer should be present, I've already stated the only conditions in which I'll agree to talk to you guys.'

Hyacinth and Nerissa had spent the best part of an hour trying to extract something useful from Oliver Jacobs, to no avail. The windowless room with cinder block walls and the purple glow from the low-level LEDs was becoming as tiresome as Oliver himself, and the faint smell of seaweed as nauseating. In addition, Oliver was annoyed following his court attendance that morning, which added to his uncooperative mood. Hyacinth and Nerissa were aware that Magistrate Darroux had denied bail, as expected. For now, at least, Jacobs was staying put.

'We've already told you you're not in a place to be demanding any kind of conditions,' Hyacinth said in a glacial tone.

'Except I am and you know it. Persuade Gray and Alicia to come on board with this, read them *fully* into the case and I'll cooperate.'

'Or *what?*' Hyacinth asked, hands on her hips.

'Or I don't talk to you,' Oliver shrugged. 'And if I do happen to have anything which might help with your case, then I guess you'll never know.' He rattled his handcuffs behind his back. 'I'm bored. I think we're done here.'

'Nerissa and I will decide when we're done,' Hyacinth said coldly. She glanced at Nerissa in frustration at their lack of progress. Nerissa paused before turning to Oliver.

'Suppose we speak to your friends,' she began, 'read them into the case, tell them what we have so far. How do we know we can trust them? I mean, come on Jacobs, they're *your* friends. I'd sooner trust a salesperson trying to sell me a timeshare.'

'You might like to read up on the Rock Palm Resort cold case they helped the Antigua police department solve last year if you don't think they're trustworthy,' Oliver replied.

'Then remind us exactly *why* you want them on board with this again?' Hyacinth said. 'What d'you want them to do?'

'What they do best. Solve crimes.'

'Surely that's the very last thing you'd want.'

'Au contraire. I know I'm guilty of drug running, I can't lie about that when I was caught with a boatload of cocaine, can I? As far as Quincy's murder goes, I'm as much in the dark about that as you are, but believe me, I'm just as eager for the killer to be found.'

'*Really*?' Hyacinth asked in disbelief.

'Yes really.'

'If we speak to Graymond and Alicia, how do we know they'll agree to help?' Nerissa asked.

'You don't.' Oliver remembered his previous conversation with his friends and their refusal to get involved. 'But if *you* ask them it might carry more weight.'

'How do we know you'll keep your word and cooperate with us?' Hyacinth asked.

'*You* don't know me, but Gray and Alicia do.' Oliver spoke calmly. He made eye contact. He was serious. 'Persuade them to help. Tell them why you want them on the case. And then ask them to vouch for my integrity.'

'Your integrity? Right. It's that little thing called trust again Jacobs,' Hyacinth said.

'I'm not asking you to trust *me*, I'm asking you to trust *them*,' Oliver replied. 'But suit yourselves.' He shrugged. 'Either way, I get to sit here in this delightful little grotto with purple mood-lighting and suboptimal airflow. Oh, and when you come back to beg for my help again, don't forget to bring my lawyer. And some air freshener. This rancid seaweed smell is beginning to impregnate these lovely prison clothes.'

'We'll talk to your friends,' Nerissa said.

'And thus I shall be delighted to cooperate with the CDSLI in solving their little murder mystery,' Oliver replied.

Hyacinth gave Oliver a look of disdain before following Nerissa out of the room.

'Get Gray and Alicia on board,' Oliver called after them, 'and then I'll tell you anything you want to know.'

For the second time that day, Frank transported Graymond and Alicia from the West Beach Club to the CDSLI headquarters at English Harbour. The mood in the Toyota minivan was sombre. Alicia dabbed her reddened eyes with a tissue and stared out of the tinted glass at the passing scenery. Frank kept half an eye on her in his rearview mirror. He knew she and her family had known the general manager of the West Beach Club for many years. He himself had been devastated to have been told the news of Leon Fayer's death by the assistant general manager of the hotel.

Frank had started working as a taxi driver for the West Beach Club shortly after Leon had joined as the GM. In fact, it was Leon who had employed him. Frank had always felt indebted to Leon for giving him a chance and Leon had always been kind to him. He secretly wiped a tear from his own eyes as he wondered how Leon's wife Betsy was holding up with the news.

The Toyota minivan pulled up outside the nondescript brick and sandstone building which housed the CDSLI headquarters, where a man was waiting to escort Graymond and Alicia inside. He was the same man who had greeted them earlier that morning. Frank recognised him as one of the bouncers at The Jungle, not because Frank had ever set foot inside the place, but because now and again he dropped customers off at or picked them up from the notorious establishment. He said goodbye to Graymond and Alicia and watched as the nightclub bouncer ushered them through the steel grille-front door of the warehouse. He knew better than to ask, but as he drove away Frank wondered what their visit to the CDSLI could possibly be about.

Delano, Mitch, Hyacinth and Nerissa were waiting in the crew room as Lloyd directed Graymond and Alicia inside. Delano thanked them for coming, offered his condolences on behalf of the team to Alicia and asked Lloyd to stick around. Leaving nothing out, he summarised the events of both cases: the payload of cocaine on the Atratus, the hundred million dollars in the cistern and Quincy's disappearance and murder. He finished with the holdup of the truck on the coastal road that morning in which Leon Fayer, Anson, and others, had lost their lives. At the mention of Leon's name, Alicia fought back more tears and Graymond placed an arm around her shoulders.

'You'll have to forgive me but I do have an ulterior motive for asking you here this afternoon,' Delano said gently, when Alicia had composed herself. They waited for him to continue.

'It all comes back to your friend Oliver Jacobs.'

'What's he done now?' Graymond asked.

'He's refusing to talk to us unless we read you into the case.'

'He's *what?*'

'We're pretty sure he knows far more than he's letting on about Quincy's murder, and he's also staying tight-lipped about his contacts here and in Trinidad. His laptop's still missing and, according to him, he has no idea where it might be. He's agreed to tell us what he knows on one condition: that you two come on board with the investigation.'

'I'm sure you don't need our help,' Alicia said.

'It's an unusual situation, I agree,' Delano replied, 'but in light of your reputation with the Antigua police department after the Rock Palm case last year, I'm very happy to invite you to assist us in any way you feel you can. It's up to you, of course, and there's no pressure from us, but we'll always welcome any extra help or insight and your involvement might just persuade Jacobs to cooperate a little more.'

'That's very kind of you but I'm sorry Officer Reid, we've already told Jacobs we're here on vacation and there's no way we're getting involved in this,' Graymond said firmly. 'And anyway, after this morning I'm certainly not letting Alicia participate in your investigation. To begin with, she needs time to grieve the loss of a family friend. I'm sorry, but we can't help you.'

'I completely understand,' Delano replied, 'and I appreciate Alicia's position. Believe me, we're feeling it too. We lost four police officers and one agent this morning. I have another agent in the ICU right now and,' he nodded to Mitch whose right arm was in a sling, 'an agent with a gunshot wound which narrowly avoided major vessels and organs.'

'Once again Officer Reid, I'm very sorry but…'

Alicia suddenly placed her hand on Graymond's arm.

'Wait a minute Gray,' she interrupted. Graymond stopped in surprise. 'Remember when Leon stepped in to help us last year with the Rock Palm case?' Alicia said. 'He never asked questions and he trusted us implicitly, even when we directly implicated him in a crime without any explanation.'

'Alicia…' Graymond began in a cautionary tone.

'I wouldn't accede to Jacobs's requests for anything, but this time around I'm prepared to make an exception,' Alicia continued. She looked steadily at Delano. 'We don't owe Jacobs a minute of our time and I've no idea why he wants us involved, but Leon lost his life over this. We owe it to him and his family — and your own people of course, Officer Reid — to find out what happened and who's behind it all.'

'Are you sure about this Miss Clayton?' Delano asked.

'I'm certain.' Alicia looked up at Graymond. 'Vacation's cancelled,' she said decisively before turning back to Delano. 'We'll help you Officer Reid. We'll talk to Jacobs. We'll do whatever it takes to solve your case and, ultimately, bring Leon's killers to justice.'

'Thank you,' Delano said quietly, 'and you too Mr. Sharkey.'

'Don't thank me,' Graymond replied. 'This is Alicia's decision, but if she's happy with it then I am too.'

'We'd better revert to first name terms if you're happy?' Delano suggested.

'Absolutely,' Alicia replied. She dried the last of her tears with a tissue. 'I do have one request of my own though.'

'Name it.'

'There are two people who will insist on helping with this case besides Gray and me, one of whom owes Leon an enormous debt of gratitude. They'll be working off the record, of course, but Owen's a native of the island and may prove useful. He was homeless for many years and still has contacts everywhere. Spencer's…' Alicia paused, 'well let's just say Spencer's helped me with a number of my own fact-finding investigations as a journalist back in the UK and he always gets results.'

'Can they be trusted?' Delano asked.

'Absolutely. Both Owen and Spencer played their parts perfectly in solving the Rock Palm Resort case. They can be wholly relied upon in confidential matters.'

'Then I'll take your word for that Alicia,' Delano nodded. 'We'll involve both of them at your request, but this is an ongoing case and there will be consequences if any of this information is leaked to a wider audience.'

'Rest assured that won't happen,' Alicia replied. 'I'll take full responsibility for them. Thank you. So shall we start by paying Jacobs another visit?'

'He's all yours,' Delano said with a smile. 'I'll have Lloyd get him back in the interview room.'

'I can't wait.' Alicia returned the smile.

As Graymond and Alicia waited for Oliver to be escorted to the small interview room on the south side, a dark blue Ford Explorer with tinted windows and government licence plates pulled into the parking lot outside. In the rear passenger seat sat Paul Griffiths, the pharmaceutical CEO and Oliver Jacobs's neighbour. He was accompanied by Duane and another plain clothes officer who escorted him into the reception area of the CDSLI building.

'Steady on,' Paul protested angrily, narrowly missing a step. He was wearing a pale green golf shirt and olive-coloured shorts with white ankle socks and white trainers.

Delano stepped into the room.

'Where would you like Mr. Griffiths?' Duane asked.

'Take him to the north room,' Delano replied.

'Will this take long?' Paul asked as Duane steered him through a door on the opposite side of the room.

'That depends on you,' Delano replied. 'Answer our questions truthfully and if we're satisfied you're innocent and have nothing to hide, you'll be back on the golf course in no time.'

'But I *am* innocent,' Paul wailed. Duane guided him along the corridor and jostled him into the room on the right, the north interview room, which appeared to mirror the south room with its whitewashed walls and wooden table, but without the rays of sunlight.

'This is highly irregular, not to mention downright embarrassing,' Paul protested angrily as Duane placed a firm hand on his shoulder and pushed him into a chair. 'I have some very important business associates staying right now. What am I supposed to tell them? This could damage my reputation irrevocably.'

'Sorry about that Paul,' Delano said, taking a seat on the other side of the table. 'I guess we should've thought of that before we brought you in. Then again, I guess *you* should've thought of that before you lied to us about where you were yesterday morning.'

'What?' Paul frowned and squirmed uncomfortably in his chair. 'I have no idea what you're talking about. Should my lawyer be here?'

'That's your call,' Delano replied. 'By all means, if you think you need your lawyer, but it will almost certainly delay your return to the golf course.'

'What's this about then?' Paul asked.

'Your alibi. Yesterday morning. You told my officers you were meeting an old friend on his boat, the Blue Moon, at English Harbour.'

'Yes. That's because I was.'

'For a start there *are* no boats called Blue Moon berthed at English Harbour, or anywhere else in Antigua.'

'I can assure you I…'

'We went through the CCTV footage for every harbour and marina on the island from yesterday morning,' Delano interrupted. 'You don't show up anywhere.'

'That's hardly proof I wasn't there,' Paul replied. 'You can't dispute my alibi with something you *don't* have.'

'Oh I completely agree,' Delano said. 'And we're not about to. We certainly wouldn't pull you away from your important game of golf without a shred of evidence, at the very least.'

'I'm not following.'

'Then how about I jog your memory as to where you were yesterday morning?' From an A4-sized file, Delano produced some still shots which Lloyd had printed in preparation for the interview. They were taken from surveillance footage outside the gift shop of the boutique hotel near Nonsuch Bay. The first of the black and white images showed Paul's face, clearly visible in the centre of the picture. Delano slid the page to one side, revealing a second picture which showed two people leaving the gift shop: a man and a woman. Although their faces were not as distinguishable as on the first picture due to the camera angle, it was obvious that the man was the same person as in the previous shot and the woman had been identified as Elena, the Spanish lady who ran the gift shop. A third picture showed Paul and Elena turning back towards the camera as Elena went to hang a sign on the shop door. The fourth and final image was of the couple walking away from the shop, their backs to the camera.

'Recognise anyone here?' Delano asked.

Paul slumped in his chair before burying his face in his hands and massaging his forehead. He let out a noise which was somewhere between a whimper and a moan.

'All right,' he said bringing his hands back down on the table in front of him. 'I lied to you. I admit it. But please don't bring my wife and kids into this. Or anyone for that matter.'

'So your wife knows nothing about your affair with Elena López?'

'No, Jennifer has no idea. Please don't let her find out. You'll ruin my life, my reputation…'

'Do your wife's feelings come into this at all or is it just *your* life and *your* reputation which matter here?' Delano asked coldly.

'Just… *Please*… I'll tell you everything, just don't let this information get out,' Paul pleaded.

'Is that what you told Quincy Moran when he found out about you and Elena?'

'*What?* What d'you mean?'

'Paul, this interview is going to move very slowly if it takes you at least three attempts to answer each question,' Delano said in frustration.

'But I don't…'

'It's going to get very tedious, not to mention a complete waste of our time, if I have to ask the same question — to which I am well aware you know the answer — multiple times. Let's start over, shall we? How did Quincy find out about your affair with Elena López?'

Paul picked at a splinter on the table top. Without looking up, he began talking.

'Elena and I have been seeing each other for about eight months. We met at the hotel at Nonsuch Bay where she runs the gift shop. I was entertaining some clients and business colleagues. Jennifer and the kids were home in New York and, well I guess I was lonely and needed some company. Elena was single and things just went from there. We started seeing each other regularly, sometimes at her place — she rents a beach house near the hotel — and occasionally at Sugar Reef Bay. We were incredibly discreet, you know. She was very respectful of the fact that I had a wife and kids and rarely contacted me when we came out here as a family. Elena and I certainly didn't see each other during those times. This was a one-off. Jennifer and the kids had stayed for longer than planned and Elena and I hadn't been able to see each other as much. I knew my business associates would be arriving soon after my family left for the airport so I arranged to meet Elena yesterday morning. Jennifer was busy organising the kids for the flight home, I would've just been in the way.'

Delano remained silent.

'As for Quincy,' Paul continued. 'Elena and I were in the pool at Sugar Reef one afternoon when Quincy showed up unexpectedly. He promised not to say a word to my wife, or anyone, about Elena and I, and I thought our secret was safe with him until a couple of months later he brought it up out of the blue. He asked for money to keep quiet.'

'How much?' Delano asked.

'Fifty-thousand US dollars a month, to be wired to a bank account in Antigua. Fortunately I have a bank account which my wife knows nothing about so I set up regular payments to Quincy's account as instructed. What else could I do? I had no choice.'

Delano knew from Lloyd's background checks that Paul was telling the truth about the money.

'So Quincy was blackmailing you,' he said.

'Yes.' Paul briefly made eye contact before looking away.

'Fifty-thousand dollars a month is a lot of money. That's a good motive for murder, no?' Delano asked. He watched Paul closely.

'Murder?'

'Oh come on Paul, I've already spoken to you about wasting time.'

'No, really, I don't know what you mean. What murder? What's this about?'

'Quincy's body was found in the cistern of Oliver Jacobs's villa. He'd been murdered.'

'Oh my… Quincy's *dead*? How? When? You've got to believe me, I had no idea.'

'That's the problem Paul, I struggle to believe habitual liars.'

'No, you have to, I didn't do it.' Paul spoke quickly. 'Fine, I may be a cheating rat but I'm not a murderer.'

'Where were you and Elena yesterday between nine in the morning and one forty-five?' Delano asked.

'We went back to her place. It's a small beach house just north of Nonsuch Bay. She drove. We were there the whole time. She dropped me back at the hotel around one-thirty and I came straight home.'

'Any witnesses?'

'No. No one.' Paul shook his head. 'Not that I know of anyway. But you can speak to Elena. And your officers guarding the Sugar Reef access road can vouch for my return of course.'

'So there's no one to say you didn't return to Sugar Reef Bay, to Villa Bella Casa, to take care of the one person who knew your sordid little secret?'

'No. But I didn't do it, okay? Ask Elena if you don't believe me.'

'She's on her way here right now. You better hope your little stories match up.'

'Do you really think I'd go back to Sugar Reef Bay, to commit murder, with my wife and kids at the house next door?' Paul asked desperately. 'And anyway, the access road was being watched the whole time by your officers.'

'What about the other way in?'

'Other way in?' Paul frowned in puzzlement. 'What other way in? There's only one way to get to the properties up there, including Oliver Jacobs's place, and that's the access road. I don't know any other way in. Surely those cliffs render any other road impassable?'

Delano paused. It was true that Paul did not pass the officers guarding the entrance to Sugar Reef Bay until he returned from his visit to Elena early that afternoon. It was possible that he genuinely had no idea of an alternative way to reach Villa Bella Casa. Delano decided to change tack.

'Tell me how well you know Oliver Jacobs.'

'I already answered that question when your agents knocked on my door yesterday,' Paul replied. The answer was firm but he spoke less confidently than before.

'Were you aware he was involved in narco trafficking?' Delano asked.

'No, I had no idea,' Paul replied instantly. 'Like I told your agents, he kept himself to himself. But if you're accusing me of being involved with a drug smuggler now, you've got that completely wrong. Sure, I've been an idiot, I was having an affair and I allowed myself to get caught, but I paid Quincy what he asked and I certainly didn't kill him. And I'm not a drug trafficker either. Hell, I'm the CEO of a pharmaceutical company. The very last illegal activity I'd get involved in would be drug smuggling.'

Delano's cell phone buzzed and he checked the screen. It was a message from Mitch. It read: *ME's report just in re: Quincy. Call Lianne ASAP.* He pushed back his chair and stood up.

'I have to go,' he said.

'What about me?' Paul asked.

'We're not done with you yet,' Delano replied, turning to the door.

'But I — I've told you, I've got nothing to do with this...'

'Then you've got nothing to worry about, have you?'

The door shut with a loud click and Paul was alone.

TWENTY-TWO

2:25 pm, Friday, September 20
CDSLI Headquarters, English Harbour

Oliver Jacobs had spent the last ten minutes lamenting the injustices of the legal system of Antigua.

'It's a complete disgrace,' he seethed to Graymond and Alicia who sat opposite him. Hyacinth stood in the far corner of the room but Oliver ignored her. 'How *dare* that miserable little magistrate deny bail? I doubt he'd even read my case file.'

'I think you'll find it's his decision to make,' Alicia replied. 'Just like in the UK.'

'Well I've got Webster working round the clock to appeal against it,' Oliver huffed. 'This can go all the way to the Supreme Court if it has to.'

'If you're telling the truth that you know nothing about the circumstances surrounding Quincy's murder, then your life may be at risk too,' Graymond said. 'It might be safer for you to stay in custody for the time being.'

'I don't see why my life might be in danger,' Oliver said with a frown. 'How do you figure that one out?'

'You're a drug trafficker Jacobs. The minute you signed up for that little side business you pretty much signed your own death warrant.' Alicia spoke wearily, as if she was explaining dental extractions to a sugar addict.

'Forget bail for now Jacobs,' Graymond said. 'If Webster's the best lawyer on the island then let him do his job. Tell us about this Ray you mentioned, the British expat you met in Jamaica.'

'Like I said, Ray is probably an alias,' Oliver replied. 'I haven't heard from him since he contacted me about this latest cocaine shipment. He's sure to know what's happened. It's probably the last I'll ever hear from him.'

Graymond and Alicia agreed that Ray — whoever or wherever he was — would be aware of Oliver's capture. He had clearly been awaiting Oliver's usual text message to confirm he'd arrived back at his mooring at Sugar Reef Bay, which had never been sent.

'Can you give us a description of Ray?' Graymond asked.

'Sure. He's of average height, average build, normally wears dark clothes, dark glasses and a baseball cap,' Oliver began.

'Not helpful Jacobs,' Alicia said. 'How old is Ray?'

'Fiftyish? Maybe. Could be older. Or younger.'

'I'll send in a sketch artist,' a voice said from behind Oliver. He had forgotten Hyacinth was in the far corner, listening in to the conversation.

'Good. Let's talk about Quincy again,' Graymond went on. 'Why did you want him to go to your villa yesterday morning?'

'I was worried about storm damage,' Oliver replied. He had a serious expression and made eye contact as he spoke. 'Quincy has — sorry, *had* — access to the property and knew the place better than anyone.'

'He knew about the cash in your cistern?' Graymond asked.

'Yes. He did.'

'Seems a little odd you trusted your pool man with that kind of information,' Alicia ventured.

'He was also the maintenance guy, knew the place inside out. He helped me block off the pipes to the cistern in the first place.'

'Anyone else know about it?'

'Just Quincy.'

'Aside from the cistern, where else did you store the money you got from drug trafficking?' Graymond asked.

'Nowhere,' Oliver replied, carefully maintaining eye contact. 'The cistern was the only place.'

'Stop playing us Jacobs,' Graymond said. 'The CDSLI found a hundred million dollars in your cistern. If you'd gotten away with your most recent shipment you were due to get somewhere in the region of seventy-five million, and that's one shipment alone. How many trips have you made to Trinidad and back in the last year?'

'A few, but the payload isn't always that much.'

'I'm not buying it either,' Alicia said. 'Where's the rest of the money Jacobs?'

'I'm telling you, that's it.'

'Jacobs, if you don't start telling us the truth, we can't help you and we're leaving now,' Graymond said, standing up.

'I *am* telling the truth,' Jacobs said insistently. 'Please Gray. Sit down. The money in the cistern is all there is.'

'Well even that's gone now.' Hyacinth stepped forward. Oliver turned in his chair to face her.

'Gone?' he asked in surprise.

Hyacinth moved to the opposite side of the table, next to Graymond and Alicia. She watched Oliver closely as she continued.

'The truck carrying the money was hijacked this morning by a group of masked hitmen. Both the truck and the money are missing.'

'Oh *dear*,' Oliver said with a sneer. 'That's a bit of a blow for the CDSLI, isn't it?'

'You don't happen to know anything about that do you Jacobs?' Hyacinth asked.

Oliver smiled slightly before replying.

'What d'you think I am? A psychic medium or something? First you accuse me of being involved with Quincy's murder, now you're suggesting I had something to do with the hijacking of a truck. And all the time I've been stuck here in a locked cell. I realise I'm a man of many talents, but this whole telepathy thing is a stretch, even for me.'

'Just answer the question Jacobs,' Graymond said sternly, 'or Alicia and I walk out of here right now.'

Oliver gave an exaggerated sigh.

'No need to be like that Gray. It was only a joke. All right, no, I don't know about any hijacking. How could I? I didn't even know you were moving the money this morning.'

'So you knew nothing about it and had nothing to do with it?' Hyacinth asked.

'*No.*'

'And what about Quincy? You sure you had nothing to do with his disappearance and murder? He was a loose end for you, after all.'

'If you can tell me how I arranged to have him killed from the confines of your dungeons here, I'm very interested to know how you think I did it.'

'Do you know who killed Quincy?' Graymond asked.

'No,' Oliver replied with a firm shake of his head.

'Jacobs,' Alicia said with a frown.

'Honestly, I've told you everything,' Oliver said, looking at each one of them in turn. 'You've got the whole story from my side, you've got the payload of drugs from my yacht, you've found my little hiding place for the cash — and, by the way, it's your problem if you've lost it all, be more careful next time I guess — and you've…'

'How *dare* you Jacobs?' Hyacinth burst out angrily. She slammed her fists down on the table. 'Six good men died this morning as a result of that hijacking. *Someone* knew we were moving the cash from your cistern. *Someone* knew the route we'd be taking and *someone* knew the number of gunmen for hire needed to overcome the police escort. Show a little more respect for the dead, and if you're lying about this, we *will* find out, and if you think you're in a dungeon now, this place'll seem like a palace compared to where you're headed.'

'Look, I don't know anything about Quincy and I don't know anything about the hit on your truck, okay?' Oliver replied.

'You'd better be telling the truth Jacobs.' Graymond gave him a warning glare as he stood up. He followed Alicia and Hyacinth to the door. Hyacinth turned back to Oliver.

'We'll send in a sketch artist so you can give us a description of Ray.'

The door slammed shut behind them.

Delano waited patiently for Lianne Henderson, the medical examiner, to answer her cell phone.

'Delano, thanks for getting back to me.' Her voice came on the end of the line. 'I've just completed Quincy Moran's post mortem. I've spoken to Officer Rivera, but there were a few things I thought might interest you too. Prior to death, Quincy suffered a blow to the right side of his forehead. The injury's consistent with a heavy object, like a crowbar or something of a similar shape and size. This wasn't the death blow, however, as there was considerable bleeding from the wound. There were ligature marks around the neck just below the level of the thyroid cartilage, along with evidence of facial congestion and signs of petechial haemorrhaging — tiny pinpoint red marks — in the conjunctiva of the eyes. There were other abrasions on the face, as well as on the hands and arms, indicating that Quincy was involved in some kind of a struggle prior to his death. Judging by his injuries and the fact that he was young and fit, his attacker would've likely been fairly strong. There was blood under Quincy's fingernails: his own, and traces of common diesel fuel and polypropylene.'

'Polypropylene?' Delano queried.

'It's a material used in a wide variety of applications, but it's commonly found in nautical ropes because it floats on water. It's also resistant to ultraviolet and it doesn't rot.'

'The rope which was used to kill him,' Delano said.

'Exactly. There was something else too. I found traces of neoprene under Quincy's nails…'

'Found in wetsuits,' Delano finished her sentence.

'Correct again.'

'The nautical theme's interesting.'

'It is. You're looking for someone with access to thick nautical rope and who possibly owns a black neoprene wetsuit. A sailor or surfer or someone with connections to the boating world.'

'Any DNA from the killer?' Delano asked.

'No, but if he, or she, was wearing a wetsuit and gloves, then that explains why. Cause of death was asphyxia due to strangulation. Livor mortis is consistent with the probability that Quincy was attacked and killed in the cistern. As for the time of death, I'd estimate it as between twelve and two p.m. That's all I got.'

'Thanks Lianne.'

'No problem. We're working on the bodies from the hijacking this morning, but it's pretty cut and dried. If I find anything, I'll be in touch, obviously.'

'Appreciate it.'

They said goodbye as Mitch entered the crew room.

'Quincy Moran's PM results?' he asked.

'Yeah. Cause of death was strangulation, as we suspected. Looks as though the killer had some kind of a maritime connection.'

'You mean like a sailor?'

'Or a diver, or surfer. Lianne found traces of diesel fuel, possibly from a boat engine, polypropylene, used in nautical rope and neoprene...'

'A wetsuit,' Mitch finished. 'I just finished interviewing Elena López, the Spanish gift shop lady. Her story checks out with Paul's although we still don't have any witnesses, just their words to go on. But she did mention that sometimes they went to Paul's boat. I did a bit of digging. Turns out he owns one of the yachts moored in Sugar Reef Bay. It's a sleek-looking sixty-foot Sunseeker Predator. He occasionally takes his wife and kids out on it, but it's mostly used to entertain clients and business associates and, of course, his Spanish lover.'

'He's still in the interview room. Go talk to him,' Delano said.

'Sure. What about Elena?'

'She can go for now.'

Mitch nodded and turned back to the door. One of the telephones buzzed on the desk in front of Delano. The display confirmed the call was being placed from the CDSLI office in Saint Lucia. Delano answered it.

'Bobby, hi.'

'Afternoon Delano, I hear you're having quite a day in Antigua.' It was the voice of the Saint Lucia CDSLI officer.

'You could say that,' Delano replied.

'I heard about Anson. I'm so sorry Delano. He was a good man.'

'Thanks Bobby.'

'How's Edella doing?'

'Not great right now. We're hoping she'll pull through.'

'I hope so too.' Bobby paused before continuing. 'I've just talked to Marcus Holland, the owner of the Garden Bay Marina. In spite of his earlier denials to your team about his connections with Oliver Jacobs, when I showed him the CCTV footage taken from his own marina of the Atratus, his memory was miraculously restored.'

'Funny that.'

'I know. Anyway, he confessed to everything and confirmed his little arrangement with Jacobs: in exchange for a nice little kickback of cocaine, Holland provided fuel, supplies and of course, complete discretion. Very convenient. Holland's in custody, very scared and prepared to give evidence at trial should it be required.'

'Good to know,' Delano replied. 'Thanks Bobby.'

'Any time. Keep me updated and let me know if there's anything else you need from me.'

'Of course.'

Delano replaced the handset and stared at the whiteboard across the room. On it were written names, places, times, dates and details intertwining the two cases: the drugs bust on the Atratus and the murder of Quincy Moran. And then there was the hijacking. Where was the truck and the one hundred million dollars now? Who had hired the mercenaries to take out Anson and the four police officers? Arrows crisscrossed the board, asterisks connected one facet of a case to another, but they had little to go on. The team were no further forward in uncovering the cartel network within which Oliver Jacobs was operating, they were no closer to identifying Quincy's killer and they had no idea where the money truck had gone. The cases were inextricably linked, but by what or whom? There seemed to be one vital piece of the puzzle missing, the piece which connected all the others. Delano knew that when they found it, everything else would fall into place.

TWENTY-THREE

3:05 pm, Friday, September 20
The Pavilion Café, the old runway ten, V. C. Bird International
Airport

Johann sat alone at a table in the far corner of The Pavilion Café
gazing at the boats moored in the small marina at Winthorpes
Bay. As they bobbed gently on the water with the occasional wave
slapping at their hulls, Johann imagined himself on his own boat.
He'd be at the helm, a glass of champagne in one hand and a
gorgeous woman beside him wearing very little. He briefly closed
his eyes and told himself that one day he'd figure out a way to
escape Rusty and the cartel. It was a happy daydream, a wistful
moment, but ultimately with little hope. He took a gulp of strong
coffee and glanced back towards the terminal as he waited for Rusty
and his party to arrive. He had only managed a couple of hours
sleep since returning from Miami and tried to suppress a yawn.
He'd read somewhere that flying while tired was more dangerous
than flying when mildly intoxicated. Twenty years ago he probably
wouldn't have noticed the lack of sleep but now, at the age of
sixty-four, he was feeling it. He took another slug of coffee and,
from the corner of his eye, spotted a black SUV making its way
towards the café along runway ten.

Johann had refuelled the Cessna since his flight that morning
and it was ready and waiting to go. The final decision as to where
exactly remained with Rusty, the pseudo-pilot. Johann downed the
last of his coffee, slipped an extra strong mint into his mouth and got
up from the table as the SUV came to a halt next to the café. Rusty
and his guests had arrived. Leaving a ten dollar bill on the table,
Johann nodded to the waitress and headed outside as all four doors
of the SUV opened simultaneously. Rusty, wearing a white shirt with
the usual four-bar gold epaulettes on the shoulders, and smart black
pants, jumped out of the driver's side and spotted Johann.

'Johann, what up dawg!' he called cheerily. He was all smiles.

'Rusty, my man.' Johann forced the usual greeting which Rusty insisted upon, along with the handshake and the macho hug. All part of the act. He hoped the strong coffee and peppermint disguised the telltale smell of alcohol on his breath.

'Johann, meet my buddies Logan and Carter, and their friends, Victoria, Madison and Brielle.' Rusty pointed to each of them in turn as he made the introductions, lingering on the last three names. As the obligatory handshakes and greetings took place, Johann noticed that the three girls, probably in their mid-thirties, were indeed hot. They were a little out of his league, but he'd enjoy the view and the company for the next few hours nonetheless. Rusty's male companions were around the same age as Rusty himself, a little older than the girls but no more than forty. Logan and Carter were in casual attire: t-shirts, blue jeans and cowboy boots. The girls wore a variety of outfits, clearly selected with the object of accentuating gym-honed figures, which did not escape Johann's notice.

'My friend Johann here has asked if he can join us for our flight.' Rusty began with the usual spiel which Johann had heard many times. 'He's taking flying lessons and is keen to pick up as many tips as possible. With my many years of experience as a pilot, well I like to give back and encourage the new ones where I can. So I hope you don't mind…'

'Oh sure, why not?' Logan spoke with a Southern drawl and a wide smile. He nodded at Johann. 'Good for you man. It must be quite a challenge to learn a new skill when you're older.'

Johann resented the older comment but had no choice than to let it go. By now he was used to the humiliation Rusty subjected him to, with comments like he was "doing well but could use the extra practice," or he "wanted to see how the experts did it." One day Johann had a mind to pull off the roughest, most badly executed landing possible, but the stakes were too high.

'It's great you're learning,' the girl who had been introduced as Victoria was saying. 'I'd love to learn someday.' Long, dark, wavy hair cascaded around her shoulders over a blue and white striped blouse with matching shorts, which were teamed with wedge-heeled sandals. Dark, oversized sunglasses covered most of her face and a dramatic shade of crimson accentuated her lips.

'Great,' Rusty said enthusiastically. 'Let's all head over to my aircraft then. Anywhere you fancy going girls?'

As the group walked across the disused runway to the Cessna, the girls entered into a lively discussion as to a possible route.

'I'd really love to fly over English Harbour and Nelson's Dockyard,' Madison said excitedly. Her blonde curls and pale pink playsuit contrasted with her perfectly tanned limbs. 'I'm a sucker for historical sites. Wasn't Nelson some guy in the British Royal Navy?'

'He was. He married a young widow from a plantation family in Nevis. You know Mads, as in Saint Kitts and Nevis,' Brielle added. Her brown hair was scraped back from her face in a tight bun. She had paler skin and wore a short floaty dress in leopard print with matching sandals. 'The girl was called Frances — or Fanny — Nisbet.'

'How d'you know all about that Bree?' Madison asked, peering over the top of her large, square-framed sunglasses.

'I once stayed at the hotel built on the old sugar plantation where Fanny Nisbet grew up. It's this really cool place called the Nisbet Plantation Beach Club. The dining room's in the Great House, Fanny's ancestral home. It's where Nelson, the British Navy guy, and Fanny met. There's even the ruins of an old sugar mill right by the entrance.'

'That sounds so cool,' Madison replied. 'I wanna go there. Can we go this afternoon Rusty? Can we fly to Nevis? How far is it? Let's go for dinner at the Great House!'

'Sure Madison,' Rusty replied with a sideways glance at Johann. 'It only takes about thirty minutes to get to Nevis. I'll call ahead and get a table booked in the Great House. Is there anywhere else you'd like to go on the way there? We've got all afternoon. How about a scenic tour of Antigua? I can show you Jumby Bay Island, one of the most exclusive private islands in the Caribbean, or we could head down to Montserrat and check out the volcano.'

'A volcano? That's pretty cool,' Madison replied. 'How about it y'all?' She glanced round at the little group as they walked. They had almost reached the Cessna.

'Rusty, how long would it take to fly to Redonda?' Victoria asked suddenly. Johann noticed that, like Brielle, her accent was slightly different to Madison's. He guessed they were from a different part of the United States, perhaps the West Coast.

'Redonda? Nobody's ever asked to go there before,' Rusty replied. 'You realise we can't land there? There's no runway. The island's uninhabited. It's essentially a giant rock.'

'Oh sure, I realise that sir, I just wondered if we could fly over and circle round a few times, you know?' Victoria replied.

'What's so fascinating about Redonda?' Madison asked curiously. 'I've never heard of the place.'

'I read an article about it once in a nature magazine,' Victoria replied. 'Few people know that it's the obscure sister island of Antigua and Barbuda, even though it's actually closer to Montserrat. It lies about thirty-five miles southwest of Antigua. The only way to visit is by helicopter as it's mostly inaccessible and landing by boat is virtually impossible. The article said it has one landing site which is poor and pretty much unprotected against the prevailing wind and swell.'

'Sounds really inviting,' Brielle interrupted, to a chorus of laughter.

'Rusty's right,' Victoria continued. 'The island's tiny and practically deserted, but it was once inhabited. Back in the late nineteenth century, they discovered bird poop — or guano as it was called — on the island as a result of it being home to massive seabird colonies over the centuries. The guano contained a valuable mineral which could be used as a fertiliser. I think it was phosphate or something. So they started mining it there. Around two hundred miners lived and worked on the island at that time. According to the article, the mining operations stopped at the outbreak of World War One and no one's lived there since, but you can still see remnants of a past civilisation there: miners' huts, broken cisterns, rusting machinery, even the old post office.'

'That's awesome!' Brielle said.

'Isn't it?' Victoria agreed. 'After Redonda was abandoned, it turned into a refuge for sea-birds, reptiles and goats and so on, but it became overrun with rats and they all ran out of food. The island basically became this huge barren rock rising out of the sea with sheer cliffs and a rugged, lunar-type landscape. It was pretty bleak and desolate. Not exactly your typical desert island.'

'Ewww, rats?' Madison pulled a face of disgust. 'In that case I'm glad we can't land there.'

'But what's so cool is that according to the article, back in twenty-seventeen a group of conservationists went to Redonda and set up a restoration programme,' Victoria continued. 'They got rid of the rats and brought the goats to Antigua, and within twelve months all the native plants and animals on the island had begun to make a miraculous recovery. You should see the before and after pictures. The island's pretty much returned to its natural, lush green state now. There's grass and even flowers and trees growing there. The birds and reptiles are thriving. The conservation work completely turned the whole ecosystem around. There are seabird colonies, land birds, rare lizards… The island even has its own indigenous lizard called the Redonda Ground Dragon, found nowhere else on earth.'

'That is awesome,' Brielle gushed. She was tapping on the screen on her iPhone. 'Lemme check out that ground dragon, I wanna see a picture. Oh look Mads, he is *so* cute! Look at him, it's the Redonda Ground Dragon, otherwise known as the pholido… wait, how d'you say that?'

Logan leaned in towards Brielle to look at the screen.

'That's its Latin name Bree,' he said. 'Pholidoscelis atratus. Pholidoscelis is a genus of lizards that belongs to a certain family. I guess the atratus bit is the name for this particular lizard.'

'Cool name,' Brielle said still examining the picture on her phone. 'I wanna go see Redonda too. Can we fly over Redonda please Rusty? And then go to dinner at the Great House in Nevis.'

'I'm sure I can make that happen,' Rusty said making subtle eye contact with Johann who gave a brief nod. They had reached the

Cessna. 'Johann, would you mind calling the Great House to make our reservation tonight while we climb aboard?'

'No problem Rusty.' Johann forced another fake smile.

Rusty opened the cargo door and offered his hand to Victoria. 'Ladies first,' he said with a smile. 'Watch your step.'

Victoria graciously took Rusty's hand and climbed aboard. 'Anywhere I should sit?' she asked.

'Johann and I will be up front. How about somewhere in the middle?'

Johann knew Rusty was never keen for passengers to be too close to the front of the aircraft for fear that they might watch a little too closely and realise who was actually doing the flying. The others climbed on board behind Victoria and settled themselves excitedly in seats which clearly gained Rusty's approval.

'Make yourselves comfortable,' he said. 'I'll just, er, check out the aircraft.'

He stepped back down on to the tarmac and began a cursory walk around the Cessna, pretending to inspect control surfaces and other moving parts. Johann had found the number of the Nisbet Plantation Beach Club and asked to be put through to the Great House.

'Remember to ask for the best seats in the house,' Rusty called over to him from the port wing. Johann ignored the instruction. Rusty rounded the nose of the aircraft and joined Johann as he finished the call.

'I've made a reservation for seven-thirty,' Johann said. 'It should give us plenty of time to detour to Redonda and perhaps fly over Saint Kitts before landing in Nevis. The hotel will arrange for a taxi to meet us at the airport.'

'Excellent,' Rusty said with approval. 'Are we good for fuel?'

'*You're* checking the aircraft,' Johann replied.

'Excuse me?' Rusty's demeanour changed abruptly.

'Yeah, we're good,' Johann said hurriedly.

'I've told you before, pull any stupid tricks and your life won't be worth living,' Rusty hissed. 'And you are sober I take it?'

'As a judge,' Johann lied.

'Good. And don't try to get funny by asking me questions about flying that I obviously don't know the answer to, like you did last time. In fact, don't bother asking me *any* questions. Just go on about how one day you hope you'll be as amazing a pilot as me, you know, crap like that. Are we clear?'

'Crystal.'

'Remember your job here.'

'To make you look like a damn good pilot. All right, I got it Rusty.' A sudden image flashed through Johann's mind of Rusty becoming stranded on the uninhabited island of Redonda with rats and lizards. He smiled slightly.

'What's funny?' Rusty snapped.

'Nothing,' Johann replied quickly.

'Get in,' Rusty said in a glacial tone.

They climbed back into the aircraft and Rusty was all smiles and congeniality once again as he shut the cargo door and made his way to the front of the Cessna with an air of importance. Johann followed him as he issued various instructions to his passengers.

'Belt up everyone! Keep those cameras to hand. You'll get some fantastic shots of the island. The visibility's great this afternoon!'

While Rusty settled himself into the captain's seat, Johann took his place in the co-pilot's seat, although of course, for the purposes of Rusty's little ruse, he behaved as if he was a passenger. Rusty stuck a set of headphones over his head and offset them from his ears before turning in his seat to the group of Americans chattering excitedly behind him.

'I'm gonna be talking to air traffic in a minute so before we start up, I thought you'd all like a quick flight brief.'

Johann rolled his eyes. Rusty's tour guide impression was beginning to wear thin.

'So, first the technical bit: we're gonna take off into wind on runway zero seven and climb to one thousand feet. We'll turn clockwise and initially set a southeasterly course, following the coastline all the way down to English Harbour. Madison, you should be able to get some great aerial shots of the harbour and Nelson's Dockyard.'

'Awesome,' Madison replied breathlessly.

'Then we'll take up a southwesterly heading, across the Caribbean Sea towards Redonda. There's a prize for the first person to spot the island!'

Rusty's quip was met with a chorus of oohs. Johann felt a wave of nausea which he was sure wasn't due to the alcohol and coffee. He drew some track lines on his navigation chart with a Sharpie while Rusty talked.

'Although we can't land, I'll fly as low as I can so you can get some pictures of the terrain down there.' As Rusty droned on about the rest of the flight an idea began forming in Johann's mind. It was an appealing thought and would certainly add to the enjoyment of the afternoon.

'Does anyone have any questions?' Rusty was finally winding up the brief. There was silence from the back although Johann suspected the only question in everyone's mind was "when are we going?"

'Great,' Rusty said, adjusting his headset over his ears. 'Then sit back, relax and enjoy the flight.'

He swivelled back round in his seat and buckled up before signalling to Johann to get started with the preflight checks. Johann stuffed another mint in his mouth as he began flipping switches as inconspicuously as he could, running through the preflight checklist in his head. In the seat next to him Rusty pulled out an actual checklist and pressed a few redundant knobs and buttons with careful precision and a pained look of extreme concentration, a truly professional pilot. Johann switched on the electrics and the radio, selecting the airport information frequency. He listened to the weather and other important details relevant to the flight, rapidly jotting notes on a kneeboard strapped to his thigh. Rusty also had a kneeboard with an official-looking form attached, which, as usual, bore no relation to the flight. Johann changed the radio frequency to ground control and nodded to Rusty to call for start. Rusty pressed the push-to-transmit button on the yoke and spoke loudly for the benefit of everyone on board.

'Good morning Antigua Ground. Cessna three one bravo foxtrot at romeo one zero with information...' He glanced at

Johann for a prompt. Johann held up his kneeboard. It had the word "tango" written on it in large letters.

'Information *tango*,' Rusty continued. 'Er, request start.'

He listened attentively as the ground controller responded with permission to start the engines of the Cessna and advised them to contact the tower for a clearance to taxy. While Rusty pressed more redundant buttons and zoomed in and out of the GPS a few times for good measure, Johann started the engines and signalled for Rusty to go ahead with the request. Taxy clearance was duly given, along with taxiway and holding point instructions, and Johann smoothly pushed the throttles forward — with his left hand this time — while steering the aircraft with his feet. Rusty pulled a navigational chart out and opened it up, positioning it in such a way as to obscure Johann's hand on the flight controls, in case anyone happened to be watching. He flapped about with the chart for a few moments, which Johann couldn't help noticing was upside down.

'I need to see the RPM gauges,' Johann said in a low voice.

Rusty glanced across at him before lowering the chart a little.

'Thank you,' Johann said curtly.

They reached the holding point and Johann brought the Cessna to a stop. He completed the pre-takeoff checks before nodding at Rusty to inform the controller they were holding at alpha one and were ready for departure. Rusty relayed the radio message and they were instructed to line up for takeoff on runway zero seven. Rusty repeated the instruction back to the controller and Johann eased the throttles forward. The navigation chart was covering the gauges again.

'Put the chart away,' Johann snarled under his breath. 'I need to be able to see what I'm doing.'

Rusty removed the chart and stuffed it into a side pocket as the controller gave them a clearance for takeoff.

'Bravo foxtrot cleared for takeoff,' Rusty confirmed.

Ahead of them stretched the wide tarmac runway of V. C. Bird International Airport with a shimmer of heat haze rising above it. It was a little different to the crudely paved, weed-strewn runway Johann had taken off from in Miami early that morning. He scanned the gauges and instruments and glanced at his watch before he pushed the throttles forward to full power and released the brakes. The Cessna began its takeoff roll. This time the aircraft was well below the maximum weight limit and as they reached the takeoff speed, Johann applied gentle back pressure to the yoke, feeling the nose wheel lift off the ground.

Rusty followed through on the controls, staring intently ahead as Johann continued to ease the yoke back. The main wheels lifted off the tarmac and the aircraft began to climb, rising above the airport terminal building on their left, the runway falling away beneath them. Johann retracted the gear and flaps and banked the Cessna gently to their right, levelling off at a thousand feet. He took up a southeasterly course on which they would meander along the coastline towards English Harbour. He gazed out of the window at the expanse of glittering blue sea ahead of him. It was a wide world out there. He had more money than he could ever have dreamed, enough to go wherever he wanted. But he lacked one thing: freedom. Johann made a silent promise to himself that, one day, he would figure out a way to escape from the man sitting beside him. One day he would slip below the radar forever.

TWENTY-FOUR

3:45 pm, Friday, September 20
St. John's, Antigua

Brandon rarely ventured into St. John's. In fact, he tried to avoid the place as much as possible. The capital of Antigua had changed a lot over the last four decades of his life. Brandon supposed that much of the reason for this was due to tourism, the numbers of which had increased significantly since he was a kid back in the eighties. Antigua's sandy beaches, pellucid waters and sunny climate attracted visitors year round, particularly from America and the United Kingdom. Cruise ships were also a big deal these days. Locals knew to avoid the capital when a cruise ship was in port. But love it or hate it, tourism was Antigua's bread and butter, its main source of income and employment. The old sugar plantations and estates lay mainly in ruins, forgotten remnants of the past, while luxury hotels and condominiums formed the contemporary landscape of the present. As to the future, while the tourists kept coming, the hotels and the cruise ships would doubtless evolve into bigger and better versions of themselves.

Brandon hustled his way through the busy streets, teeming with locals and tourists. Two cruise ships were docked at the pier to the west of the town which meant that the population of the island had increased by a few thousand for the day. Traffic was stationary in both directions, cars and trucks were bumper to bumper, and horns and engines competed with reggae music booming from oversized beatboxes in shop doorways. Brandon turned a corner, onto a much quieter, narrower street. Ahead, about halfway along, he spotted the large white sign hanging over the doorway. The words Gabe's Grill were painted in faded yellow letters on the sign with a seven-digit phone number painted in black underneath. A set of steps led up to the doorway of a small wooden shack with peeling yellow paint and a bright green corrugated metal roof. A handwritten menu was stuck next to the door listing a variety of soups, salads, burgers, hot dogs and street tacos. It was hard to imagine that such an extensive menu could come from such a small building, but Brandon knew that his longtime friend Gabriel Flynn, the proprietor, chief cook and bottle washer of Gabe's Grill was one of the best culinarians on the island.

Through the open door the rich cooking aromas of melted cheese, sizzling burgers and caramelised onions intensified. Brandon stepped inside to familiar surroundings: a haphazard selection of wooden tables and chairs arranged on a linoleum floor. Colourful signs advertising local beer lined the walls between large sash windows. The place was packed with locals and a smattering of tourists who had ventured off the beaten track. Brandon weaved between the tables to the bar at the rear where a man wearing a blue apron over a black t-shirt and jeans expertly shuffled burgers around on a large open grill.

'Gabe, my bro, what up?' Brandon called over the counter.

The man turned in surprise. His face broke into a wide smile.

'Brandon, how are you my friend?'

'Good man, I'm good,' Brandon replied.

Gabe reached into a glass-fronted refrigerator and pulled out two bottles of Wadadli beer. He flipped the tops and passed one to Brandon. They clinked the glass and took a sip in unison. The beer was cool and refreshing. Brandon placed his bottle on the bar and slid onto a stool.

'How's business Gabe?' he asked.

'You tell me,' Gabe laughed, waving an arm around the crowded room. 'While the beer's cold and the grill's hot, life don't get much better than that.'

'Good for you man,' Brandon replied. 'What's the special today?'

'Grilled shrimp tacos with corn salsa, garlic, cilantro and lime.'

'I'll have it to go.' Brandon took another sip of beer.

'So what's happ'nin' down at English Harbour?' Gabe asked, pulling a handful of shrimps from the refrigerator and throwing them onto one side of the grill plate with a loud sizzle. 'I heard about the bust down there, night of the storm, seventy-five million US of cocaine on some high-class yacht, right?'

'Word travels fast,' Brandon said. 'But you know that's why I'm here Gabe.'

'I guessed as much. You want extra garlic?'

'Sure.'

'What you wanna know my friend?' Gabe turned to Brandon.

'Where would I find Vinnie Trickett?'

Gabe placed both hands on the bar top and looked directly at Brandon.

'Vinnie? He's involved? How? Ain't this a bit out of his league?'

'I'm not sure if he's involved with the drug bust, but he was in some kind of a fight with a man who was found murdered yesterday morning, a man who *was* involved. So there's the connection.'

'The murdered man; you mean Quincy Moran, right?'

'Like I said, word travels fast.'

'It's a small island.'

'Sure is. You know anything about it Gabe?'

'Word on the street is that Quincy was found dead in the dried out cistern of a million dollar mansion up at Sugar Reef Bay. Don't know nothin' more than that. You think Vinnie did it?'

'That's what I need to talk to him about. Where can I find him?'

'Last I heard he was living in a place on West Cut Street, between a car bodyshop and a gym, but not one of those gyms with treadmills and exercise classes.' Gabe finished wrapping the shrimp tacos in paper and slid the package across the bar to Brandon.

'Thanks Gabe,' he said downing the last of his beer. 'Appreciate it man.' He placed a twenty on the bar and stood up.

'Any time my friend,' Gabe said, acknowledging the generous tip. Brandon picked up the warm tacos and left as a group of five tourists wandered into the tiny shack. Business was booming for Gabe.

Brandon ate as he walked back to his car, savouring the grilled shrimp, freshly caught that morning, marinated in the strong flavours of garlic, cilantro and lime. Gabe was a magician when it came to the culinary arts. Brandon had a rough idea of where West Cut Street was but he retrieved a dogeared paper map from a side pocket in his car and confirmed its location, just to be sure. He called Hyacinth to check she was en route from the hospital where she had been visiting Edella and gave her Vinnie's address. According to Hyacinth, Edella was in a critical but stable condition. Brandon finished the tacos and tossed the paper on the seat beside him. He started the engine and pulled out onto the main road, joining a slow-moving ribbon of traffic heading north.

The house in which Vinnie Trickett currently resided was, as Gabe had described, situated between a car bodyshop and a seedy-looking gym in a less wholesome neighbourhood of St. John's. Heading out of town, Brandon drove along a deserted road. Here, the bars, restaurants and boutiques selling fake designer gear to tourists gave way to dilapidated single-storey buildings and run-down stores. According to the map, West Cut Street was up ahead on the right. He slowed and turned into a road lined with an assortment of shabby, unkempt residences. Stray dogs and scraggly chickens roamed between groups of elderly men drinking beer in the late afternoon sun and gangs of youths loitering in the shadows. About halfway down on his left, Brandon spotted the car bodyshop and the gym. Between the two was a low-rise building of wood and cinder block, with crumbling front steps and metal grilles over the front door and windows. Brandon slowed to a stop a short distance from the house, on the opposite side of the street. He waited a couple of minutes before he spotted Hyacinth's car in his rearview mirror, moving slowly. She pulled up behind him. As they approached the house together they could hear strains of reggae music from somewhere inside. Two young men in their late twenties wearing sleeveless vests, baggy shorts and flip flops sat in threadbare armchairs in the front yard. The strong smell of marijuana hung in the air.

'You lost?' one of the youths said, slurring his words.

'We're lookin' for Vinnie,' Brandon replied. 'He here?'

'Might be,' the youth replied. 'Who's askin'?'

'If you could let him know the CDSLI want to talk to him that'd be great.'

'CDSLI hey? You make an appointment?'

'No, but we'd be happy to come back with an arrest warrant if Vinnie would prefer that.'

'What's it about?' the other youth asked. He inhaled deeply from a joint and blew smoke in the officers' direction.

'Perhaps if you let Vinnie know we're here you'll get to find out too,' Hyacinth said.

Suddenly, Brandon spotted a movement in the alley between the house and the gym. Vinnie was climbing out of a window.

'Hyacinth,' Brandon said, nodding in the direction of the alley. Vinnie was half jogging, half running through to a desolate patch of ground behind the buildings. Brandon and Hyacinth followed in pursuit but it was hardly a challenging exercise. It took less than a minute for Brandon to outrun Vinnie and wrestle him facedown to the ground in a cloud of dust.

'Woah, careful man,' Vinnie said coughing and wheezing in an alarming manner as he attempted to wriggle free. 'Eughh, what's that garlic smell?'

Brandon yanked him roughly to his feet and marched him round to the front of the house. The threadbare armchairs were empty and the front yard was deserted.

'Nice to see your homeboys standing by you,' Hyacinth remarked. 'You got yourself a loyal crew there Vinnie.' She glanced at his t-shirt which had the words "a friend with weed is a friend indeed" printed on it in bright green lettering.

'Nice t-shirt. Profound,' she said, nodding at Vinnie's chest. 'Come up with that all by yourself did you?'

'Funny,' Vinnie spluttered. He tried again to shake himself free from Brandon's grip. 'Loosen up man,' he said with a pained expression. 'What's this about anyway? I ain't done nothin' wrong.'

'Then why did you run Vinnie?' Brandon asked. 'You got somethin' to hide?'

'I ain't got nothin' to hide. You're CDSLI, right? I'm clean these days.'

'That's great to hear Vinnie!' Brandon replied. 'So if we search this property we won't find anything illegal?'

'Well,' Vinnie hesitated. 'I can only speak for myself of course.'

'Be thankful it's not about the drugs then,' Hyacinth said.

'It's not?'

'No. Not today, at least. I can't promise about tomorrow though.'

'So what did I do to deserve the pleasure of a visit from you guys then?'

'We were kinda hoping you could tell us. You know anyone by the name of Quincy Moran?'

Vinnie paused and frowned, as if trying to recall an important memory. Finally he shook his head.

'Sorry man. That name don't mean nothin' to me.'

'You got into some kind of argument with him at The Jungle last week. One of the bouncers had to break it up.'

'Oh *that* guy? Yeah, I remember now. I never got his name though. What did you say it was again?'

'Quincy Moran. What was the fight about?'

'I wouldn't call it a fight. More like a playground scrap.'

'About what?'

'Ohhh he was accusing me of sleeping with his girl, somethin' like that. But from what I could see he wasn't that into her anyway. It was just an excuse to pick a fight. No one picks a fight with Vinnie Trickett an' gets away with it.'

'Is that cos your loyal crew always have your back?' Hyacinth asked, glancing at the two empty armchairs. Vinnie ignored her.

'You happen to run into Quincy again after the fight?' Brandon continued with the line of questioning. 'You know, like to finish it off? Show him that no one picks a fight with Vinnie Trickett and gets away with it?'

'Nope. No way. I didn't mean it like that, man.' Vinnie shook his head firmly.

'So you haven't seen Quincy since that night at The Jungle?' Brandon asked.

'No man,' Vinnie protested. 'Why? The son of a bitch accusing me of somethin'?'

'Quincy's dead,' Brandon replied. 'He was murdered yesterday.'

'Shit. No way.' Vinnie's bloodshot eyes widened and his already dilated pupils became even more prominent. His jaw dropped in disbelief.

'Where were you between eleven and two yesterday Vinnie?' Brandon asked.

'Hey man, I ain't got nothin' to do with this.' Vinnie was instantly on the defensive. 'Sure, we had a… thing… but it was nothin'. I ain't no killer and I didn't have nothin' to do with no murder.'

'So where were you yesterday between eleven and two then?' Brandon asked again.

'Here,' Vinnie said, pointing at the ground. 'With my crew.'

'They'll vouch for you will they?' Hyacinth asked.

'Yeah man. My alibi's solid.'

'That's great Vinnie, but we will need to actually ask them ourselves,' Brandon said.

'No problem man.' Vinnie turned to the house and yelled loudly. 'Jett, Richie, get yo asses out here now. CDSLI wanna talk to you.'

The two young men appeared at the doorway, joint-free, with slightly sheepish expressions.

'You okay man?' the taller, skinnier one of the two said, noticing Vinnie's scuffed appearance.

'Yeah Jett, I'm fine, no thanks to you two scaredy cats. CDSLI want to know where we were between eleven and two yesterday afternoon.'

'Errrr…' Jett appeared to be deep in thought.

'We was here,' the other man, Richie, said suddenly. 'We was here hangin' with Roots and Shaq.'

'Yeah, that's right. We was here the whole time,' Jett echoed, nodding sagely. 'Roots and Shaq came round for…' The sentence was hastily aborted by stern looks from Vinnie and Richie.

'Either of you two know Quincy Moran?' Hyacinth asked.

'Who?' Jett asked.

'Nah. Don't know that name,' Richie replied.

'That guy at The Jungle last week,' Vinnie offered helpfully. 'He picked a fight with me over some girl.'

'Oh *that* guy,' Jett said with wide eyes.

'Yeah, him. These officers are here cos some jackass took him out,' Vinnie went on. 'He's dead, man.'

'No shit,' Richie said, adding quickly, 'we didn't have nothin' to do with that, officers. We was here the whole time.'

'Any of you boys familiar with Sugar Reef Bay?' Brandon asked.

Jett and Richie returned the question with blank looks. Vinnie was apparently a little more informed.

'Ain't that the place with the Hollywood mansions?'

'Yeah, that place.'

'I know it but I ain't never been there,' Vinnie said. He gestured to the rundown house in front of them. 'This might come as a surprise but I'm in a different league.'

'You know anyone called Oliver Jacobs?' Hyacinth asked.

Three heads shook in unison.

'You sure about that?' Brandon said.

'Who is he?' Richie asked.

'He was involved in a drugs bust early on Thursday morning at English Harbour,' Hyacinth replied. 'You hear anything about that?'

There was a sudden flicker of recognition on the half-stoned faces of the men.

'Don't know nothin' about no drugs bust,' Jett replied.

'Oh please Jett, I've seen better acting from the donkey at my niece's kindergarten nativity play,' Hyacinth said wearily.

'Maybe we will take a little look around the property after all,' Brandon said, starting for the front door.

'No, wait,' Vinnie said quickly, a look of alarm on his face. 'Did you say a drugs bust at English Harbour?'

'Something jog your memory all of a sudden?' Hyacinth asked.

'We might have heard about that...' Vinnie began hesitantly.

'Yeah, wasn't that Ray's...' Jett stopped himself a little too late.

'Who's Ray?' Brandon asked.

'Sorry, what?'

'I'm getting bored of this,' Brandon said with an impatient tone. 'If you don't answer the question, all three of you are coming back to English Harbour with Hyacinth and me.'

Vinnie frowned at Jett before replying.

'Okay, okay, I'll tell you what we know, but we didn't have nothin' to do with no drugs bust. Or no murder either.'

'Who's Ray?' Brandon asked again.

Vinnie's reply was reluctant and stilted but he appeared to be telling the truth.

'Word on the street is that Ray's this new kid on the block with links to one of the newer cartels outta South America. Ray's s'posed to be a British guy, speaks with a James Bond accent, you know, all smooth and proper. I ain't never met Ray, but I heard of him 'bout a year ago. Don't know where he came from, outta the blue somewhere, but he's this high level dealer — calls himself an independent entrepreneur or somethin' — who started undercutting the other major dealers on the island and disrupting the supply chains. Word is he's causing a serious headache to the other players, screwing their profit margins. They're losin' business and even the loyalty of other OC groups, shit like that. Anyway, let's just say as far as they're concerned, the competition ain't exactly welcome. They had a sweet little setup goin' on till Ray gatecrashed the party.'

'Ray have a last name?' Hyacinth asked.

Vinnie shook his head.

'Above my pay grade darlin'.'

Brandon and Hyacinth exchanged glances. Vinnie's information on Ray matched what they knew from Oliver Jacobs. This time he was telling the truth. Brandon released his grip and Vinnie breathed an audible sigh of relief.

'Will that be all or is there anything else we can help you with today, officers?' Vinnie enquired sweetly after a pause.

'Get those sorry-looking chairs re-covered,' Brandon replied nodding to the forlorn-looking armchairs. 'They're an eyesore to this lovely street.'

'I'll get right on that,' Vinnie replied.

'And if we find your alibis don't check out, we'll be back,' Hyacinth called over her shoulder as she and Brandon started back to their cars.

'I'll look forward to that,' Vinnie called after them, adding cockily, 'good talk, by the way.'

When they were out of earshot of the three men, Hyacinth spoke.

'You think they're telling the truth about Quincy?'

'Honesty isn't one of their strong suits, but today I think they just might be telling it to us straight,' Brandon replied. 'We know the quarrel between Quincy and Latoya was because Quincy thought she was cheating on him, so Vinnie's story about the reason for the fight at The Jungle checks out. As for Jacobs, the mention of his name didn't seem to ignite any sparks of recognition in any of them.'

'Which leaves us with the mysterious Ray,' Hyacinth said. They had reached their vehicles.

'We know Jacobs is on his payroll,' Brandon said, 'but that's pretty much all we got on him, other than he's a British expat with a James Bond accent who's spent time in Jamaica, where Jacobs hooked up with him. If Vinnie's correct and Ray is linked with one of the new, emerging cartels out of South America, the cartel could be any of a number linked with the new crime organisations which are popping up all over the place. Sure, the older generation of cartels were vast criminal enterprises, well established, far reaching and highly influential throughout South and Central America and the Caribbean, but these new COs are just as deadly and are equally forces not to be tangled with.'

'If Ray's been operating out of Antigua for a year, how is it we've only just heard of him?' Hyacinth asked.

'Apparently we're not the only ones who are behind the curve. Remember Vinnie said Ray's giving the other major dealers here in Antigua a severe headache? Ray may be less entrenched and less powerful than the other players, but he's clearly ruffling feathers and making a dent in profit margins.'

'We need to find him. He's the kind of person who'd have the resources to eliminate Quincy and hijack an armoured truck carrying a hundred million dollars.'

'Let's get back to English Harbour,' Brandon said. 'If Ray's our guy, then we'll have to hope Jacobs gave the sketch artist a decent physical description for us to work with. Right now it's all we've got.'

TWENTY-FIVE

Rising defiantly out of the Caribbean Sea to a height of almost one thousand feet, with steep cliffs on all sides, the rugged, uninhabited rock discovered by Christopher Columbus on his second voyage to America in 1493 loomed closer. Johann had set the autopilot of the Cessna Titan on a southwesterly heading, almost directly into the sun, with a leisurely speed of one hundred and sixty knots and a height of four thousand feet. With one hand on the yoke and the other occasionally pressing knobs and buttons which had no direct bearing on the aircraft's controls, Rusty had simultaneously provided a comprehensive spiel on the history, geography, culture and nightlife of Antigua, talking loudly over the noise of the engine. While their passengers seemed to be impressed by his knowledge, Johann, who had heard the tour guide patter more times than he cared to remember, ignored him.

As they neared the tiny island of Redonda, however, Rusty's knowledge appeared to dry up and, to Johann's relief, they sat in silence. He disconnected the autopilot and took the controls to begin a gentle descent to a thousand feet and then lower still. It had been some time since he had flown over Redonda, but the once eerie moonscape of the island now indeed resembled a much greener haven. Sure, with its craggy cliffs and rocky terrain, the place was never going to be a tropical beach paradise, but even so, as Johann banked the aircraft closer to the island, he was captivated in some way by the strange charm of the uncommon, lesser-visited attraction.

'Rusty, this is awesome,' Logan said loudly from behind the camera lens of his phone. 'I had no idea we'd be able to fly so low over here.'

Johann increased the angle of bank as they rounded a sheer cliff face. It was met with an excited chorus of delight from the back, but he sensed Rusty stiffen in apprehension.

'Rusty could we go even lower?' Madison asked. 'I'm getting some pretty cool pictures for my Instagram.'

'Er, sure Madison,' Rusty replied hesitantly, but Johann was already lowering the nose of the Cessna. He increased the bank angle still further and, as they flew nearer to the edge of the cliff, they almost seemed to brush the rocks and trees and foliage below.

'Awesome!' Madison cooed, tapping at the screen of her phone.

Suddenly, Johann pushed the throttles forward and raised the nose sharply, putting the Cessna into a steep climb before pulling the power and banking the aircraft sharply to the left, back down towards the rocky terrain. Two large seabirds soared on thermals a little way out to sea.

'Are those frigate birds?' Brielle asked excitedly. 'Oh my gosh, I have to get a picture. Rusty, could we…'

'Erm, well…' Before Rusty could manage a reply, the Cessna suddenly banked sharply in the opposite direction towards the birds. There was a buzz of elation from behind him but Rusty was unusually quiet. Johann glanced sideways. It was clear that Rusty's constitution wasn't built to withstand aerobatic manoeuvres, even of the gentler variety. Beads of sweat began trickling down the side of his face and, behind his sunglasses, he briefly closed his eyes, as though he was about to pass out.

'Rusty, you are just the most amazing pilot!' Brielle called from the back with admiration.

'Thanks.' Rusty croaked out a weak reply. For an alarming moment Johann wondered if Rusty was about to throw up. He decided to ease off the steep turns and, as they reached the southern tip of the island, he banked one-eighty degrees to north and dropped to a height of just below a thousand feet. They were now skimming along Redonda's west coast. He glanced below to where he could see a few of the abandoned buildings of the past, emerging from the cliffside. He remembered the wood and stone buildings from when he had flown over the island at low level a few months before: the derelict huts, the miners' barracks and other smaller constructions, even some old abandoned cart wheels. He frowned to himself. There was something different about the buildings to when he had last seen them. They appeared to have undergone renovation works of some kind. He knew that a number of conservation and environmental groups had made exploratory visits to the island in recent times, but surely their mission had been to restore native biodiversity and ecosystems rather than a bunch of crumbling miners' huts. Even so, he noticed that a number of the buildings had had crude repairs made to the roofs and masonry. Where there had once been gaps in the walls, there were now wooden doors in the doorframes and shutters over the windows. There even appeared to be well worn tracks leading to and from the buildings, through the fresh grass and foliage.

Perhaps the conservationists had converted the abandoned buildings into small research stations or storage huts. That had to be it. But Victoria had mentioned that following the great success of the Redonda Restoration Programme, the conservation team had commenced a long term monitoring project, thus visits to the island were far less frequent these days. Yet the pathways were clear as if someone had hiked along there very recently.

Johann glanced across at Rusty who still appeared to be shaken from the unscheduled manoeuvres. His eyes were half closed and he had apparently not noticed the buildings beneath them. Johann doubted that Rusty would have known what they were like before as he clearly had no interest in the island. They reached the northernmost tip of the rocky outpost and, with Rusty in his incapacitated state, Johann wondered what to do next. As he began to circle back round, Rusty managed to revive himself.

'If you guys are happy, we'll head over to Nevis,' he said without turning in his seat. He kept his head facing forwards and his eyes fixed on the horizon in an attempt to quell the nausea. Johann smiled to himself. The consequences he undoubtedly faced as a result of going rogue with the flight controls would be worth it.

'Oh sure, that'd be great,' Carter replied.

'That was awesome Rusty!' Brielle called from the back. 'I just got the coolest pictures from back here.'

The others agreed that Rusty had executed some unusual but highly skilled low-level manoeuvres for an aircraft not necessarily designed for this type of flying. As they took up a northerly heading towards Saint Kitts and Nevis, they settled into their seats for the flight which would take around fifteen minutes. To their left, the sun, a bright golden ball still high in the sky glinted on the deep blue of the Caribbean Sea below, which stretched to the horizon in every direction. The rhythmic hum of the engines was almost hypnotic and, after the excitement of soaring over Redonda, the group relaxed, content to gaze out of the windows and daydream. Johann set the autopilot to a leisurely cruise at five thousand feet. He decided it was probably prudent to maintain straight and level flight for the rest of the journey. His mind drifted back to the recently restored miners' huts and buildings on Redonda. Who had completed the work? And for what purpose?

The mystery intrigued him, but he knew the only viable way to visit the island, the most far-flung corner of Antigua and Barbuda, was by helicopter. The low passes he had made confirmed what was already widely known: that landing there by boat was virtually impossible. In the distance, he could just make out the shadowy contours of Saint Kitts and Nevis, the cloud-shrouded mountains and rainforests and white, grey and black sandy beaches of the islands basking in the late afternoon sun. This time the scenic flight would take them on a gentle course around the western side of Saint Kitts before a leisurely cruise down to Nevis. Beside him, Johann ignored a fierce glare from Rusty. For now, at least, Johann was in control.

5:10 pm, Friday, September 20
CDSLI Headquarters, English Harbour

It was early evening when the remaining five members of the CDSLI reconvened. They stood in a tight circle around the whiteboard as Brandon and Hyacinth relayed the details of their visit to Vinnie Trickett, Jett and Richie, to the amused laughter of the others.

'Unfortunately we only have their word as to where they were between eleven and two yesterday,' Brandon said, 'with no way of checking their alibis. But if those goons managed to pull off a murder and a theft from inside the walls of a property being surveilled as closely as Villa Bella Casa was yesterday, then I've been underestimating them all this time. Not to mention the hijacking of the armoured truck with its police escort. If they coordinated that between them, they deserve a whole new level of respect from the CDSLI.'

'On the subject of Vinnie, I spoke to Latoya,' Nerissa added. 'I asked her why Quincy thought she was seeing Vinnie behind his back. She said she knew of Vinnie but certainly wasn't having an affair with him — or anyone else — and has no idea why Quincy got it into his head that she'd been cheating on him.'

Mitch reported that following his interview with Paul Griffiths, Paul had confirmed that he and Elena López did indeed occasionally conduct their clandestine liaisons on board his Sunseeker yacht moored in Sugar Reef Bay, but he had denied owning a wetsuit.

'I searched his property and the yacht with a team of officers but we didn't find a wetsuit or any other items of clothing made from neoprene,' he continued. 'Paul definitely used the yacht more for entertaining purposes than actually sailing it. We took samples of rope from the Sunseeker but none came back as a match to the rope used to strangle Quincy. There was no sign of Jacobs's laptop either. We came up with nothing at both the villa and the yacht. The only thing we got on Paul is that he was being blackmailed by Quincy over his affair with Elena, which he admits to. Otherwise we got nada and I had to let him go. He's got motive and potentially means and opportunity, with only Elena's word that he was where he says he was yesterday, but we still have no evidence to suggest he was at Jacobs's villa yesterday morning, and no witnesses. As for the hit on the armoured truck, he claimed to have no knowledge of that and we were unable to find anything connecting him to a hit squad or mercenaries. We checked his bank records but there was no evidence of a large amount of money leaving any of his accounts within the last few hours. The hitmen may have agreed on other forms of payment with whoever contracted them but we got nothing on Paul for now.'

'And then there's Jay Palmer,' Delano said, 'the debt-ridden restaurateur who also has means, motive and opportunity for Quincy's murder, and no alibi at the time of death. If his cleaning lady's telling the truth and he didn't arrive back at his home in Cedar Valley until after one o'clock yesterday afternoon, then we still have no idea where he went after he left Hamilton Bay. When I questioned him about it, he was adamant he came straight home and that she's mistaken. Right now it's her word against his until we can prove either way. He denied any knowledge of the hijacking and we found no connections between him and any mercenaries or other groups who might have been responsible.'

'And finally, we have Oliver Jacobs and this man.' Hyacinth produced a black and white sketch of a man's face. The image had been drawn by a sketch artist following Oliver's description of his contact in Antigua, known only as Ray. The man was clean-shaven with short cropped hair. The eyes and lip line had a hardness about them but otherwise the face in the picture was featureless and unremarkable.

'That could be any white guy,' Brandon observed wearily.

'Which is a pretty accurate summary of Ray,' Hyacinth said as she stuck the sketch on the whiteboard and continued. 'Although we know very little about him, Ray is very much a person of interest in this case. Lloyd's still working on locating him with what we do have but, so far, he's not having much luck. It seems as though Ray — or whatever his real name is — lives well and truly off the grid.'

'Here? In Antigua?' Nerissa asked. 'That's a tough call, especially for a white guy.'

'Ray has no last name and no address,' Hyacinth went on. 'He communicates with Jacobs via prepaid cell phones which he buys with cash, probably from a range of stores, and swiftly disposes of when he's finished with them. I reached out to a number of our own contacts, even down in Trinidad and Tobago, but surprise

surprise, although some of them had heard of him, no one was able to tell me anything much about him. According to Vinnie, Ray isn't connected to any of the major cartels currently on our radar, but supposedly has links to one of the newer South American cartels. He's a high level dealer who's been running his little sideshow out of Antigua for a year or so. Up until the night of the storm he'd managed to evade detection by the CDSLI as well as other major dealers and COs for whom Antigua is the command and control hub for drug movement. The dealers and criminal organisations are aware of him, of course. Or at least, they're aware that he exists. He's screwing their profit margins and supply chains and generally upsetting their apple carts, but, according to our reliable source Vinnie, they just can't smoke him out.'

'If the cartels can't find him, with all the resources at their disposal, then there's little hope for us,' Mitch said despondently.

'But we have an advantage over them right now,' Brandon said. 'We got Jacobs. Ray must be mad at him for getting caught in that storm.'

'You can bet Ray was watching when the Coast Guard towed Jacobs and the wreck of the Atratus into English Harbour yesterday morning,' Nerissa said. 'If he knew Quincy was in on the whole thing too, then he had a very strong motive for wanting Quincy dead.'

'In which case there's another life in danger,' Delano said.

'Jacobs,' Hyacinth said. Delano nodded.

'Then Magistrate Darroux just saved his life this morning by denying bail,' Nerissa said.

'You think Jacobs realises that?' Hyacinth asked.

'Probably not,' Delano replied. 'He's still insisting that his lawyer appeals, but nothing's going to happen over the weekend and Darroux's a stickler for doing things by the book. There won't be any bribes changing hands, that's for sure. Hyacinth, put out an APB for Ray with the sketch artist's drawing. Send it to as many agencies as you can think of, the DEA, the US Coast Guard, every partner agency we work alongside in the Caribbean Border Interagency Group, the whole alphabet soup from A to Z.'

'All-points bulletin's already out boss,' Hyacinth confirmed. 'I'll make sure I've covered all the agencies and task forces currently operating within the region.'

'Good,' Delano replied. 'As for the hit on the armoured truck, I don't think that would've been too much of a problem for Ray.'

They were interrupted by Lloyd who strode through the door from the reception area. He was followed by Graymond, Alicia and two men, roughly of the same age, each with a CDSLI visitor's pass clipped to their shirts. Lloyd introduced them as Spencer Warne and Owen Rapley. Spencer, dressed in a denim shirt and white shorts, was a friend of Graymond and Alicia's from England. He was currently on vacation, staying with Owen, the man who had once been the prime suspect in the Rock Palm Resort cold case. The team knew he was found to be innocent and exonerated the previous year when the case was closed after twenty-three years. Owen had subsequently been employed by Leon Fayer as a groundsman and, more recently, as a part-time tennis coach, at the West Beach Club.

'Thanks for the introductions Lloyd,' Delano said. He stepped forward and shook hands with the four latest arrivals.

'I'll do anything I can to help find Leon's killers,' Owen said, visibly upset. 'I owe it to Leon. He gave me a second chance in life.' He had apparently come straight from a tennis coaching session at the West Beach Club and was still dressed in his tennis whites, which showed off a lean, muscular physique.

Suddenly, there was a noise from a desk at the other end of the crew room. It was an animal-like sound, halfway between a bark and a howl.

'This is ridiculous.' The words almost exploded with indignation. 'Why don't we just go out on the streets of St. John's with a megaphone and invite every damn local and tourist on the island to join in with the case?'

'Wendell, calm down,' Delano said as a stockily built man in a grey shirt and black pants lumbered across the room towards them.

'No, I will *not* calm down,' Wendell Rivera replied fiercely. 'Do you have any idea how many laws you're breaking here Delano, letting these — these *tourists* and — and *him*,' Wendell pointed to Owen, 'a former suspect in a *murder trial* for heaven's sake, just barge in and gatecrash a highly confidential meeting?'

Delano turned to Wendell and, in contrast to the police officer's threatening, angry tone, spoke quietly.

'Just to be clear Officer Rivera, I personally invited Mr. Sharkey and Miss Clayton to assist us with this case in light of their relationship with Oliver Jacobs…'

'*Relationship?*' Wendell interrupted. 'They're his *friends* for crying out loud! They're in league with him, as thick as thieves. It's obvious they're deliberately infiltrating our investigation for inside information.'

'Wendell,' Delano said firmly. 'May I remind you of the invaluable assistance Graymond and Alicia provided to the Antigua Police Force last year in solving one of your most notorious cold cases, the Rock Palm Resort murder?'

'Oh don't give me all that,' Wendell spat out. 'We were closing in on the killer anyway.'

'You were doing nothing of the sort,' Delano replied. 'The case had been ice cold with zero leads since the late nineties and you know it.'

'Well this is *my* case and I am forbidding these people to be here.'

'This is a *joint* case between the police and the CDSLI.' Delano was unfazed. 'If you need someone to explain to you how that works, I'm happy to get Assistant Commissioner Henry on the phone.'

Delano knew that Wendell was still smarting from his reprimand from the Assistant Commissioner the previous week for withholding details of a case from another officer.

'Are you threatening me?' Wendell said nastily. He stood in front of the whiteboard in the middle of the group, breathing hard.

'It's more of a promise than a threat,' Delano replied. 'So if you'd kindly stop talking…'

'How *dare…*' Wendell began, but once again Delano cut him off.

'I'd appreciate it if you'd also step aside, away from the whiteboard, so we can all see the case notes so far.'

Wendell glanced behind him and, with a glare in the direction of the newcomers, sullenly stepped to one side of the whiteboard.

'Spencer, Owen, my apologies on behalf of Officer Rivera,' Delano began as Wendell fumed silently behind him. 'It's been a stressful day for us all. Alicia mentioned that you might be able to help us in some way with this case. I believe Lloyd has brought you up to speed with what we have so far?'

'Yes, he has,' Graymond nodded. He noticed the sketch artist's impression of Ray attached to the whiteboard. 'Has Jacobs's description helped at all?'

'Not so far,' Delano replied, 'but we've put out an all-points bulletin to our partner agencies operating in the Caribbean.'

'That's good. But if you want my honest opinion I still think Jacobs is playing us. He's holding something back and not telling us the whole story.'

'I agree,' Delano said. 'And that may well be to his detriment. If Ray's out there somewhere, he may be looking to tie up any loose ends. Like Jacobs.'

'If he's tying up loose ends, d'you think Ray was responsible for Quincy's murder?' Alicia asked.

'He's one of a number of possible suspects.'

'If Ray's out to unfriend anyone who's become a liability to his business then Jacobs had better sleep with one eye open,' Alicia said. 'And Webster had better forget appealing against the magistrate's decision to deny bail. Prison may be the thing keeping Jacobs alive right now.'

'But if you don't have any luck finding Ray, Jacobs may come in handy as bait,' Graymond added.

'It crossed my mind,' Delano said, 'but we're not the CIA and we don't have the kind of resources to ensure an operation like that would go without a hitch. And then we might lose Jacobs for good. Ray's been clever enough to stay off our radar for the last year. He's also successfully evaded the major cartels. He's smart and apparently covers his tracks well. We'd need a foolproof plan with enough surveillance and backup to make sure we could protect Jacobs and take Ray down. If we hit a wall with this case I might be able to convince the DEA — the US Drug Enforcement Administration — to help us out. They have far more resources and expertise at their disposal. Right now though, let's work on ruling out the other suspects for Quincy's murder and find the money and the armoured truck. And I'll talk to Harvey Webster, tell him to drag out the appeal.'

'I knew Quincy,' Owen said suddenly. The four members of the CDSLI and Lloyd looked at Owen in surprise.

'How?' Mitch asked.

'When I was living on the streets sometimes I used to hang out at this homeless shelter in St. John's. It must've been about five or six years ago now, this teenage boy came with his mom one Christmas Day to serve Christmas lunch to a group of us homeless people. Quincy would only have been about fifteen or sixteen back then but we hit it off right away. Quincy was a keen tennis player, so sometimes we'd talk about technique, ways to improve his game, that kinda thing. He used to show up with his mom every few weeks or so, more in the summer when school was out. I wasn't at the shelter all the time — I moved around quite a lot — but we'd always catch up when we saw each other and became friends over the years.

'When Quincy started working as a pool maintenance man and a gardener, his visits to the shelter dropped off a bit, but I still saw his mom, Junella, and she always told me how Quincy was doing. After the Rock Palm case was closed, my name was finally cleared and I got myself together again — thanks to Leon — I ran into Quincy a few months later at The Jungle. We arranged a little fishing trip together last January, rented a boat out of English Harbour and sailed round the coast to Green Island. On the way back, Quincy said there was somethin' he wanted to show me. I was sworn to secrecy, but he said he'd been doing some work for this guy who owned one of the mansions up at Sugar Reef Bay. He didn't say what but it was pretty clear it was something shady.'

'What did Quincy want to show you?' Hyacinth asked.

'The million dollar properties up at Sugar Reef Bay are known for their unrivalled privacy and exclusivity. Most people assume there's only one way to get up there, via the single access road. But there's another way. Through the cliff.'

'*Through* the cliff?' Brandon said with a frown.

'Yeah. When we were about level with the headland at Sugar Reef Bay, Quincy navigated a course through some rocks to a tiny cove at the foot of the cliff where we pulled the boat up on shore. It was a pretty narrow stretch of sand; there'd only be space for two small craft to land there, at the most. The other thing is there are manchineel trees growing there.' He paused and glanced at Spencer. 'They're poisonous,' he added. Spencer's eyes widened in fear at the very thought but he motioned to Owen to continue.

'Off to one side there's a small cave, concealed by the rocks. It's pretty rough and rugged, the waves seem to collide on the rocks from all directions, but once you're inside it opens out into a narrow passageway.'

There was silence in the crew room as Owen went on.

'The passage winds its way up fairly steeply through the cliff. It's not very pleasant; it's pitch dark in there, damp, slippery and in some places you're bent almost double. Quincy told me it dates back to the nineteenth century and was created by smugglers as a secret passageway to bring their contraband ashore without attracting the attention of the customs officers. It takes about half an hour to reach the other end of the passage.'

'Where does it lead?' Hyacinth asked. They waited for Owen's reply. Even Wendell appeared to be hanging on every word.

'The secret passage opens out in a concealed corner of the garden of Villa Bella Casa.'

TWENTY-SIX

10:35 pm, Friday, September 20
V. C. Bird International Airport

The effects of the Krug Champagne were beginning to wear off as Johann executed a perfect landing on the brightly lit runway of V. C. Bird International. Rusty, who was stone cold sober, took the credit for a wonderful afternoon and for piloting them so skilfully between the islands. The girls informed him that they particularly enjoyed the flight over Redonda. Dinner in the Great House at the Nisbet Plantation Beach Club on the island of Nevis had also proved to be a huge success. The food had been sensational while champagne and cocktails flowed freely in every glass, with the exception of Rusty whose tumbler contained iced water.

Johann taxied the Cessna back to its parking spot on runway ten between the Learjet and the Britten-Norman Islander. When he had shut down the engines and completed the after-landing checks, he thanked Rusty profusely for such expert flying and tuition. Gushing with compliments, he emphasised how much he'd learned and what a privilege it was to fly with such a talented pilot. Rusty moved his index finger across his neck in a discreet throat-slashing gesture at Johann, as a warning to shut up, before making his way to the rear of the aircraft where he opened the cargo door and let down the steps. He was all smiles as they stepped out onto the tarmac into the warm night air. Johann was the last to disembark, behind Victoria. As she reached the top of the steps, she turned to him and spoke quietly.

'It was a pleasure to meet you Johann.'

'Oh, er, thanks.' Johann felt the heat rise in his neck.

'Or should I say *Captain* Johann?' Victoria half whispered.

'What?' Johann was unsure how to respond.

'I know you were the one flying this plane,' Victoria continued. 'Rusty's no more a pilot than I am.'

Johann was briefly taken aback before he replied anxiously: 'You can't say anything. It's supposed to be a secret.'

'But why?' Victoria asked. 'Why d'you do it Johann? Why not take the credit for yourself?'

'Because I… I can't. Please don't say anything.'

'Come on Victoria,' Brielle called from outside.

'Sorry Bree, I forgot my purse. One second,' Victoria replied. She turned back to Johann. 'JHR Airways, that's you, right?'

'Yes, but…'

'You're based in the wooden hut with the tin roof over there?'

'Victoria, I can't…'

'Good to know.'

Victoria stepped elegantly down onto the tarmac with a broad smile.

'Got it,' she said to the others, waving her purse.

'You don't wanna leave that behind,' Maddison said. 'Carter's just called for a taxi. It's waiting right over there in the parking lot.'

'Shall we go ladies?' Carter asked. They said final goodbyes as the five Americans made their way across the deserted strip of tarmac towards a lone taxi parked next to a dimly lit building belonging to an airport handling company. When they were out of earshot, Rusty turned to Johann.

'You son of a bitch,' he said through gritted teeth.

'Excuse me?' Johann adopted an innocent expression.

'I know what you were up to,' Rusty continued in a low voice.

'Sorry, I'm not following you.'

'Cut the crap Johann, you knew exactly what you were doing over Redonda. Those steep turns, the sharp climbs and descents…'

'But the girls loved it…'

'I don't give a flying flamingo whether the girls loved it. I nearly threw up all over the cockpit, dammit, and you nearly blew both of our covers by your crazy stunts.'

'Sorry Rusty,' Johann said apologetically. 'It won't happen again.'

'You can be sure of that. And while we're at it, you can forget the excessive compliments at the end of every flight.'

'I thought you wanted me to…'

'You're supposed to be thanking me for the flight you jackass, not giving an Oscar speech.'

'Fine, I'll tone it down a bit,' Johann replied.

'You better. Anyway, to business. I've got a job for you first thing tomorrow morning.'

'Isn't it time I had a day off?'

'I'll tell you when you can have a day off, and it's not tomorrow. I've got four suitcases to be flown to Puerto Rico first thing in the morning. Be at the hut by nine-thirty sharp. The cases will be waiting for you inside. I'll file your flight plan to San Juan International as usual. Departure time will be ten-thirty local time.'

'Can't the cases be dropped off by the aircraft? You know I hate carrying them across the tarmac, especially when I have to make multiple trips back and forth. It's too risky.'

'That's your problem. Deal with it,' Rusty said harshly. He broke off to answer his cell phone.

'Glen, what up?' There was a pause, a furrowed brow and a few grunts before he spoke. Johann turned away, pretending not to be listening.

'Damn the magistrate,' Rusty was saying into the phone. 'No, there's not a thing we can do about it now. It's the weekend. The courts barely manage to function on weekdays let alone Saturdays and Sundays. Who's his lawyer? Webster, yeah, I know him. He's no stranger to greasing palms but Darroux won't be bought for any price. That old crank's a stickler for the rules. What about the British friends? How are they involved? Right. Right. Yeah man, tell him to keep a close eye on them.' Rusty paused for a moment. Johann kicked a small pebble across the tarmac and thought of Victoria.

'Are we any closer to identifying Ray?' Rusty began talking again. He sounded irritable and tense. 'Yeah Glen, I know the CDSLI is looking for him too. That's why we need to get to him first. So you're saying you've still got nothing? For heaven's sake Glen, it's not good enough. I don't care what it takes. Just find the bastard. He's been the bane of my existence for the last year. Right now Oliver Jacobs is our only link. He's our only hope of getting to him. Jacobs *must* know more than he's saying. If I was a gambling man I'd say his British friends know more than they're letting on too. The timing of their supposed vacation is just a little too perfect. Johann? Yeah, he's all set for Puerto Rico in the morning. Listen Glen, I gotta go. Yeah man, keep me posted. Remember, whatever it takes.'

Rusty hung up and glanced over at Johann.

'You didn't hear any of that, okay?'

'Any of what?' Johann replied casually.

A black SUV suddenly approached from nowhere and skidded to a halt in front of the Cessna. With its engine still running, one of the rear passenger doors swung open.

'Nine-thirty sharp tomorrow Johann,' Rusty said, climbing into the back. 'Set your alarm. Don't be late.'

The passenger door slammed shut and the SUV sped away into the darkness. Johann stood still on the tarmac next to the Cessna. It was a clear, cloudless night and he gazed upwards at the multitude of stars twinkling in the darkness above him, great luminous spheroids of hydrogen and helium suspended in the vastness of space, held together by their own gravity. Johann had always been fascinated by the stars and the myriad galaxies and constellations. He was accomplished at celestial navigation and familiar with many of the patterns and pictures which illuminated the darkened sky; silver glitter sprinkled on black velvet.

It was almost midnight when Johann reached his Subaru, the only vehicle still parked in the small lot. As he climbed in he reached for the bottle of Captain Morgan hidden under his seat. Savouring the warm sensation of the dark, potent liquid in his mouth and throat, he closed his eyes and rested his aching head against the seat. He thought of the abandoned huts and buildings on Redonda with their recently installed doors and shuttered windows and restored masonry. And then he thought of Victoria and wondered if he'd ever see her again.

09:20 am, Saturday, September 21
JHR Airways headquarters, the old runway ten, V. C. Bird
International Airport

Johann had slept badly and was suffering from a hangover which he blamed on the Krug. He parked the Subaru in its usual space in the small lot furthest from the airport and popped two Tylenol tablets, washing them down with a generous swig of Captain Morgan. He hauled himself out of the car and retrieved his flight bag from the trunk. He was wearing navy cargo shorts and an old shirt from his airline days but without the four-bar epaulettes, which he felt were a little pretentious. As he trudged across the parking lot towards runway ten he felt the clean white shirt already sticking to his back with sweat. The mercury was nudging eighty degrees with no lift in the breeze or cloud in the sky to hold back the heat of the sun.

Approaching the wooden hut with its tin roof and drab-looking JHR Airways sign, Johann noticed two men standing beside it. One wore smart navy linen shorts and a white linen shirt. The other man, in less conservative attire, wore a matching shirt and shorts in lime green with an orange pineapple print. Draped around his neck was a camera with an oversized lens.

'Help you?' Johann asked gruffly, placing his flight bag on the ground as he fumbled in his shorts pocket for the key to the hut. The two men were standing directly in front of the door. It was impossible to ignore them.

'We're hoping so,' pineapple man replied brightly. 'You the person to talk to about arranging a flight?' His white skin was pink with mild sunburn and he spoke with a British accent, which briefly reminded Johann of England.

'What kind of flight?' Johann asked cautiously.

'Me and Owen here saw you do scenic flights round the island.' The man tapped the sign on the door. 'Got anything available this morning?'

'Sorry, I'm fully booked this morning,' Johann replied abruptly.

'This afternoon then?'

'Afternoon's fully booked too.' Johann glanced at his watch. The time was approaching nine-thirty. He needed to be loading the Cessna, not talking to these idiots. And the four suitcases full of cocaine would be inside the hut in full view the moment he opened the door. This wasn't ideal. Rusty had filed the flight plan to Puerto Rico with a ten-thirty departure time. He wouldn't be happy if it was delayed. His people were waiting at San Juan Airport. Johann needed these men to leave right now.

'I said I'm booked solid,' he said insistently. 'I got nothing available today.'

'Oh. Shame.' There was disappointment in the man's voice. 'How about tomorrow?'

'Sorry.'

'You're fully booked again?'

'Something like that.' Johann hadn't had a day off all week and he'd barely slept the last few nights. He was exhausted and was looking forward to spending a lazy day in his hot tub with a Mai Tai and the latest copy of Boat International. It was his favourite read when he needed to forget about flying. 'Try somewhere else,' he added. 'There are plenty of tour companies here who do scenic flights.'

'Yeah we looked into those. They're all really expensive. We want to do a tour of the island but we're kind of on a budget. And you're cheap. Cheaper than all the other tour companies. So we were hoping you'd have a couple of spaces left.'

'Sorry again, but I'm just really busy,' Johann could feel his heart begin to race. He needed these men to leave.

'You don't look very busy,' the other man said, glancing around the deserted area in front of Johann's hut.

'Well, my next tour's booked for later this morning,' Johann stammered. 'The customers are being picked up from their hotels right now.'

'Could you fit us in first for a short flight?' Pineapple man asked with a hopeful look.

'No dammit, I…'

'How long have you got?' Pineapple man kept talking. 'Like I said, we're on a budget, but there's supposed to be an uninhabited island called Redonda over near Montserrat with really impressive seabird colonies. Have you heard of it?'

Johann was about to brush off the two men once more when he stopped himself.

'Redonda?' he said in surprise. 'Yeah, I've heard of it. Matter of fact I flew there yesterday. You're the second person to ask about it this week. Why does everyone suddenly want to fly over Redonda? The seabird colonies have been there forever.'

'Yeah, but it has a really interesting history too,' the man replied. 'I was telling Owen here about it last night.'

'It sounds a pretty cool place,' Owen added. 'I've lived in Antigua all my life and never knew anything about it until Spencer mentioned it.'

'It's almost impossible to get to,' Johann said.

'Yeah, if you go by boat and try to land there. But anyone can fly over it,' Spencer said. 'Did you know the island has recently undergone a restoration programme thanks to a bunch of conservationists? There's plants and animals there which have been pulled back from the brink of extinction thanks to the project, as well as a surge in the number of land and seabird colonies. Last year some of the frigate birds and booby species on the island had their best breeding year on record.'

'Into birdwatching, are you?' Johann asked in a bored tone. He wasn't particularly interested in nature or wildlife or any of this conservation crap, but Spencer's enthusiasm about the island reminded him of Victoria's passion for it the previous day. He also thought of the puzzling restoration work which had been carried out on the buildings there.

'Birdwatching? Nah, I'm not into it that much,' Spencer replied. 'I love nature and birds and animals, but they're more of a side interest. Exploring abandoned buildings is my thing. Have you heard of Rock Palm Beach?'

Johann confirmed that he had. It was a spectacular white sand crescent beach on the southeastern coast of Antigua. He'd been there a few times.

'Do you remember there used to be an abandoned hotel there called Rock Palm Resort?' Spencer asked.

'I used to fly over it,' Johann nodded. 'I heard it was destroyed by a hurricane back in the nineties. Aren't they rebuilding on the site now?'

'Yeah, they are. After twenty-three years of the hotel lying derelict, a luxury resort company bought up the site late last year,' Spencer replied. 'I used to think that every derelict building was haunted, but after exploring the old Rock Palm hotel that all changed. These days it's sort of like a hobby of mine to check out forgotten, abandoned places.'

'Good for you,' Johann said. He suddenly remembered he was on a tight schedule, which was being made even tighter thanks to these two intrepid explorers.

'I heard there's some abandoned miners' huts on Redonda,' Spencer continued, apparently oblivious to the fact that Johann was in a hurry, 'from the days of the guano mining back in the nineteenth century. I know we can't land there, but any chance we could fly low over those huts so I can get some pictures?'

Johann paused again. He was keen on the idea of flying over the buildings again to get another look at the restoration work himself.

'How much would it cost for a flight over to the island?' Spencer was asking.

'Hold on a moment,' Johann said. He pulled his cell phone from his flight bag. 'Let me make a call. I can't promise anything but I'll see if I can, er, reschedule the tour that's booked for this morning.'

'Awesome, thanks man,' Spencer said with a wide grin.

Johann stepped away from the two men, ensuring they were out of earshot, as Rusty's voice came on the line.

'There a problem Johann?'

'No, no problem Rusty,' Johann replied hastily, 'just a small matter I need to discuss with you.'

'What small matter? Make it quick, I'm very busy.'

'Yeah, sure Rusty. I've got two men outside the hut. They're insisting I take them on a scenic flight over Redonda. I can't get rid of them. I was wondering if there's any way we could postpone the Puerto Rico trip to this afternoon? I know we'll have to refile the flight plan and so on, but would it be…'

'What is it with Redonda?' Rusty interrupted in an irritated tone. 'What's the attraction? First the Americans and now these two. It's an uninhabited rock with a handful of birds and a bunch of lizards crawling around on it. What's so appealing about that?'

'I completely agree,' Johann replied, 'but I'm thinking if I can get these men off my back…'

'Tell them you're fully booked all day. They'll have to find another tour company to take them over there.'

'I've tried that. They said they're on a budget and JHR Airways is cheap. Which it is.' Johann couldn't resist the last part.

'I've already filed the flight plan,' Rusty said firmly. 'You're departing for Puerto Rico at ten-thirty this morning and that's the end of it. So tell the two men to beat it or I'll send Glen over.'

'Yeah, okay, I will, I just thought…'

'Who are they anyway?' Rusty asked suddenly.

'Well, one's Antiguan. The other's a white guy with a British accent.'

Rusty paused at the mention of the British accent.

'What're their names?' he asked.

'I think the Antiguan's called Owen and the British guy is Spencer.'

There was another silence at the end of the line.

'Last names?'

'Hold on a moment, I'll ask them.' Johann stepped over to the two men.

'Spencer Warne and Owen Rapley,' Spencer replied with a hopeful look.

'Thanks.' Johann stepped away again and relayed the details. Rusty repeated the names out loud. Johann wasn't sure whether he was talking to himself or speaking to someone else.

'What did you say their interest in Redonda was again?' Rusty asked.

Johann hesitated. Rusty was a dangerous man. Sometimes it was in everyone's interests to be economical with the truth.

'Just the birdlife, the indigenous plants and lizards,' Johann replied casually, 'that kind of thing, nature, the environment. It seems that the conservation project or whatever it was has made quite an impact.'

'Tell them you'll take them.'

'Really?'

'Yes. You can go to Puerto Rico later this afternoon. I'll file another flight plan and send the details to your phone. I'll let my men on the ground there know your flight's been delayed.'

'Right. Okay.' Johann wasn't exactly sure what had just happened.

'Take a cooler full of beer too,' Rusty added. 'You know, the Champagne Package. Fly them around Redonda, wherever they want to go, throw in a few of those low passes and a couple of barrel rolls too for some extra excitement.'

'Seriously?' Johann asked in surprise.

'Yeah, why not? Oh, and get them talking.'

'About what? Seabird colonies?'

'No. There was a drugs bust at English Harbour in the early hours of Thursday morning.'

'I heard about that. It wasn't one of your shipments though, was it?'

'That's the thing. It wasn't. The man who was busted was a British expat called Oliver Jacobs. He was caught in the storm off the southwest coast of Antigua and had to make a Mayday call to the Coast Guard. When they towed him back to English Harbour they found over two thousand kilograms of cocaine stashed on board his yacht in plastic drums.'

'No shit. But that's…'

'Over seventy-five million dollars' worth of the stuff. Exactly.'

'But who…?'

'Good question. If he's not working for me then who *is* he working for?'

'I thought the Ramirez cartel ran this island?'

'It does. Except for the last year we've known about a rival dealer operating from these shores. We think he's linked to one of the newer cartels — out of South America; Colombia or Bolivia at a guess — who specialise mainly in cocaine. Members of the cartel appear to be past masters at staying under the radar. No matter how hard we've tried to identify key personnel within the cartel, work out how they're moving the shipments around, where their stash houses are and so on, we've come up with nothing. As you can imagine, Ortega's not happy with the situation. He's ordered us to do whatever's required to take care of the man who seems to be running the show here in Antigua, and anyone associated with him. According to our sources, he goes by the name of Ray.'

'This guy Jacobs, the one whose boat…'

'Careful what you say,' Rusty hissed. 'Are the two men in earshot?'

'No, don't worry, they can't hear a word,' Johann replied hastily.

'Make sure of that,' Rusty said before continuing. 'Oliver Jacobs is being held in custody by the CDSLI. And he ain't sayin' much. His bail application's been denied so he's stuck in jail. Which means we can't get to him right now. His lawyer's appealing but we know how long that'll take, such is the legal system out here.'

'Can you pull any strings?'

'Let's just say we're pursuing other avenues. Which is where you come in.'

'Me? How?'

'The two men standing in front of your hut right now are connected to Oliver Jacobs through one of his friends, a man called Graymond Sharkey.'

'Is that his real name?'

'Yes, it is. Spencer Warne and Owen Rapley may know something which could help lead us to Ray, whom we believe Oliver Jacobs was working for.'

'How am I supposed to get them to talk? I can't just ask them straight up about it.'

'You'll think of something,' Rusty said impatiently. 'Ply them with a few beers for starters and get the conversation flowing. Use your initiative.'

'I'll try.'

'Good. Well, get going then and report back to me on landing. I'll reschedule your Puerto Rico flight for later this afternoon.'

Johann hung up and turned back to Spencer and Owen.

'Looks like we're going to Redonda,' he said.

'That's awesome! Thanks man,' Spencer said excitedly. 'How much?'

'I'll just charge you for the half-island tour,' Johann replied, unlocking the door of the hut and ignoring the suitcases which had been placed in one corner. 'Seventy-five US dollars each.'

'Seventy-five US each? That's a bargain,' Spencer said, extracting the cash from a fake designer wallet.

'Need receipts?' Johann asked as he placed the notes in a small metal container behind the counter.

'Nah, we're cool,' Spencer replied. 'Do we have to sign anything?'

'Not unless you really want to.'

Spencer and Owen shook their heads. Neither of them were big on paperwork.

'You the pilot?' Spencer asked.

'Yep. My name's Johann by the way.'

'Is that what the J stands for in JHR Airways?' Owen queried.

'Yeah, they're my initials.' Johann opened a small refrigerator stocked with various-sized bottles of beer and champagne. 'Drinks for the flight?'

'Iced water thanks,' Spencer said.

'Same for me,' Owen added.

'The beer and champagne are included in the price,' Johann said.

'I don't drink,' Spencer said.

'Me neither. I ain't never goin' back there again,' Owen echoed from behind.

'I'll take an iced water though,' Spencer said.

'Okay, if you're sure.' Johann closed the refrigerator door and pulled out four bottles of water from a chilled cabinet. He placed them in a cool box, snapping it shut. With his flight bag in his left hand and the cool box in his right, Johann ushered Spencer and Owen out of the hut before closing and locking the door.

'Need help with that cooler man?' Owen asked.

'Thanks, I'd appreciate it.' Johann willingly accepted any offers of carrying heavy items across the tarmac in ninety degrees heat. He directed the two men towards the Cessna Titan, parked on the edge of runway ten between the Learjet and the Britten-Norman Islander, as usual. Spencer and Owen waited for Johann to complete the external checks of the aircraft before he opened the cargo door, let down the steps and motioned for them to climb aboard. They strapped themselves in as Johann took his seat up front and commenced the routine preflight checks. Air traffic control had a LIAT flight inbound from Barbados and were keen to get the Cessna Titan airborne as soon as possible. In less than fifteen minutes, they were climbing away from the airport. Johann made a leisurely turn onto a southwesterly heading, as he had done the previous afternoon, and retracted the gear. He was on his way to Redonda once more.

TWENTY-SEVEN

10:45 am, Saturday, September 21
Redonda, Caribbean Sea

The volcanic island of Redonda rose out of the turquoise blue sea, a tiny speck in the distance which loomed closer as the Cessna approached it at low level. Spencer had provided a surprisingly informative running commentary on the island for the duration of the flight to which Johann and Owen agreed he had clearly done his research. In addition to his extensive knowledge on Redonda's birdlife, reptiles and the highly successful conservation project, details of which Johann remembered from Victoria's account the previous day, Spencer also enlightened them with amusing anecdotes relating to the mythical Kingdom of Redonda. According to Spencer's in-depth account of the island's eccentric history, it was famous for its unusual monarchy with a number of people laying claim to the "throne" of the rocky outpost. The first was a man by the name of Matthew Shiel who allegedly founded the kingdom in the late nineteenth century, with Queen Victoria's consent. Legend even had it that a pub in England declared itself to be an embassy of the micro-nation in order to gain diplomatic immunity from a smoking ban. Spencer informed his captivated audience that the pub's owner was bestowed with a knighthood by the latest king of Redonda, the name of whom Spencer couldn't recall.

Johann descended to a thousand feet as they reached the island and they could clearly make out dense patches of wild grass and foliage over the dark, maroon-coloured volcanic rock. Johann flew as close as he dared until they could almost make out every blade of grass and wild flower, every crack and crevice in the sheer cliff face and every foam-crested wave which crashed on the rocks below. Owen spotted a goat skull while Spencer snapped endless photos of the seabirds soaring over the island and the surrounding sea.

For the first time in many months, Johann relaxed. He enjoyed Owen and Spencer's company and amusing banter immensely. He also enjoyed flying without a conscience, without the knowledge that he was breaking the law on more levels than he cared to admit, even to himself. He was flying for the pleasure of others with no pretence, no deception and without committing any felonies. The two men also seemed to be enjoying Johann's company as they laughed and joked together. Johann had once been a sociable animal, in another life, in another country. These days he had no friends to speak of and his social life consisted of moving in Rusty's circles of acquaintances, for the most part posing as a rookie pilot or a passenger.

As he flew low over the abandoned miners' huts built into the side of the rock, he suddenly felt an urge to confide in Spencer and Owen.

'You know, when I flew over these buildings yesterday I noticed there's been some renovation work carried out since I last flew over here.'

'Really?' Spencer refocused his camera lens on the buildings immediately beneath them. 'What sort of renovations? Can you bank a little sharper to the left? Yeah, perfect. Thanks Johann, great angle for these pictures. I wish I had your flying skills.'

'Someone's made a few repairs to the roofs and masonry of those buildings down there,' Johann continued as the wings of the Cessna almost seemed to brush the tops of the stone structures. 'They've even replaced the rotted wooden doors and window shutters.'

'Who has?' Spencer asked curiously, bringing his camera down from his face.

'I don't know,' Johann shrugged. 'It could be the conservation people but since their project to remove the goats and rats was successful, I heard their visits are only occasional these days.'

'That's correct,' Spencer replied.

'And yet you can see well-worn tracks leading to and from the buildings down there. They look recent to me.'

'Yeah, I see them,' Owen said. 'They're definitely recent. Wild grass is resilient. It grows up in no time at all. Those tracks look as though someone's walked along there within the last couple of weeks. If the conservation team don't come here anymore, then who does? Who's making those tracks and why?'

'I don't know,' Johann replied.

'Where do they lead?' Spencer asked.

'It looks like they head down that way,' Owen said, pointing. 'But the grass thins out a bit and the track disappears.'

'Hold on,' Johann said. He rolled the aircraft into a steep turn and dipped to little more than a hundred feet above the sea. 'Can you see the track now?'

'No, but I can see what I'm guessing is the island's only place to bring a boat in,' Owen replied. 'It looks fairly treacherous. You'd need a lot of skill and experience to navigate those rocks and the swell looks pretty rough. I wouldn't want to chance it.'

'Someone must be though,' Spencer said. 'Other than by helicopter, there's no alternative way to land here. What about the building renovations Johann? How recent are they?'

'I last flew low over here about five or six months ago. I was on my way from Guadeloupe to Saint Kitts. The buildings were as derelict as they'd ever been back then, all crumbling stonework and the wooden doors and windows had long since rotted away. These repairs are new.'

'They can't have been made as part of the conservation project,' Spencer said. 'From a conservationist's point of view I'm guessing any manmade interventions would be kept to a minimum to protect the terrain and encourage the natural habitation to flourish.'

'Maybe it was pirates,' Owen said jokingly. The question went unanswered. Johann increased the power and they climbed back up to a thousand feet.

'Anything else you guys want to take a look at?' he asked, turning to his two passengers.

'I guess it's time to head back,' Spencer replied, glancing at his watch. 'This is far more than we were hoping for Johann. Thanks for agreeing to take us over here.'

'Not at all,' Johann said turning the Cessna onto a northeasterly heading. 'I've enjoyed it myself. And I nearly forgot, I know you're not much into the wildlife, but have you heard of the Redonda Ground Dragon?'

'The what?' Spencer asked.

'The Redonda Ground Dragon. One of my passengers yesterday mentioned it.' Johann thought of Victoria. He wished he'd had more opportunity to talk to her. 'It's a lizard indigenous to the island, found nowhere else on earth.'

'No way,' Spencer said. 'You mean that piece of rock down there is the only place in the world you can see that type of lizard?'

'Yeah, apparently. Amazing really, isn't it?'

'The Redonda Ground Dragon.' Spencer repeated the name of the lizard to himself. He took a last glance at the rocky, volcanic slopes of Redonda as Johann set the course back to Antigua.

'It's got some kind of weird Latin name too,' Johann went on. 'The pholido… I can't remember now, the pholido atratus I think it was, or something like that…'

'Atratus?' Spencer queried. The name seemed familiar somehow. 'Isn't that…'

'Check out the red chest of that frigate bird,' Owen interrupted suddenly. 'Those things are huge up close,' he said in awe. 'Their wingspan must be, what, over six foot. No wonder they seem to be able to soar forever.'

They admired the frigate birds which had taken flight close by, disturbed from their nests by the noise of the Cessna.

'If you guys want to come flying again sometime, I can always work out some sort of special deal if you're on a budget,' Johann said. Money was no object. Persuading Rusty to sanction the idea might be more of a problem, but if Johann could demonstrate that the flight benefitted Rusty in some way, perhaps with information on Oliver Jacobs or Ray, he would surely be accommodating.

Johann had enjoyed the laidback company of Owen and Spencer immensely and hoped it wasn't the last he'd see of them.

'We'd love that,' Spencer was saying. 'We'll definitely take you up on it if you're willing to offer us a good deal.'

'Yeah, I'd be happy to. That's no problem.'

In the distance they could make out Antigua's western coastline with its dazzling white sandy beaches, vivid turquoise water and colourful harbours. For Johann, the idyllic paradise setting was quickly obscured by thoughts of the impending flight to Puerto Rico, which hung over him like a heavy black cloud. No matter how brightly the sun shone or how vibrant the colours of the Caribbean, nor how much money he had accumulated in the rented storage facilities, it wasn't enough anymore to relieve him of the guilt of the world he had become involved in. But there was no way out. He was trapped forever in his private hell, until the CDSLI or the DEA finally caught up with him, or he became another faceless victim of the cartel. Either way, Johann knew he was a dead man walking.

1:45 pm, Saturday, September 21
English Harbour

Wearing handcuffs and the dark blue prison scrubs, Oliver Jacobs climbed into the small RIB secured to a private jetty in a secluded location at English Harbour. He smirked slightly as Delano instructed him to sit down on one of the bench seats around the edge of the boat.

'Didn't realise weekend sailing trips were part of my custody package,' he said with a sneer. 'Is there a picnic included? Where's the drinks cooler? Mine's a beer.'

'Shut up Jacobs,' Graymond snapped. 'If there was any way we could've left you behind in your miserable cell, believe me we would have.'

'There's no need to be like that Gray,' Oliver replied, pretending to sound hurt. 'I thought you and I were friends.'

'There's an element of trust where friends are concerned Jacobs. That is very much lacking in this particular friendship.'

'Well forgive me if I forgot to mention the alternative route to my house,' Oliver said defensively. 'But if you'd been through what I have over the last forty-eight hours, *you* might've forgotten about a little-used passageway.'

'You didn't forget,' Graymond replied. 'You deliberately withheld the information. You've been playing us the whole time, asking for our help with the case, pleading with us to find Quincy, but you knew he was dead all along, didn't you?'

'I swear I didn't. You have to believe me about Quincy. I'd never have sent him to the villa if I'd have known…'

'I don't believe a word you say anymore. Why did it take Owen to tell us about the passage through the cliff?'

'I swear I didn't…' Oliver's voice faltered and Graymond glanced at him suspiciously. Something about Oliver's response puzzled him. Something wasn't adding up but Graymond couldn't work out what. It almost seemed as though Oliver wanted to tell the truth, but something — or someone — was holding him back.

'Jacobs, if you thought you were here for your scintillating conversation you're mistaken,' Delano interrupted. 'The moment we're done with you, you're going back to your cell.'

He pushed Oliver roughly onto the seat as the rest of the team climbed aboard. Brandon was at the helm; Nerissa, Hyacinth and Mitch, still with his arm in a sling, sat next to Oliver and Delano, while Graymond, Alicia, Owen and Spencer took their places on the opposite side. They avoided eye contact with Oliver.

It was during their preparations to explore the secret cliff passage leading to Villa Bella Casa that Owen remembered the manhole which opened into the garden from the passage was protected by an advanced security system.

'*Another* one?' Mitch had asked in disbelief. 'How many security systems does one property need?'

'If I had a hundred million dollars in my cistern I think I'd want a few security measures in place too,' Hyacinth had said. 'Lloyd, did you find anything relating to the manhole on any of Jacobs's devices?'

'No.' Lloyd had shaken his head firmly. 'I've double-checked his iPad and cell phone. Other than the main security system for the villa, there's nothing on either device to suggest there's any other surveillance at the property. There are no apps, no notifications, nothing. I'll bet you anything it's all on the missing laptop. Along with everything else that actually matters. The person who removed the laptop knew that all along.'

'Well we've searched the homes and belongings of all suspects relating to Quincy's murder, as well as a number of people connected to Jacobs, excluding Ray, of course, who continues to evade detection,' Nerissa had said. 'The laptop was nowhere to be found.'

'Then where is it?' Delano had asked. There had been a note of frustration in his voice. And it was a question which had remained unanswered as they continued with their plans to explore the cliff passage.

Owen had explained that the secret passageway, which led from the small cove at the foot of the cliff to the garden of Villa Bella Casa, widened out into a cave-like room at the top. As far as he could remember, there was a small ladder leaning against one wall of the room. Immediately above was a manhole cover which opened outwards into the garden of Villa Bella Casa. From the garden side, the cover was completely camouflaged by fake turf, identical in colour to the grass and impossible to locate unless you knew exactly where it was hidden. The other thing Owen had remembered from Quincy's secret tour was that the manhole opening was protected by an advanced security system which had been installed by Oliver earlier that year. In order to open the manhole cover, a scanning device required a retina scan and right index fingerprint from one of only two people: Jacobs himself, or Quincy.

'So that's why Quincy's killer needed Quincy alive to get into the grounds of Villa Bella Casa without detection,' Brandon had said.

'Yeah, looks that way,' Owen had replied. 'From the garden side you can just lift up the manhole like any other. It wasn't locked or anything. The retina and fingerprint scanners are only on the cave side. So the killer could leave freely. He — or she — only needed Quincy for access.'

'But what about when the killer planned to return, to retrieve Quincy's body and the money?' Nerissa had asked. 'If he or she intended to use the secret passage again, how would the manhole open without Quincy?'

No one could provide an answer to that question. Brandon had suggested that the missing laptop was probably instrumental somehow, which didn't help them much. For now, with Quincy's body lying on a cold metal tray in the hospital mortuary, there was only one other person who could pass the scanning device in the cave and open the manhole cover. Lloyd wasn't sure he could easily hack the device and therefore the CDSLI had no choice but to take Oliver with them. If the tunnel and manhole cover contained evidence which could lead to Quincy's killer, they needed Oliver's right eye and index finger.

As Brandon navigated the RIB through the harbour towards the channel to the sea, the others sat in silence. It was hard to talk over the noise of the powerful engines anyway. The channel was busy with motor cruisers, sailing yachts and a couple of fishing trawlers, lazily meandering their way in and out of the harbour. Further out to the sea, the breeze was fresher and cooler.

The boat ride to the small cove at the bottom of the cliff at Sugar Reef Bay took around an hour. The RIB bounced over the waves while hazy rainbows formed around it from the sea spray caught in the sun's light. As they approached the steep cliffs at the edge of the bay, thick with trees and dense tropical foliage, Brandon pulled back the throttles and reduced the speed. He manoeuvred the RIB closer to the shoreline. Waves crashed on the rocks which encroached menacingly out into the sea and seemed to guard the cliffs themselves.

'I don't see any sandy coves,' Brandon said, setting the throttles to idle.

'It's here somewhere…' Owen shielded his eyes as he surveyed the shoreline.

'Where is it Jacobs?' Delano asked.

Oliver glanced straight ahead before looking back at the cliff.

'We're nearly there,' he replied. 'When the rocks just over there line up with the headland… like now… turn to port. You'll see the stretch of sand in a minute.'

Sure enough, from behind a ridge of jagged grey rocks emerging from the churning water, a small sandy cove came into view.

'Go slowly,' Oliver warned. 'Turn to port slightly. There are rocks immediately below the surface of the water up ahead.'

Brandon followed Oliver's guidance, manoeuvring the boat carefully towards the tiny cove.

'Can we get the RIB all the way in?' Delano asked.

'Yes, if you do what I tell you,' Oliver replied. 'Turn ten degrees to starboard now. There are more rocks just over there. I can take the wheel if you want me to, but obviously someone will need to remove these.' He held up his cuffed hands.

'Not a chance Jacobs,' Delano said.

Oliver's knowledge of the small channel was impressive and they reached the cove without a hitch. Brandon cut the engines and hauled the outboards up out of the water moments before they felt the hull of the boat hit the sand. One by one they climbed over the side and Graymond and Owen guided the RIB higher onto dry ground, tying it to a wooden post pointed out by Oliver. As Owen had described it, the cove was more of a narrow stretch of sand, barely visible from the water and shielded by rocks. Behind, the sheer cliffs of Sugar Reef Bay rose above them, up to the garden of Villa Bella Casa.

'Oh, I should've mentioned, watch out for the manchineel trees,' Oliver said suddenly with a smirk.

Spencer looked around in alarm. Following the earlier warning from Owen, he had read up on the dangers of the fearsome trees. He cast a wary look at one which stood a few feet away as if it resembled some kind of hideous apparition.

'Where's the cave Jacobs?' Delano asked.

'Over there.' Oliver nodded to the edge of the strip of sand where the waves surged closer to the shore over rugged boulders. They made their way towards it. The entrance to the cave was dark and low-level, almost obscured by the craggy rocks immediately in front of it. It was only visible from a few feet away.

'Careful not to slip,' Oliver said. There was more sarcasm than concern in his voice. 'The mouth of the cave is quite low, you'll have to bend double to get in. And sorry girls, you might get wet feet on the way in.'

'Then I'll be sure to wipe my boots all over that Persian rug in your living room,' Hyacinth replied frostily.

'Touché,' Oliver said. He turned to the entrance to the cave.

'Brandon and I will go first,' Delano said. 'Mitch and Nerissa, you're with Jacobs. The rest of you stay close behind.'

They switched on their flashlights and crouched low, stepping into the narrow entrance of the cave. It opened out into a small passageway, barely wide enough for one person at a time and they walked in single file. Owen's description of the tunnel had been accurate. It wound its way up steeply through the cliff and without the aid of their flashlights it would have been pitch black inside. Spencer imagined the smugglers of the past, sneaking through the darkness with their spoils glittering in the light of hurricane lamps, the smell of paraffin wafting from the lanterns as they hurried along the narrow passageway.

The rocky walls surrounding them were damp and slimy, and the air was cool and clammy with the smell of salt and seaweed. The path underfoot was slippery and undulating, treacherous in places. Sometimes the height of the tunnel lowered to the point where they were forced to bend almost double as they walked.

'Hope no one's claustrophobic?' Oliver asked.

'The only claustrophobic thing here is you Jacobs,' Hyacinth said, 'so be quiet for everyone's sake and keep walking.'

'It is kind of, you know, cramped in here,' Spencer's voice said from somewhere near the back. He was red-faced and sweating, and working hard to keep up with the rest of them. 'I don't s'pose we're nearly there yet, are we?'

His remark was met with amused chuckles.

'Spencer does have a point,' Hyacinth said. 'It is pretty cramped and confined down here. And the tunnel's slippery and quite tricky to navigate under foot in places. It's not surprising Quincy's killer only made off with Jacobs's laptop. I doubt any of us could've carried much more. It explains why the killer deleted the footage from the video recorder and left it in the study rather than trying to take it with him.'

'He probably knew the footage could also be viewed on Jacobs's other devices anyway and didn't want to weigh himself down unnecessarily,' Nerissa added.

'Speaking of that surveillance footage, when I watched it yesterday, something struck me,' Owen said suddenly. 'I've known Quincy for a long time. That look on his face when he was spraying the cameras with the paint, it was a look of utter fear, desperation, terror even…'

'You mean like he was being threatened? Coerced into doing it?' Nerissa asked.

'Exactly,' Owen replied.

'Which confirms our theory that someone accosted him on his way over from Hamilton Bay, forced him out of his truck and into a boat somewhere close by,' Delano said. 'They must've taken it to the little cove down there before Quincy was forced through this passageway by his killer and up to the villa. He probably had no choice but to blind the cameras and reveal the location of the hundred million dollars.'

'After which he was strangled and left in the cistern while the killer deleted the surveillance hard drive and made off with the laptop, back down this tunnel to the cove, evading the officers at the access road and the gates of the villa,' Hyacinth finished. 'Sound about right to you Jacobs?'

'I already told you, I don't know who murdered Quincy,' Oliver replied shortly.

'What did you really want him to do at the villa?' Nerissa asked. 'Or did you lure him into a trap in order to have him silenced?'

'He was the maintenance man. I asked a perfectly reasonable thing of him, in light of my absence in the storm: to check on my property. Fine, he may have known about the money and the cistern, but I knew it was only a matter of time before you guys would be all over the place like bees round a honeypot. You really think I'd be stupid enough to ask him to start moving the money out of the cistern? That's the last thing I'd want him to do. And no, it wasn't a trap.'

Graymond remained silent throughout the discussion. Once again, something puzzled him but he couldn't work out what. He knew Oliver was a professional liar who certainly hadn't been straight with them following his arrest, but when it came to Quincy, there was a grave note in his voice, a flicker of sincerity. Oliver may not have been telling the whole truth, but Graymond knew there was a hint of fact somewhere in the story to which he was sticking. They just needed to work out which part.

After nearly an hour of negotiating the tunnel through the cliff, the passageway suddenly opened out into a narrow antechamber with a crudely constructed ladder leaning against one wall. To the right of the ladder were two small terminals attached to the rock behind. They were positioned at eye level and backlit with blue lights. The contrast of advanced technology against the rocky walls of the crudely constructed tunnel was a strange sight.

'You're up Jacobs,' Brandon said, stepping aside to allow Oliver through. He obediently moved towards the terminals and positioned his face close to the retina scanner. There was a low beep. Lifting cuffed hands to the device below, he placed his right index finger onto the reader. Another low beep. He glanced upwards at a square in the ceiling above them. There was the sound of a click.

'You just go up the ladder and push on the manhole cover,' he said, stepping back. 'It's attached to gas springs; should be real easy to open.'

Brandon climbed the stepladder and reached above him. He pushed on the base of the manhole cover, a smooth square of metal set into the uneven surface of the rock. To the faint hissing noise of gas moving around a piston rod in a cylinder, the cover opened above them and rays of sunlight and warm air flooded the antechamber. One by one they climbed up the ladder and through the opening above into a corner of the garden on the south side of Villa Bella Casa. A large hibiscus plant partially obscured their view of the property.

'There's camera seven, the first camera Quincy sprayed,' Mitch said, pointing to a camera just visible under the roofline of the villa.

'His killer's not visible on any of the camera footage though,' Nerissa said. 'If Quincy was under duress, how did the killer get him to spray the camera right over there?'

'The killer probably had a gun pointed at Quincy the whole time, even from way back here,' Delano said. 'Once Quincy had the first couple of cameras blinded, the killer could approach the villa knowing that he wouldn't be on any surveillance footage from that side of the garden. All he had to do next would be to ensure Quincy covered the remaining cameras with paint, then he could move freely around the outside of the property.'

'So if the killer had a gun all along, why go to the trouble of strangling Quincy when he could've just shot him?' Spencer asked suddenly.

'Good question,' Delano replied. 'Think about where he was murdered, down in the cistern with all those stacks of hundred dollar bills. If Quincy had been shot, or even stabbed, his blood would've been all over the money. It was more effort, but a blow to the head and strangling Quincy was the cleanest way to kill, with no risk of spoiling the hundred dollar bills or making them traceable in any way.'

'It sounds like the killer had it all worked out and came prepared,' Spencer said.

'It was a well executed plan, for sure,' Delano agreed. He pulled his cell phone out of his pocket.

'It's Lloyd,' he said. 'Oh man, I wonder what he wants, I've got a whole bunch of missed calls from him.' Delano tapped on the screen. 'Lloyd, hi, you're on speaker.'

'Delano, where the hell've you been?' Lloyd's deep voice echoed from the phone. 'I've been trying to reach you for the last twenty minutes.'

'Sorry, we've been in the cliff tunnel heading up to Villa Bella Casa. There's no cell reception in there. What's up?'

'We've had an anonymous tipoff about a haul of cocaine. It's on a private flight leaving for Puerto Rico in forty minutes from V. C. Bird. Duane's on his way over to Sugar Reef to pick you up and take you straight to the airport. He should be there any minute now. I've contacted the airport authorities and they're watching the pilot and the plane, but are on standby and awaiting further instructions from you.'

'Thanks Lloyd. I'll meet Duane at the gates of the villa,' Delano replied quickly. 'Nerissa, Hyacinth, you're with me. Brandon, Mitch and the rest of you, stay here and see if there's anything else about this tunnel which could lead to Quincy's killer.'

'Sure boss.' Mitch and Brandon nodded in tandem.

'You got any other details about the flight, Lloyd?' Delano spoke into his phone.

'Duane will brief you in the car. Earl Bextor and Rusty McChannen will meet you at the airport and bring you up to speed with any latest developments,' Lloyd replied. 'The aircraft is bound for Puerto Rico at seventeen hundred hours this evening.'

TWENTY-EIGHT

4:30 pm, Saturday, September 21
The old runway ten, V. C. Bird International Airport

The dark blue Ford Explorer with tinted windows and government licence plates, flanked by two airport vehicles in a glare of flashing lights, hurtled onto the tarmac of runway ten with tyres screeching, stopping abruptly in front of the Cessna Titan. The engines of the aircraft were already running, the blades of the twin propellers were spinning, and the pilot was preparing to taxy towards the main runway. The doors of the Explorer flung open and Duane, Delano, Nerissa and Hyacinth leaped out onto the tarmac. They surrounded the Cessna, approaching cautiously, their weapons pointed at the lone pilot seated in the cockpit. Delano ran to the cargo door on the port side. He felt the strong breeze of the slipstream from the port engine's propeller as he yanked open the door and boarded the aircraft.

'Put your hands behind your head, stand up and turn around slowly,' Delano shouted as he moved quickly towards the cockpit, his gun aimed at the pilot. The pilot didn't move. Delano, now a few paces away, repeated the instruction.

The pilot, a man in his mid-sixties and a little out of shape, looked straight ahead out of the window. The game was finally over and Johann knew it. He watched as Rusty emerged from one of the airport vehicles parked in front of the aircraft. The deputy chief of airport security looked directly into the cockpit and they made eye contact. Johann's expression was one of desperation and defeat, but Rusty wore a cold, hard look of betrayal. A Judas kiss. Rusty was about to disown him. Johann was alone. He brought his hands up slowly and placed them behind his head before he stood up. Sweat poured down his back, soaking his white airline shirt as he turned to face Delano and the other officers who had boarded the aircraft. Four guns were pointed directly at him and he felt sick.

His knees shook and he tightened his grip around the back of his head to stop his hands trembling.

Delano quickly stepped forward and, in the confined space of the cockpit, roughly pushed Johann round, forcing his hands down behind his back before placing handcuffs on his wrists. Delano pulled the headset off Johann's head and flung it on a seat before manhandling him back down the aisle towards the cargo door, passing the other officers. Nerissa moved to the cockpit to shut down the engines. Her private pilot licence and knowledge of aircraft frequently came in useful with the airport interdictions. While Hyacinth conducted a rapid search of the cabin, Duane retrieved four large, brown leather suitcases from the rear. He unlatched them and opened them side by side.

'Boss,' he called to Delano who was guiding Johann down the aircraft steps onto the tarmac. 'The anonymous tip was right on.'

Duane was joined by Hyacinth who took a snapshot of the open cases with her phone before kneeling beside him to examine the contents more closely. Inside the cases were large rectangular packages of white powder wrapped in clear cellophane and packed tightly together.

'Cocaine,' Duane said, passing some of the white powder through a gloved hand. 'Probably weighs something in the region of...' He surveyed the contents in front of them. 'There's maybe close to two hundred pounds' worth here.'

'Roughly three million US dollars then, maybe more,' Hyacinth said in a low voice. She glanced through the open cargo door at Delano and the pilot who stood next to him. In contrast to Oliver Jacobs and the many drug traffickers they had arrested during her time with the CDSLI, who were usually rude, insulting and unrepentant, there was something different about this man. He had said nothing so far and hung his head low with a look of shame, remorse, perhaps even relief. He was about to go down for drug trafficking, and possession and exportation of cocaine, amongst other things. He was facing a life sentence in prison and he knew it. But he stood quietly on the tarmac, almost as if he had been waiting for this moment for some time. Hyacinth gazed momentarily beyond Delano and the pilot to Rusty, whom she recognised as the deputy chief of airport security. He was flanked by three other security officers who stood ready and waiting for the order to spring into action. Her gaze suddenly met his and she looked away. There was something about him she had never liked. Perhaps he was just a jobsworth, a clipboard man who always did things by the book, nothing more than an officious busybody. But sometimes she wasn't so sure.

'This disused runway seems more like a hub for drug traffickers than a biz jet parking lot every time we come here,' Duane was saying behind her. He was still examining the packages of cocaine.

'I agree,' Hyacinth agreed, turning back to him. 'Makes me wonder sometimes, who is actually running runway ten? Airport security or the cartels?'

'There's a lot of private jets parked over here,' Duane replied without looking up. 'What with the anonymous passenger manifests, high net worth individuals demanding complete privacy and blocked flight plans it's a security nightmare.'

'You're tellin' me.' Hyacinth glanced warily in Rusty's direction once more. He was approaching the Cessna. Johann, the pilot, stood forlornly beside Delano. 'Who was the snitch who turned this guy in again?' she said quietly to Duane.

'Anonymous tip. Came from a burner. Lloyd's still working on it but he's not too hopeful.'

Outside on the tarmac, Rusty stepped towards Johann as Delano took a call on his cell. Hyacinth watched as her boss tensed and frowned and asked for more details.

'Who's he talking to?' Nerissa asked from behind.

'I don't know, but by the look on his face I'm pretty sure it's not good news,' Hyacinth replied. While Delano continued talking on the phone, Hyacinth noticed Rusty had pulled Johann aside and was giving him some kind of stern talking to. She was out of earshot but it didn't look like Rusty was offering any constructive comments. She watched the look of anguish on the pilot's face before turning back to Duane.

'The hell happened?' Rusty hissed to Johann in a low voice.

'How should I know?' Johann replied helplessly. 'You're the security guy round here. You tell me.'

'A little more respect if you don't mind.' Rusty raised a fist and cuffed Johann's jaw. Johann reeled from the punch and tried to regain his balance.

'Those men you flew to Redonda this morning, did they see the cases in the hut? They ask any questions? You think they're the rats?'

'No, they didn't see anything,' Johann protested. He opened and closed his jaw a few times to check it still worked.

'You find out what they know about Oliver Jacobs?'

'I tried to ask but they didn't seem to know anything.'

'They've been read into the darn case. They must know something.'

'No, honestly, they didn't know much at all.' Johann ducked as Rusty raised his hand again.

'They talk about anyone called Ray?' Rusty asked.

'No. Didn't mention that name.' Johann shook his head firmly. 'What's gonna happen to me Rusty?'

Rusty didn't reply. Delano, the CDSLI officer was approaching with a serious expression. He had finished his phone call. Johann knew deep down that Rusty would wash his hands of him now that he'd been caught. He was of no use to Rusty now. He was a liability. He wondered who the CDSLI's informant was. Who had supplied the anonymous tipoff? Rusty genuinely didn't appear to know either. Surely it wasn't Spencer and Owen, his new friends from that morning. He was certain they hadn't seen the suitcases in his hut.

'Rusty, we got a problem,' Delano said.

'What's up?' Rusty asked. He signalled for four other airport security officials to join them.

'Can your men take care of things here? I need my team,' Delano said.

'Sure.' Rusty gave brief instructions to the security officers. They quickly boarded the aircraft to take over from Duane, Nerissa and Hyacinth who joined the others on the tarmac.

'What's happened boss?' Nerissa asked.

'Brandon just called from Jacobs's villa,' Delano replied. 'Jacobs, Mitch and Alicia have gone missing.'

'What?' Hyacinth asked. 'But how…'

'Brandon says they were in the garden at Villa Bella Casa when some kind of alarm went off in the villa. They split up: he and Gray took the north side while Spencer and Owen went round the south side to check the place out, to find the reason for the alarm. Mitch and Alicia stayed with Jacobs at the entrance to the tunnel. Brandon said they searched the place, found nothing which might have triggered the alarm, but when they go back to the manhole, Mitch, Alicia and Jacobs were nowhere to be seen.'

'Where'd they go?' Duane asked.

'That's just it, they'd completely vanished.'

'All three of them?' Nerissa asked.

'Yeah. Mitch's badge and cell phone and the sling were on the ground a few feet away from the tunnel's entrance, possibly indicating signs of a struggle. If that's the case, it looks like Jacobs somehow managed to take both Mitch and Alicia hostage. The only direction they could be heading right now is back through the cliff tunnel to the cove. Brandon thinks Jacobs may have had as much as a twenty minute head start. He's going after them but once he's in the tunnel he'll have no cell reception.'

'I hope Mitch and Alicia are okay,' Nerissa said. 'Where could Jacobs be taking them?'

'That's the thing. It's hard to tell,' Delano replied. 'We know he'll use our RIB as a getaway boat so I called Melford at Deepwater Harbour and asked if he could send another boat to rescue Brandon and the others. He said they just don't have anything small enough to even get remotely near the little cove down there.'

'What about tracking the RIB? It has an onboard GPS, doesn't it? If we could see where Jacobs is taking it, Melford could send a boat to intercept it,' Rusty said helpfully.

'I thought of that too but Lloyd can't locate the RIB. The radio and GPS are offline.'

'Jacobs must have disabled them,' Hyacinth said.

'It looks that way. And anyhow, Melford said both lifeboat crews are already out on rescue missions and he can't get hold of Max to captain a third boat. The Coast Guard can't help us right now.'

'This is bad,' Duane said with concern. 'I hope Max is okay too.'

Delano's cell phone rang again.

'Brandon,' he said quickly, answering it. 'You're on speaker with the rest of the team and Rusty McChannen, airport security.'

'Er — Delano.' They heard Brandon's voice from the phone's speaker. 'Spencer thinks he might have something. I'll put him on.'

'Delano, sorry, I know you're busy and all that, but I think I know where Jacobs is taking Mitch and Alicia.'

'Go on Spencer,' Delano replied.

'It's the place where I think he might be hiding the rest of his money. At least, well, I'm not sure, but…'

In the background a jet took off from the main runway. The team, along with Rusty and Johann, leaned closer to the phone in order to listen.

'Spencer, just say where…' Delano said loudly over the noise of the jet engines.

'I'd kind of like to check something first, before I do,' Spencer replied. 'Owen agrees, we think the pilot we flew with this morning, Johann Ryan, could tell us for certain if…'

'Johann Ryan?' Delano frowned. 'But he's standing right next to me. He's just been busted for drug trafficking. He was about to take off to Puerto Rico with an aircraft full of cocaine.'

'Say what?' Spencer asked in surprise. 'But that can't be, I mean, he does scenic flights and tours of the island, he's not…'

'No, it's true. I am.' Johann interrupted. 'I'm a drug run…'

'Shut up Johann,' Rusty said roughly.

'Wait.' Delano spoke. 'Spencer, what is it that Johann could tell us for certain?'

'The name of the Redonda Ground Dragon. The Latin name.'

Delano frowned in confusion but looked at Johann for a reply. He nodded at the pilot to go ahead.

'It's the pholidoscelis atratus,' Johann said, equally puzzled.

'That's it. I knew it.' Spencer repeated the name: 'The pholidoscelis *atratus*.'

'The atratus…' Delano repeated. 'That's…'

'It's the name of Oliver Jacobs's yacht,' Spencer said. 'The Atratus. The name's been in plain sight the whole time, yet it's so obscure that nobody connected the dots. Why would they? Jacobs named his yacht after the Latin name for the Redonda Ground Dragon, the island's indigenous lizard found nowhere else on earth.'

'Which would explain those recent renovations made to the buildings on Redonda that Johann pointed out to us this morning.' They suddenly heard Owen's voice. 'As well as the cistern here at the villa, we think Jacobs is storing the rest of his cash in the abandoned miners' huts on Redonda. It's the perfect location to hide something.'

'You mean Redonda as in that volcanic rock stuck out in the sea over near Montserrat?' Hyacinth queried.

'Yeah, *that* Redonda,' Owen replied.

'Didn't that place have a mining station on it at one time?' Nerissa asked.

'It did.' Spencer's voice again. 'And then a couple years ago there was this extensive conservation programme to regenerate the plants and animals and ecosystem of the island. It was reported to be a huge success, but now the conservationists have done their bit and cleared off, hardly anyone ever visits the island anymore, partly due to the fact that it's almost inaccessible by boat. Realistically the only way to get there is by helicopter and there are far nicer places to fly in the Caribbean than a rock in the middle of the sea.'

'So how does Jacobs take his cash there?' Nerissa asked.

'There is one small landing place. A skilled yachtsman who knows every inch of the water there could just about pilot a boat in.'

'Well, Jacobs sure knows how to sail,' Nerissa commented.

'It's got to be where he's headed with Mitch and Alicia,' Spencer said. 'What's the top speed of the RIB Delano?'

'Around forty knots, maybe forty-five at full power.'

'Then they could already be halfway there.' It was Brandon's voice. He had made a quick calculation in his head. 'They'll easily get to the island before we've even made it down to the cove.'

'What if we took a helicopter from here?' Hyacinth asked suddenly. She glanced up and down the old runway. 'There must be a tour company who could help?'

'Rusty?' Delano said, turning to the security officer. 'Any ideas?'

'There may be a tour company with a chopper and a pilot available, but it might take a bit of time to organise,' Rusty replied. 'I'll make some calls. See what I can do.'

'Can I help?' Johann asked suddenly.

'*You*?' Rusty said with a slight sneer. 'I can hardly allow…'

'Wait Rusty, he might be able to,' Delano interrupted. 'What are you thinking Johann?'

'I can't fly helicopters and we can't land on Redonda in this,' Johann nodded at the Cessna, 'but we could at least fly over there and see if we can spot them from the air, get an eye on what's happening, maybe even see if your boat's there.'

'Johann's the ideal person for this mission.' It was Spencer's voice again. 'He's already flown to Redonda twice this week. He knows the layout of the island perfectly from the air.'

'I think it sounds like a good idea boss,' Hyacinth said. 'I think we should do this.'

'I agree,' Nerissa added. 'Time's critical here. The clock's ticking. Alicia and Mitch's lives are at risk with every second we waste standing here. We've already lost Anson, Edella's in the hospital and Mitch is wounded. Johann's our best bet to save Mitch and Alicia now.'

'You're right,' Delano reluctantly agreed. 'We need to get to Redonda as soon as possible. But it's not enough to just fly overhead. We've got to land there.' He looked at Johann who shook his head.

'It can't be done,' he replied. 'It's impossible in an aircraft. A helicopter, yes. But a fixed wing's no good.'

'Then we really need a helicopter,' Hyacinth said.

Rusty was just ending a call with a contact from a helicopter tour company.

'No can do,' he said. 'That was Mike, a good friend of mine. He's got his own tour company with two helicopters and a fixed wing aircraft over at the main terminal. Says both his choppers are out on tours right now and won't be back until later. Neither of them are close enough to get back within the next thirty minutes. As for the other tour companies based here, there are a couple, but their helicopters are all out too — it's busy today — except for one company but their pilot isn't available.'

Delano glanced at Johann. 'You can't fly helicopters, can you?'

'Sorry.' Johann shook his head.

'How about floatplanes?' Spencer was still on speaker.

'Er, well, I used to have a seaplane rating many years ago,' Johann replied hesitantly, 'but it's long expired.'

'When did you last fly one?' Spencer asked.

'Twenty, no, thirty years ago now,' Johann said. 'I'd be very out of practice. I wouldn't like to…'

'I bet you'd be fine,' Spencer cut in. 'There's a small floatplane docked near the marina on the north side of runway ten.'

'He's right,' Duane said suddenly. 'It's owned by a Florida-based company. They have a small office near the Pavilion Café. I can run over there, see if the plane's available?'

'Go,' Delano said. 'And preferably see if the pilot's free too.'

Duane was already sprinting away in the direction of the small café.

'The cocaine's secure,' one of the security officers called from the cargo door of the aircraft. Another officer was strapping the brown leather suitcases onto a large trolley.

'We've made a preliminary search of the rest of the aircraft but the wing lockers and other baggage holds are empty. There are no other drugs stashed anywhere on board,' the first security officer continued. He handed Delano some paperwork to sign.

'Is this it, Johann?' Delano asked. 'Do we have it all?' He had a gut feeling Johann would answer truthfully.

'That's everything,' Johann nodded.

Delano scanned the paperwork and began flipping the pages over, scribbling his signature on each one.

'Boss...' Duane was back, slightly out of breath. 'I talked to the guy at the floatplane office over there. The plane's available. It's about three-quarters full of fuel. Only problem is that they had a booking this afternoon but it was cancelled at the last minute so the pilot went home and now he's not answering his cell. The receptionist guy thinks he's probably gone fishing or snorkelling, which is how he normally spends his time when he's not flying. He doesn't think we'll be able to get hold of him till later this evening.'

'So we got a plane to get us there but no pilot,' Delano said with a note of frustration.

'Pretty much, yeah.'

'You get the name of the guy in the office?' Delano asked.

'I think his badge said his name was Sean Manetti.'

'I know him,' Delano replied with a faint smile. He appeared to consider his options for a few seconds before turning to Johann.

'How much floatplane flying have you done?' he asked.

'Enough, I guess,' Johann replied. 'I used to fly them in Scotland. I've got about two hundred hours on that type of aircraft, but, like I said, it was a long time ago now and I'm not sure...'

'Duane, how many passengers can the floatplane take?' Delano asked.

'It seats four, including the pilot.'

'It's probably a Cessna 182 or something similar,' Johann said. 'I'm very familiar with that type of aircraft. It's just that I'm used to landing on wheels instead of floats.'

'Could you land on the water close to Redonda?' Delano asked.

'I guess so,' Johann replied. There was a note of apprehension in his voice. Delano made up his mind.

'Hyacinth, Nerissa, we're going to Redonda. Johann you're with us. Duane, take care of things here and get the suitcases over to Rochelle.'

'Aye aye, captain,' Duane replied.

Delano handed the paperwork to Duane and pulled Johann, still handcuffed, firmly towards him.

'Hold on a minute, you can't just…' Rusty began in protest but Delano cut him off.

'Unless you can get me one of those tour choppers in the air in ten minutes, we're going to Redonda in the floatplane and Johann's flying it,' he said firmly.

Before Rusty could respond, Delano began escorting Johann across the tarmac towards the floatplane office with Hyacinth and Nerissa close behind. Hyacinth winked at Rusty who stood speechless.

'I'm getting Earl on the phone,' Rusty called after them, quickly recovering himself. 'He won't be happy with this at all. He'll be speaking to air traffic control, ordering them to deny permission for takeoff. Captain Ryan's just been caught with an aircraft stashed full of cocaine. We simply can't allow…'

'Tell Earl we'll discuss this later,' Delano called back over his shoulder. 'And you can also tell him that the floatplane will be taking off with or without the permission of air traffic control.'

'The floatplane company will never allow this…' Rusty shouted. 'I'll be speaking to them too.'

'We'll see,' Delano called back without looking round.

'You sure about that boss?' Hyacinth said in a low voice.

'I think our friend Sean Manetti will be more than willing to help us out,' Delano replied with a smile.

TWENTY-NINE

5:01 pm, Saturday, September 21
The floatplane jetty, V. C. Bird International Airport

Sean Manetti, who manned the desk at the floatplane office, was initially reluctant to allow a retired pilot without the proper credentials to take the controls of a floatplane worth over a quarter of a million dollars.

'Absolutely no way,' he said with a firm shake of his head. 'My boss will never agree to this. It's illegal.'

'I'd be more than happy to speak to your boss,' Delano offered. 'And while I'm asking about the floatplane, he might be interested to hear about your little brush with the CDSLI last month.'

'You can't tell him about that,' Sean said in alarm. 'I could lose my job.'

'Which is why we agreed to let you off on this occasion,' Delano continued. 'However, I could always…'

'How many flying hours did you say you had in a floatplane again?' Sean turned to Johann.

'About two hundred. Give or take.'

'I'm sure that will be fine,' Sean said quickly. He grabbed a sheet of paper and slid it across the counter towards Johann with a pen. 'If you could just sign here. It's a disclaimer for…'

'We're not signing anything today Sean,' Delano said, tossing the sheet of paper into the trash.

'No, of course you're not. Which is absolutely fine by me,' Sean replied. 'Then you'll just be needing these…'

He retrieved a set of keys from behind the counter and handed them to Johann. Hyacinth had removed his handcuffs before they entered the office with a stern warning that if he tried anything funny he'd regret it.

'We'll take four lifejackets as well thanks Sean,' Delano added.

Sean was about to protest again before he stopped himself. He briefly disappeared into a cupboard behind the desk where he retrieved four lifejackets which he dumped on the countertop.

'I'm sure your enthusiastic, friendly service really draws in the customers,' Delano commented as he handed out the lifejackets to the other three. Sean scowled.

'Delano, if it's okay with you, I think I'll forgo the jacket,' Johann said hesitantly, placing his lifejacket back on the counter. 'It'll be more comfortable to fly without it.'

Delano paused before replying. Technically, Johann didn't need to wear one.

'No problem.' Delano nodded. He put on his own, securing it tightly. The four of them left the office and walked quickly to the floatplane which was docked at the jetty. It bobbed gently in the water in the last rays of late afternoon sunshine.

'I just need to check it over,' Johann said.

'Go right ahead,' Delano replied. With Hyacinth close by, Johann began inspecting the starboard side of the aircraft from the jetty before stepping on the floats to check out the port side. It was much newer than his Cessna Titan. Its blue and gold stripes which ran along the length of the fuselage were crisp and clean, as opposed to the faded, peeling retro brown and orange stripes on the Titan. Johann detached the mooring lines securing the floatplane to the jetty and they climbed on board. Delano was next to Johann, in the front; Nerissa and Hyacinth sat in the back.

Freed from its mooring, the floatplane began drifting gently away from the jetty. As Johann familiarised himself with the cockpit layout and began the preflight checks — which were not dissimilar to those of a land plane — he allowed the plane to drift backwards further with the wind. He found a preflight checklist in a side pocket although he felt strangely confident that he could recall the most important aspects of float flying from his distant past. He remembered that when flying floatplanes, the water, obstacles and wind needed to be considered before deciding on the takeoff direction. He knew that a downwind takeoff required a longer water run and when the wind direction was opposite to the current, the pilot had to decide which of the two would have the strongest influence on the takeoff run. The best takeoff performance was achieved when the plane departed against the current into the wind.

As they fastened their belts, Johann turned the key in the ignition. The engine started first time and idled smoothly. The plane was well-maintained and in good condition. He glanced at Delano for confirmation that he should continue. Delano nodded and, with one hand on the yoke and the other on the throttle, Johann made a brief radio call to the tower. Through his headset Delano listened to the exchanges between the pilot and the air traffic controller. So far, so good.

'Just a few more pre-takeoff checks on the water and then we're good to go,' Johann said.

'We're ready when you are captain,' Delano replied. He was beginning to like Johann Ryan. He couldn't imagine how he had ended up trafficking cocaine between Antigua and Puerto Rico — and wherever else — and sure, the pilot was looking at many years in jail when this was over, but for now, he deserved to fly one last time.

Johann took a careful glance around for boats and other floating obstacles, in and on the water. They had drifted some distance from the coastline now, far enough away from the small harbour for Johann to complete the preflight checks. When he was satisfied with the handling of the floatplane and that they were ready to go, he radioed the tower once more. There was still no sign that anything was wrong.

'We have permission for takeoff,' Johann said, turning to Delano who had listened to the radio exchange. Suddenly Delano realised that, in spite of Rusty's threats, Earl Bextor would never kowtow to his junior. He clearly had no intentions of instructing air traffic to deny permission for the floatplane to take off. Delano had a good working relationship with the airport's chief security officer and knew that Earl would sooner trust him than Rusty, his clipboard-wielding deputy.

'Let's roll,' Delano said, 'or ski, or whatever the word is.'

'Yes sir.' Johann scanned their surroundings once more before easing the throttle forward. The floatplane began gathering speed as it skimmed across the water, sending a mist of sea spray from behind the floats. He maintained the heading and felt the resistance from the water as the floatplane gained enough speed for the planing attitude. Johann quickly settled into the feel of the controls, as if he had flown on water just yesterday. Carefully applying the right amount of back pressure on the elevator to ensure the correct pitch angle of the aircraft, he held the yoke sensitively between the fingers and thumb of his left hand. Too much pressure and the stern of the floats would be forced deeper into the water. Too little and the bows would remain in the water, causing excessive drag.

As the floatplane settled onto the plane, the surface of the water or the "step" as it was sometimes known, it bounced from one wave crest to the next. Johann maintained a constant pitch attitude which allowed the floatplane to skim across each successive wave. He felt the wind and the current and the waves as they gathered speed. With only a part of the floats now touching the water there was less drag and the floatplane reached takeoff speed. Johann pulled back a little more on the yoke, sensing a slight acceleration as the hydrodynamic drag disappeared. And then he felt the lift from the airflow over the wings.

He gradually eased the nose up, cautiously at first. When the floats were clear of the water, he established a positive rate of climb and raised the flaps. As height and speed increased, he banked gently onto a southwesterly direction, into the setting sun. He knew it was the last time he would ever take off from V. C. Bird International, or any airport for that matter, from land or sea. As they soared over the patchwork of greens and blues below, Johann tried not to think about how much he would miss flying. He'd miss the views, the feeling of being high above the world and all its cares, the feeling of being in control of a machine that could actually fly, the feeling of soaring through clouds as if he was as light as a feather. Setting course to the island of Redonda for one final time, Johann told himself that this would be the greatest flight of his life.

5:20 pm, Saturday, September 21
Redonda, Caribbean Sea

Johann flew a direct track to the island of Redonda. He knew that, in general, once a floatplane was in the air, it flew much like a land plane, although floatplanes had a slower rate of climb and cruise speed than their land-based counterparts. The floatplane was considerably slower than his own Cessna Titan and it took double the time to reach Redonda, but within fifteen minutes they could see the island's craggy silhouette rising out of the sea, the setting sun behind it.

'We're almost there,' Johann said. 'How d'you want to do this?'

'How close to the island can you land?' Delano asked.

'I can get you pretty close,' Johann replied. 'I'm familiar with the surrounding water by now. We'll land on the leeward side. It's a little calmer there.'

He glanced at his watch and then at the sun, rapidly descending towards the horizon. 'Daylight's fading fast now. It's not much more than twenty minutes before sunset.'

'We got waterproof flashlights,' Delano said, producing a small black cylindrical item from his pocket.

'I'll start a gentle descent,' Johann said, smoothly pulling back on the throttle. 'You're aware the noise of the engine will alert anyone on the island of our presence? We'll lose the element of surprise.'

'Perhaps,' Delano replied, 'but we'll take our chances.'

The muffled ring tone of his phone sounded from one of his pockets. He pulled it out.

'Go ahead Brandon.' He listened intently for a few minutes before replying. 'It's a good plan but be careful. As for us, it's a long story but we're almost overhead Redonda right now. No, not by sea; by air, we're in a floatplane. I'll explain later. The pilot? The same one we caught red-handed at the airport bust but we'll get to him later too. What's your ETA? Great, get here as soon as you can.'

Delano hung up and relayed Brandon's side of the conversation.

'Brandon and the others got back through the tunnel to the cove with the manchineel trees and guess what? The RIB was still there, on the shore, but its outboard engines had been completely disabled.'

'I wasn't expecting that,' Hyacinth exclaimed in surprise. 'So how did Jacobs get away? Did they swim?'

'He must've arranged for another boat to come and get them.'

'But *how*? And with whom? He's been locked up in a cell the whole time.'

'Maybe Ray picked them up,' Nerissa said.

'But how would he know they were there at the cove, at that time?' Hyacinth asked. 'I just don't get it. If Ray's doing all this, how is he keeping one step ahead of us the whole time?'

Neither Nerissa nor Delano had an answer.

'Are they all still stuck down there at the cove?' Hyacinth asked.

'Not exactly. Brandon called Lloyd back at HQ, told him they were stranded and that with the Coast Guard unable to get a boat to them they'd have to go back up through the tunnel to Villa Bella Casa. The only other option left was for Lloyd to send a car to come and get them.'

'So we're on our own now?'

'We would have been except Lloyd had an idea. Remember Paul Griffiths, the pharmaceutical CEO from New York, who owns the villa next door to Jacobs?'

'You mean the guy cheating on his wife with the Spanish gift shop lady? Used his yacht as a love boat for his sordid little affair?'

'Yeah, that guy,' Delano nodded. 'Turns out the love boat's about to come in useful. It's moored right there at Sugar Reef Bay and comes with a handy little tender. Lloyd called him and asked if he'd be up for striking a deal: we'd make sure all knowledge of his affair with Elena López went away if we could borrow his Sunseeker.'

'That's imaginative,' Nerissa said with amusement, 'although not entirely ethical. Technically I don't think we're supposed to blackmail potential suspects, but — desperate times and all that — we need a boat. Is Paul on his way to the cove to rescue them?'

'This very minute,' Delano replied. 'And then they'll head straight over here, to Redonda.'

'In the Sunseeker?' Hyacinth asked. 'They should make it within the hour.'

'Delano, I can see a boat down there, on that little stretch of sand,' Johann interrupted. 'It must be the sole landing place on the island for sailing vessels.' He gently banked the aircraft and the three officers looked out of the windows in the direction he was pointing.

'Whose boat is that?' Hyacinth asked.

'It looks like Jacobs's go-fast,' Delano replied in surprise.

'But it can't be.' Nerissa voiced what the others were thinking. 'That boat was impounded with his yacht when we busted him on Thursday morning.'

'It's definitely Jacobs's,' Hyacinth confirmed. 'I recognise that Miami Vice-style hull and the camouflage paint job. It's a typical drug-trafficker's boat: long, sleek and extremely powerful. See those multiple outboard engines? Some of these boats have a top speed of up to a hundred miles an hour.'

'So if it's Jacobs's, then how did he get it out of the impound?' Nerissa asked.

'Not so much *how*, but *who* got it out,' Delano said.

'Ray,' Hyacinth said in a low voice. 'He must be with them.'

'I can see people down there,' Johann said.

'It's Jacobs and Alicia. And Mitch,' Hyacinth said. She paused. 'Is that...?' She stopped herself in surprise and looked in alarm at Delano and Nerissa. 'Oh my gosh, we've got this so wrong.'

'I don't understand...' Nerissa began, her eyes wide in astonishment as she stared at the little group below them.

'Wait, I know one of those guys too,' Johann said in surprise. 'That's Max Moran. I met him in a strip club in Miami. He works for Rusty McChannen.'

'What?' Delano asked. It was his turn to be surprised. 'Max doesn't work for Rusty, he's a lifeboat coxswain with the Antigua Coast Guard. And I hardly think he's the type to hang out in a

Miami strip club. Rusty, yes, I can see that, perhaps, but not Max. You must be mistaken.'

'No, I'm not. I recognise him. He's definitely the same guy from Miami,' Johann replied insistently.

'So how did you and Max come to be acquainted?' Delano asked curiously. Johann paused. Perhaps he should have stayed quiet about his association with Max. He wasn't sure if he would help or hurt himself by answering the question. But perhaps it was too late to consider that.

'A few years ago I was doing some flying work out of Miami. While I was there, I met two Antiguans: Rusty McChannen, the airport security guy, and Max Moran. He works for Rusty. They're high-level dealers and fairly prominent within the Ramirez cartel. It's one of the most powerful cartels run by one of the most powerful drug lords, Alejandro Ortega. You'll know of him.'

'Yeah, we know Ortega and the Ramirez cartel well,' Delano said. 'Both have brutal reputations. But how are Max and Rusty involved?'

'They pretty much run the whole of Antigua as a drug transhipment zone between South America and the United States and Europe. They've got a nice little enterprise going on. Rusty has top-level clearance in airport security and takes care of the drug shipments that arrive and leave by air. Max works for the Coast Guard and is obviously ideally positioned to oversee the maritime side of things, the harbours, marinas and seaports. I first met them in a strip club in Downtown Miami. I kept in touch with Rusty, on and off. A couple of years later I was made redundant back in the UK and Rusty offered me some flying work out here. According to him, I'd be doing scenic flights for tourists. It sounded legit, almost too good to be true. Turns out it was. Looking back I can't believe how easily I was taken in by his lies.'

'But by then he had you right where he wanted you and there was no way out,' Hyacinth said. 'You had to keep flying or you were a dead man.'

'Exactly,' Johann said as he banked the aircraft over the southern tip of the island. They were getting closer now. 'That's how the cartels operate. Through fear. I just had to hope I'd never get caught.'

'It's all falling into place,' Delano said quietly. 'Max and Rusty have been hiding in plain sight the whole time and I never even saw it.'

'How could we?' Hyacinth asked. She checked the time on her watch. 'How long until the others get here? Twenty minutes?'

'More like thirty,' Delano said. 'We're losing daylight fast. It'll be dark soon. We'll have to do this without them.'

'Look down there,' Nerissa said. There was a note of panic in her voice. The others followed her gaze out of the starboard windows where two men below were pointing what appeared to be large assault rifles straight at them.

'It's Mitch and Max,' Delano said.

'They're shooting at us,' Johann said in alarm. He increased the power and banked the floatplane away from the island as sharply as he dared. 'Those semi-autos aren't for show. Delano, what d'you want me to do?'

'We should wait till the others get here,' Nerissa said.

'No.' Delano shook his head. 'We go while we still have daylight. Johann, get us down on the water as quickly as you can.'

'If you're sure. I'll try and get you as close to that stretch of sand with the boat as I can.' Johann banked the floatplane into the direction of the wind and continued descending as he checked the tide and looked for any obstacles in the water. 'You got a spare cell phone?' he asked suddenly. 'If we keep an open line I can fly back and forth over the island once I've set you down and let you know what's happening from the air, where everyone is and so on. If it would help?'

'Yes, it would.' Delano wrestled a phone from one of his pockets and handed it to Johann. 'It's your own cell phone. I'm breaking all the rules by giving it back to you but we could really use your eye in the sky right now. Give us regular sit-reps once we're on land. You can return it to me when this is over.'

'Yes sir,' Johann replied, attaching his cell phone to the kneeboard strapped to his thigh. 'Are you ready to go now sir?'

'Take us all the way down Johann.'

They made eye contact briefly.

'I'm sorry for all this, for my involvement with…' Johann spoke solemnly, unsure of how to finish the sentence. 'Please believe me, it's not what I signed up for. Not at all. It was never meant to be like this.'

'I believe you,' Delano replied. He knew Johann was telling the truth. 'And I see how things went for you. But you're aware of the consequences, right? You know you're facing a life sentence?'

'Yeah. I know that.' Johann looked away sadly.

'Seventeen thirty-five ain't good news for a guy like you.' Delano was using the local name for the national prison of Antigua and Barbuda, in St. John's. He looked Johann in the eye again. He felt sad for him. 'If you tell us everything you know we may be able to consider putting you into a witness protection programme…'

Johann nodded. He understood it may be the only way. The idea of looking over his shoulder for the rest of his life wasn't exactly appealing but it was surely better than prison. And certainly better than being hunted down by the formidable Ramirez cartel. But there was no time to think about that now. He had a floatplane to land, a skill he had not revisited in nearly thirty years.

They were flying due south of the island on the leeward side, heading in a northerly direction. For now at least, Mitch and Max and their deadly assault rifles were nowhere to be seen. The failing light didn't help but Johann was confident he could get the little floatplane down safely on the water, even if the landing itself lacked his usual finesse. As far as he could recall, landing a floatplane was a lot like landing a land plane with a nose-wheel, except a floatplane didn't have brakes. He scanned the area around his proposed landing spot on the water once more. It was becoming increasingly difficult to identify any obstacles and rocks but he wanted to touch down as close to the island as possible. The three CDSLI officers would be vulnerable to attack from Mitch and Max above them while they were in the water and needed as short a distance to swim as possible.

Johann pulled the power and commenced the descent for the last few hundred feet, setting the floatplane into a glide towards the sea and extending the flaps. Just as when landing on tarmac, he knew it was important to touch down at the slowest possible speed. The sheer cliffs of Redonda loomed ahead of them on the starboard side and the water churned and boiled on the rocks below them as the floatplane passed four hundred, three hundred, and then two hundred feet. Johann continued to guide it closer to the water, trimming the control surfaces to maintain the final approach speed. They passed one hundred feet and the others watched in silence as the sea rose up to meet them. Johann scanned the rocky shoreline ahead and to his right in order to accurately judge their height above the surface of the water. He kept a trickle of power on to control their descent rate for the final few feet.

As the orange ball of the sun slipped below the horizon in a hazy palette of pinks and reds, casting a pale glow across the waves — the last of the daylight — they dropped below fifteen feet above the water and Johann squeezed the yoke towards him, adding another trickle of power to maintain the landing attitude. They scudded over the tips of the waves as he held the floats just above the surface of the water until he was ready to touch down. He reduced the power and felt the floats touch the water. He pulled the throttle to idle as the floatplane pitched forward from the sudden contact with the waves. He squeezed gently back on the yoke and, as the speed decreased, he felt the floatplane drop off the plane and slow to taxying speed, rocking a little on the swell of the current.

'Good job, Johann,' Hyacinth said from the back.

'Thanks.' He breathed a sigh of relief. Holding the yoke fully back, he allowed the floatplane to drift towards the island. He kept one hand on the throttle and a close eye on the surrounding rocks, ready to power away should the floatplane drift too near.

'This is as close as I can get you,' he said, glancing round at them. 'Is it good enough?'

'It's ideal,' Delano said.

'The landing shore and the boat are just over there,' Johann added. 'D'you see them?'

'Yeah,' Delano replied. 'We got it from here. Keep us informed with your eye in the sky.'

'Yes sir, I will,' Johann nodded. 'Take care. And good luck.'

'You too, Johann.' Delano unlatched the door and pushed it open. Releasing his seatbelt, he scrambled out, stepping onto the float and then jumping into the water. Nerissa and Hyacinth climbed over from the rear seats and joined him. Hyacinth, the last to leave the floatplane, thanked Johann again and closed the door firmly before jumping off the float. With the engine idling, Johann watched the three heads bobbing in the water as they swam to the small beach on the rocky shoreline. He waited until they were almost there and well clear of the floatplane before manoeuvring further out into the sea. He quickly reconfigured the flaps and trimmed the control surfaces ready for takeoff before confirming the direction of the wind and the current. He flipped on the floatplane's lights and scanned the dark water around him for rocks and obstacles. It looked clear ahead. He glanced across to the shoreline where he could just make out the silhouettes of three figures emerging from the murky water, one by one, like a scene from a movie with a United States SEAL Team on a classified mission. The three officers had reached dry land and now it was time for the second part of the last flight of Johann's life. He held the yoke and eased the throttle forward. The floats began advancing through the water once more.

As the floatplane became airborne, Johann set it into a climbing turn back towards Redonda. He quickly levelled off at just over a thousand feet and banked around the steep cliff face. In the twilight, he spotted four figures walking closely together over the rocky terrain. They were heading for the abandoned miners' huts. The woman and a man led the way. The man was wearing what looked to be dark-coloured pyjamas, or perhaps they were prison scrubs. With their hands tied behind their backs, they appeared to be hostages of the two men immediately behind who were wearing powerful headlights. The men carried assault rifles which were pointed straight at their hostages. Johann recognised one of the men with the rifles: it was Max Moran. As he flew overhead, he watched as the four figures looked up at the floatplane. He flew on a little further, out to sea, before making a one-eighty degree turn.

He was now flying in the opposite direction and scanned the coastline, frantically searching for the three CDSLI officers. Suddenly, he saw the golden beams of three flashlights near to the tiny cove. They were standing next to Jacobs's go-fast boat, pulled up high on the beach. Johann's phone buzzed on his kneeboard. He answered it and put it on speaker. He heard Delano's voice. The sentence was broken as the CDSLI officer recovered his breath.

'We're here... on the beach... which way Johann? Where are they?'

'I can see a small path on the north side of the beach which winds its way up the cliff,' Johann replied. 'It's steep, but it looks passable. When you reach the top, turn left. You should be able to make out the path with your flashlights, even though it's almost dark now. It leads to the abandoned miners' huts where Max and the other guy seem to be heading with the two hostages, the man in the prison scrubs and the woman.'

'They're emptying the huts of the rest of the cash,' Delano said, 'loading it into Jacobs's go-fast down here on the beach. They must be using Jacobs and Alicia to help move it all to speed things up. There are already stacks of currency bundles stashed in the back.'

'Then they'll be heading your way once they've reloaded with more cash,' Johann said. His voice had a sense of urgency. 'Hurry Delano, you need to reach the top of the cliff before they make it back there.'

'We've found the path,' Delano replied. 'We're on our way up. You're right, it's pretty steep.'

Flying in the opposite direction once more, Johann made a low pass over the abandoned buildings as four figures — the two shooters and two hostages — headed towards them. The shooters looked up towards the floatplane, their headlights following the direction of their eyes. Johann watched in alarm as they pointed the assault rifles upwards, aiming straight at him. In an evasive manoeuvre, he banked the aircraft as sharply as he could and braced himself for the shots. He knew he was well within range and vulnerable to being hit. But he felt nothing and the floatplane continued flying.

He banked around and watched as the party of four below him reached the abandoned miners' huts. The two armed men: Max and the rogue CDSLI officer whom Delano had referred to as Mitch, pushed the man in the prison scrubs and the woman inside one of the huts before disappearing after them. Johann doubled back to check on Delano's progress. In the distance, he could see lights on the water, perhaps a few miles out. He followed the cliff wall until he had Delano, Nerissa and Hyacinth in his sights once more. They had made good progress and were over halfway up the uneven cliff path, but there was still some way to go. The rocks seemed to become steeper the higher they climbed.

'Delano, you need to hurry,' Johann said. He tried to speak calmly. 'Max and Mitch are inside the miners' huts with the hostages but I'm guessing it won't be long until they're on their way back.'

'Thanks Johann. We're moving as fast as we can.' Delano's reply was breathless as he scaled the cliff path with Nerissa and Hyacinth close behind. 'We'll try to catch them off-guard, use the element of surprise to our advantage.'

'I'll keep you updated with their position,' Johann said. 'And it looks like your rescue boat is on its way.'

'The Sunseeker?'

'Yeah, I can see lights on the water from what looks like a decent-sized yacht. It's probably about ten minutes out.'

'Can you guide them to the landing place?'

'Sure, I'll head out to them now, but I'll be right back. I won't leave you.' Johann eased the throttles forward a little to increase his speed as he flew away from Redonda towards the approaching vessel. He saw the open line to Delano's cell go dead on the screen of his phone and guessed Delano was calling someone on the yacht. As he reached the Sunseeker with its bright lights reflecting on the water, his phone buzzed. It was Delano.

'I've told them the game plan and that you'll guide them to safe harbour. They'll follow you in.'

'Got it,' Johann replied. He circled overhead the yacht and descended slightly. His slowest speed was still considerably faster than the Sunseeker and so he flew a holding pattern over the yacht, moving closer towards the island with each lap. It was a starless night and the darkness wrapped itself around the island like a shroud. Without Johann's guidance it would have been treacherous for the Sunseeker to approach the waters surrounding Redonda.

As it neared the rocky island, the yacht slowed and held its position some distance away. Undoubtedly it was equipped with depth sounders and other detection equipment to ensure it didn't run aground. With the engines idling, it bobbed up and down on the waves. Johann watched from the air as three crew members launched a tender into the water and jumped in, before setting off to the small cove. Johann flew from the Sunseeker to the cove in wide arcs, lighting the narrow channel through the rocks like a beacon, keeping the small boat in his sights. Whoever was at the helm of the tender appeared to be an expert skipper. Johann watched tensely as it navigated through the channel, flanked by the jagged lines of rocks on both sides. The tender reached the landing stage and the three dark shapes clambered out, hauling the boat far up onto the beach beside Jacobs's go-fast. Three flashlights quickly became unified in a northerly direction, upwards along the cliff path. When Johann was satisfied that the team from the Sunseeker were safely on track, he circled low over the upper path until he spotted three more figures. They had extinguished their flashlights but he could see that Delano, Nerissa and Hyacinth were nearing the abandoned huts, gaining ground on the shooters and their hostages who were still inside.

'See anyone down here?' Delano asked.

'Nobody,' Johann replied. He banked a little steeper in an attempt to get a clearer view. Suddenly, two lights emerged from one of the miners' huts. They were the headlights of Mitch and

Max who were still carrying their assault rifles. Before Johann had time to react, the two men turned and aimed the rifles upwards, at the floatplane. Johann swore under his breath and banked sharply, dipping the port wing towards the ground. It was too sharp for the floatplane and he corrected the manoeuvre quickly, reducing the bank angle. He was certain he hadn't escaped the volley of bullets but the control surfaces seemed to be intact.

'Delano, the shooters are coming back your way, they're headed straight for you,' he said urgently.

'Thanks Johann, I hear you. Can you draw them out further?' Delano's voice sounded through the speaker on the phone on Johann's knee. 'Nerissa, Hyacinth and I are going to climb higher to avoid them and then double back to the rear of the buildings.'

'I'll do my best,' Johann replied quickly. He felt himself taking fast and shallow breaths as he levelled off and banked in the opposite direction. He knew there would be bullets coming his way but he continued with the turn.

'Any sign of the hostages?' Delano asked.

'No, just Mitch and Max as far as I can see. The other two must still be inside the huts.' Johann circled low over the two men who took aim once more at the floatplane. As another round of bullets struck the airframe, Johann flew a little further away, towards the incoming party of three from the Sunseeker. Out to the east, the dark silhouette of the yacht skulked low in the water, like a mysterious ghost ship. Those who remained on board had extinguished the lights. The hull bobbed on the waves in darkness, watching and waiting.

'Sit-rep Johann?' Delano's voice. 'There's a lot of gunfire noise down here.'

'That'll be Mitch and Max shooting at me. But your crew from the Sunseeker is getting closer.'

'How close?'

Aware the floatplane was taking the impact of bullets from powerful assault rifles, Johann scanned the instruments in the cockpit more intently than usual. Suddenly he noticed that the fuel gauge for the starboard wing tank was showing a rapid decrease in fuel. There could only be one reason for this.

'Dammit, I've been hit,' Johann said.

'You okay?'

'Yeah, the latest round of bullets must've punctured one of the fuel tanks. There's enough fuel in the other tank for now though. Delano, the shooters are headed straight for your agents from the Sunseeker. They're close, maybe two, three minutes away.'

'My guys are expecting them. They're armed and ready.'

'I see you've reached the miners' huts. Be careful down there.'

'We're going in.' Delano's voice sounded through the speaker of the phone as Johann circled over the abandoned buildings and watched as the three officers disappeared inside. With one eye on the fuel gauges, Johann flew back towards the crew from the Sunseeker. From the lights of the floatplane he could see they had nearly reached Mitch and Max, but the two men were apparently unaware of their presence. Instead they were looking upwards with their rifles trained on the plane. Johann braced himself as they took aim and followed his flight path.

Suddenly he noticed the needle on the other fuel gauge begin to fall. The bullets from the assault rifles had punctured the other fuel tank in the port wing. The floatplane was now dumping fuel at an alarming rate from both tanks.

'Damn,' Johann muttered under his breath. He glanced at his watch and made a rapid calculation in his head. He guessed he had no more than ten minutes before he would be completely out of fuel. Sure he could set the floatplane into a glide and land on the water, but then what? Maybe the Sunseeker would sail over and rescue him. Then again, maybe it was better if nobody rescued him. He thought maybe he'd prefer to just drift out to sea and disappear forever instead of being picked up by the CDSLI. If that happened, he knew two choices lay ahead of him: a new name and a new face in some kind of witness protection scheme or a life sentence in prison. Neither option appealed. Pushing the thought from his mind, he circled low once more, perhaps for the last time, over the volcanic rock with its sheer cliffs. As he strained his eyes to make out what was happening below, he was startled to see that the shooters were lying face down on the ground with the three members of the Sunseeker crew standing above them.

'Delano, it looks like your agents have taken down the two shooters,' he said.

'They've just radioed to say they have them in custody,' came the immediate reply. 'They ambushed them, caught them completely off-guard. And we have the hostages, Oliver Jacobs and Alicia.'

'You do?' Johann spoke with relief. 'Are they okay?'

'Yeah, they're fine. Everything's good. Johann, what's your fuel status?'

'The bullets from the assault rifles have punctured both fuel tanks,' Johann replied calmly. 'I'm haemorrhaging fuel like crazy now.'

'How long do you have?'

'Seven minutes maybe. Eight maximum.'

'Get out of here Johann.'

'I'm not leaving you Delano, but I'm gonna have to put this thing down on the water soon.'

'Get out of here. Your job's done. The hostages are safe and we have Mitch and Max in custody. There's nothing more for you to do. We got this.'

'But what about…'

'The Sunseeker's waiting to take us back to Antigua. Fly away from here Johann. That's an order. And good luck.'

Johann understood.

'Thank you sir.' It was all he could manage to say.

As he banked away from the island into the darkness he was startled to realise he was blinking back tears from his eyes. The screen of his cell phone went dead and he knew Delano had hung up. It was the last time he would hear from the CDSLI officer. He glanced at the GPS. He would never make it to Antigua. The wing tanks were losing fuel by the minute. Suddenly, in the distance, he saw a faint string of lights, like pale golden beads. It was part of the northwestern coastline of the island of Montserrat. If he could put the floatplane down somewhere close to land, he could abandon it and swim ashore. And disappear.

With the needles of the fuel gauges falling closer to the red with every mile, Johann set his course towards the northwest corner of Montserrat. And then he remembered the exclusion zone. Over the time he had spent flying around the Caribbean, he had developed an interest in the islands, especially those in the Leeward chain close to Antigua. Montserrat was particularly interesting because of its volcano. In the summer of 1995, the Soufrière Hills volcano, which had been dormant for centuries, suddenly became active. The eruption obliterated much of the southern part of the island and soon buried the capital, Plymouth, in almost forty feet of mud and ash. The airport and harbour were also completely destroyed, and an exclusion zone was imposed on the southern half of the island which was deemed uninhabitable and unsafe for travel. Johann knew that this part of Montserrat had been evacuated and visits were severely restricted. Which meant that there would be no one around to notice an aircraft gliding silently down towards the darkened stretch of sea on the southwest coastline of the island.

He took up a southerly heading, along the west coast of Montserrat, flying at just below a thousand feet. He watched the lights of the northern, inhabited part of the island become further apart and finally fade into nothing as he approached the exclusion zone in the southern half. The fuel gauges were both showing he was empty of fuel and he knew it was a matter of minutes, perhaps seconds, before the engine would stop.

He was approaching what he thought was a point roughly abeam the ghost town of Plymouth when he heard the engine splutter and knew he was out of fuel. As the engine cut out completely, he adjusted the flaps, trimmed the control surfaces and set up a smooth glide towards the sea. There was very little light and he hoped there were no rocks or obstacles in his landing path. He continued the descent, maintaining a broad scan of the water around him. The wind was light and he could just make out the shoreline on the port side from which the darkened ruins of the former capital city rose up steeply.

The waves rolled onto the desolate stretch of what had once been a white sandy beach lined with palm trees. It was now a stark, barren landscape covered by the pyroclastic flow from the volcano and layers of ash from previous eruptions. The place was eerily deserted. No one noticed the floatplane glide silently towards the sea, or the mist of spray behind the floats as they touched down onto the water. No one heard the splash as a lone figure clambered out of the plane onto a float and jumped into the water. No one saw the figure swim towards the shoreline or watched the plane drift silently away from the island, out to sea, the waves slapping lazily against its floats. And no one saw the figure half-crawl, half-drag himself onto the deserted, ash-covered beach before collapsing, facedown in a heap, dishevelled and soaked through.

THIRTY

The shoreline of Plymouth, Montserrat

Dazed and exhausted, Johann rolled over onto his back and opened his eyes. His face was covered with sweat and ash and his head was pounding. What he wouldn't give for a generous swig of Captain Morgan's finest right now, he thought to himself. He'd take it neat. He felt something vibrate in the pocket of his shirt. He had removed his cell phone from his kneeboard before jumping from the floatplane. It was the only possession he had with him now. He eased himself up onto his elbows and pulled the phone out of his pocket. Rubbing ash out of his eyes, he tried to focus on the screen. The phone appeared to have miraculously survived the swim. There were three missed calls from a number he didn't recognise along with a text message from Rusty which he ignored. He slid the phone back into his shirt pocket. He knew he needed to dispose of it soon, before someone put a trace on it in an attempt to track him down.

He sat up in a fresh cloud of dust and ash, coughing as he rested his elbows on his knees. Except for the waves lapping gently on the shore a few feet away, there were no other sounds in the warm night air. He scanned the horizon, twisting his neck painfully to the left and right but there was not a single light to be seen. He was in the middle of nowhere, inside a volcano exclusion zone. There would be no one for miles around. The downside offered by the invisibility the exclusion zone provided was that he would have to hike in the darkness to one of the towns in the north of the island. It would take half the night. And then what? He had been so focused on flying and landing the floatplane, he hadn't considered his next steps. In spite of Delano letting him go, he was still a wanted man by various law enforcement agencies and the notorious Ramirez cartel. Information was doubtless shared between the islands by the cartels and the drug enforcement agencies. Sure, he had survived this far, but what now?

He felt his cell phone vibrate in his pocket again. With a shaking hand, he pulled it out and looked at the screen. It was the same unknown number. He was familiar with the usual "No caller ID" notification which showed on the screen when Rusty or his henchmen called from one of their latest burners, but this number was visible. He gazed at the screen as the phone continued to vibrate. It would soon go to voicemail. Suddenly he made up his mind. For reasons he would never later be able to understand, he answered it.

'Hello?'

'Oh hi, I'd like to speak with Captain Johann Ryan.' A female voice spoke with an American accent. It sounded familiar.

'You're er, you're speaking with him.' Johann spluttered out the words. His throat felt dry and raspy from the dusty air.

'Oh hey Johann, it's Victoria Lorenzo here. You and Rusty McChannen took my friends and me on a scenic tour of Redonda yesterday, and then we flew to Nevis for dinner at The Great House.'

'Sure Victoria, I remember you.' Johann's pulse quickened.

'Awesome. I hope you don't mind me calling you after-hours and all but I was wondering if we could do it again before I fly back to the States on Monday.'

'Uhhh, I'm sorry Victoria but I don't think…'

'Oh I forgot to say, the others have plans tomorrow so it will just be me, but I'll pay for a full aircraft. And dinner's on me too, naturally.'

Johann ached at the thought that any other time he would have been elated to have been asked such a thing from a woman like Victoria. She was beautiful, intelligent and with a body to die for. She could have the flight and dinner for free for all he cared. But she was a day too late for that.

'Victoria, I'm sorry but…' His voice faltered and he coughed.

'Johann, are you okay?'

'I'm fine.'

'I came by your hut this evening, on runway ten, but it was all shut up, and your plane wasn't parked in its usual spot. Are you out on a night flight or something?'

'Not exactly, no.'

'I heard there was some kind of drama at the airport this afternoon. There was a bunch of crime scene tape everywhere when I got here.'

'Yeah, there would be.' Johann's reply was more to himself than Victoria.

'I know Rusty's game Johann,' Victoria said suddenly, to Johann's surprise. 'Logan and Carter, how d'you think they're connected to him? The Ramirez cartel. They're all involved. And I saw how you're enthralled to Rusty. He's an evil son of a bitch. How did you get mixed up with him? What does he have on you? I know you're a good man. I saw it in your eyes yesterday.'

Johann was speechless. Had Victoria really seen all this from yesterday's flight alone?

'Where are you?' she asked.

'I can't say,' Johann forced the words out. 'Goodbye Victoria.'

'Don't hang up Johann,' Victoria said quickly. 'Let's talk. Can I meet you somewhere?'

'No.'

'Where are you?'

'Why d'you want to know? Are you working for Rusty? Is this a trap?'

'On the contrary. Rusty works for me. I come from a family who've been involved with drug cartels and organised crime groups for four generations, since the nineteen-thirties. I know how they operate: drug trafficking, protection rackets, assassinations, extortions, kidnappings, the usual criminal activities. For the last few years dad's been prepping me to take over the family business — he wants to retire — but I can't do it Johann, I can't live this life, I'll never sleep at night again if I do.'

Johann thought he understood. But even so, she could still be luring him into a trap.

'I'm sorry Victoria, but I can't help you. I can't even help myself right now.'

'That look in your eyes when you were with Rusty, I just... I know how you feel.'

'Thanks. But even so, it's too late to...'

'I'd really like to see you again Johann,' Victoria interrupted. She was clearly not used to being told no. 'It'd be good to talk at the very least. I liked you. There was something about you.'

The surge of adrenaline which was released in Johann's body at Victoria's words was tainted with a mixture of excitement, cynicism and disbelief.

'That's very nice of you Victoria, but I'm sorry, it's too late for anything like that.'

'Why don't you let me be the judge of that?' Victoria sounded resolute. 'Where are you? I'll come to you.'

Johann let out a rasping laugh.

'Good luck with that,' he said. 'You'll need a boat or a helicopter.'

'I have both at my disposal, but I'm sure you'd prefer me to take the boat. It's a lot less conspicuous. Send me your location.'

Johann was taken aback at Victoria's reply. Was she for real after all? But then again, he'd known her for less than a day. It could so easily be a trap. How could he possibly trust her? It was through trusting someone that he had gotten himself into this mess. He vowed he'd never trust anyone again.

'Johann?'

'How do I know this isn't a trap? How I can trust you?' he heard himself say. Suddenly his heart and head were pulling in two different directions.

'You can't possibly know,' Victoria replied. 'Trusting someone is a risk you take. We all have to. You have to make a choice.'

Johann quickly weighed up his options: he could either hike to the nearest town, which would potentially take a few hours, where word would undoubtedly get back to local law enforcement officers, and worse, the cartel, in record time, or he could accept Victoria's offer of a boat ride and get off the island, preferably without raising any alarms. Assuming he could trust her. The only flaw in the plan was that she could still be working on behalf of Rusty, or perhaps some drug enforcement agency. It was a risk, a chance he'd have to take. He made his decision and took a deep breath.

'How soon can you make it to Montserrat?' Johann asked.

'Montserrat? As in the island Montserrat?' She disguised the surprise in her voice well.

'Yeah. I'm on the southwest coast, on the shore of Plymouth, the old capital city.'

'You mean you're inside the exclusion zone? How did you end up there?'

'It's a long story, but I sort of... I ran out of fuel and had to make an emergency landing.'

'Oh my gosh, are you sure you're okay?'

'I've been better, but I'm fine.'

'Does anyone else know where you are?'

'I don't think so. Not so far anyway. It's pretty deserted out here. I don't think anyone saw the plane go down. I landed on the water a little way offshore.'

'You ditched your aircraft?'

'Not exactly no, it was a floatplane.'

'A floatplane? Where is it now?'

'Adrift somewhere in the Caribbean Sea. I can't see it now, it's too dark. I guess it'll follow the tide and wash up on shore somewhere, but it's not flyable; the wing tanks are all shot up with bullet holes.'

'I need to hear this story Johann, but there's no time now. Stay right where you are. I'm coming to you.'

'Is Rusty looking for me?'

'Let's just say you're a wanted man by a few people right now. I'll grab a few things and then I'll head down to Montserrat.'

'How soon can you get here?'

Victoria paused to make some mental calculations in her head.

'How far is it from Antigua? Thirty-five, forty miles? I'll be with you in an hour.'

Johann wondered what kind of boat Victoria had at her disposal. To cover the distance between the two islands in one hour it clearly had some horsepower behind it.

'How d'you know you won't be tracked or followed?' he asked suddenly.

'No one knows about this conversation except you and me. As for the boat, I've personally disabled its tracking system. Don't worry Johann, ain't nobody gonna find you through me. D'you have a light or something so you can signal to me when I reach your position? I'll probably have to anchor offshore and bring the tender to you.'

'I've only got the light on my cell phone.'

'Hmmm. That's too risky. Its signal can easily be detected by anyone looking for you. It'll lead them straight to you. Once you've sent your location to me, switch your phone off, take out the battery and throw it into the sea as far as you can. Just get rid of it.'

'I will. What kind of boat should I be looking for? Just so I know it's you.'

'You know Morse Code right?'

'Of course.'

'I'll signal the code for a V to you three times with a flashlight.'

'As in V for Victoria?'

'As in V for Victorious. Which is what we'll be when we've escaped the cartel once and for all.'

'I hope you're right about that.'

'Me too. Listen Johann, I gotta go. I'll see you in an hour.'

Victoria hung up and Johann stared at the screen of his cell phone in a daze. Was their conversation for real? He tapped on the screen and within a few seconds he had disclosed his exact location to Victoria. He powered off the phone and removed the battery before hurling them both into the sea. It came as no surprise to learn that he was a wanted man. He dared not think how many people were looking for him at that moment. He hoped Victoria would find him first. He made a note of the time before lying back onto the ash. Placing his hands behind his head he gazed up at the few stars in the night sky and thought of Victoria.

THIRTY-ONE

9:20 pm, Saturday, September 21
Paul Griffiths's Sunseeker, off the coast of Redonda

As Delano manoeuvred the tender alongside the bathing platform of Paul Griffiths's yacht for the final time, Graymond and Owen helped Alicia, Brandon and Oliver onto the boat. They were the last of the group to leave the island of Redonda. They joined the others in the aft seating area which was becoming crowded, even for the sixty-foot super yacht. On the port side sat Mitch and Max, sullen, silent and in handcuffs, flanked by Duane and Nerissa. Hyacinth was with Paul at the helm. As Alicia and Oliver, exhausted but relieved to have been rescued, sat down wearily on the expensive cream leather seating opposite Paul, Spencer emerged from the galley with tumblers containing an orange-coloured liquid, decorated with orange slices and umbrellas, which he placed on the table in front of them.

'Fruit punches,' he announced cheerfully, 'and a selection of cookies. There's a well-stocked bar in that sideboard unit over there.' He nodded to the opposite side of the saloon as he pushed the large plate of chocolate chip cookies towards them. 'And boy am I glad to have you back Alicia.' He shot a suspicious glance at Oliver but said nothing.

'Welcome aboard,' Paul said to them. 'You guys doing okay?'

'We're fine,' Alicia replied. 'Thanks for the rescue boat.'

'Not at all. I'm glad to be of help. Sounds like you've been through quite an ordeal.'

'The tender's secure,' Delano said, joining them. 'Melford's sending a boat and crew to collect the money stashed in the miners' huts. Turns out the calls made to the Coast Guard this afternoon were both hoaxes.'

'You're kidding?' Hyacinth turned in her seat. She glanced to the aft of the yacht. 'Max?'

'Yeah.' Delano nodded. 'He wanted to keep both crews busy and get them as far away from Redonda as possible. The boat should be here in around twenty minutes. Nerissa, you and I will go back to Redonda with the crew. The rest of you will head back to English Harbour. Paul, our private jetty has Jacobs's yacht berthed there right now, so I've arranged for you to dock at one of the other jetties. The Coast Guard will instruct you when you enter the harbour.'

'No problem,' Paul replied. 'Help yourself to refreshments, by the way. Spencer's been acquainting himself with the onboard beverages…'

'Non-alcoholic only,' Spencer interrupted him. 'I don't drink these days.'

'There's plenty of rum available if anyone needs a proper drink,' Paul said.

'There's an awesome sound system on this skiff too if anyone's interested?' Spencer added. 'I can put on some reggae vibes, or…'

'Thanks Spencer but we'll stick to the sounds of the ocean for now,' Delano replied. He caught Duane's eye which held a look of amusement.

'We tested it out earlier,' Duane said, briefly glancing in Spencer's direction before returning his attention to their captives.

'What about Rusty McChannen?' Hyacinth asked suddenly.

'Wendell picked him up at the airport earlier,' Delano replied. He smiled slightly. 'They found a burn phone in his office which showed a number of calls made to Max's cell this afternoon, as well as to three other accomplices: Glen Polito, Lamont Ashley and Emil Wincott. They've been arrested too. Wendell also discovered details of a number of offshore accounts in Rusty's name, along with various aliases. Wendell's running them down now for links to the Ramirez cartel.'

'I bet Officer Rivera's in his element,' Nerissa said wryly.

'You could say that,' Delano replied with a laugh. 'And we're his new best friends forever. Well, for the time being, at least.' He picked up a fruit punch and a cookie from the table before returning to the aft seating area where he was joined by Brandon.

He munched on the cookie before he looked directly at Mitch and Max.

'Why d'you do it?' he asked. 'Two good men like you. Why sacrifice everything for this?'

'I've only got two words for you Delano,' Mitch snarled. 'My lawyer.'

'Afraid all the good ones are taken,' Oliver called from inside.

'You'll need more than a good lawyer to get you out of this one,' Delano said, ignoring Oliver and looking at the two men. 'You'll need the best of the best. Then again, you could just help yourselves and confess to what I fear is a mounting number of offences, including murder…'

Delano's voice tailed off as he turned to Max.

'Your own cousin,' he said quietly. 'Could you sink to any lower than that?'

'*Quincy?*' A shocked voice spoke from inside. '*You* murdered *Quincy?* You *bastard*, you…'

'Sit down Jacobs.' Graymond stepped forward and placed a firm hand on Oliver's shoulder as the man in the prison scrubs stood up angrily.

'Why should you care?' Max said, turning to Oliver with a sneer. 'You're the reason he got caught in the first place. And anyway, you should be thanking me, I saved your life in that storm remember?'

'*You killed my Quincy.*' To everyone's astonishment, Oliver began to blink back tears. The hardened, sarcastic demeanour was replaced by something between a wail and a sob. He buried his face in his cuffed hands.

'*Your* Quincy?' Max asked scornfully. 'What d'you mean, *your* Quincy? What was he to you?'

It was indeed a question in everyone's minds at that moment. All eyes were on Oliver as he tried, unsuccessfully, to suppress more sobs before finally breaking down with a wail of anguish.

'I loved him,' he cried weakly, through his tears.

'*You* and *Quincy?*' Max asked with a horrified look. 'But — that's crazy — Quincy was your *maintenance man*, your pool boy, your *gardener,* dammit. He had a girlfriend.'

'I know about Latoya.' Oliver tried to recompose himself. 'But he loved *me*. And I loved him. Latoya was just a cover. We were taking our time with the relationship, our feelings for each other. And Quincy wasn't ready to come out to his family yet.'

'Quincy was *gay*?' Max asked in disbelief.

Oliver nodded slowly.

'I didn't know,' Max said. 'Even his mom didn't... He kept it from us. We had no idea.'

'So just to be clear Jacobs, you were having an affair with your pool boy?' Hyacinth asked coldly.

'He wasn't just my pool boy,' Oliver replied.

'That's quite obvious,' Hyacinth said. 'He was also your partner in crime, your accomplice in this whole drug trafficking racket you had going on, your...'

'But more than that, he was my...'

'He was your lover, yeah we hear you.'

'I guess that explains why you wanted to use your one phone call to talk to Quincy, rather than calling your lawyer,' Nerissa said suddenly.

'Incidentally, what *was* the purpose of that phone call?' Delano asked. 'What was it really that you wanted Quincy to do?'

Oliver paused. He wiped a single tear from his cheek before fixing his gaze on the deck of the yacht.

'I had one message for Quincy: to go to ground and keep his head down. We had an understanding that if either of us was captured, we'd get word to the other one to let them know, and warn them, so they knew to be careful.'

'So you had a coded message?'

'Sort of. We agreed that whoever was caught would make the call. If it was Quincy, he'd be calling me to say he wouldn't be able to come and do the pool and garden. If it was me, as you know, my message was to ask him to go check on the place.'

'But you never intended for him to actually go to the villa?' Delano asked curiously.

'Not exactly. The plan was that Quincy would drop whatever he was doing and head straight there...'

'Through the cliff tunnel…' Delano interrupted.

'Yeah, he couldn't risk being spotted anywhere near the villa from the access road. So he was to go straight there and start unloading the cash from the cistern. We guessed it'd probably take a few trips, but the plan was that I'd stall you guys as long as I could to give Quincy as much time as possible.'

'Which is why you gave us a London address when we arrested you,' Nerissa said.

'Yeah. Except you were a bit quicker than I thought you'd be with finding my place in Antigua.'

'So Quincy was to empty the cistern of the cash,' Delano brought Oliver's narrative back on point, 'and then what?'

'He was to take all the money down to the cove with the manchineel trees where he'd have a small fishing trawler waiting. He'd load the cash onto the boat and sail it round to a large yacht I've got moored in a small marina in the north of the island.'

'Whose name is the yacht registered to? Yours or Terry Dove's?' Delano asked.

'Er, it's in Gray's name actually.'

'*My* name?' Graymond said in surprise. 'Seriously Jacobs?'

'Sorry Gray. Anyway, we guessed that Quincy would probably have to make a couple of trips or so, sailing back and forth between the cove and the marina, but when he was done, the plan was for him to secure the parasols in a certain way as a message to me that the money was secure, all was well and he was waiting for me on the yacht.'

'But he never secured the parasols,' Hyacinth said. She remembered the strange expression on Oliver's face the night they drove away from Villa Bella Casa after the first search. Granted they hadn't found the cistern with the money, but she remembered trying to work out if Oliver's look was one of puzzlement or bemusement. Now she realised that he was perplexed as to why Quincy hadn't fixed the parasols to confirm that all was well.

'The parasols were the first things I looked at when we got to my villa,' Jacobs went on. 'I knew instantly that something had gone badly wrong with the plan but I couldn't let on, obviously. I guess in my heart of hearts I hoped he'd just forgotten or simply hadn't had time or something. Quincy had assured me he'd go straight to the villa, so if he hadn't been there, then where was he?'

'He had every intention of dropping everything and going straight to Sugar Reef Bay but he was held up by one of his employers,' Delano said. He considered the outcome of this for a moment. If Jay Palmer hadn't arrived unexpectedly to check on Quincy, Quincy would have already made it to Oliver's villa and started removing the cash from the cistern. He would have lied to Max about his whereabouts and might still be alive. But Delano knew he was only trying to alleviate his own conscience. He should never have called Max to give him the heads up about his cousin. But how could he have known about Max, a trusted coxswain for the Coast Guard? Or Mitch, one of his own agents? Delano felt sick at the thought that the two men had been deceiving him the whole time, right under his nose, and he never even saw it. A man was dead because of his phone call to Max. It wasn't Jay Palmer's fault that Quincy had been murdered; it was Delano's.

'What about the surveillance cameras around the villa?' Brandon was asking Oliver. 'How was Quincy supposed to evade those? You must've known we'd retrieve the footage.'

'The cameras were rigged to ensure a blind spot between cameras seven and eight where a narrow, unmarked track from the entrance to the cliff tunnel leads to the sliding doors in the study, on the southeast corner of the villa. From there you can make your way through to the dining room without being detected. Quincy didn't need to tamper with the cameras or the NVR at all. The footage could keep rolling as far as we were concerned. In fact, even better if it did. Which is why I honestly couldn't help you when you kept asking me about it. I couldn't think of any reason why Quincy would take the recorder. That certainly wasn't in the plan.'

'But Quincy didn't tell Max about the blind spot between the cameras. He knew that if anyone got hold of the surveillance footage, they'd see he was spraying the camera lenses against his will,' Delano said. 'He couldn't make it too obvious; he knew Max was watching nearby, but he wanted us to know that there was someone else with him, even if his captor was never seen and remained out of shot.' He shot a glance at Max who scowled and said nothing. 'What was the rest of the plan Jacobs?'

'There's a go-bag with two sets of fake ID: passports, driving licences and so on, stashed on the yacht. One for Quincy and one for me. Along with the money, we were all set to disappear. Quincy was to stay on board the yacht with the cash and keep a low profile while my lawyer pulled some strings and got me out of jail. Harvey Webster assured me he'd have me out on bail by sunset. I'd planned to make my way to the marina where I was to join Quincy on the yacht. We were going to sail away together before anyone even realised we'd gone. But other than discovering Quincy hadn't managed to carry out his part of the plan for some reason, that damn magistrate wasn't budging with his decision to deny bail and was refusing to take any bribes from Webster. It was turning into a nightmare.'

His cuffs jangled together as he paused to wipe a tear from his eye. Alicia watched him closely. She thought of the conversations she and Graymond had had with him the day after their arrival. She now knew why he had been so anxious for them to find Quincy. The look of horror on his face was genuine when Wendell had broken the news, somewhat dispassionately, of Quincy's murder. Alicia had been aware of inconsistencies in Oliver's behaviour but had assumed it was part of an act to hide the truth. Now she realised Oliver had cared deeply for Quincy and had struggled to mask his emotions when he learned of Quincy's death. Suddenly Oliver leaned round toward Max.

'Just tell me one thing, why did you have to kill him?'

Max shrugged before replying in a callous tone.

'Quincy was a liability. Once Delano told me he was the person you'd made your one phone call to from custody, I knew he was involved. I'd had my eye on him for a while. I knew he was up to something but I could never quite work out what. He was sneaky. He covered his tracks well, I'll give him that. But then suddenly, with one phone call, I had the answer. Of course, first I had to get him to show me where you were hiding the money. I'd heard rumours there was another way up to Sugar Reef Bay, other than the access road. Quincy was good enough to show me.'

'You threatened him. What was he supposed to do?' Oliver spoke through his tears.

'Well, the alternative was that I'd shoot him. I suppose he thought if he cooperated I might spare him his life.'

'The fact he didn't show you the blind spot between the cameras in the garden was his insurance policy,' Delano said.

'I guess so,' Max shrugged.

'I hope you rot in jail for what you did to Quincy,' Oliver said in a low voice mixed with emotion and anger.

Max laughed scornfully.

'Right back at you Jacobs,' he said with disdain. 'You're not exactly going to a five star hotel yourself.'

'We got company,' Paul called from the cockpit.

Through the darkness they could make out the lights of a rapidly approaching vessel.

'The Coast Guard,' Delano said. 'Paul, ask them if they can come alongside us and send a tender across to collect Nerissa and me. This is as close to Redonda as they'll be able to get. Wendell and Lloyd will be waiting for you guys back at English Harbour with a team of officers.'

Paul relayed Delano's message over the radio to the coxswain of the approaching vessel which was quickly acknowledged. Within minutes, the rescue boat was alongside the yacht. A tender arrived with four other crew members of the Antigua Coast Guard. Delano and Nerissa climbed aboard and they set off for Redonda once more.

'Time to go,' Brandon said as the tender disappeared between the rocks which flanked the treacherous passage to the island's only landing place. Paul eased the throttles of the Sunseeker forward and, with a roar of powerful engines, the yacht gathered speed as it sliced through the waves and the darkness. There was a low mist rising over the sea. It was almost as foreboding and sinister as the three handcuffed passengers on board the luxury yacht, a bizarre assortment of murderers, drug dealers and master criminals.

THIRTY-TWO

It was over an hour since Johann had spoken to Victoria and he was beginning to think she wasn't going to show. He sat on the ash-covered shoreline in the darkness listening to the waves, the rhythmic sound almost trancelike and hypnotic, as he anxiously scanned the horizon. His eyes stung from tiredness and smarted with the dust but he dare not close them for fear of falling asleep. Suddenly, he thought he heard another sound over the waves, the low noise of an engine. He blinked a few times and strained his eyes into the gloom over the water. He wasn't sure if he could make out the faint glow of distant lights. Or perhaps he was hallucinating.

And then through the shadows he saw it, the distinct shape of the hull of a sleek motor yacht. The lights were dimmed and at times the engine noise seemed to get lost in the sounds of the waves. The dark shape moved closer, like a silent, mysterious ghost ship. Johann stood up in anticipation. He waited and watched intently for the signal, ready to run if it wasn't her. But then he saw it: three short flashes and one longer flash, the Morse Code for the letter V. She signalled three times. Within minutes there was another engine noise. It had a higher pitch than the first. Johann hurried to the edge of the shore as the dark shape of a small boat with a faint light emerged from the gloom. Johann could just see the outline of the petite frame of the skipper. He held his breath as the boat reached the shore.

'Johann?' It was Victoria's west coast accent.

'Over here.' Johann ran towards the boat as Victoria jumped out. He helped her pull it up higher onto the shore.

'Thanks.' She stood facing him. 'I got here as quickly as I could. Are you ready to go? They'll be searching for you as soon as it gets light.'

'Yeah, I know,' Johann nodded.

'Good. Then we need to get moving. We've got a lot to do tonight.'

'We do?'

'Yes, and not much time to do it in. You have any belongings with you?'

Johann held out his hands.

'I got nothing. The CDSLI seized it all on runway ten this afternoon.'

'Your cell phone?'

'Over there in the sea somewhere.'

'Then let's go.'

They pushed the tender back into the water before climbing in. Victoria started the outboard engine and, with one hand on the rudder, she guided the small craft back to the yacht. As the skiff bounced gently over the waves, Johann felt the cool breeze on his face and a renewed energy and excitement began to stir inside him. Victoria's yacht skulked in the darkness ahead of them as they sped towards it. Pale blue low-level downlights reflected on the waves and seemed to accentuate the sweeping lines of the vessel.

Victoria skilfully manoeuvred the tender to the aft bathing platform. The yacht was impressive close-up. The sleek, luxurious craft was probably around forty foot in length. Victoria quickly tied the tender to the bathing platform and signalled for Johann to climb onto it. He scrambled out and turned to offer his hand to Victoria but she was already pulling the tender out of the water behind him.

'Help yourself to a drink.' Victoria gestured towards the cockpit. 'Looks like you need one,' she added with a smile. 'There's a wet bar over there. You should find something you fancy. Captain Morgan, right?'

'Yes,' Johann said in surprise. 'How did you know?'

'I did some homework after yesterday's flight,' Victoria replied. She secured the tender and joined Johann in the cockpit. He found an open bottle of Captain Morgan rum in the wet bar along with two tumblers which he placed on a large teak table. He poured two generous measures of the rum into each tumbler before handing one to Victoria. She was wearing a black t-shirt and faded denim jeans. Her long, wavy hair was windswept and she wore less makeup than the previous day, although her eyes seemed to be darker in the pale light of the cockpit. As they raised their glasses, their eyes met and they paused.

'To new beginnings,' Victoria said.

'I'll drink to that,' Johann replied and they clinked glasses.

THIRTY-THREE

9:30 am, Sunday, September 22
CDSLI Headquarters, English Harbour

Fresh coffee and donuts were laid out on one of the wooden desks in the crew room of the CDSLI. Along with Duane and Lloyd, Delano, Nerissa, Brandon and Hyacinth were joined by Graymond and Alicia, Spencer and Owen, and Wendell. The mood was buoyant and the adrenaline was still flowing in spite of the fatigue from the events of the previous night. The morning sunshine, heralding another beautiful day on the Caribbean island, streamed through the jalousie windows. Wendell was anxious about commencing proceedings and keen to launch into what the rest of them knew would be a wordy account of Rusty's arrest at the airport, along with his accomplices Glen, Lamont and Emil, but first, Hyacinth had news from the hospital.

'I just talked to Edella. She's out of the ICU and has been transferred to one of the private rooms. She's recovering well and will hopefully be ready to go home in a few days. She said to say hi to you all, she's sorry she missed the excitement and can't wait to hear all about it.'

'That's fantastic news,' Nerissa said. The others echoed with a chorus of agreement before Lloyd excused himself to continue working on Oliver's laptop which had been recovered from Max's house. Oliver had been surprisingly cooperative, providing passwords, codes and information required to access the encrypted files stored on the laptop. It was all a little too straightforward. Lloyd was suspicious that there was something Oliver wasn't telling them and was determined to find out what. Wendell opened his mouth to speak before Hyacinth cut him off again.

'How did it go with the Coast Guard last night?' She looked over at Nerissa and Delano.

'We retrieved every last one hundred dollar bill stashed in the old miners' huts,' Delano replied, taking a sip of coffee. 'And there were a lot of them. The money's next door waiting to be counted but it'll take a while; the contents of Jacobs's cistern were small change compared to what we recovered from Redonda.'

'To think he'd been using those old buildings and miners' huts to hide the cash the whole time, and no one ever knew,' Brandon said.

'It was the perfect place,' Delano continued. 'It was free of rats and goats thanks to the conservation programme last year and was rarely visited, mainly due to the inaccessibility of the island. Jacobs used the below ground cistern of his villa to store the cash — and sometimes the drugs — temporarily, before moving it to Redonda. He and Quincy would take the cash through the tunnel down to the cave at the bottom of the cliff. They'd wait until nightfall when they'd load it into Jacobs's go-fast boat. Some nights they'd make multiple trips back and forth to Redonda. The boat's powerful engines combined exceeded a thousand horsepower. That, and the length of its V-shaped racing hull, meant it could reach speeds of up to sixty miles an hour in calmer seas — they could make it from Sugar Reef Bay to Redonda in around forty minutes — and it was capable of carrying around one thousand kilograms of money — or drugs — per trip.'

'Impressive,' Spencer said in awe as he bit into his third donut of the morning. He frowned at Alicia as she looked at him in disgust. 'What?' he said defensively. 'It was hard work making endless drinks for you all last night.'

'Jacobs's go-fast, with its camouflage colours and phenomenal top speeds, is your typical drug runner's boat,' Delano continued. 'Just like the rum-runners of the past, drug smugglers love the sea: it's vast, the authorities can't patrol all of it and evidence can be tossed overboard in seconds.'

'On the subject of Jacobs's boat, how did Max get it out of the impound yesterday?' Duane asked.

'Very easily,' Delano replied. 'He's a senior member of the Coast Guard. Or at least, he was. He had access-all-areas clearance.

Brent was the officer on duty yesterday at the impound. When Max showed up saying he had instructions to move Jacobs's boat because we needed it as part of the ongoing investigation and that he'd return it later in the day, Brent didn't even think to question him. Why would he? Like us, he had no idea what Max was up to.'

'So Max takes the boat from the impound and drives it round to the sandy cove at the bottom of the Sugar Reef Bay peninsula,' Owen said. 'How did he know when and where to go?'

'Mitch told him,' Delano replied. 'Mitch and Max were in league the whole time, along with Rusty McChannen.'

Wendell finally got a word in and was keen to hold on to the moment.

'We spent most of the night questioning them. They pretty much confessed to everything in the hope of making some kind of deal. The three of them were in bed with the powerful Ramirez cartel, which I know you're all familiar with. Antigua's an essential transhipment route from the drug producing countries of South America — Colombia, Peru and Bolivia, to name a few — to the United States and West Africa, from where the drugs move northward to Europe.' It was turning into a lecture already. 'Max and Rusty were ideally positioned to oversee the lion's share of drug trafficking on the island. Between them they worked together, controlling almost all the shipments of drugs which passed through Antigua; Rusty took care of the airport side of things while Max oversaw the maritime smuggling operations. Mitch came in handy with the inside knowledge he obtained through his position with the CDSLI.'

'The hijacking of the money truck…' Owen said suddenly, thinking of Leon.

'Exactly. Thanks to Mitch's tipoffs they were always one step ahead of us, but we'll get to that.' Wendell disliked being interrupted. He took a hurried sip of coffee lest anyone else dare to speak, and continued. 'As I was saying, Rusty, Max and Mitch pretty much ran the whole show when it came to the movement of drugs on the island. Between them they had the monopoly on the streets and, more importantly, the shipments destined for further afield. That is until around a year ago when they became aware of a rival who was undercutting them with other major players in the business and disrupting their regular supply chains. The problem with the new guy was that no matter how hard they tried, they just couldn't track him down. He was a ghost. The only information they could ever find out about him was that his name was Ray. But then the trail went cold every time. It wasn't until the night of the storm, when the lifeboat crew went out to rescue Oliver Jacobs on his yacht — aptly named the Atratus, after the Latin name for the Redonda Ground Dragon, in a brazen nod to the island where he was stashing his drugs money — that Max realised they may finally have found a link to the competition.'

'I think the storm was a gift as far as Mitch and Max were concerned,' Delano added. 'After realising the sheer quantity of cocaine that Jacobs had on board the Atratus, along with the amount of cash in his cistern, they knew they were close to discovering the identity of their unwelcome rival and threat.'

'The other gift they received that morning was, of course, delivered by you Delano,' Wendell said, retrieving the narrative after another hasty sip of coffee.

'Yes, thank you Wendell, I'm aware of that,' Delano said. There was a note of shame in his voice.

'Don't beat yourself up about it boss,' Brandon said kindly. 'It was a perfectly legitimate phone call made out of professional courtesy to Max. Any one of us could have done it. How were you to know?'

'Thanks Brandon, but even so...'

'I agree Delano. Could've been handled differently.' Wendell had taken a bite out of a donut and was talking with his mouth full. There was a line of sugar along his upper lip which he was apparently oblivious to. 'Quincy's death warrant was signed the moment you told Max about the phone call from Jacobs.'

'Death warrant?' Hyacinth said with a raised eyebrow. 'There's no need to be so dramatic Wendell.'

'Well forgive me Officer James but that's exactly what it was,' Wendell replied sanctimoniously. 'Max had no idea that Quincy, his own cousin, was involved with Jacobs until Delano called him with the information.'

'If Mitch was passing inside information along to Max and Rusty, then surely if the call to Max about Quincy hadn't come from Delano, it would have come from Mitch?' Nerissa said.

'Eventually, yes,' Wendell agreed. 'But if you recall, that morning Mitch was the only CDSLI officer not present when Lloyd revealed the person to whom Jacobs had made his one phone call.'

Nerissa frowned as if trying to remember.

'Where was he then?' she asked.

'He was with the Coast Guard bringing the Atratus ashore,' Wendell replied. 'Mitch wasn't privy to that information until much later in the morning. By the time he learned about the phone call, even if he'd have passed the information to Max straight away, Quincy most likely would have been and gone from Villa Bella Casa. And, more importantly, he'd still be alive.'

'Thanks Wendell,' Delano said quietly. 'I think we get that. Let's move on, shall we?'

'Of course Delano.' Another bite of the donut. 'Where was I? Oh yes, Max. After Delano's phone call...'

'Moving on...' Nerissa reminded him.

'Max knew time was of the essence — everyone would be wanting to know where Jacobs was hiding the rest of the money — so he called Quincy straight away, said he needed to talk to him urgently and could they meet somewhere.'

'But Quincy was over at Hamilton Bay with Jay Palmer,' Hyacinth said.

'Palmer had just left when Max called,' Wendell went on, frowning at his notes. 'Max told Quincy to meet him at the bottom of the dead end track near Tamarind Point. Quincy agreed — it's on the way to Sugar Reef Bay, after all — but when he arrived, Max pulled a gun on him and threatened him.'

'Why didn't Quincy answer my calls when I tried to reach him?' Hyacinth asked suddenly.

'Like I said, Max got to Quincy first. He told Quincy it was a serious matter and not to take any other calls until they'd spoken in person,' Wendell replied, 'especially from the CDSLI. Quincy was already running scared after Jacobs's call so I guess he thought it would be prudent to speak to Max first before going to the villa, just in case Max knew something.'

'Did Quincy know about Max's involvement with the cartel?' Nerissa asked.

'It's difficult to say. Max, Mitch and Rusty had deep covers with responsible jobs in high positions. None of us had any idea that they were linked to the cartel. Perhaps Jacobs and Quincy had their suspicions, although Jacobs swears otherwise. I'm sure it became immediately obvious to Quincy though, when Max forced him to reveal the alternate route to Villa Bella Casa, in order to avoid the surveillance officers at Sugar Reef Bay.'

'Poor Quincy,' Owen said.

'Well he shouldn't have gotten involved with Jacobs in the first place.' Wendell said loftily.

'You really have no compassion at all, do you Wendell?' Hyacinth uttered in disgust. Wendell ignored the remark and continued talking.

'At gunpoint, Max ordered Quincy to take them to the cove at the bottom of the Sugar Reef Bay cliff in his little fishing boat. They entered the tunnel through the cave, just like you did yesterday, and made their way up to the garden of Villa Bella Casa.'

'Which explains why, when it only takes thirty minutes to drive from Hamilton Bay to Sugar Reef Bay, it seemed to take Quincy a whole hour,' Brandon said.

'Yes, exactly,' Wendell nodded. 'As we all know, the next we see of Quincy is when he appears on camera seven, spraying the lens with black paint.'

'If Max came with the spray paint, he premeditated this whole thing,' Graymond said.

'You think Max tried to persuade Quincy to change sides?' Owen asked suddenly.

'It's unlikely,' Delano replied. 'Quincy may not have revealed the nature of his relationship with Jacobs to his cousin, but I think their love for and loyalty to each other — Quincy and Jacobs I mean — meant that Quincy was never going to betray Jacobs. According to Max, Quincy was pretty tight-lipped. The only thing he gave away was the location of the below ground cistern and, ergo, the money.'

Wendell frowned as Delano continued.

'Quincy probably decided to disclose the information about the cistern in the hope that the hundred million dollars would be enough of a bargaining chip to save him, but Max had no intentions of that happening. Max's identity as a key player in one of the largest narco-trafficking operations in Antigua was at stake. Quincy knew too much and needed to be silenced.'

'So he was struck with a crowbar and strangled with a length of nautical rope,' Hyacinth said. 'Rochelle surmised that the killer had some kind of maritime connection, but we never dreamed it was the coxswain of the English Harbour Coast Guard!'

'Standard nautical rope's pretty common round here with all the harbours and boats and so on,' Owen said. 'But why did Max go to all the trouble of strangling Quincy when he had a gun? Why not just shoot him?'

'Too messy,' Delano replied. 'Too much blood. It had to be as clean a job as possible. Max had every intention of coming back another time, when we'd finished searching the place and the dust had settled, to dispose of Quincy's body and retrieve the money.'

'Except we got there first *and* discovered the cistern before he had a chance to do either of those things,' Hyacinth said.

'Much to his and Rusty's annoyance,' Delano added with a smile. 'Rochelle also found traces of black neoprene at the crime scene. When we searched Max's house we found a wetsuit made from the same neoprene. And the traces of Quincy's blood recovered from the crime scene suggest he put up quite a fight before Max struck him with the metal bar. Max was wearing gloves, which we also found at his house; together with the wetsuit, they explain why he left no DNA and no prints behind.'

'Just as an aside, why did Quincy call Latoya from the villa?' Nerissa asked suddenly.

'According to Max, Quincy tried to call her in a last, desperate attempt to summon help, but Max cut him off before he'd had a chance to say anything,' Delano replied. 'Which is why the call only lasted a few seconds and Quincy never said anything. After that, Max confiscated the phone and threw it off the cliff. Once he'd taken care of Quincy and closed up the cistern, he had one final job: locate Jacobs's laptop and the recorder for the surveillance system. Max realised it would be difficult to carry both through the tunnel back to the cove, due to it being steep and slippery, so he elected to take only the laptop. The best he could do with the NVR was to erase everything on the hard drive, believing that even if we recovered the deleted footage, his backup plan of having Quincy blind the cameras would protect his identity.'

'So then Max leaves the villa with Jacobs's laptop, being careful to reset the alarm system to avoid raising suspicion, and retraces his steps back through the tunnel to the cove at the bottom of the cliff,' Nerissa said. 'He returns Quincy's fishing boat to its mooring and goes back to the dirt track near Tamarind Point...'

'Where he gets in Quincy's truck and drives it over the edge of the cliff, jumping out at the last second.' Wendell couldn't bear to be sidelined any longer. The others glanced at him as if they'd forgotten he was there.

'Why go to all the trouble of doing that?' Spencer asked with a puzzled expression.

'To offer an explanation for Quincy's disappearance, which was sure to be flagged up sooner rather than later,' Wendell replied. 'But of course, we know by then that Quincy was already lying strangled to death on the floor of Jacobs's cistern.' Wendell seemed to have a knack of emphasising the details everyone else would rather forget. 'Let's face it, the dirt track was pretty remote. It was unlikely Quincy's truck would be discovered for at least a couple of days. But unfortunately for Max, his best laid plans were foiled yet again, this time by two tourists who happened to be out exploring and reported the truck.'

'Out of interest, was Quincy's little black book containing the names and numbers of everyone he worked for ever recovered?' Nerissa asked.

'No,' Wendell shook his head. 'My guess is it was in the truck when it went over the cliff and was thrown clear. The waves probably took it, along with some of Quincy's other personal effects which we never found.'

There was a pause, almost as if in some kind of solemn salute to Quincy's unfortunate demise.

'I'm curious; how long were they working together, Quincy and Jacobs?' Hyacinth broke the silence. 'What came first? The personal or the professional relationship?'

'According to Jacobs, he employed Quincy as his gardener, handyman and so on when he moved to Villa Bella Casa eighteen months ago,' Delano replied. 'Over the next six months their relationship began to develop and Jacobs confided in Quincy about his drug trafficking activities. They started doing cocaine together at weekends and Quincy helped him convert the cistern into an airtight storage bunker for the drugs and cash. It was Quincy's idea to move the excess cash to Redonda when there was too much for the cistern. He was aware of the successful conservation programme which had taken place on the island a couple of years before. Together, they renovated the miners' huts and moved the cash across when they needed to. For six months Quincy kept his head down and worked diligently at his other jobs, but then it seems the money and drugs started to take over his life and began affecting his work. A number of his employers, like Jay Palmer, became increasingly frustrated with his poor quality of work and unreliability.'

'Poor Quincy,' Hyacinth said quietly. 'I feel so sad for him, getting involved with Jacobs like that. It's not fair. He wound up dead in Jacobs's cistern and Jacobs is here, alive and well.'

'Albeit facing a life sentence in seventeen thirty-five,' Brandon said. 'Jacobs might wonder sometimes if he'd been better off with Quincy's fate.'

They were interrupted by Lloyd who had been pecking away at Oliver's laptop on the other side of the crew room.

'I've been through every damn file, folder and database on this computer,' he said reaching for his cup of lukewarm coffee. He took a sip and placed the cup back on the desk where it would be forgotten again. 'I've finally struck gold and recovered the files OJ *didn't* tell us about. I've got names and numbers for his contacts throughout the Caribbean, from Colombia to the Cayman Islands. I've also got information on strategic locations and pickup points at Brighton Port and other harbours in Trinidad. There are details of trade networks and supply chains, as well as connections to arms smuggling and money laundering. Seems OJ had his fingers in all kinds of pies. We're just at the tip of the iceberg here.'

'Perhaps it would be quicker to say what illegal activities Jacobs *wasn't* into,' Hyacinth murmured.

'Probably,' Lloyd agreed. 'Anyway, there's a lot of information here. It looks as though OJ had connections with some of the newer, up and coming cartels and organised crime groups. There are some names here I'm not familiar with. I'll get it all sent over to your tablets.'

'Thanks Lloyd,' Delano said. 'Did you find anything on Ray?'

'Nothing.' Lloyd shook his head firmly. 'There's no reference to him whatsoever. And believe me, I've been through everything on here at least a dozen times.'

'Ray's still out there,' Nerissa said. 'Who is he? Why can't anyone find him?'

Her question remained unanswered as Delano took a call on his phone. He placed the caller on speaker. It was Pat, one of the team of law enforcement officers who had been sent to retrieve the armoured truck involved in the heist en route from Villa Bella Casa. Mitch had admitted that the hijacking in which four police officers, CDSLI officer Anson and Leon Fayer had lost their lives, had been carried out by a group of mercenaries for hire, contracted by Rusty and overseen by Glen. The masked men had been instructed to take out the convoy and seize the truck containing the hundred million dollars. Mitch had confessed to supplying Rusty with inside information on the route and timings of the truck, as well as details of the police escort accompanying them. He had also admitted to ensuring he sustained minor injuries during the heist to make it look as though he was another innocent victim. The truck's journey was fated before it had even departed Villa Bella Casa.

Mitch had also provided the truck's current location: it was parked in an abandoned warehouse in a rundown area of St. John's. The money was being stored temporarily at the same location. Pat confirmed that they had secured both the truck and the money and had made a number of arrests. Delano thanked Pat who said he'd check in again later. They had the money but there was still much to be done, including counting it all and confirming its authenticity.

The last few details of the case were finally coming together. Mitch and Max's versions of the events at Villa Bella Casa the previous evening had been largely corroborated by Alicia and Oliver. Max had taken Oliver's go-fast boat from the impound, mooring it briefly in Sugar Reef Bay where — thanks to Lloyd's hacking programme which had been stolen by Mitch — he had hacked remotely into the alarm system of Villa Bella Casa, setting off the alarm at a time confirmed to him by Mitch.

As the group split up within the grounds of Villa Bella Casa to investigate the reason for the alarm, Mitch took Alicia and Oliver hostage at gunpoint, forcing them back down the cliff tunnel to the cove where Max was waiting with Oliver's go-fast. Mitch had deliberately dumped his badge, sling and cell phone to make it look as though he'd been involved in a struggle, when in fact it was to ensure that he couldn't be tracked. He disposed of Alicia's phone in the sea. Max had already disabled the CDSLI's RIB and was ready to leave for Redonda.

Delano was confident that, between them, Rusty, Mitch and Max had provided enough information to bring down a large part of the Ramirez cartel's command and control centre in Antigua.

'There are still a couple of things I'm curious about,' Hyacinth said suddenly. 'What was Jay Palmer up to between eleven and one o'clock on the morning Quincy was murdered? He said he was at home in his office but his cleaning lady swears his car wasn't in the parking lot.'

'I can help there,' Lloyd volunteered. 'His financial problems raised a number of red flags so I dug a little deeper and found some gambling debts which he'd kept hidden from his partner and business associates. He'd been borrowing money from a loan shark in St. John's. On his way home from Hamilton Bay, Jay went via the loan shark to beg for more time to repay his debts and secure another payday advance.' He glanced at Brandon.

'I spoke to the loan shark who confirmed Jay's alibi for the times we couldn't account for,' Brandon said. 'I also spoke to Jay who admitted to the whole thing. His cleaning lady was telling the truth.'

'Seems like an awful long time to spend at a loan shark's shop though,' Nerissa remarked.

'Apparently there were a few discussions about Jay putting the restaurant on the line,' Brandon replied. 'He said he stayed a little longer than usual to try to thrash out some kind of deal.'

'Did they?' Nerissa asked.

'No.'

'So it may have been a waste of time, but at least it gave Jay an alibi,' Hyacinth said. 'The other thing I'd like to know is where are Mitch, Max and Rusty hiding all their money? They've obviously been skimming off a considerable amount of cash from their criminal activities for the cartel, yet their lives are far from extravagant. Where's the money going?'

'According to them, most of the money doesn't venture anywhere near Antigua,' Delano replied. 'It's being deposited in all sorts of offshore accounts held by all sorts of shell corporations throughout Central America and the Caribbean. The other way they've offloaded a proportion of their cash is through the purchase of a four hundred acre private island in Saint Vincent and the Grenadines. As we know through Johann Ryan, the pilot we busted on runway ten yesterday, Rusty and Max also enjoy the occasional weekend in Miami, frequenting plush hotels and bars, VIP lounges and strip clubs. Don't worry Hyacinth, those boys knew how to spend their cash!'

'Speaking of Johann Ryan, we could never have pulled off last night without him,' Brandon said. 'Does anyone know what happened to him? I heard Mitch and Max shot up the floatplane while he was flying over Redonda.'

Delano remained unusually silent and it was Wendell who answered the question.

'The floatplane was found drifting in the sea a few miles northeast of Guadeloupe in the early hours of this morning. The Coast Guard's recovering it as we speak. They've confirmed the wings are peppered with bullet holes and the plane is completely empty of fuel.'

'Any sign of Johann?' Hyacinth asked. There was a note of concern in her voice.

'No,' Wendell shook his head. 'We've no idea what became of him.'

There was an uncomfortable pause before Brandon spoke again.

'What about the anonymous tipoff which led us to him?' he asked. 'Who did that come from?'

'We traced it back to some tourist who'd been hanging around the airport plane-spotting over the last few days,' Wendell replied. 'He probably didn't imagine for one moment that he'd stumbled onto something like this. We found nearly ninety kilograms of cocaine — that's around three point two million dollars' worth — in the suitcases Johann had onboard his aircraft.'

'Rusty knew about it?' Nerissa asked.

'Rusty orchestrated it. He took care of all the paperwork, the flight plans, airport passes, everything. All Johann had to do was fly the drugs out of and the money into Antigua. He was just a courier, albeit a very rich one I'd imagine.'

'No, he was far more than that,' Hyacinth said suddenly. 'He came good in the end. Sure, he was a trafficker and deserves jail time for what he did, but he was one of the bravest of us all last night. He risked his life to help us, flying low over Redonda, drawing Mitch and Max away from the miners' huts with their assault rifles so we could rescue Jacobs and Alicia. Not only that, it's thanks to his information on Rusty and Max that put us onto them in the first place.'

'It's true,' Delano agreed. He remembered his final instructions to Johann and wondered what had become of the disgraced airline pilot. It was perhaps one of those mysteries that would never be solved. Delano knew that sometimes justice didn't come in black or white, but in shades of grey, somewhere in between. This was perhaps one of those times.

THIRTY-FOUR

3:30 pm, Sunday, September 22
CDSLI Headquarters, English Harbour

'You asked to see us.' Graymond and Alicia sat opposite Oliver Jacobs in one of the interview rooms at the CDSLI headquarters.

'I did.' Oliver spoke gravely. 'I just wanted to check Alicia was okay after yesterday's — ordeal, and to apologise for everything I've put you through.'

'I'm fine thanks Jacobs,' Alicia replied a little frostily, 'and apology accepted, although I had no idea you cared that much.'

'Then please forgive me for not showing it,' Oliver said. 'I'm so sorry if I haven't been more thoughtful towards you both. I guess I've just been a mess since the news of Quincy's death. He was my love, my life, my everything.' He gave a dramatic sigh. 'I'd finally found happiness and a fulfilling relationship, and then it was snatched from me so cruelly.'

Graymond and Alicia exchanged glances.

'You're not a character in a Shakespeare play, Jacobs,' Alicia said.

'No, of course not. Sometimes I let my heart rule my head, that's all.' Oliver appeared to blink back tears before composing himself. 'Tell me, did the CDSLI officers recover the money from my cistern?'

'They did,' Graymond replied.

'All one hundred million dollars of it?'

'I believe that's what the final amount was, yes.'

'Ah. Good. They have special machines to count it all and check for counterfeit bills I understand?'

'Yes, I think they do.'

'Good to know. And how will you both be spending the rest of your vacation?'

'We'll be staying for Leon's funeral and heading home after that,' Alicia replied. 'What about you Jacobs? What's next?'

'Oh Webster's working on all the legal stuff as we speak.' Oliver replied somewhat casually for a man facing life in prison. 'Nothing happens very fast in these places, does it?' He rolled his eyes in frustration. 'The CDSLI has, naturally, laid the charges against me on thick: possession, possession with intent to supply, possession with intent to transfer, drug trafficking, being concerned with the supply of cocaine, importation, the list just goes on and on. I'll probably have to face trial before a judge and jury in the High Court due to the quantity of drugs seized. But until then I'll be remanded to Her Majesty's prison. It'll keep Webster busy I suppose. He's appealed on my behalf against that wretched magistrate's decision to deny bail, as you know, but we're not moving very fast on that one either. And the ridiculous thing is that after all the corruption on this miserable island, no one at the courthouse is taking any bribes.'

'Oh how terrible,' Alicia said in a mocking tone. 'You'd think people would be more accommodating round here.'

'It's not exactly ideal, is it?' Oliver said, ignoring Alicia's sarcasm.

'Perhaps I should remind you that the wretched magistrate saved your life,' Alicia replied curtly. 'If you hadn't remained in the custody of the CDSLI, Rusty McChannen would've arranged for you to mysteriously disappear the day you walked out of here.'

Oliver paused before replying.

'Yes, of course Alicia. You're quite right. I'm a lucky man, especially after what happened to my poor Quincy. The best thing I can do now is learn from this. It's time for change. Time to turn over a new leaf. I owe it to Quincy.'

'Well, you'll have plenty of opportunities to think about that,' Graymond said. 'You're going down for a very long time Jacobs.'

Oliver didn't reply.

'We'd better be going,' Alicia said, glancing at her watch. 'I promised Spencer we'd be back at the hotel to say goodbye before he leaves for the airport.'

'Just one last question,' Oliver said suddenly as Graymond and Alicia stood up to leave.

'Make it quick,' Graymond said.

'Did the CDSLI ever find any leads on Ray, my contact here in Antigua?'

'No, they didn't.'

'They must've put out an interagency APB with the picture the sketch artist drew from my description of him?'

'They did. They got nothing back.'

'Nothing? Oh how disappointing. So he's just lost in the wind then? Vanished into thin air?'

'It would appear so, yes,' Graymond replied. 'Anyway Jacobs, we have to go.'

'Sure.' Oliver nodded in understanding. 'Thanks for stopping by.'

'No problem. And rest assured, I'll be visiting you in prison as many times as you visited me.'

'Touché Gray. Touché.' Oliver watched as the door was opened for Graymond and Alicia by the guard posted outside. 'Then I guess it's goodbye.'

'Goodbye Jacobs,' Graymond said over his shoulder. As they were ushered through the door, Oliver overheard his whispered comment to Alicia: 'If I didn't know Jacobs better, I'd say this Ray doesn't even exist.'

Before the guard outside had closed the door behind them, Oliver strained his ears for Alicia's reply.

'You know what *I* think Gray? I think Jacobs *is* Ray...'

The door slammed shut and Oliver Jacobs sat alone in the silence with a strange smile on his face.

Delano had an announcement to make. It was never going to be an easy one, but now was the right time. He gazed around the crew room at his team who had started on the inevitable reports and statements, and the small mountain of paperwork which followed the action and excitement of an investigation. The network within which Rusty, Max and Mitch operated had been exposed and, in addition, the CDSLI had obtained a number of fresh leads on the inner sanctums of the Ramirez cartel. They were working closely with partner agencies throughout the Caribbean, and Brandon was preparing a joint statement with the Coast Guard and the Caribbean Division of the DEA. The CDSLI intended to use the events of the last few days to send a strong message to cartels and drug traffickers throughout the Caribbean: they were being hunted down, it was a year-round open season with no let up.

'Everything okay, boss?' Hyacinth asked, glancing up from the file in front of her.

'Yeah Hyacinth, it's good thanks, but there's something I want to share with you all,' Delano replied. One by one his officers looked up from their desks. He had the attention of the room and took a breath.

'I want to thank you all for the outstanding work you've done over these last few days. It hasn't been easy, I know, but none of you has shown anything other than courage, professionalism, tenacity and, in some cases, extreme bravery in the line of duty. You're an exceptional team. Your achievements are highly commendable and will, I'm sure, be recognised accordingly. In addition, we've also had to mourn the tragic deaths of one of our own, Anson, as well as Leon Fayer, who was known to many of us.'

Delano paused and swallowed hard before continuing.

'The culmination of these things has led me to make a personal decision which I've been considering for some time now.'

The room was silent. Outside, a cloud drifted across the sun. The rays of light which splayed across the floor disappeared into shadow.

'It's been my privilege to lead this team for the past five years,' Delano continued, 'but now it's time to move on to new and different challenges.'

'What are you saying boss?' Hyacinth asked quietly.

'As of the end of this week, I'll be retiring from the CDSLI,' Delano replied. He paused as there were gasps from both sides of the room. 'It's one of the hardest decisions I've ever made, but it's the right one and I'm excited for what the future holds.'

'What will you do?' Lloyd asked. 'We could always use more muscle on the door at The Jungle,' he added with a touch of humour in an attempt to lighten the mood.

'Thanks Lloyd,' Delano smiled, 'but I was planning on a more fulfilling future than Friday night exchanges with Jett and Richie.' Returning to a serious note, he continued. 'I plan to realise a lifelong ambition, a dream I've always had. It's a risk, but life is short; we've seen that more than ever in the last few days. I'm setting up a little beach shack — a bar and grill — just off the beach at Sugar Reef Bay. It'll start small, perhaps with a simple menu of chicken, ribs, snappers, sometimes lobster, all freshly grilled. On the drinks menu I'll have ice cold margaritas, mojitos, daiquiris, rum punch...'

'I'm there already!' Brandon interrupted.

'There'll be tables and chairs on the sand — nothing fancy — and brightly coloured parasols. And reggae tunes to set the vibe, of course.'

'Oh boss, I don't want you to leave but this all sounds pretty exciting!' Hyacinth said with tears in her eyes.

'What about Tamesha?' Duane asked.

'She's totally on board with this,' Delano replied, smiling broadly at the mention of his daughter's name. 'She's even offered to help paint the beach shack and toss a few ribs on the barbecue to earn a bit of cash towards her college education.'

'Good for her!' Hyacinth said. 'I'm happy for you boss, but I do have one question: who's going to lead this team when you're gone?'

Delano paused and glanced at Brandon who stepped forward.

'For now, I will be,' he said, 'with Nerissa as my second-in-command.'

'With a view to these roles becoming more permanent,' Delano added.

'I can definitely live with that!' Hyacinth said, her face brightening.

'Me too,' Lloyd agreed. 'Congratulations on the promotions Brandon and Nerissa, and good luck Delano. I'll be at the opening night party, you can count on it!'

As the team settled back at their desks, Delano gazed around the room with pride. He'd miss them, but it was time to move on and he was excited for the future. He leafed through his own pile of paperwork and was about to return to his desk when he spotted the headlines of a local newspaper from that morning. They read, "Pilot Charged In Drug Bust At Antigua Airport." He thought of Johann Ryan and dared to hope that somewhere, he too was starting out on a new chapter in his life.

THIRTY-FIVE

5:55 pm, Sunday, September 22
Jolly Harbour Marina, Antigua

In the deep orange glow of a perfect Caribbean sunset, a man and a woman walked along a palm tree-lined jetty, away from a maroon rental SUV parked in a secluded corner. The man, with short-cropped brown hair and dark aviator sunglasses, wore a baseball cap low over his face. He was perhaps in his late fifties or early sixties — it was hard to tell — with a physique which had clearly once been sporty and muscular, but had perhaps seen less active days over recent years. He wore a white linen shirt, navy shorts and deck shoes. The woman who accompanied him was quite a few years younger. Her heart-shaped face, framed by a neat, dark brown bob, was also almost completely obscured by oversized sunglasses with darkly tinted lenses. She was wearing an understated olive green sundress over a slim, toned physique, and a simple pair of flat sandals.

The couple exchanged few words as they walked along the jetty. It wasn't a leisurely stroll, but neither did they appear to be in a hurry. They kept their heads low, but seemed to be aware of their surroundings. They stopped and turned to examine a sign as a group of tourists passed them from the opposite direction.

Day was beginning to yield to night and the western skies were darkening. Shades of deep crimson were enveloped in a velvet of midnight blue from above. The lights from the bustling marina and the boats moored in the crowded harbour — from humble sailing vessels to luxury super yachts — were warm and inviting. Strains of reggae music from a nearby bar, the enticing aroma of grilled chicken drifting from a dockside diner, and the lazy slap of water against the boats accentuated the carefree, Caribbean vibe. The couple meandered anonymously between tourists, holidaymakers and deckhands, to where a sleek, expensive-looking, nameless yacht was berthed. It was the fourth time they had casually made their way from the SUV to the yacht that evening and it would be their last. But unlike the previous trips, this time they were empty-handed. The man stepped onto the bathing platform with surprising agility. He disappeared inside the yacht while the woman untied the mooring lines from the jetty. She cast off and joined her companion on board.

Within minutes, the berth was empty. The yacht had slipped discreetly away with barely the ripple of a wake as it left the harbour, unnoticed, blending seamlessly into the darkness of the ocean beyond. Under twinkling stars in the expanse of the night sky it smoothly gathered pace, little by little. Inside the saloon, the lights were dimmed. Johann Harcourt Ryan and Victoria Lorenzo gazed at the glittering marina behind them before turning to face each other. Victoria poured expensive champagne into two flutes and passed one to Johann, who sat at the helm.

'We did it Johann,' she said in a low voice. She had removed the oversized sunglasses and her cheeks flushed with excitement as she spoke.

'Yes. We did it,' Johann replied as Victoria leaned towards him and kissed him. They clinked their flute glasses and took a sip of champagne.

'I didn't think we'd pull this off, but we did. *You* did. I wasn't even sure we'd get past that guy at the storage rental place when we were loading my cash into the SUV, but your powers of persuasion almost had *me* captivated…'

'Almost?' Victoria asked playfully.

'Okay, you won me over on that very first flight to Redonda.'

'You mean *Rusty's* flight?' Victoria said with a mischievous smile. They laughed before Johann spoke seriously.

'Did you see the breaking news on the TV at that roadside store we stopped at? Rusty and his henchmen were arrested last night. The CDSLI and a whole bunch of other drug enforcement agencies throughout the Caribbean are hoping to make further arrests in the near future, thanks to new intel on the Ramirez cartel.

Rusty and Max won't be bothering us for a while, but the cartel will undoubtedly have a price on our heads.'

'Which is why you and I will never become complacent,' Victoria replied solemnly. She produced two passports and driving licences from a small handbag.

'Your new identity. I had them made up yesterday night, just in case we ever need them.'

'Where were you thinking of using them?' Johann asked. He gazed at the compass, briefly lost in thought.

'That depends on where you'd like to go.'

Johann considered his answer.

'Some place where we'll blend in, I guess. Where we'll be lost in the crowds forever. As far away from Antigua as possible. Maybe we should head to Europe? We could disappear in Paris, or Rome, or Prague.'

'That's how everyone would expect you to think,' Victoria replied. 'But what's the very last thing anyone would predict you'd do?'

'Stick around here probably,' Johann shrugged.

'Then that's exactly what we'll do. And we'll always be one step ahead of them, trust me. So, tell me where you want to go.'

'Can it be anywhere?'

'Anywhere.'

'There's a place I've always wanted to visit, but…'

'Where?'

'How about we start with Panama?'

'Panama? Sure. Why Panama?'

'The old Panama City was seized and plundered by one of my heroes. He was a Welsh pirate in the seventeenth century. His name was Captain Henry Morgan.'

'Panama sounds like the perfect place.'

They set course for Panama as the distant lights of Antigua faded into the darkness behind them. And they raised their glasses once more.

AUTHOR'S NOTE:

The boats: my sincere and grateful thanks to Steven Saint and James Cable for their invaluable insight into sea rescue missions. The factual parts are, of course, theirs, while the errors and occasional departure from accuracy are mine. It was an honour to spend time with such knowledgable, competent and, above all, courageous professionals.

The planes: John, you're an incredibly talented, skilful pilot, but more than that, you're my best friend. Thank you for your ideas, your inspiration and for sharing my dreams!

The original source of the concept for this book: must remain anonymous. But perhaps one day our chance encounter on a beach in the Caribbean may be revisited…

Printed in Great Britain
by Amazon